Hu 2.0

BRENT LADD

HU 2.0
HUMANITY'S
LAST HOPE

A JERICHO THRILLER

NEW YORK

LONDON • NASHVILLE • MELBOURNE • VANCOUVER

Hu 2.0

Humanity's Last Hope

Published in New York, New York, by Morgan James Publishing. Morgan James is a trademark of Morgan James, LLC. www.MorganJamesPublishing.com

Proudly distributed by Publishers Group West®

Morgan James BOGO™

A **FREE** ebook edition is available for you or a friend with the purchase of this print book.

CLEARLY SIGN YOUR NAME ABOVE

Instructions to claim your free ebook edition:
1. Visit MorganJamesBOGO.com
2. Sign your name CLEARLY in the space above
3. Complete the form and submit a photo of this entire page
4. You or your friend can download the ebook to your preferred device

ISBN 9781636981338 paperback
ISBN 9781636981345 ebook
Library of Congress Control Number:
2023930491

Cover & Interior Design by:
Christopher Kirk
www.GFSstudio.com

Morgan James is a proud partner of Habitat for Humanity Peninsula and Greater Williamsburg. Partners in building since 2006.

Get involved today! Visit: www.morgan-james-publishing.com/giving-back

The present belongs to us,
but the future is in our children's and their children's hands.

To AJ, Thomas, and Noah.
May your lives be full and your generation's stewardship wise.

1

NOTHINGNESS . . .

A sudden feeling of pain flashed forward like a melding of one's senses, each sense overloaded to its limit. A surge of fear and confusion whirled as the agony pushed beyond understanding. A shrill scream filled the air, engulfing the room . . . then nothing.

The sound of an electrical discharge preceded ragged, raspy breathing, fast at first and then in sync with the ticking of time—smooth and constant.

Bright white changed to a monochrome blur that focused on an unknown world. There were shapes and borders, each unfamiliar. The sudden need to escape filled his soul, building until it might burst, but something held him back from executing. A movement to the right called to his blurry attention, calming the growing emotional cyclone at its limit.

A mechanical arm, boney and rigid, appeared and began wiping and sucking away the viscous material that clung to the newly born adult body. White pigment-less eyes tracked in time with the machine's orchestrated movements. There was a return sensation in his consciousness every time it made contact. It was soothing and non-threatening.

An adult male lay prone, naked on a birthing table, too weak and exhausted to move. His bald head and almost skeletal form set against a bulging midsection with no belly button. Alabaster skin covered all six feet and one inch of the ungainly creature. If you were to guess, you would say he was in his mid-twenties and dying of something horrible. You would be only half right. A mirror slid out from a wall, extending and reflecting an unfamiliar face. It was gaunt and alien. A calming female voice interrupted the newborn's self-scrutiny.

"Subject 25, welcome. My name is Azraelle. I will be your interface."

The words had feeling but no meaning.

> **Day 2.** I am moving Subject 25 out of the birthing chamber and into his living space. The feeding tube has been a success, and he is showing cognitive acceleration on par or better than past subjects. His physical advancement is ahead of schedule, as he is able to wriggle on his own. I estimate erect movement within eight to ten days.

Subject 25 crawled across the cool floor in starts and stops, battling gravity and losing. Each time he fell, 25 obstinately tried again, his will to succeed strong. The composite floor was smooth with just a touch of texture to allow traction. The problem was that the texture had worn through his jumpsuit, causing scabs on both knees. And it hurt, forcing him to crawl with his knees up. It was something he was mostly failing at. The feeding and water tubes were placed three feet off the floor, causing him to crane his neck to use them. 25's skeletal shape was slowly filling in while his ungainly potbelly was fading. The room contained several banks of indirect UV lighting, which was proven to help the skin and eyes as they developed. At first, he hid from the bright glow, but now it was second nature.

> **Day 14.** Subject 25 has shown sufficient progress to move past termination to initialize restart. I will commence with the ALMA (Advanced Language, Math, and Arts) program and continue physical therapy until he is fully developed. He is quick-witted and eager to learn, even astute, having already developed a sense of self and a determination of will.

Subject 25 moved awkwardly, like a toddler learning to walk, teetering from side to side. The lone trilacycle in the middle of the room rose from the floor. It was a machine designed to work every muscle group at the same time. He straddled the black seat and began his morning session. Music filled the room with band-associated information to go with it, including the name, genre, and decade. The written information was gobbledygook to him, but the rhythm had an energizing feeling. Sweat poured off his newly pigmented skin. It had a slight olive color, and the faintest of hairs were sprouting on his limbs. His muscles struggled to move as form and function began their dance against resistance and gravity. He listened and watched a floating image in front of him as his body strained.

The multipurpose room was a twelve-by-twenty space with padded walls and several configurable apparatuses that could be deployed for physical training and therapy. The floating image in front of him was a technology known as Hollowvision. It used lasers capable of ionizing air molecules to create a three-dimensional view, which allowed the spectator to move or lean and see it from every perspective.

A calm voice matched the images and words as they appeared.

"Apple"

"Aple," Subject 25 repeated poorly.

"Duck"

"Dook"

"Duck."

He tried again, only slightly better.

Day 28. Since initiating phase one, subject 25 has found comfort in routine and is progressing well. His brain is responding and functioning at capacity, and he is nearly ready to begin training in earnest. Interfacing through the Azraelle sensors has had total success. Based on previous subjects, 25 is most capable and progressing ahead of schedule.

The chime for first meal sounded. It was a single tone that repeated every few seconds.

Subject 25 gazed at an image in the mirror, one that was now familiar to him. He ignored the meal alert and focused on the details in front of him: ears, nose, pale green eyes. There were all his and based on the images he had seen of other humans on the Hollowvision, he would fit right in. His body had begun to fill in, with muscle definition showing. Hair had started to grow on his scalp, and his grasp of his four-room world was solidifying, along with images of something much grander. He opened his mouth and let his tongue move about freely. Using his facial muscles, he scrunched and stretched his face, making various poses as he grew more comfortable in the skin he was in.

An urging from Azraelle pulled him from his actions, and he stepped next to the Vaculet, an evacuation machine for when nature called. There were two footprints etched on the floor next to the wall. Subject 25 turned his back to the machine and placed his feet on the prints. As he started to squat, two padded arms extended and cushioned the edge of his butt cheeks. A curved appendage with a pipe-like support moved up between them and sucked onto his undercarriage. The mechanism began to noisily suck out any waste products his body had created and was ready to release. The sensation was intense and a bit overwhelming. Once finished, it rinsed everything with warm water, and then an infrared light quickly dried him off.

Subject 25 pulled his white jumpsuit back up and padded in matching soft shoes toward the galley. As he sat alone at the small table, spooning a beige protein gruel, a cycle of thoughts spun through his mind. It was as if an anxious feeling was sneaking up on him. The walls in his world were closing in. He shook the feeling from his mind and slurped another bite, as lifeless black sensors up on the wall watched his every move.

The eating area was made up of an all-white collection of cabinet-filled walls and a few functioning FDMs, or food delivery machines. The feeding tubes had retracted back into the wall now that he could stand, and he was given a limited selection of synthetic protein tastes from which he could choose. He spied something shiny in the corner of the floor and moved to investigate. A small bearing ring from some previous repair or damage had been overlooked. He collected it up and turned it over in his fingers. It was cool to the touch and a perfect fit for his pinky.

"Subject 25, are you ready to begin?" Azraelle said.

25 pocketed the ring, deciding to hang on to it as a keepsake, and stood. "Ready," he said, without looking back.

An image of a book appeared in front of him. *One Hundred Years Of Solitude*, by Gabriel Marquez. The pages flipped open to a specific passage. Subject 25 read the section aloud. "It is enough for me to be sure that you and I exist at this moment." Subject 25 struggled with pronouncing the word *exist*.

"What do you make of that sentence?" Azraelle asked in a calm voice.

He looked up from his food as he answered. "That I am alive?"

"And what does that mean?"

Day 42. 25 has taken to the training well and has excelled. He is showing signs of restlessness and dissatisfaction, much like subjects 12 through 23. With an occasional outburst, he finds and learns to control his emotions. Further evaluation is needed before proceeding to the next phase or termination and restart like many of the others. Will consider the later response based on the next two weeks' progress.

Subject 25 entered the multipurpose room. The trilacycle rose from the floor. His eyes, now finally fully developed into a creamy brown, scanned the white padded walls, looking for something that was not there. He wore a frown that spread across his chiseled face.

"You are late Subject 25."

He mumbled to himself, "Took a left at the last hallway," even though there was no left.

"Discipline and protocol are imperative for your success."

"You keep talking about *my* success, but I don't have a clue what you mean. You show me images of a planet I've only seen in pictures and expect me to give one hundred percent for something I have no interest in. This is my world . . ." He gestured to the twelve-by-twenty room. ". . . and I have a hard time believing in something I can't touch or see with my own eyes."

A moment of silence followed as Subject 25 held on to his frustration, eying the black orbs that watched without answering. Eventually, he climbed onto the trilacycle and began his session in silence.

"Please report to the galley; it is time for your debriefing." The Azraelle suddenly reported.

"Would you make up your mind?" He climbed down and headed past his small berth with his bed and dresser, the head with its noisy Vaculet, and into the galley with its mixture of stainless and the ever-present white of his world. These four rooms were the only earth he knew, other than a brief memory from the birthing chamber. As he took his seat at the small stainless-steel table in the galley, six opaque glass panels in the room transitioned to a clear view of the outside world. 25 stood transfixed.

At first glance, it was nothing but darkness. Then Subject 25 moved to one of the windows. On the other side, a black void with tiny pinpricks of light filled his view. The closer he got, the more spots of light filled his vision. It was beautiful and awe-inspiring, but at the same time, his world seemed a lot smaller.

25 had no words as the ramifications set in.

"Subject 25, you are aboard the SS Hollanbach."

"SS?" He asked.

"Space Station."

Hidden behind the dark side of a moon was a gray cigar-shaped tube with a cluster of seed-like pods on one end and a looped array on the other in the shape of a dish. Small porthole-style windows populated the cylinder, giving it a tentacled look. It was exactly ninety meters long by twenty meters wide. The fully automated ship was the result of the latest technology of the time, and its location was by design—keeping it hidden from warring factions. The dish on the far end was a Na-TECC converter, which stood for "sodium thermo-electro-chemical converter." It peaked out just past the shadow of the moon to get rays from the sun and use them to generate power by thermally driving a sodium redox reaction that pushed electrons through a solid electrolyte. This generated enough raw power to support two ships the size of the SS Hollanbach. There were no moving parts and simple table salt could be used as an activator. The power was stored in a graphene-based supercapacitor, giving the ship plenty of power and a long life expectancy.

The SS Hollanbach rotated to generate gravity, providing its occupant a realistic freedom of movement. The ship was divided into several sections. The top end, close to the converter, was dedicated to the ship's automation. Computers of every type ran redundant chores and maintenance operations, including Azraelle's AI. A bevy of robotic machines capable of cleaning, repairing, and replacing anything on the ship via 3D printers and onboard tools were stored and recharged there. Azraelle, named after the Greek god of life, death, and rebirth, was in charge of the incubating, birthing, and raising of the ship's humans. She (if you could call it that) was a specialized computer with limited AI and a mandate to complete her task at all costs. Over the last fifteen years, she had sent five pods back to earth and been forced to destroy and recommence all the other candidates due to incompatibility issues with her directives.

The middle of the ship contained the living and birthing quarters where a mixture of oxygen and nitrogen filled the area, giving the fragile human breathable air and just enough room to train and educate. It was not ideal but sufficient for his needs.

The bottom of the station housed several pods capable of returning the subjects to the nearest planet once their training and education were complete. There had been no contact with the five pods that had previously left and as per her programming, Azraelle would continue until there were no more viable samples in inventory.

Since first arriving on the station, the ship was cut off from any incoming and outgoing communications as a safety measure. All information currently onboard was frozen in time with the current affairs of civilization relative to fifteen years ago. The downside was obvious, and the upside was they had not been discovered by any of the warring factions who might have survived the war and been looking for the ship. Secrecy was at the very core of their survival.

25 turned his face from the glass separating him from the cold vacuum of space, his mind reeling.

The soft, friendly voice spoke up. "During a worldwide civil war, a group of dedicated scientists and technicians launched and hid the SS Hollanbach behind the moon. This ship is equipped with onboard genetic samples and automated growing incubators capable of birthing adult specimens to be educated and trained for reinsertion on planet Earth. Since then, it has been my mission to send these trained and educated humans back."

"And I'm what . . . the twenty-fifth subject you've tried this with?" he asked.

"The SS Hollanbach is a purpose-built ship for the continuity of the human race."

"Terrific."

2

Day 56. Subject 25 has passed phase one and is ready to begin phase two. He has command of his first language and a physical presence sufficient for the requirements ahead. His brief bouts of anger and frustration have been growing. There is concern over his behavior and emotional state, but as long as he continues to progress and stays within my tangential parameters, I will push for launch at 180 days.

A soft chime ended, waking 25 from his morning slumber. He leaned up on one elbow, letting the sleep depart and his head clear. His bed was just wide and long enough for his needs, with matching white linen. He sat up and pulled the covers off, revealing a firm and muscular physique, with a full head of curly sandy-brown hair and an expression of annoyance. Judging eyes scanned the room with concern. He pulled the ring from his pocket and moved it mindlessly from finger to finger, staring at the shiny metal surface.

"Good morning, Subject 25. It is day fifty-six of your existence."

"Thanks for the update," he countered with no small amount of sarcasm.

A song started to play, and 25 glanced up at the screen to see its information.

Some singer named Elvis Presley and a song called "A Little Less Conversation." It had a good beat and catchy lyrics with a gritty sound. 25 stood and danced a bit to the beat, enjoying the feeling.

"Next," he said, and Azraelle's playlist jumped forward several decades to something that sounded smoother and more electronic. He stopped dancing and went back to getting dressed and pulling on his shoes.

25 was being educated on a broad spectrum of topics, from basic survival techniques to more advanced subjects, like metallurgy and chemistry. He was trained in self-defense and was taught weapons use and handling. Things that would help him take what was left on Earth and improve his environment.

"Today, you will meet your counterpart," Azraelle announced.

25 stopped and looked toward Azraelle's sensors with sudden interest. "Counterpart? You mean you created more of me?"

"Every cycle consists of three phases and two subjects, male and female. Past experience has shown the best results come from an insertion between fifty and sixty-five days."

"Best results? I take it you've had bad results?" he asked.

The question was followed by a moment of silence. "Yes."

25 left his cabin with a million different thoughts flowing through his mind. *Another human.* He hurried down the hallway that connected his four-room world.

He had read and seen images of the great civil war on Earth. It had been devastating to both the planet and humanity. As a one-off—and now perhaps one of two—he felt no connection to those humans or responsibility to fix what they had destroyed. He was created to play the role of Adam, and it made him feel like a lab rat. With every step, his anger grew. He was no plug-and-play drone. If being human was what he thought it was, he would do things his way . . . like Napoleon or Churchill.

Though it wouldn't hurt to look at the female. Perhaps he could find some way to make . . .

A panel on the back wall of the galley slowly opened, quelling his rantings mid-thought. Beyond it was a mirror image of his galley. On the other side sat a female on a small matching stainless-steel table. She stood and gazed at 25 like he was some sort of aberration.

"Subject 25 meet Subject 24," Azraelle said.

No words were spoken.

The living quarters on the ship actually contained two identical spaces connected at their galleys by a removable wall, allowing for the simultaneous raising of a breeding pair. Each was individually raised until they were deemed ready to interact, then the couple would learn, train, and work together, just like they would have to on Earth. Once their education and training were completed, they would be escorted to the bottom of the space station where one of the launch pods could be fired off for their journey to the planet Earth. At that point, another set of specimens would be harvested, thawed, and grown. The whole process took just over six months.

The ship's gene pool contained a collection of DNA, frozen eggs, and sperm samples. It was located between the computerized sections and the living quarters of the ship. Currently, there were sixteen viable pairs left. When that was done, the mission of the SS Hollanbach would be complete, and Azraelle would be free to take the ship off station and continue deeper into the universe, using her AI to glean and learn as she went.

25 watched as 24's eyes traced his narrow waist, across his flat stomach and broad shoulders, and finally landed on his face. He knew he had the face of a man with the look of a boy. A small smile grew as she took a tentative step toward her new partner, not sure what to do next.

Everything 25 had been feeling and fostering vanished in a heartbeat as the female stepped forward. She had a smoothness in her movements that seemed effortless. Short blonde hair topped aqua blue eyes and her shape . . . It was very different from his. Of all the females he had learned and read about, she was different because she was real and standing right in front of him; it wasn't a Hollowvision. His heart raced as he tried to comprehend what to do next, as undisciplined eyes danced across her form, unsure of what to focus on. She had full hips, a thin waist, and firm breasts. She had a strong chin, pink lips, and a button nose. There was a stray piece of hair that obscured her left eye, but the intelligence within seemed to radiate out. She was intoxicating and intimidating all at once.

The female lifted a finger in his direction, and he returned the gesture, much like the Creation of Adam fresco on the ceiling of the Sistine Chapel. *Touch.* It was something new to feel another human, and they quickly pulled their fingers back, feeling awkward and vulnerable.

After another few minutes, "25," she spoke.

"24," he countered.

They stared at each other for a few more minutes before the spell was broken by a disrupting voice. "I will let you two get to know each other."

24 stood about five foot seven, with perfect creamy skin and a pair of matching dimples that expressed themselves without effort. She moved to the table and sat down as if her legs were suddenly feeling weak. A glance back at the tall man in front of her allowed him to internalize a question. He hoped she found him appealing with his olive skin.

Eventually, 25 joined her at the table, and he found his voice again. Once the conversation started, it lasted an hour or so before the two-tone chime sounded for the second meal.

Over the next few weeks, 24 and 25 trained and studied together. As the only two human subjects on the ship, a bond between them grew quickly. They found commonalities in each other as well as many differences. 24 was a natural-born follower, eager to learn and dedicated to her task. 25, not so much. He was given to the occasional outburst, mainly focused on Azraelle and the confined quarters that held them prisoner. He often refused to follow the rules or did his own version of a drill.

Azraelle had sensors and image collectors throughout the ship. She used them to interface with the two humans and to watch their every move, constantly observing and judging. Even the slightest missteps were corrected, as their successes were positively reinforced. This seemed to agitate 25, who was happy to express his individualism.

A single padded pole about six feet tall with two motion-detecting eyes near the top pushed up through the floor in the utility room. 24 and 25 had just finished their morning studies, and it was time to train physically.

"Level three." Echoed through the room, and 24 stepped forward.

Three soft tones rising in pitch followed as she lowered her body into a fighting stance. 24 was wearing a white textured leotard that wicked sweat away and provided muscle support. The tightly fitting outfit showed off every curve and detail but flexed easily with motion.

25 leaned against the wall to watch his partner's action, but his eyes kept drifting and focusing on the differences in her body. It was mesmerizing to watch, and he didn't know what compelled him to do so. A warm feeling coursed through his body, and he let the feeling envelop him rather than fight it. A smile grew on his face that he couldn't hide.

24 noticed his dopey look. "What?"

"Nothing," 25 replied as the tips of his ears suddenly burned. "You got this."

24 returned her attention to the upcoming fight.

The pole, called an E-Chung, spun and turned erratically, using moving extendable side posts for feet and hands to simulate hand-to-hand combat. 24 had mastered the E-Chung's first two levels and was trying for the third. Today was going to be her day. Her mind flipped between her task and the image of 25's goofy face.

The sudden machinations of the E-Chung had 24 jumping, weaving, and ducking, just to keep from taking a hit. It forced her to the defensive side of the fight almost immediately, hardly giving her a chance to get a punch or kick off.

"Watch the back fist and leg sweep!" 25 called out from his place on the wall.

It was too late. A sudden reverse in direction caught 24 in the side of the head just as a lower arm on the E-Chung swept across both of her feet. 24 went down in a *humph*. She rubbed the bump on her head and got back up to reengage. Three soft tones chimed, and the fight continued.

"Okay, keep your hands up," 25 encouraged.

Again, the speed of the E-Chung was too much for 24, and she ended up in a heap with the wind knocked out of her.

"Let's take a break," 25 said as he squatted next to her.

"Let's?" 24 countered as she rubbed the side of her head.

"It's hard work seeing you get the crap beat out of you," 25 said.

24 seemed confused as she twisted and looked at her butt. "There is no crap coming out of me."

"It's a figure of speech. Meaning beat-up. Something I picked up in one of my slang courses."

"Yes, you're learning slang, while I am learning French."

"Hey, it's one of the few options we had a choice about, right? Might come in handy if we find a city."

"The chance of a city surviving on Earth is 12.5 percent," Azraelle interrupted.

25 rolled his eyes and put on some charm as he looked back at 24. "It's still a chance," he said with a raised eyebrow.

24 smiled at the effort.

"That means there is an 87.5 chance there will be no cities."

They glanced toward the all-seeing orbs that governed every room—a black pair of lenses that articulated and followed their every move, always watching and listening.

25 gave it a sour expression.

"Subject 24, please return to your training."

25 stood and stepped up to the visual receptors and challenged back. "She's had enough, for now, Azraelle."

"It is imperative that you master the E-Chung. Should there be any enhanced survivors on the planet, they will surely have, at minimum, this speed and skill set."

"This speed and skill set," 25 mocked back. "If 24 dies of a concussion in training, then your whole plan goes down the drain. How am I supposed to repopulate the earth by myself?" He mocked with a dose of sarcasm. "What are you going to do, then?"

"There are measures and backups in place should one of you falter. Beginning with a full restart and a—"

"What? Are you kidding me?"

"25!" 24 called out. "I'm okay. Let it go."

There was a moment of deadly silence. "Please disregard. You are right; we will return to training later. It is time for a biological break."

The chimes for second meal sounded.

"I'm tired of taking orders from you. I'm ready for some me time. That's what I think."

"25, please," 24 pleaded.

"Take your little plan and shove it!" 25 yelled at the lifeless orbs staring back at him. The extreme emotion surprised 25, and he fed off it, ripping the arm off the E-Chung and swinging it at Azraelle's sensors.

"This is not my plan. I have been purpose-built to resupply the earth with viable breeding pairs by the Tenet Project team. It is of the utmost . . ." The voice died abruptly.

The impact had smashed the orbs from the wall, and sparks flew and then died.

"25! What was that?" 24 yelled.

"That is what I like to call a bit of satisfaction." He dropped the arm, then turned and left the room, a pleased look plastered across his face as his anger faded.

A small mechanical robot entered and began cleaning up and repairing the damage.

24 stood and headed for the galley, tears filling her eyes. 25's unfamiliar emotion and response left her confused and a little scared.

Day 79. Subject 24 is showing continued improvement in her language and aptitude learning. She has been behind on her physical training but ahead in every other category. Anticipate complete immersion and qualification by day 180. She will excel in the mission. Subject 25 continues to struggle with finding his way. He is a quick learner but often procrastinates or just disregards the lesson. His individuality may prove valuable on earth but not here.

25 placed a set of ER viewers over his eyes and stepped onto the multidirectional mat. The goggles were used to give the wearer a fully immersive enhanced-reality experience. The image on the screens came to life, and 25 was transported to Earth's surface. There were destroyed buildings and burned-out cars. The wind blew an assortment of trash across his path. The ER viewer provided shooting practice within a variety of scenarios in the environment, from black-clad bad guys to rabid dogs attacking from behind and the side. The experience was connected to the subject neurologically. The curriculum worked the mind and reflexes, giving the player vital fundamentals in handling, aiming a firearm, and discerning hostiles in split seconds of time.

24 watched from the side of the training room with amusement as her partner moved and ducked, firing off his ER pistol in an unheard and unseen battle. He looked dorky and vulnerable without the aid of seeing what he was reacting to. It was one of her favorite things because the moment he took off the ER viewers, he would be back on guard, his eyes always looking for a way out, but for now, he was just a boy in a man's body.

25 was often difficult to read. One second he was making eye contact with just a hint of a smile. It gave her a rush of emotion she was still trying to understand. The next, he was angry, and she couldn't get far enough away. Was it like that with all males? They seemed to carry their emotions on the outside—easily corrupted and changed. She would need more time with him if she was to figure it all out.

25 finished his training and stepped off the mat. He looked up to 24 and released a breath. A smirk followed, and his eyes twinkled as he handed the ER viewer and gun to 24. Fingers touched fingers as the exchange was made, and both could feel the intensity that grew in their bodies from it. They let the moment linger before it was broken by 25.

"1650. Let's see you beat that."

24 took the pistol. "Challenge accepted." She stepped onto the mat, and her mind filled with the requirements of their mission. If the world had truly destroyed itself, it would be up to 24 and 25 to not only repopulate it but to build a modern version. Something that was compatible and user-friendly to humans and the environment. The knowledge they carried would be the difference between living in a cave or rebuilding a modern society. After all, knowledge was only a generation away from being lost and sending humankind back to the Stone Age. It would be up to them to prevent this from happening and pass on their experience to future generations.

24 pulled from her thoughts, realizing that she had been shot and killed. The game was standing by, waiting for her to reset and start over. She glanced up at the score. *Zero.*

25 closed his eyes and let his mind drift. It was a cleansing process he had adapted to help him reset after a particularly intense learning session. The speed and intensity they had been required to follow were brutal. Every waking moment seemed to be filled with uploading information or skills into their brains and muscles. Sometimes at night, his head would pound with the punishment it had taken throughout the day, or his muscles twitched involuntarily.

He lay on his bed, sweat still glistening on his forehead, as he pondered the day's events and slowly let it all go.

Today was the first time he had really felt like his world was so small and tight he could not go on. In the beginning, when he had no perspective of his outside world, the ship had been everything to him, but once Azraelle opened all the windows, it made him feel like one of those twentieth-century sardines that came all smashed together in a can, another thing he had learned in slang class.

24 had done a lot to change his perspective. She was dedicated to the mission, and her diligence sometimes rubbed off. If they could just hold on a bit longer, they could get out of this place and into their brand-new world.

He sat up and stepped to the small round porthole in his berth next to the storage dresser. The stars lit the backside of the moon, giving it plenty of detail. He felt like he could just reach out and touch its roughly textured gray surface. 25 imagined taking a stroll over its scalloped indentations and appealing open spaces and never coming back to the same place. It was hard to perceive. Without protective gear, he wouldn't last fifteen seconds out there. A Hollowvision instructional had shown him that exact scenario.

Supposedly, the earth was just on the other side of the moon. Though he had never seen it, except in pictures and motion visuals, the colors he'd been shown seemed improbable. His life and everything he could touch or see around him was a limited palette. Growing up in a cylindrical white world, the kind of color the earth had was as extreme as fire to an infant's fingers. Even the moon out his window was monochromatic. A planet filled with color seemed more like science fiction than fact.

The more he learned on the SS Hollanbach, the more he was convinced he was not the right man for this job. The whole idea of supposedly traveling through space to this "earth" and landing there to start anew seemed beyond reach. Living in a constrained artificial tin can with nothing but a dictate of something better was unfathomable. It went against 25's instincts, and he found himself more and more annoyed, to the point of battling just to stay the course.

Maybe that would change when they got to Earth . . . if they got to Earth.

24 had become his rock, his go-to confidante. She was special and marvelous in everything. The way she cocked her head when she wasn't sure of an answer or the sideways glance she'd give when 25 tried to be funny. 24 could mesmerize the soul just by the way she ate her food. She could even placate Azraelle, which was no small task, but his favorite was her eyes, especially when they made contact with his. It was like a charge of energy being released right into your gut. It felt like a drill boring into the back of his head while floating on a cloud.

25 pulled back from the port window and looked at the two orbs ominously staring at him.

"What's on your mind, Azraelle?"

"What's on your mind, Subject 25?" Her voice was a combination of soothing and judgmental.

"I feel like I can't . . . breathe."

"Adjusting the oxygen level."

"No." He calmed slightly. "I can't breathe in this cooped-up world you have created. I need a change. Something different; I don't know . . . maybe some context." 25 picked at an imperfection along his cuticle as he spoke.

After a beat, Azraelle replied. "Please find Subject 24 and report to the galley."

25 looked up at the cold spheres spinning in his direction; there was never an emotion to go with her words. He gave a subtle nod and left his room, still unfulfilled.

24 was already sitting in the galley, drinking from a water tube and repeating various French phrases that matched a floating screen in front of her. As 25 entered, the small screen vanished and a large image of Earth materialized in the space between them. 25 walked through the projection and sat next to 24.

The face of an older man with dark skin and white curly hair appeared. He had kind, intelligent eyes and square-framed glasses.

"Hello, I'm Doctor Honeywell. I was the lead biologist on the Tenet Project. It included a secret build and the launch of a space station with the sole mission of preserving humankind in its original form; and if everything is going to plan, you are watching me now, preparing yourselves to return to Earth. Let me begin with some context."

The Hollowvision of the doctor faded out and a 3D view of Earth returned. 24 and 25 shared a glance before turning back to the projection.

"A series of global pandemics shook the human race to its core. This was not like any previous quarantinable contagions but four distinct viral outbreaks with world-ending ramifications."

The continents on the spinning globe were slowly covered in red.

"The first—a virus known as Marburg Virus G—spread across the globe, instilling fear in every doorknob and stranger."

An image of the virus and its name appeared. It looked like a U-shaped yellow caterpillar with green, red, and blue dots all over it.

"The WHO and CDC worked diligently to combat this plague and help develop a vaccine that would save the world. People were encouraged to get the vaccine to help slow the spread. The encouragement led to government mandates that caused a rift between those who were vaccinated and those who were not. You see, many humans were opposed to the vaccines. They believed the future of humankind was in those that survived the pandemics through natural immunity. Natural selection, after all, has been a part of all species throughout time. A vaccine so quickly produced held too many variables. While the other side believed one death was too many and any way to save lives was worth it."

A bold graphic showing the evolution of natural selection popped up on the Hollowvision.

"As all this was happening, the Metaverse was taking over the minds and imagination of most of the civilized world. Many people never left their homes. Everything they needed was within arm's reach, and the threat of sickness just on the other side of their doors didn't help. The difference of opinion grew and polarized humanity. Those in power saw it as an opportunity and acted. It was easy to affect opinion in the Metaverse. People who live in a false world are subject to the whims of it."

A view of hundreds of computers being controlled to manipulate reality was projected.

"What the public didn't know was that this vaccine held additional mRNA markers that were designed to modify the human genome. They used Cas9 to cut the DNA and alter the cell's gene. Over the course of the next six years, four more pandemics swept the earth, forcing additional vaccines to be developed using the same modified Cas9-mRNA injections. This ultimately gave the three pharmaceutical companies that developed successful vaccines the power over life and death."

Images that matched the narration appeared.

"By the time it was over, there had been a shift in world dominance and humanity. The pharmaceutical companies who had patented and now owned the genetic modifications that were part of millions of humans started flexing their muscles. These modifications not only allowed them to do a host of things, like monitor and modify health and prevent sickness. This allowed these companies to charge a monthly fee to everyone who used their modifications, turning on a faucet of financial boon and placing the hand of control over a vast portion of the world."

24 leaned back against the table.

"The gap in humanity grew, and what became known as the Vaxxer Age emerged. Humans effectively divided themselves into two groups: the vaccinated and the non-vaccinated. Over time, cities polarized themselves and became uniformly one or the other. Detroit in Michigan, for example, was a non-vaxxer city, whereas Tokyo in Japan was a vaxxer city. There were harsh travel restrictions, as you can imagine. A vaxxer city wanted nothing to do with a non-vaxxer, and the marketing spin doctored by those in power only added fuel to the growing fire."

Images of extreme poverty with emaciated humans hidden behind barriers and fences moved through the air.

"That riff continued as big corporations fought against one another to oversee the planet. The key was in getting control of the non-vaxxers."

Images of blocked highways and marching protesters appeared.

"Pro-vaxxer campaigns and pride marches soon gave way to a new moniker, Hu 2.0, for 'human version 2.0.'"

Hate-filled groups were shown carrying anti-non-vaxxer signs and marching through the streets chanting, "No 1.0s."

"It gave the vaxxers a superiority complex, partly because they truly believed they *were* better than the original version of man. This upgraded version of man, or Hu 2.0, was the next evolutionary step. Soon, other enhancements became available, like heart and eyesight improvements, lab-grown organs, and chip implants, but these things are not always for the best. 2.0s embraced a new version of man, and as long as you made your payments, everything went great. To be clear, the 2.0s were not bad. Many of my friends were 2.0s."

25 leaned forward and placed his arms on his knees.

"Eventually, a global war broke out. Not country against country, but intercorporate war, fueled by a need to control all humanity. They pitted Hu 2.0s against Hu 1.0s. The result was a loss of billions of lives and a consolidation of power and wealth such as the world had never seen. Many of our most advanced technologies were destroyed: the Metaverse, our space program, and even our most modern cities. As the Hu 1.0s started to lose the war, a dedicated group of scientists began the Tenant Project and started work on the SS Hollanbach. A plan to insure the continuance of us, our original species. A way to say goodbye to disease with a path for a better future for all, without the strings of corporate power controlling everything. For surely, by the time you are watching this, the world has destroyed itself. You are humanity's last hope."

The image disappeared, and silence filled the room. It was heavy and thick.

After a beat, 25 spoke in a whisper. "It's not my responsibility to fix what others have broken."

Two black orbs followed, as 25 left the room. They seemed to linger after him before returning to their view of 24, still sitting at her table and looking like her own world was breaking apart.

"24, I am detecting an unacceptable level of hostility growing in Subject 25. I will look to you to help curb that angst until you arrive on Earth."

24 looked up at the sensor that connected them to Azraelle. "Of course," she said as tears flowed.

Day 86. Subject 25 seems to have only grown more agitated. Subject 24 has had little effect on redirecting his focus. I see no path forward that allows for success. Will begin the termination sequence after four bells. It will be unsettling to have to eliminate Subject 24 as well, but there is no place for a lone female on this ship waiting until the next male catches up.

25 placed his used food bowl in the evacuator, an automated cleaning system that sterilized, cleaned, and returned the bowl in seconds. The last two days had been sullen and quiet. 24 had been respectful and helpful, but the constant closeness made it impossible to just turn it all off. Azraelle seemed to always be watching and pushing them forward. Just once, he wanted to go the other way. He lay back on the galley table and stretched his back on the hard, cool surface.

24 watched as she finished her dinner. She had a strong sense of compass that led her forward on an efficient and effective path. Dedication was one of her strengths, and she was determined to fulfill her mission. The problem was trying to get a read on her partner. He seemed way too preoccupied with himself, constantly pushing back against the system. She had no idea what was to be gained by his actions and didn't understand how they were going to succeed on Earth if he kept up like this.

Letting his mind wander, 25 spoke without looking. "What do you think about taking a walk with me on the moon?"

24 looked over at her partner and allowed the fantasy to breathe. "Craters or mountains?"

"I'm thinking just the flat areas, somewhere we could have a picnic. Preferably on the other side so we could see Earth. That is if it really exists." He stood and walked to the porthole window, which had a perfect view of the dark side of the moon.

"The earth exists," 24 replied.

"Oh? You've seen it, or are you just taking that on faith?"

"No . . . but I've read all about it, and I can describe it in great detail," she said as she stood and approached 25.

"So faith. I could say the same thing about the Jabberwocky. Yet it doesn't exist," 25 said.

"That's ridiculous. You know, sometimes you seem like you don't want to go with me to save humankind."

25 turned from the window to look at 24. "*Save humankind*. You say that like it's been programmed into your brain." He tapped the side of his head to punctuate his words.

"I guess it has, but it's why *we* exist. And being programmed doesn't mean you don't have control."

25 looked at 24 with a dour expression. He knew he would never convince her, so he decided to let it all go and just enjoy their moment. "Yeah, yeah. I've heard it all, but luckily my feelings for you are not connected in any way to our mission or the programming."

24 stepped closer to 25. "Feelings?"

"Sure. You are the most amazing woman I have ever known."

"Jerk."

"What? That shouldn't change the impact of my statement—just because I have not met another real woman."

"No, you're right. It shouldn't," 24 conceded. "So what is it that makes you think I'm amazing?"

25 took her by the hand and led her over to the table where they sat down, side by side. He turned and looked straight into her aqua-blue eyes, smiling coyly. "You are intelligent, gentle, and kind. You don't let circumstances get to you, and I think I would have lost my mind completely by now if you hadn't been here."

24 smiled at 25's comments. "I think you might still be losing your mind."

"Undoubtedly . . . Oh, and I find you super attractive. Like I could kiss you right now."

24 had no words.

25 leaned in and touched lips with his partner. There was an awkwardness followed by a subtle pleasure that grew as they explored the texture and softness of each other's lips. A white-hot burning filled their bodies as 25 placed his arm around 24 and pulled her closer. Eventually, 24 pulled back and opened her eyes, trying to catch her breath.

"Wow."

"Yeah, wow," 25 replied.

The ship's chime sounded four times, indicating it was bedtime. 24, like a trained seal, pulled out of 25's arms and looked a mixture of ashamed and hungry for more. She reached back in and pecked 25 on the lips before turning for her berth. "Good night . . . partner."

25 couldn't help but let the corners of his mouth reach for the bulkhead. "Just when things were getting interesting," he said to himself as he watched her leave the room. The view suddenly seemed more magnificent than normal.

The moon was especially detailed that night as he looked out his window after a visit to the head. 25 let his mind drift in imagination, choosing a path they could follow on their proposed picnic. He pulled the small bearing ring he had collected and moved it through his fingers, knowing now what to do with it. He placed it next to his bed for later, reliving the feeling that had taken over his body as they kissed. He couldn't wait to feel that again, so he let his imagination progress until he had 24 in a firm grasp and her lips pressed to his. The automated lighting in his room dimmed, and he reluctantly tore himself from the fantasy.

Climbing into bed, he let the day's events melt away. He was looking forward to tomorrow for the first time in weeks.

24 sat in bed with her arms around her knees. She swayed slowly back and forth, letting her mind fill with warm, fuzzy thoughts.

"24."

She looked up at the ever-present lenses of Azraelle. "Yes?"

"I am sorry to report that Subject 25 has not fulfilled his parameters."

"What do you mean?"

There was a pause. "He has been set for termination and rebirth."

"What. No! Please. I can make this work. It is working. Didn't you see us in the galley?"

"I see everything, 24. My programming is very specific," Azraelle said.

"I am making progress. 25 is making progress. We can do this together. Just give us a few more days."

Silence filled her plea. "There is nothing left to do but to start over," Azraelle said.

"Start over? I can't go through all this again. Please, just give me a little more time; you'll see."

"I know." The voice replied as though it hadn't heard the last of her sentence.

A panel slid over the door, sealing her into the small room. A small vent on the ceiling started to release gas into the room.

24's pleading quickly turned to panic when she realized what was happening. She banged on the panel and tried to pry it open. "Please, Azraelle! I can make this work. I can fix him. Don't do this!"

24 put her arm over her face and tried to breathe through her clothes. She pleaded for a few more minutes until she realized it was hopeless. She let gravity pull her to the floor, and the tears flowed. There was nothing more she could do but die.

Day 86, addendum. Termination proceedings have begun. Subjects 24 and 25 are no longer viable. Once the bodies are disposed of and the ship cleaned, I will resume birthing duties, as the next pairing might prove more successful. This is another example of inherited traits versus learned behavior. Control of the human species is variable and unpredictable at best. Will attempt to raise the next subjects in total isolation until they depart.

25's eyes fluttered open. His room was dark, and there was a hissing sound coming from a vent. He tried to stand, but his legs failed him. He dropped to the floor, unable to move. His mind flickered with the possibilities of what might be happening, interspersed with flashing images of 24 and their time together.

Just before he closed his eyes for good, the hissing stopped. The silence was followed by a flashing red light and a firm male voice he had never heard before. "Proximity alert: impact eminent."

Then his world ended.

3

The SP TigerShark was designed for a single mission. It didn't feel or make decisions about anything. Just a series of ones and zeros routing one way or another. The moment it came out of its arc around Earth and started to slingshot beyond Earth's gravitational pull and toward the moon, it began a series of soundings, much like sonar on a submarine. It was looking for something. The Space Probe TigerShark was just over twelve feet long with a variable diameter that started at three feet and narrowed to one. It had a slight spiral as it moved through space. Once a sounding was returned, tedious analytics were engaged to process the information, with a single focus at its core: seek and destroy. It used sophisticated intelligence to avoid the space junk that ringed the planet. A lifetime of broken satellites and space weapons destined to float in a slow spiral back to Earth.

A confirmation code was dispatched back to control, "SS Hollanbach confirmed," and the targeting system took over, adjusting its trajectory in minuscule quantities. At fifty kilometers to target, the electromagnetic rails powered up and at ten kilometers, it fired a single spent plutonium ball down the rails, exponentially speeding up with each foot of travel. The hardened heavy metal was not explosive and would do little more than punch a hole in anything it encountered, but to a spaceship, it would be devastating.

The sound was distant but alarming. Everything he felt seemed muddled and slow. Even his brain refused to engage. It was like swimming in a viscous gel. His eyes fluttered open to a familiar sight now painted in red. A face stood over him, her arms shaking his body as her voice slowly became clear.

"25, we have to go!"

A slightly concerned male voice repeated his mantra. "Proximity alert: impact eminent."

24 shook him again, and it seemed to register this time. He sat up on the floor of his room, where a red warning light was flashing, painting the space in a metronome of red and black.

"We have to go now!" 24 shouted.

"Okay . . . Where to?" He asked as his head tried to clear itself from the poisonous gas that had taken him to the brink of death.

"Off the ship. Follow me."

25 stood on wobbly legs and followed his partner out of his berth before realizing he had forgotten something important. He stumbled back into his berth and grabbed the ring off his nightstand just as the ship shuttered. Running as fast as he could down the hall and into the galley, 25 caught back up with 24. They repeated the pattern in reverse—galley, hall, berth, head—coming to a sealed hatch at the bottom of the space station. 24 tried the lever. Nothing.

"Open the door!" she screamed at the two orbs looking down at her. They stared unblinking, like a menacing ghoul with no soul. No reply.

The ship shuddered again, this time starting to list.

"You're the one that stopped the termination order. Azraelle, you know this is the only way. Either 25 and I live right now or no human does."

The only reply was the repeated warning that echoed throughout the ship.

The SS Hollanbach suddenly, violently shook as multiple muted explosions started taking down the upper half of the ship. Loss of oxygen and depressurization happened almost instantly. Sparks shot out as electrical systems failed and death chased its way toward the two humans at the bottom of the ship. Suddenly, the hatch turned green. 25 didn't wait. He pulled the lever, and the door opened. The ship's systems died; the gravitational rotation slowed, making them lighter with each second that passed.

25 grabbed 24 by the wrist as she was suddenly sucked back toward the approaching melee. He pulled her into the room and used all his strength to close the door against the pressure difference. Once shut, 25 slammed the lever down, sealing them inside. He held onto the handle as his body became weightless. The oxygen was low, and they both had to hyperventilate just to breathe. They wouldn't last long.

25 crawled along the pipework inside the room toward an exit hatch to his right. It was flashing a green light, and he had no view of what lay on the other side. He reached for the handle, still trying desperately to breathe.

"Stop!" 24 shouted. "I don't trust her; she could still be trying to kill us."

"What are you talking about?" 25 asked.

"Azraelle . . . she selected us for termination last night."

25 looked at his partner like she was crazy.

"Something about us not meeting the parameters of her mission statement," she added.

Then it all made sense. The hiss in his room last night; the complete loss of motor skills and the blackness that followed.

"That bit—" A familiar voice interrupted him.

"Subjects 25 and 24. I have prepared an escape pod for you. You have twelve seconds until you pass out from a lack of oxygen."

"Bite me, Azraelle. You tried to kill us!" 25 yelled.

The entire ship shuttered again as it started to die.

"Circumstances have changed." Azraelle started having problems with her voice as her processors shut down. "I am also . . . one who pumped . . . reversing agent . . . your rooms . . . prevent . . . term . . . . -ation. Pl . . . hurry . . . now have six sec . . . Due t . . . incomplete training and dysfunctional behavior . . . a nine percent chance of success . . ." A warbling sound followed and then nothing.

"I'll take action over odds any day." 25 yelled back at her as he took one last breath and opened the hatch.

The view through the front glass was indescribable. At first, the sun blasted the cockpit, blinding 24 and 25 onboard the escape pod, and then it moved to the right and a blue variegated sphere appeared, filling their hearts and minds.

"Earth," 25 exclaimed. "It's real."

24 had no words as she gawked. Then, "I told you it was real" finally moved past her lips.

"What do they call it when faith becomes reality?" 25 asked.

"Science.," 24 surmised.

"No . . . home."

25 and 24 gazed at the planet as they moved past the moon and began the trip to the big blue marble.

"It's beautiful."

"From here it is. But for all we know, that blue could be due to cobalt 60 and more than a few hours of exposure is lethal."

"I guess we'll find out together."

Less than ten minutes ago, the duo had popped the hatch to an escape pod access room. A flashing green light above EP5 pulled them to the fifth escape pod. 25 had shoved 24 inside and slammed the hatch behind him. He blew the restraining bolts holding them in place, and the ship's automation quickly took over. The craft's ion-beam emitters pushed them away from the failing SS Hollanbach just before it exploded. They had watched in silence as their only known home was destroyed. The last image was a ripped-up section of the head, Vaculet still attached to its wall as it drifted past. The pod then course-corrected and spun around toward the front as they cleared the moon, opening their view to a whole new world. 25 reached for 24's hand and gave it a reassuring squeeze as he waited for the inevitable failure or destruction of their capsule, but it never came.

Filled with fear and trepidation, they had lost everything but their lives. They felt unprepared for what was to come and hoped a few months of training would be enough to find their way and survive the path ahead. Could they overcome the dim future Azraelle had forecast right before her circuits were extinguished? They still had each other, and that was truly the only hope that still burned.

Once free of the moon's gravity, the ship increased in speed, leaving the remains of all they had ever known behind, perhaps destined to drift through space for eternity.

"How did you know that hatch wouldn't just open us up to outer space?" 24 asked.

"I didn't. Took a chance."

She looked over at her partner, not liking the cavalier way he did things.

"We would have died either way," he added.

A sober nod agreed with his estimation.

"What do you think it was that destroyed the ship?" 24 asked.

25 had no answer.

The escape pod was small. It had two seats and a tiny standing area behind them with a small suction hose for a toilet and a single food delivery machine. Their chairs would double as beds with the most amazing skylight and a view few would ever see. The pod used its ion emitters to move through space slowly, gaining speed over time.

24 and 25 wore matching white jumpsuits with a rough texture. The cabin was heated, and the air supply was controlled with generated O2 and scrubbers.

25 unbuckled himself and let his body drift out of his seat. It was a marvelous sensation. Soon, 24 did likewise, and they floated free-form around the small space, playing like two five-year-olds. They ended up in each other's arms, eager to explore their passions. 24 pulled 25 close and kissed his lips in an awkward fashion. 25 liked the sensation and replied with a kiss of his own. Electric current consumed them with a feeling beyond description. After a while, 25 pulled back. He was breathing hard. His hand reached into his pocket and came back with the bearing ring he had held onto all these months.

"I've been saving this for something special, and I know that something is you." He placed the ring on 24's left-hand ring finger. "I'm pretty sure this is the right finger." The fit was surprisingly perfect.

"It's beautiful and so shiny. I love it." 24 pulled him back and returned the gift with a passionate kiss that no longer seemed awkward. They explored each other as if learning a new skill, no longer being watched over by Azraelle. Hands, lips, and finally other things. It was a collection of passion and instinct that led to an unexpected pleasure for both. Leaving them both dizzy and satiated.

After a time, they drifted off to sleep, each floating freely, umbilically connected by the loving grasp of hands.

25 twitched with the sudden realization that he had not been consumed by an explosion in space; it was only a dream. He grabbed onto the back of his chair, controlling his floating form.

"Hey, wake up," 25 said gently.

24 stirred and tried to sit up, but being in zero gravity, her body just folded. She didn't go anywhere.

25 gave her a small push, and she drifted over to the wall where she could grab a railing and move her feet to the floor. Earth had gotten much larger since 24 had last seen it. The thing that caught her eye were two large areas of light that populated a darkened continent.

"I think those are cities!" she exclaimed.

25 spun to look, and sure enough, what looked like mega-large population zones glowed and sparked below against a mostly darkened landmass.

Everything they had been taught and expected was wrong.

4

The first effects of Earth's exosphere affected the quality of their ride; it got rough. That was followed by an intense jarring as the craft skipped and finally dove through the thermosphere, where the heat became so intense that the view outside the window turned traumatic. The small cone-shaped capsule with the single observation window was designed and built for this very moment.

24 and 25 had strapped themselves in their seats and hung on, as there was nothing more they could do. The ship was completely automated, and their survival was not determined by their actions.

Eventually, the view grew bluer as they entered the stratosphere from the mesosphere and raced toward terra firma, some thirty kilometers below. The rough ride smoothed out, and they saw scattered clouds as they dove. Two wings deployed from the sides of the craft with a sudden jolt. Their descent became slower, more controlled. Both 24 and 25 were sweating and gripping their chairs in fear. This was something they had never trained for or experienced. It was like giving birth. There was nothing you could do but grit your teeth and breathe until you got to the other side.

At 20,000 feet, the craft turned ninety degrees and locked in on its final trajectory. At 10,000 feet, the craft seemed to be moving too quickly, bent on total destruction. Though 24 had relaxed, she tensed back up as the ground came rushing toward them; the thought of eminent impact front of mind.

At 2,500 feet, retro rockets fired, slowing the craft just enough to allow it to plow into the earth. The craft skipped, slid, and crashed into a grove of small trees, coming to an abrupt rest.

25 rubbed the back of his neck from the sudden stop and pulled his harness off with his free hand. He leaned over to help 24 do the same. The front screen was cracked. Inside the cabin, electrical circuits were sparking, filling the space with smoke. A small fire broke out and an internal clock in 25's head started ticking. They needed to get out fast.

The craft came to rest on a steep incline wedged between two trees, with the middle third bent and broken from the impact.

25 shoved the exit hatch open and pulled 24 out just as the small fire took hold and grew. He could see their gear lockers were still intact, but the hot flames prevented him from accessing them.

24 jumped down to the ground and wobbled away from the ship. 25 followed right behind her and quickly shoved her behind a large boulder. They waited there for several minutes for an explosion that never came.

Black smoke rose in the air as the fire consumed the capsule. 25 peeked his head out from the boulder, finally determining they were out of harm's way. He stood and helped 24 to her feet. He embraced her as emotion overcame adrenaline.

"We made it."

"Yes . . . but we lost everything," 24 said, looking back at the raging fire that had held all their supplies.

"Not our lives. We'll be okay. Come on," 25 mumbled.

24 started to rise and then looked at the ground she was lying on. It was soft and organic, all things she had never experienced growing up on a spaceship. "Everything is so different here. Even the air smells weird. It's difficult to describe; there's no metallic element to it. I hope it can sustain us," 24 said as she looked around. There were a few birds and squirrels that moved about, but otherwise, the only sound was the wind through the trees and the popping of their space capsule burning to the ground.

25 felt like he had bigger problems to worry about. His mind ran through the four principles of survival: water, fire, shelter, and food.

They were standing on the edge of an open field surrounded by trees. The spaceship had left a furrow across the land before colliding with the trees on the edge. The field had a variety of shorter plants that had made a home there. Taking 24 by the hand, 25 moved across the meadow.

It was strange walking on the uneven surface, which was soft with every step. They found themselves having to lift their feet as they walked, each stumbling multiple times across the ground. The SS Hollanbach's hard even floor was no representation of this world, and after two days at zero gravity, they were like children learning to walk all over again.

24 and 25 had seen images like this on the Hollanbach, the wild open forest. They had even heard its accompanying soundtrack, but experiencing it for real was unlike anything either could have prepared for. "I feel like that couple that was kicked out of the garden and had to fend for themselves."

"You mean Eden?" 24 asked.

"Yeah, that's it."

"Not sure if that was real or not. It might be an allegory."

"Well, this is plenty real to me," 25 finished.

"Yes, it is. Look." 24 stopped and placed her hand on the soft petals of a flower growing in the meadow. "It's so beautiful."

Sturdy trunks of trees filled the area with dappled light, while smaller plants and shrubs grew throughout. The uneven ground slowly rose into the distance.

25 joined her, and they shared a moment of magic. A bee buzzed and landed on the flower. This was truly an amazing place.

A snapping of a stick off to their right had them both frozen. Then a small deer moved through the woods, seemingly unconcerned by their presence. They watched as it foraged on new growth before continuing on. 24 squeezed 25's hand as they watched in wonder.

"We need to find some water and put some distance between us and that column of smoke. If there is anything or anyone bad around here, they are on their way."

"And if there is anything good around here, the same is true," 24 countered.

"Better to be safe than sorry."

24 couldn't argue with that logic.

The rear hatch slammed on the IVC Stryker II, as automated twist locks sealed it in place. It was a purpose-built personnel carrier with the ability to withstand most attacks.

"Go, go, go!" implored the sergeant behind the controls as his team engaged the drive system. Eight tires spun across the loose gravel and left the comfort of the hangar in Fort Camden. The convoy consisted of two Strykers. Each was heavily armed and filled with some of the best warriors in New Kansas.

The eight-wheel-drive transport military vehicle, with its wedge-shaped nose and squared-off rear, was the preferred armored transport of the COE military. It had imaging and targeting capability with a small-caliber rail gun and a plasma cannon mounted on top. Inside, a driver and navigator sat up front at the cockpit-inspired controls, while eight warriors were seated in two bench seats that ran the length of the rear cargo area. Additional gear was stored on the floor between the squad. A powerful bank of Li-S batteries and triple e-motors pushed the 40,000-pound sophisticated chunk of armored steel at up to 80 kph.

Since first detecting an incoming ship from space, the defense systems alerted their operator, who passed the message up the chain of command. A team was quickly scrambled to intercept. It had been years since the last detection, and they had been unable to track and find it. Things were different now. Technology was on the rise again.

The war against the 1.0s had all but been won, and though costly in both dollars and human life, stability and growth were becoming commonplace. With the COE, Congress of Earth, now controlling a majority of all useable land, peace was surely within sight, and it was just a matter of time before the last 1.0 city, Zion, fell.

Commander Weng pulled the last strap on his boot and stood. He glanced over at the nine-year-old girl playing on the floor. She was a marvel of modern technology. Her left arm was so realistic, he often forgot it was a prosthesis. He watched as she deftly combed the hair on her Play-with-me-Maggie doll. His eyes wandered upward to the hideous scar that ran across the top of her head, mostly hidden now by beautiful, curly brown hair. He flashed back to the night six months ago when news of a bloody drone crash had reached him. Flashes of gore and body parts moved in his mind before he repacked them in a mental metal case and locked them back away. He didn't have time for this.

"Carlyle, on station please." The HSR, or home social robot, lit up.

"On station," it replied as it moved from its charging port and into the room. It looked like an upside-down, white bowling pin with a glowing blue human-like graphic for a face and a small revolving tank-like carriage for a base.

Weng knelt down next to his young daughter and kissed her head.

"Ruth, Daddy's gotta go. Carlyle will take care of everything until I get back."

"Okay, Dadda. Are you making the world safe?" she asked with innocent eyes.

"Always, darling." He stood and grabbed the go-bag he kept in the closet and left the house. Just before closing the door, he gave one last demand. "Carlyle, guard."

The CHR's face turned red and a concerned voice replied as a small-caliber barrel poked out of Carlyle's midsection. "Guarding."

Ruth didn't seem to mind. She was far too busy with her dolls.

The PCD R-2 was parked on a section of the roof. As Weng approached the driver's side, the door slid open and the instrument panel powered up. By the time he sat down and put on his harness, the four external disk-like rotors had spun up. All Good's latest version of their personal commuter drones (PCDs) was popular with the elite class. They were fast, had good range, and were fully automated. The cockpit of the R-2 carried two passengers in comfortable seating with a small space behind the seats for storage. It was shaped like an egg with a tapered butt. The four three-foot rotors were attached to the sides equidistant from each other. They could individually articulate to make the PCD quite maneuverable. Weng had paid extra for a custom color, a dark purple paint job to match his upgraded irises.

His eyesight was just one of the many medical upgrades he had opted for, including the muscle burst stim, which gave him a ten percent faster reaction time, and the A2 auditory implants, which enhanced his hearing and could connect directly to transmissions, allowing him to speak and listen without any additional device.

"Fort Camden. Emergency response."

"That is restricted airspace," came a voice from the cockpit.

"Override. Commander L. Weng, ID #256419."

A brief moment passed before the vehicle's computer replied. "Confirmed."

The drone lifted into the air and banked right, quickly reaching maximum speed, leaving the protection of his gated and armed neighborhood behind. A preset path placed them in the highest priority air lane.

Weng used the onboard screen to link with COE command and track the path of the unidentified object hurdling toward Earth. Its trajectory was somewhere southwest of his destination, and it would impact just about the same time he got to the fort. They had received confirmation just a few moments ago, once the UFO's trajectory was confirmed. Now that it had entered Earth's atmosphere, it had lit up the early warning system and alerted the military to take action.

New Kansas was alive this morning with the hum of automation. Its tallest buildings gleamed in the morning sun. The glare hid the corrosion that lived just under the surface. Something only a local would notice.

As the world's last remaining mega-city, it carried a population of just over three million. The war had taken its toll, and the once-gleaming example of modernization and coexistence had started to decay and fracture. The city was filled to its tipping point, bleeding outward beyond its protective wall, now used as a foundation for a high-speed train.

Cars from many eras plied the streets, fighting for every inch along their journeys. Smaller two-wheel electrics seemed to make up most of the traffic, often piled with loads beyond the apparent laws of physics. Weng thought of it as a well-orchestrated symphony, from the street level congestion below to the almost empty air lane four levels above, reserved for special people. He looked out the window. The sun was off to his right, the sky a perfect blue without a cloud in sight. *That will change,* he thought.

Below him were the other designated lanes of transportation, including three other air lanes, each separated by a thirty-foot safety margin. Sequential roundabouts served as intersections and off-ramps. The streets were for people who couldn't afford a PCD, and some of those people could be dangerous. Air lane one was next, just above the street with all the delivery and worker drones. Each with a specific task and destination in mind. It was always congested, and the homogenization of design styles was nonexistent. Air lane two above that was for general public use. All PDs could access and navigate these designated lanes. It was rarely not filled with commuter drones whisking their owners to myriad destinations and automated taxi drones taking fares to every destination.

Above that was air lane three, the fast lane. It was reserved for those who could afford it and local law enforcement, known as Control. It was the lane to fly in if you wanted to see the most expensive drones on the planet. Each was tricked out with sophisticated and personalized upgrades, including the ability to change color to match their owner's whims. The final and highest air lane in the skyway system was rarely used. It was for high-ranking officials and corporation leaders. It also had the best views of the city and the busy life below. It was the air lane Weng was currently traveling in.

The ADS, or automated drone system, maintained the distance, height, and speed of each vehicle. Access was highly controlled and any unauthorized person trying to enter a lane they were not approved for would be in for a surprise, as their drone would automatically redirect them to the nearest control officer. They could be fined or imprisoned, depending on the circumstances.

Weng had always been surprised by how humanity could adapt. Since the start of the Vaxxer War, the planet had been torn apart as two sides fought to destroy the other, but life in the city had gone on. Dentists worked mouths, grocers filled orders, factories pumped out the latest tech, and babies continued to be born. Inside the city, as bad as things got, you would never know just how horrible it was outside.

As lead commander, who reported directly to President Caleb, Weng had a unique perspective on the war and the people they were close to eradicating once and for all. He took great pleasure in his work and often shared the pride in a job well-done that his hand-picked group of warriors were famous for. It allowed him a lifestyle above most, and Weng used this notoriety to leverage his way up the food chain.

Weng looked down the row of seasoned fighters riding with him in the follow vehicle. UBT1 was the acronym for Unit B Team One, and they were some of the deadliest fighters at Fort Camden. Each had distinguished themselves in battle over the years, and he would be proud to fight alongside any man or woman there. President Caleb had personally requested Weng's presence on this mission, making it a top priority.

Each warrior carried the compact KRISS Vector EM1, a lightweight weapon capable of rapid-firing small flechettes via an electromagnetic pulse at over 8,000 kph. The projectile was small and needle-like, but because of the speed it traveled, it was devastating.

The captain who ran the squad for Commander Weng was a man named Oscar, but everyone just called him "Cap." He was in his early forties and had made a name for himself during the battle of Philadelphia, just after New York fell. Now, he ran the most elite unit of fighters out of Fort Camden in the New Kansas area.

His second was a man named Santee. He was a wiry little guy who fought like a tornado. Nobody messed with the man they affectionately called "Nado."

"Commander, how do you like the OE2s?" Nado asked with a head gesture in his direction. The OE2, or Ocular Enhancement v2.1, was a hardware upgrade for one's eyes. It essentially removed the front of the eye and revamped the remaining portion with two elements. One was a bio-neutral receptor grid grown on the backside of the eye. The other was a full lens replacement that upped resolution and vision. It allowed one to zoom in on small details and long distances with stunning clarity not previously possible. The entire operation took about four hours and cost what most soldiers made in six months. Weng had added that upgrade color: dark purple.

"They're great. I can see a crumb of the cake you had for breakfast on your shirt from here."

"I ain't no cake-eater," Nado countered.

The commander just smiled as the other soldiers started to razz Nado. What the others didn't know was Weng had also upgraded his hearing and muscle speed as well. Making him one of the premier warriors on the planet. He let the conversation go on for a few moments more as the general pre-operation trashing dialogue bounced from warrior to warrior.

He listened to communication in his inner ear and affirmed its reception. "Copy, sir." He then called out to the squad. "Listen up. We have confirmation of a spacecraft entering and touching down twenty clicks from our current position. Who or what is responsible is not known, so we treat them as hostiles till we know. Suit up. I can't afford to lose anyone." His voice was carried through a closed and encrypted system each fighter wore as part of his tactical gear.

"Nav, drop a drone on these coordinates," Weng said.

The navigator fired off a drone, and it sped off to the suspected landing site, sending a video feed of everything it saw.

The BDS II, or bio-suit, was a sterile outerwear that protected the wearer from all known biological and viral threats. Weng pulled one from his pack and slipped into it, sealing it closed with a specialized rubber zipper. He then donned the headgear to go with it. The helmet had a large viewing screen covering his entire face.

It was capable of heads-up display and full peripheral vision, with details like biometric data, infrared imaging, visual feeds from other team members, and access to telemetry from surveillance drones and command. The aerial image of the drone appeared as his screen booted up. The filter on the back of the helmet used a specialized ultraviolet array to kill anything in the air the wearer might breathe in. It allowed for effortless breathing, even when running.

Once suited up, Commander Weng checked the curved screen on his wrist for an update.

"Five minutes to target."

The path narrowed, and 24 and 25 had to travel single-file. It soon took them along a berm that dropped off steeply to the left. 25 picked his way around a few roots that made the terrain uneven. He was finally getting used to the smell of the air, and he liked it. A sudden cry from behind him dopplered down and away. He spun to see the flash of a white jumpsuit to his right as 24 fell. She cartwheeled down the hillside in an uncontrolled tumble, coming to a sudden stop at the bottom.

25 quickly worked his way down the slope to the unmoving figure below. He knelt down and cradled her head.

"Ugh," she moaned as her eyes flickered open.

"You okay?"

A brief nod followed.

25 picked a couple of sticks out of her hair and helped her to a sitting position. He pulled her close and held on, still reeling at the thought he had almost lost her.

24 looked up into his eyes, and they met. An intensity neither had felt before threatened to overwhelm them, even with the sudden scare still fresh on their minds. He pressed his lips to hers and let his heart race. They held there for a long time, exploring each other until 25 pulled back.

"What is it?"

"I just . . . am so happy right now. You have given me a reason to live, to fight, to love. I feel truly blessed to have you in my life," 25 said with sincerity.

24 blushed and started to repay the compliment when her eyes suddenly focused past 25. "I think someone's watching us," she said.

25 turned toward the direction she was looking, and sure enough, through the brush, it looked like two eyes were staring back. He helped her to her feet, and they moved to investigate.

As they came around the bushes, they were caught off-guard at the sight before them.

A capsule, identical to the one they had taken to Earth, was half-buried in the ground. A tree limb had removed the front polymer window and impaled the two occupants, most likely killing them on impact. They stared on in ghoulish disregard, having long ago been dinner for the locals. As they approached, a rat scampered away, sending both 24 and 25 into a near panic. Once they calmed, a closer look revealed their previous counterparts. The couple had made it past Azraelle and all the way to Earth, just to die in their capsule.

25 wiped the accumulated grime from the breast of one of the corpses. It revealed the number S-7. He stepped back and looked for the insignia on the ship. Faded letters told the story—SSH EP4.

24 stepped next to him. "Spaceship Hollanbach, Escape Pod Four," she spoke unnecessarily.

"That means only four other capsules have made it down here."

"And we're number 24 and 25," she added.

"I think Azraelle was taking her job too seriously," 25 said solemnly.

The implication that so many previous couples had been killed for non-compliance to her standards was staggering. They shared a moment of silence before their current circumstances returned to 25's mind. He climbed into the cockpit, past the two bodies, and rummaged through the gear lockers. Everything they had lost on SSH EP5 was here. He passed one of the backpacks to 24 and put one on himself. He then pulled out a case the size of a carry-on and two weapons. He handed one of the weapons to 24 and then dragged the case out with him. He pulled a small handheld device from his pack and powered it up. A red dot appeared with a green square off to the side. He held it up.

"We need to go this way." He pointed west.

5

The Stryker II pulled to an abrupt stop, and the rear hatch lowered to the ground, forming an exit ramp. The two drivers remained onboard, ready with the weapons system set to react as needed. Cap exited first and used hand signals to have his men spread out and survey the area. The surveillance drone hovered on station, giving every warrior a heads-up overhead view. Weng walked out last, pausing on the ramp to get a better view of the area. He stood six feet, one inch, with an athletic build. His broad shoulders and hardened pecks capped a muscular core chiseled by an overzealous workout routine. He wore a tactical belt around his waist with a personal uplink interface and a ZIP-Nine pistol with extra ammunition and a customized tanto sword strapped to his back.

The sword was made with traditional samurai techniques, including layered and hardened steel, a full tang, and a razor-sharp edge. It was not a weapon carried by warriors but Weng had made it his signature piece and had relished opportunities to use it. Each time with a slight nod to his ancestors and a violent streak that he loosed when needed. With it and his many violent victories, Weng had become the poster child for the COE forces.

His trained eyes briefly scanned the premises, looking for anything of interest. His ability to consume information at a dizzying rate and then prioritize an action plan based on that information had helped propel him to the ranks of the Warrior class. Now, he took his orders directly from the president, living a life most envied and would kill to have. But he would give it all away for just one more minute with his deceased wife. The thought of her tugged at the edge of his mind. *She would have loved it out here.* He dismissed the thought and engaged his heads-up display to include the view of the warrior on-point.

Cap placed an all-call through the headsets. "Warriors. Quick reminder: we are in open country, and it is not safe here. Our mission is clear, but we need to get in and out efficiently; no mucking about . . . Nado."

Nado used the small targeting screen mounted to his KRISS Vector EM1. He spun and started following the vector on his display to their objective.

They quickly crossed the small meadow scarred by the craft's impact. At the edge of the woods, the squad approached the last remains of the burned-out craft. It was unrecognizable. Weng stepped next to the smoldering black hulk and removed his bio helmet. He inhaled and tried to place the acrid smell. "Graphene. This ship came from Earth," he said to no one as he looked around for more evidence.

"Sir, we have two sets of human spoor heading across the meadow."

Without another word, Weng spun and headed after his quarry. This is what they had come here for.

The footprints faded and returned, depending on the condition of the ground, but the two humans leaving the trail were not trying to hide. The warrior on point held a small tubular device with a simple directional arrow for a readout. It was a Gen-One SNIF. An air particle reader that was more accurate than a purebred hound dog. After sampling the air directly above a footprint, it took three seconds to calibrate and then indicated a direction to follow. Even if the spoor petered out, the Gen-One SNIF could still find its way.

A small alert caught Commander Weng's attention, and he flicked his wrist to answer the curved screen. The image was three inches wide, narrowing as it connected on the other side with a clasp. A strong face appeared, one with perfect hair and the blackest eyes on the planet. Weng knew it was true because President Caleb had paid a hefty price for the one-off upgrade. As the commander in chief of the Armed Forces, President Caleb was responsible for winning the war against the 1.0s, but as president of the COE, he was too busy to get involved in its daily efforts. This was an exception.

"Status," Caleb demanded.

Weng stopped walking and put his BDS II containment helmet back on, casting the image to his head's display. "Just as we expected, sir, it's one of ours, or at least the same build style and materials. There's not much left to identify it, though." He sent an image of the blackened hulk. "Once the graphene ignited, it burned itself to the ground."

President Caleb looked over how little was left of the craft. "Did anyone survive?"

"I have two human tracks leading away from the craft. Currently in pursuit."

"Make sure you eliminate them before they come in contact with anyone, and then burn the bodies. I don't want anything they're carrying to get loose."

The screen blinked off before Weng could reply. He jogged to catch up with the others.

Cap had stopped with his men along a narrow part of the trail. When Weng caught up, he looked at what had caught their attention. There was a large scuff and some of the trail had broken away.

"Somebody went over the side and the second one followed behind," Cap posed.

"We are close, sir," Nado added.

"Open the case," Commander Weng tossed out casually.

"Chen, open the case," Nado sent the command over the radio.

Sergeant Chen was the driver for the lead Stryker II. He ran the op from the cockpit maintaining communications and the onboard weapons systems. "Affirmative, case open."

A hatch on the lead Stryker II opened, and nine small drones the size of a pack of cigarettes flew off in the direction of Unit B Team One. They would spread out and use a modified Lidar to see through the thick forest and send a real-time 3D picture of the terrain below—and anything with a heartbeat moving under the thick tree canopy.

President Caleb looked out the glass wall of his high rise. As president of the COE, Congress of Earth, it was his duty to be the face of the world. He represented the best of humankind and the future of this great and powerful, albeit fractured, authoritarian society. Fractured because five major corporations ruled the world, and he was their interface to the masses. Five chairmen, each with their own agenda and power plays. On top of all that, he was also expected to win the war. A war that had drug on for almost two decades. It was an impossible ask, but somehow, he was managing—knowing the moment he didn't, there would be someone else ready to take his place.

He checked the clock on the wall. One of the antiques he used to add a sense of nostalgia to his space. His offices and living quarters were located on the top floor of Government House, a sixty-story, oval, bronze-glassed building that was the heart and mind of the city. It had long since lost any connection to the people below. Their collective voice now just a murmur to be disregarded.

A soft tone sounded and Caleb double-checked his reflection in the mirror. Perfect, not a hair out of place. The pristinely combed hair was a hybrid that grew each hair in a specific direction giving him the same hairstyle, no matter the situation.

His personal office was a combination of black lacquer and glass, with a magnificent view of the city and art on every wall. His desk was situated far from the front doors so any guest would have to pass his personal e-conference table, sitting area, small bar, and large marble sculptor of a woman leaning into an unseen wind, with her loose clothes blowing backward and a rifle raised and ready. She was called "Determination," one of the symbols for the 2.0 movement. A power walk—that's what he called the journey every person who came to meet with him had to endure to get a seat across from his desk.

Caleb strolled to his e-conference table and sat in a leather padded chair. The only chair around a projector table that had a liquid-oil-like surface. He watched as a realistic polished wood table formed around him and slowly populated with five other realistic but virtual individuals. These five, along with himself, were the true holders of world power.

There was Chairman Chou, who ran Allegiance Financial, the finance and banking giant that controlled all currency and cash flow for the masses. The man was nearly seventy, with thick black hair and not a wrinkle on him.

Rachel Tee ran UH Concerns, the utilities and housing conglomerate that controlled everything from street repairs, home rentals, and the electrical grid. She had porcelain-white skin, burnt-red hair, and matching irises.

Simon Bogachev was the chairman of All Goods, the consumer products mega-store that built and sold everything from automated teapots, robots, and drones to the sunglasses on everyone's face. He was a rotund man in his fifties with a quick wit and an intensity that could melt butter in the freezer. His salt and pepper hair seemed to have a mind of its own, as if he had just gotten out of bed, every hour of every day.

Karla Brown was the power behind Grocery Giant. It was a farm-to-home business solution for food and groceries. She prided herself on her quality-to-cost ratio but never missed an opportunity to make a little more. The mint-green eyes she had chosen were decorated with an assortment of facial paint that seemed to require every color of the rainbow to make her latest statement against her dark skin—whatever that statement was.

Giles Favreau was the one who had started the original consolidation of power. Once the war broke out, he used his billions to wage his own secret war on his competitors and slowly gobbled them all up. While the world was looking the other way, his company, Pharma One, had consumed the entire medical industry, including hospitals and their doctors.

He used this leverage to push only *his* products through the system, a system he now owned and controlled. He then set his sights on his direct competitors, the most prolific part of his business: the pharmaceutical world. With all the companies clamoring to get their products out and Pharma One controlling their downstream, it was only a matter of time before they capitulated. These companies controlled all the bio upgrades, including the vaccines.

The concept of corporate weaponization was new to the world, and soon, chairs from other disciplines followed suit. It caused the war to fracture, and neighbors battled neighbors until the consolidation of power eventually stabilized things. From the ashes, five major corporations now controlled everything, including the government and military. The wealth and power these five possessed were unimaginable, god-like.

President Caleb welcomed his masters to the meeting and tried to look comfortable among them. The virtual room was a collection of polished woods, many now extinct, and famous art. A large glass wall gave the view of an impossibly beautiful waterfall in a lush forest. Except for the occasional transmission glitch, each person was a perfected version of their real self.

Simon Bogachev was the first to speak. "I hear you have news?" He said the question more like a command.

"Yes, good news. As you know, we have been trying to locate and destroy the spaceship named SS Hollanbach for some time. The 1.0s responsible for the operation that launched it died without giving us its location. They were very dedicated. Our relatively non-existent space program managed to launch two SW TigerShark probes on a seek-and-destroy mission last fall, compliments of our predecessors. The first probe ran afoul of some space junk, and we lost contact with it a month ago. The second probe made it to the back side of the moon, confirming our suspicions." He looked around the room before continuing.

"As of 21:00 hours yesterday, we confirmed the Hollanbach's location and launched a hardened plutonium ball with an electromagnetic pulse. Here is the result."

He pressed a button on a small remote in his hand and watched with the others as a virtual, 3D string of images appeared above the table. They showed an attack probe firing a small cannonball-sized chunk of black metal at a large cigar-like metal ship hiding in the shadow of the moon.

The ball easily tore through the ship's skin and out the other side. The impact seemed to do little harm at first, but within a few seconds, the ship started to spark. One section of the Hollanbach imploded and another section exploded. In the video, the seemingly peaceful craft was completely destroyed. A small escape pod shot out away from the explosion and disappeared from view.

"Was that another craft?" Chairwoman Brown asked with sudden concern.

Caleb proceeded as though he hadn't heard her. "Now that the Hollanbach is destroyed, we will see no more attempts at polluting our world with impure virus-filled humans. The attempts by the council have failed. We can now fully concentrate on cleaning up the remaining 1.0s and putting all this behind us. Soon, all humankind will be yours to do with what you like."

Caleb adjusted his chair. "To answer your question, Chairwoman Brown, yes, that was a ship that escaped the Hollanbach's destruction. We tracked it to Earth where the capsule was destroyed." He showed them an image of the burned-out capsule. "There is currently a warrior unit in pursuit of two humans on foot who left the landing site."

The words made everyone else at the table look anxious, and some murmuring followed.

"Not to worry. I have this well in hand, and I expect their demise and clean-up evidence within the hour." There was an unusual moment of silence. "This will be the last of such concerns," Caleb added.

His words seemed to mollify the others.

The conversation soon turned to matters of state and the business of running a war. A business that was booming. If President Caleb didn't know better, he would think they didn't want the war to end, but there was a limited number of 1.0s left out there, and with every day that passed, fewer still.

A young girl with short white hair and dark skin stepped up behind Caleb and whispered in his ear. His assistant, Cin, was efficient and proactive, one of his favorite qualities about her, besides her figure. She was well acquainted with the communication lockout that happened when the CEOs got together. It required her to speak in person, but she was never afraid of interrupting such a meeting.

"You'll have to excuse me . . . I have an ongoing operation that is critical to the security of the state." With that said, Caleb said his goodbyes and clicked off.

Tactical boots stepped next to the tarnished metal skin of an older spaceship.

"They were here," the warrior on point said as he moved his handheld SNIF from side to side.

"Chen, use our current position as a starting point," Cap ordered.

"Copy," came the reply.

The mini drones fanned out and began an extended search.

Weng took in the site of the older spaceship that had crashed some years before. Somehow, it had landed here undetected. The two obvious passengers still harnessed in for the ride weren't as lucky. Their skin was partially intact and long since dried out, giving them a surprised skeletal expression. A faded EP4 stenciled on the surface of the craft had been wiped clean recently.

"Sci Officer Katrina, document everything and get biosamples to the lab. Then burn what's left," Cap ordered.

"Yes, sir," Science Officer Katrina replied as she stepped forward. A soldier next to her handed her a weapon from his pack. It looked like a cross between a blowtorch and an electromagnetic paintball trainer, used for war games and training.

An image of two humans moving below the canopy popped up on Commander Weng's face shield. It gave distance and direction from where they were standing.

"Cap, we're wasting valuable time. I have a visual of the targets. Get the vehicles to rendezvous here, and once Sci Officer Katrina is done, they can coordinate back up with us."

Cap barked orders, and the squad moved off quickly, closing in on their targets.

Sci Officer Katrina swallowed, her mouth suddenly dry as she watched her team move off. She was new to field operations, replacing the last science officer who had been infected by a 1.0. This was not the place to screw up—alone in the woods, especially on her first off-base mission. She had something to prove because joining the military was against her family's desires. For Katrina, it had been a source of pride, even if finding the right place for her here had taken a few twists and turns. Now, she was in her element and just needed to deliver on this first assignment.

At twenty-five, she had long, curly strawberry-blonde hair with cream-colored skin. Katrina had not gone for the more flashy upgrades that most 2.0s did; instead, she was happy with her natural chestnut eyes and everyday-girl appearance.

She spent her upgrade money on keeping her vaccines up-to-date and the monthly fees associated with that. Every major vaccine came with a need for a monthly booster. It was as simple as walking through one of the many LIFE-ARCHes throughout the city. Every time a person passed through a LIFE-ARCH, the signal realigned the biomarkers in their body, upgrading and inoculating them to the latest known disease and auto-billing their account. If your payment did not clear, it would turn off the biomarkers, and you would become susceptible to myriad diseases that were now part of daily life for the 2.0s.

The darker parts of the city were ripe with the dying and infected—something a true 2.0 would never let happen, but progress had a way of leaving many behind, the shiny skin on the outside blinding many to the rotted center.

Katrina had personally known friends and family who'd passed away because they couldn't make their payments. This scared her almost as much as the two corpses staring blankly at her. She could only imagine the death sentence they carried.

She moved closer with caution, making sure her helmet was properly sealed. First up were a few samples. She opened her kit and extracted a gleaming pair of scissors, taking samples of hair and nails from each. Using tweezers, she placed the samples, one at a time, in her bioanalyzer and closed the door. Every few minutes, she scanned her surroundings to make sure she was still alone. It took ten seconds for each sample to be analyzed, and the results were transmitted back to the lab on base via her link to the lead Stryker. Both vehicles were currently making their way to rendezvous with her, and Katrina would feel a lot better once they arrived. She gathered her thoughts and repeated the process with the other sample.

Next, Sci Officer Katrina took a reverse-curved blade from her kit and cut open each spacesuit. She instinctively held her breath as human dust filled the air in front of her. She removed a slice of dried black skin from under each suit and loaded them into the handheld bioanalyzer. Once that was done, she packaged up all the samples and put everything back in her kit. She didn't realize she was sweating until a drop from her forehead fell into her eye, making her jump. The BDS II she wore would protect her from any viral transmission, but there had been many stories in the news about people dying over the slightest imperfections in their bio suits. The 1.0s were a death sentence to some, and standing so close to two of them was nerve-racking. She glanced down at the readout on the bio-analyzer. A brief description flashed on the screen: Female, African American, age 25, COD exsanguination. *American* . . . something the past held dear but carried no memory for her.

Once finished, she stepped back and grabbed her weapon, feeling slightly braver with it in hand. The XL21 was a plasma-based discharge weapon that shot a scarcely controlled plasma flame up to thirty feet. It was not typically used in warfare but rather as a bio-eliminator. Any living or dead organic tissue could be ionized almost instantaneously. Sci Officer Katrina flicked the safety off with a practiced rhythm and aimed the weapon. A snap of a twig spun her around, looking for the source. She used the barrel of her weapon to point where she looked. Left then right, as a feeling of dread suddenly returned. A squirrel shot across her

6

25 watched as 24 picked her way through the trees. They had said their piece to their doppelgangers and were working hard to get the image of the desiccated corpses out of their minds. The forest was thinning out and underbrush was more prevalent. 25 was looking for a place near some running water where they could make camp and reevaluate their situation.

His searching eyes found their way to the back of 24 as she hiked in front of him. 24 had a way of walking that shimmied her backside as she moved. He didn't know why, but he could look at it all—A root sticking out of the ground caught his foot, and he went down in a *humph*.

"You okay?" she asked, looking over her shoulder.

"Yeah, wasn't looking where I was going," he said as he stood back up.

"You weren't watching my butt, were you?"

A sudden flush bloomed across 25's face. "No," he lied. "But it is a nice butt."

24 let a small smile dance across her lips and then continued on. "It's okay; I was doing the same to you earlier."

"Hold up," 25 said in a whisper as he raised his hand in the air. "Do you hear that?"

A subtle humming sound could be heard in the distance. 24 nodded as fear clouded her face.

"We're being tracked. Come on!" 25 started to run, and 24 followed right behind. The buzzing sound quickly overtook them and then continued past. 25 paused to listen and catch his breath. He changed direction and made it about ten feet before figures materialized from the trees. He froze as the buzzing drones returned. They were surrounded. 24 raised her weapon to fire, but 25 placed his hand on it and pulled it to the side. "It's of no use," he whispered as the armed soldiers closed in. "Let's see if they're friendly."

"Do you speak English?" one of the men shouted.

25 nodded.

"Lower your weapons, or we will fire on you where you stand," the voice added.

25 tossed his weapon to the side, and slowly, 24 followed suit.

"On your knees, hands behind your head. . . . Nice and easy."

25 and 24 were quickly surrounded. A female warrior secured their hands behind them and picked up their guns. She showed one to the main authority, whom she called "Cap."

"Keltec P68s—old-school but still effective."

Commander Weng stepped over to the two captives kneeling on the ground in front of them. He let his eyes wander from one to the other.

A readout from the crash site samples scrolled across his helmet's display. *Samples viable, Hu 1.0: 1 male, 1 female, no known viruses, please advise.*

"What are your names?"

"24."

"None of your business," 25 replied.

"Did you arrive in the capsule we found?"

No answer.

"If you did, I just want you to know that we are responsible for destroying your little science experiment on the SS Hollanbach."

That got a rise out of 25 as he fought against his shackles.

"We've done nothing to deserve this treatment!" 24 shouted.

"I don't remember inviting you down here, do you, Commander?" Cap asked.

Weng stood back up, his eyes never leaving the prey.

"Maybe they need a little encouragement to open up," Cap said, watching from the sidelines.

Weng nodded and stepped behind the two captives, letting their fear percolate for a few more minutes. He withdrew his sword and used it like a pointer as he played a simple child's game.

"One potato, two potato, three potato, four. Five potato, six potato, seven potato, no more." As he pointed to the last person, with lightning speed, he delicately sliced the jugular of 24's neck.

Blood flew onto one of the nearby warriors, who panicked and grabbed a small can of disinfectant spray, then covered his pant legs on his protective suit. The rest of the warriors in the group stepped back as fear of contamination from 24's possibly infected fluids rose.

25 screamed in horror as he watched 24's precious lifeblood flow.

24 looked helplessly over to 25 as he pleaded and screamed for help. She was becoming pale. She tried to speak, but nothing came out.

"You got about fifteen more seconds to talk before it's too late to save her."

25 babbled, "What do you want to know? Yes, we are from the SS Hollanbach! We were birthed and trained there."

"To what purpose?" Weng asked.

"To restart human life on this planet!"

"That seems a bit farfetched . . ." Weng said.

"Please, just help her! I'll tell you everything. We weren't here to hurt anyone. I just need you to . . ." 25 blathered.

24 fell over, no longer strong enough to stay upright. Her white jumpsuit was covered in her blood. She looked one last time at 25 and mouthed the words *I love you* before her eyes fluttered close.

25 fell over next to her; his face close to hers. His hands were still bound behind his back. "I love you too," he managed between sobs. "24 . . . 24!" He looked up at his captors, uncomprehending their motives and methods. Unfamiliar emotions overwhelmed him, and he found it difficult to breathe.

"Sorry, I lied. There was never any chance of saving her." Weng shrugged his shoulders and turned. "Finish them off and burn the bodies." He tossed the directions callously to the captain. An alert on his personal interface sounded, and Weng focused on the familiar image that appeared on his heads-up display.

"President Caleb," he dutifully replied.

Captain nodded to Nado to follow up on the commander's order.

25 reached his bound hands out and felt for 24's left hand. He fingered the ring on her finger and pulled it off and palmed it, just as a soldier used the butt of his rifle to push him away from her. Blood had soaked the front of his jumpsuit, and tears flowed down, mixing the two liquids.

Nado pulled his KRISS Vector EM1. He stepped up to 25 and placed the barrel of the weapon on the top of his head, pointing down. The speed at which the flechettes fired required a downward angle or the bullet would blast through the human, and who knows what else.

25 moved his head back and forth trying to make himself harder to kill as he squeezed 24's ring in his hand. His face was a mask of horror and uncontrolled emotion, covered in tears, blood, and dirt.

Nado was enjoying the little resistance 25 was putting up. It would make the kill that much more fun.

"Commander Weng, do you have the enemy in custody yet?" Caleb asked.

"Just finishing them off now, sir," Weng replied.

Finally, 25 calmed, accepting his fate. He lowered his head and squeezed his eyes shut, trying to picture 24. He landed on a moment in the ship where she had looked up and smiled coyly at his antics. Hers was the face of an angel, and he locked it into his mind.

Nado started to squeeze the trigger.

"On second thought, bring 'em in alive. I want to do some testing."

Weng's hand shot up in the air. "Hold up!"

Nado released his finger on the trigger, disappointed.

"I can get you *one* alive now, sir," Weng said.

"Efficient as always, eh, Commander? Okay, *one* will do, but bring both bodies." The president cut off the transmission.

25 lay on his side in a fetal position on the floor of the lead Stryker II. Sealed in a black body-shaped bag next to him was 24. She was no longer moving or breathing, and it seemed impossible to accept. One moment, she had been

holding his hand, energy coursing between them, and the next, she'd been captured and killed. Her last whispered words played over and over in his mind as he tried to come to terms with his situation. *I love you.* He felt hopelessness consume him.

Feeling so numb, he didn't notice the rough ride as the two vehicles bounced over the uneven ground meandering their way through the trees and back to the main road. He didn't even have the energy to sit up. The soldiers had bagged him in some kind of clear suit, like a prize. He could breathe through a port, but it took significant effort to push the air in and out. The same warriors, all dressed in black tactical outfits, now sat glaring down at him with judging eyes.

How could such a small cut spill so much blood?

He gave up trying to process it all, and just let go. He was cried out and emotionally drained. They could do what they wanted to him; his mission no longer mattered. Azraelle should have finished her job on the ship, saving him all the heartache.

Then a beam, a reddish-purple smoke ring, shot through the vehicle at an incredible pace. It melted through anything it touched. The soldier across from 25 had his arm removed as if it had been sliced off with a laser sword. It fell in front of 25's face and twitched a jiggy dance.

"Plasma weapon! We're under attack!" the sergeant in the driver's seat yelled as the Stryker spun to a halt. A second ring shot through the cab and left the man behind 25 in two pieces. The weird thing was there was no blood. Body parts just came apart, each piece cauterized during the cut. The warrior in the co-pilot's seat immediately returned fire. The plasma cannon on top of the Stryker rotated up and locked in on the coordinates of the last incoming firing position and blasted several bursts.

25 knew from his lessons that plasma weapons were extremely effective under certain conditions. They could shoot through any material not protected by an E-arc shield. No amount of armor would stop them. The problem was, you had to get close because the weapon's range was just under fifty yards, and it was slow—about the speed of an arrow. Plus the energy they put out was easily identified and traced back to the source, sometimes before the first shot reached its intended target.

Weng exited the lowering ramp at full speed, leaving the other warriors in his dust. He spun around to take cover behind the wheel well of the lead Stryker. A quick inspection with his enhanced OE V2 vision spotted six targets moving in formation to his right. He didn't hesitate but fired from his position and darted head-first in their direction. His upgrades allowed him to aim, focus, and fire on the run with extreme accuracy, and by the time he had run twenty feet, all six targets were down. He regrouped behind a large stump and retargeted for his next run. Four more sat to the left. He paid no attention to the battle being raged behind him but was more concerned with eliminating as many enemy combatants as he could. Cap could handle the coordinated engagement.

As he sprinted toward the four unsuspecting shooters, his enhanced muscles propelling him at close to 58 kph, shots from the side and behind filled his senses. They had set a trap. Commander Weng had run into an organized phalanx. Before he could escape, an explosion cartwheeled him into the sky. They say, it's not the fall that kills you, but the sudden stop at the end. Commander Weng hit hard, jarring him from the fight and consciousness.

Meanwhile, Sci Officer Katrina was the last out of her Stryker. The raging battle outside was confusing and fluid. She held on to her training and took a knee to survey her situation. There were several soldiers firing to her left, and she spun and took aim. The rear Stryker exploded, slamming her to the ground and ending her plan.

Smoke filled the lead vehicle, and 25 slithered his way to the back corner of the floor. The containment bag made it difficult to move and rolling seemed to be the only effective method.

Several blasts over his head ended the sergeant's and copilot's fight. The rig shuddered, and more black smoke spewed. The few fighters still inside fled the metal, soon to be a coffin, firing in all directions as they ran down the ramp.

25 lay on his side, listening to the muted sounds of the battle through his containment suit.

The fight took all of three minutes, which seemed like a lifetime to 25, as warriors fought the attackers in the open. No one wanted to be roasted alive in a metal can, and the best defense was always a strong offense with this squad. 25 could hear the sound of unfamiliar weapons firing from multiple positions with the occasional high-pitched scream only a dying human can make interspersed throughout. He stayed low on the floor of the vehicle, curled up like a sow bug.

Nado and Cap took cover at the hood of the second Stryker. Returning fire in controlled and efficient bursts, they covered each other as they stood back to back. A bullet pinged off the armored steel next to them. *A bullet? Old-school, huh?* They returned fire with their KRISS Vector EM1s, flechettes rapidly firing through the air. It sounded like a giant metallic bow, releasing three arrows a second. They left a devastating swath as they went. Trees and humans put up little defense against their power.

Nado took a plasma blast from the side, and his head just fell off, eyes still blinking in confusion, while the rest of his body continued the fight for another second before falling over. Cap spun and put down the shooter. He knew he needed to move, or he would suffer the same fate. He sprinted in an arc, trying to make himself a difficult target to hit, all the while firing back in the enemy's direction. Every type of weapon seemed to be pointed back his way as impacts and ricochets filled his vision. Somehow, he managed to avoid them all, until a barrage of bullets dialed in and riddled him to the ground.

The smoke was acrid and several small fires had broken out in the vehicle. 25 looked around; no one inside was left alive. He coughed as the smoke made its way into his suit. He needed to get out and quickly. Rolling his way over a partial body and down the ramp onto the ground outside, he came to a sudden stop with the aid of a dark green boot.

When he looked up, a large Black man, the likes he had never seen before, stared back with a mix of contempt and relief. He had variegated dreadlocks that reached down beyond his shoulders and an unkempt full beard. There were two visible ring piercings on his nose and dark, powerful eyes that looked beyond the surface. His clothes were a mottled dark green with several different weapons strapped to various parts of his body. He wore a half helmet that had a partially clear visor covering just the eyes.

"We got him," he shouted to no one 25 could see. With a flick of his wrist, a knife appeared and the man cut the bag off 25.

Another man in similar attire ran up and reported, "Perimeter secure, but I wouldn't stay here long; they'll have eyes in the sky and a much larger response force on us in no time."

The man who seemed to be in charge nodded.

Once 25 was out of the bag, he stood on wobbly legs, struggling to comprehend. "You shot?"

25 shook his head.

"You don't look like much," the tall man said.

25 just stared back at this massive example of a human, unsure how to reply. The guy was at least six-foot-five and 240 pounds.

"I'm Finley. What's your name?"

"25," he choked out.

"25?" Finley started to laugh. "You hear that? 25!"

Several other soldiers laughed as well.

It was all too much for 25. His world spun and went black.

It started with a single muted cough, then several more followed. Sci Officer Katrina's eyes fluttered open, and immediately, her head started to spin. It took a Herculean effort to sit up and not spin back to the ground. Dust fell from her head. Her helmet was nowhere to be seen. She allowed herself a moment before trying to figure out what had happened. There was a plasma attack, and she had left the lead Stryker to return fire from behind a nearby tree. flechettes, bullets, and plasma rings filled the sky as 1.0s attacked them, and her unit fought back. She had seen several of her fellow warriors go down, and the last thing she remembered was a plasma blast causing an explosion at the rear Stryker.

Katrina looked around. Several trees had been left fractured stumps, as lightning had struck them. 1.0 soldiers and 2.0 warriors lay scattered about. She was lucky to be alive. There was no sign of movement or the enemy, so she spent the next few minutes checking the corpses of her friends. No signs of life. She pulled a weapon from the ground, held it up, and continued to investigate. A moan to her left erupted, and she identified a wounded 1.0 trying to sit up. She dispatched him with little regard, double-checking that her BDS II bio-suit was still functioning.

The follow Stryker was a complete loss, so she moved up to the lead vehicle. Here, there were more bodies from both sides of the conflict. Smoke poured out of the vehicle as the fuel cells burned. She knew better than to go near that smoke. It was lethal. A slight movement to her left had her spinning and pointing her KRISS Vector EM1. Commander Weng stepped through the bushes and smoke, pointing his sword in her direction. There was blood on the blade and on his face. His eyes looked vacant.

"Stand down, Sci Officer Katrina," he said through gritted teeth.

She glanced at his body, where she noticed his left arm was missing. Just a shredded dripping bloody stump below the elbow. Katrina lowered her weapon, and Commander Weng took two more steps forward, then collapsed.

25's body shook and bounced. He opened his eyes and noticed a worm's-eye view of the trees above moving passed. Two soldiers were at his head and two at his feet. It took a second more before he realized he was being carried. No, it was more than that . . . being *rushed* through the forest. He cleared his head and tried to sit up. A large beefy hand appeared.

"Stay down."

So he did, rubbing the welts on his wrist where he had been shackled. A quick self-inspection told 25 he was not physically injured.

Twenty minutes of jostling came to an abrupt stop with a simple command: "Ho." The four soldiers who had been carrying him dropped the stretcher a few feet from the ground and bent over taking deep gulps of air with hands on knees.

25 stood and looked around at the group. It was a motley bunch of men and women of different races and sizes. Most wore variegated camo fatigues. Some of the clothes looked like they were second-hand or perhaps manufactured by hand. A few had older bullet holes with dried blood. Two were nursing fresh wounds.

"We can't stay here long," a thin woman with matted hair and a nasty facial scar said.

"How many?" Finley asked. The large man seemed to be in charge.

"Sixteen," came a somber statement from the back. It was a sobering number.

"Are you telling me we lost sixteen brothers and sisters for this rat turd?" A stalky man with a shaved head grabbed 25 and pulled a knife up to slice his throat.

Finley called out, "Kay! Don't waste their lives. This was the job we signed up for and nothing more."

Kay pressed 25 up against a tree, lifting his feet into the air.

25 didn't fight back. He raised his chin in defiance. After losing 24, he lost his fight but not his pride.

Finley laid his hand on Sergeant Kay's shoulder. "Come on Kay. Let's all live to fight another day."

Kay pressed his knife into 25's throat, the soft skin yielding.

"What's the point?"

Blood started to weep around the knife's edge.

"The point? The point is us, man. It always has been, Kay."

The man slowly lowered his knife and then threw 25 to the ground and spat on him before distancing himself.

25 rubbed his neck. Blood came away on his hand. This was a new experience, and he almost fainted at the sight of it.

Finley stood over him. "You better be worth it." He reached out a hand to help him up, but 25 got up on his own.

The squad had stopped at a high point where they could look out across the forested hills. The sky was clear. To the east was a column of smoke, lifting through the trees. The battleground. Further off, the hint of a large city, some thirty or forty kilometers away. To the west, there was nothing but trees, with one exception—a small black spot situated in the bowl of a hill some five kilometers away. Someone passed 25 a canteen, and he gulped the contents.

The girl with the scar stepped up to 25. "Can you walk?"

He nodded while still guzzling the water.

"Good because I'm tired of carrying your butt. I'm Major Christine Helen, and yeah, I know you're 25." She gave him a partial smile and moved away.

"Okay, let's move out," Finley announced.

The squad of only eight soldiers returned to their double-time march. Slowly jogging down the hill, continuing away from the battlefield, with 25 keeping pace in the middle.

7

Giles Favreau breathed in the complex essence of the caramel-colored liquid resting in the leaded glass. The mid-fifties CEO of Pharma One had an affinity for all things rare and extraordinary, and this twenty-five-year-old single-malt scotch was one of the last bottles in existence. At five-eight and tipping the scale at 290 pounds, he was a man of excess. Extreme wealth had brought him power and the ability to live his life to the fullest. It included the very finest in hard-to-get gourmet food, and he was always happy to overindulge. It also allowed him to explore some of his depraved instincts. The extra pounds didn't seem to bother him; he was one of a kind. In the kingdom of the blind, the man with one eye is king, and in a world filled with rationing and limitations, the man with excess is king. Giles was the king.

The room was cavernous with aged copper wall panels and polished stone floors. Pin-prick lighting cast small glowing pools across the room. A combination of antiques and modern furniture filled the space in a maze fitting a madman. Giles was drawn to possessions with a myopic lust, and whether it matched the piece next to it, or not, was never a concern for him.

He let wants be his needs and needs be his passion and mission forward. Several of his wants sat scantily clad and ready for his beck and call. Young men and women plucked from poverty and given a once-in-a-life chance to live in luxury, provided they always pleased their master. A master that would easily cast them aside based on his whims and moods.

After all, he had taken Pharma One from a multi-national corporation to a corporate dynasty with a monopolistic structure and emotional hold over the entire city. Every person paid a monthly health subscription to Pharma One. And his sway on the other chairmen was absolute. A simple withholding of one of his vaccines during a pandemic was all he had to do to bend them to his will. Though he had never had to resort to that. The threat was always there, and he was more than ready to execute should the need arise.

The Congress of Earth, or COE, was built and run by Giles. The presidential puppet Caleb was his to command, and the only thing standing in his way of total and complete domination of the planet was the 1.0s. They were like gnats that kept buzzing in his ear but were too quick to kill. He stepped to a digital map of the world displayed on his wall. It had all the current population centers remaining. Most of the planet was a groveling collection of tribes and residual nationalists trying to eke out a living by taking what others had. There was no structure. As the world slowly crawled back from its brink, it would be a race to see who would prevail. Most population centers were a mess, but given time, he would control them—all of them. It wouldn't take much to bend and change the current dynamic in his favor, he thought. His eyes lingered over an icon of Zion to the west. A city of 1.0s had been built with purpose and structure, much like New Kansas.

Right now, New Kansas had a slight edge in population, but Zion's laser containment grid made it impossible for current weapons technology to make a dent on the city. Giles needed a way inside. Perhaps a new strain of a virus that was particularly nasty. He had tried that before, but the 1.0s used herd immunity and allowed a certain number to die off, just to permit the rest to build new, stronger immunities. A sickness that would devastate New Kansas might only inconvenience Zion. He turned from the map, frustrated.

It wasn't the need to be the grand puppet master that pushed Giles forward every day. It was an internal compulsion that drove him for more. Enough was never enough, and the only way to make him feel better about himself was to control and dominate others. The more, the better, and Giles wouldn't rest until everyone was under his thumb. If he worked it right, they would pay him for the privilege.

Hu 2.0

He moved to the left and admired his proud gluttonous form in the beveled mirror. The image helped calm his rising blood pressure. He was wearing a custom-tailored plaid vest with a gold pocket watch over a pink silk shirt. His dark gay mohair pants and polished black loafers all held his bulk in a fashionable ensemble. His hair was bleach-blond and cut short. An upgrade, where a bald head would have been. His eyes were aqua blue with advanced optics and night vision capability. He wore a prototype MindLink, a small square mounted on the side of his head under the hairline, with internal wires connecting to his brain. The direct neural interface improved the bandwidth between his cortex and digital tertiary layer, increasing the speed over one thousand times. It also allowed a data uplink between his brain and the computers running his business. It was in beta testing, and once perfected, it would change how business and communication were done forever. For now, he was happy to have the only one in existence. The thought almost kept him from advancing its launch to the public, perhaps a downgraded version.

With a mere thought, he connected to Pharma One's computer system. As fast as his mind determined a task, it could be sent out and delivered. Division presidents had given their marching orders, and house waitstaff ran to fill every whim. It was good to be the king.

He looked up at the screen displaying the ongoing warrior operation in the field. Giles was ever-monitoring the world around him with informants and spies at every level. The spaceship that had crash-landed and the two unknown astronauts that flew it—he knew it all first. His mind was torn between the fear of what diseases those two might be carrying and the excitement of what he could do with it. He connected silently through his MindLink.

"Caleb, I need you to do something for me."

An improvised tourniquet was the only thing keeping Commander Weng from bleeding out. Sci Officer Katrina struggled to pull him along the ground, away from the battlefield and back toward Fort Camden. The going was slow, and she estimated they had maybe traveled 500 yards of the twenty-plus kilometers still to go. It was futile. She fell to the ground, ready to concede. The black smoke from the burning batteries was almost gone as she looked back, trying to gather her remaining strength. Her head was pounding, her mouth dry as sandpaper.

The battle had been intense and confusing. The sudden attack had elite warriors moving in an uncoordinated fashion, each trying to stay alive and counter the offensive. The chaos worked at first, but the surrounding force had the advantage and used it to kill some of the best warriors she had ever trained with. It was devastating and impossible to fully comprehend, so she just clung to her training. *When in doubt, rely on your training. It will get you through.*

She flashed back to an early combat exercise she had participated in. Eight recruits had been placed in a demo Stryker attached to a modified crane. Each strapped in and blinded with blackened goggles. She remembered sweating so hard; her mouth was dry then too. They were craned up into the air and left hanging. The instructor had been purposefully vague. Without warning, they were dropped into a deep pool and flipped at the same time. It was violent and disorienting.

Katrina panicked as the cold water rushed in, consuming her body. Taking a huge gulp of air at the last second, she fought with her harness until it finally unlocked. She felt the soldier next to her push past. She used her hands to find her seat bottom, taking that information to form a mental picture and directing her to the rear hatch exit. A struggling body to her right was felt with her hand as she held it out in front, trying to feel/swim her way out.

She paused, indecisive about whether to help a fellow soldier or save herself. She was running low on air, and with each second that passed, the vehicle sank deeper. A muted sound stopped her, and she reached for the man's harness only to be met with panicked arms grabbing her and holding on. Now they were both in trouble. She managed to free a hand and get his harness unlocked, but that only set the frenzied teammate loose. He clawed over her and used his feet to kick off her torso, trying to escape. Only he went in the wrong direction. Katrina's remaining air was knocked out of her, leaving her no choice but to swim for it.

She clipped her shoulder on the edge of the exit door and prayed she was swimming in the right direction. Being underwater in total blackness was very disorienting. A person in this situation could easily swim down as opposed to up and never know it, till they hit the bottom or ran out of air. Once free of the vehicle, Katrina had to make a choice and make it quickly. Her body spasmed for air, and small flashes of light danced across her periphery. She angled ninety degrees from the submerged vehicle, estimating she had a fifty-fifty chance of guessing right. Every part of her being said *breathe* as her hands pulled through the water. She finally broke the surface in a short-lived, air-gulping, celebratory moment before her instructor yelled at her for being so slow. The soldier she had freed was forced to be rescued, and she had watched as they used him as a learning moment on how to do CPR to resuscitate him. Three days later, she requested a transfer to the sciences division.

The memory faded, and Katrina stood back up on exhausted legs. She tried to pull Commander Weng's body a little farther, foot by foot. Wisps of dust followed the heels of his boots. After about ten minutes, a soft buzzing approached from above, and she dropped back to the ground, lying prone. There was no more energy to give. Whoever it was that was coming could take them both. As the sound grew closer, she recognized it as one of their recon2 drones—they were saved. She waved briefly at the emotionless lens that stared back and then let her eyes close with relief.

Several warriors, with guns ready, appeared a moment later. They walked right past Katrina and the commander, their focus on something else.

"Hey! We need some help here," she yelled, but they ignored her, continuing on their mission. She sat up, trying to understand what was happening. Then a second wave appeared, and soon medical attention was administered.

A few moments later, the first wave of warriors returned, carrying the slightly burned body bag with the female astronaut they had captured and killed.

Katrina wanted to scream at their poor choice of priorities, but something felt wrong, so she kept it to herself.

Soon, three vehicles arrived on the scene and evacuated them back to Fort Camden.

As 25 came around a thicket, the forest stopped, like someone had drawn a line. Trees on one side, burned earth on the other. The ground was not dark brown but black. In the distance were several partial buildings and structures, all black as well. The skeletal remains of a once proud city reached up like a hand from the grave. To the right was a large metal tower. The kind you launched a rocket from—also black. A few pieces of a rocket remained at the base, most of it destroyed and blackened, like everything else. Where there was once life and promise now stood the shell that had held it.

"What happened here?" 25 asked no one in particular.

"2.0s; that's what happened. New Topeka, lost our best and brightest that day," said a man next to him. 25 looked up as they passed under the tower, which had serious fuse and burn marks. That it was still standing was a testament to the will of its builders.

25 let his mind go back to a happier time. A time when 24 was part of his life. The smell and feel of her body. He refocused, and the video of Doctor Honeywell played in his mind. *The Vaxxer War and the division of humanity. The 1.0s versus the 2.0s. Was it still going on? Had humanity somehow survived but not evolved?*

His time on the SS Hollanbach seemed so long ago and everything he had trained for was irrelevant. This was not a planet in need of repopulation. It was a planet controlled by might and fear. What could one man do against that? He suddenly had the urge to turn and run away. He could lose them in the trees and fend for himself like he was trained to do. Finley stepped next to him as if he was reading his mind. "Just up here. Come on."

As they marched around the corner of the largest chunk of a building, 25 paused. A machine he had never seen before faced him. It was the size of a semi-truck trailer with rounded corners, painted a mottled gray with four arms sticking out. Two in front and two in back. Each arm held a pair of large tandem propellers currently pointing to the sky. The middle was currently open to the world. One end had a segmented glass front. 25 tried to figure out its purpose—some sort of transport.

A hand slapped him on the back, encouraging him forward. "It's a Vortex TT, a transport. Part drone, part tilt-rotor, and it's our ticket outta here." 25 walked up the ramp, eyes scanning left and right. The well-worn walls were lined with side-by-side seats. The floor was some type of ribbed metal, and small port windows let the day's sun stream in. He took one of the seats and strapped in as the side door closed. A humming grew in volume, and soon the Vortex TT rattled and lifted off. It stayed just above the trees as it rotated counterclockwise and flew west.

A sudden rattling and shaking jarred 25 from a daze. It had been a few hours since they lifted off. He looked out the window. The transport was approaching a city. 25 noticed that it sprawled amongst trees and agriculture. There was an aqueduct or small river that flowed through the middle of it, and some kind of dam and power plant sat to the south. Unlike the cities he had studied on the Hollanbach, this one had no outlying homes or infrastructure; it was all contained within a large oval perimeter wall. A monorail could be seen running along the top edge of the oval. The raw forest beyond the city grew in every direction, with nothing else as far as he could see. Between the buildings and the small lake to the south was a landing strip and a military base.

Councilwoman Avery looked out the armored window from the top floor of the operations building as the Vortex TT banked and dropped onto its landing pad. The laser containment grid over Zion was temporarily shut down, allowing the troop transport ingress. She watched as three soldiers escorted their prize across the busy flight pad and down the stairs. The afternoon sun was getting low in the sky, casting harsh shadows across the ground below as soldiers and support staff went about the business of the afternoon. She stepped next to a COMMs unit and spoke naturally.

"Finley, have our guest put in the cage." The voice-activated communications system routed the message to any soldier with an earpiece. In this case, just to Finley.

"Roger that," came his reply as he gave a brief wave up to the operations room above.

"And welcome back," Avery voiced, with genuine concern.

She watched as Finely handed their prize off to two soldiers who escorted the newcomer to a six-by-six cage in a holding area for prisoners that had not been assigned a cell yet. The man they had collected looked to be about six one or two with solid shoulders and a trim waist and hips. His sandy brown hair was full and messy, and he had a smattering of a young beard across his face. All in all, first impression was: handsome. Something she had no time for. A closer inspection revealed dried blood on his jumpsuit. She spun from the window and returned to her duties.

At five-foot-nine, Avery stood taller than most women. She had shoulder-length, curly brown hair set against jade-colored eyes and a doubting expression that was well-earned.

As the last remaining councilwoman of the 1.0 republic, she had a heavy weight on her shoulders. Her efforts, along with a few key others, had kept the lights on and the doors open, just.

Avery turned as her number one, Finley, the leader of ground-based operations, entered the battle-hardened room and stepped toward her. The room was an open space with several command boards and monitoring stations. Concrete walls told the story of form over function and electronic ozone and body odor fought for dominance. Soldiers and technicians worked tirelessly, monitoring systems and communications, to help keep the city safe. If Zion's structures were her exoskeleton, this room was her blood.

"How many?" she asked.

"We lost sixteen, two walking wounded."

Avery gave a solemn nod.

"He better be worth that, Avery. The guy seems like no one special to me," Finley said, holding her gaze until she broke it.

"This guy?" she asked. "So only one?"

"Only one."

Avery's hopeful expression dipped as did her mouth. She turned and stepped away from the command console that was squelching maintenance dialogue. Finley followed. "I hope you're wrong about him. What else can you tell me?"

Finley was dirty and exhausted. A single stray dreadlock hung across his face, and he was too tired to move it. Taking a moment to collect himself, he looked over at his boss, the leader of the 1.0s, with questioning eyes—a woman who had sacrificed everything, like most here. Her smooth almond skin was just starting to show its age, mostly around her eyes. At twenty-eight, she had a curvy figure that held a determination of will like nothing he had ever seen.

Avery was the most recent in a line of council leaders the 2.0s had systematically targeted and killed over the years. Each time gaining ground in the war and causing mass casualties to the 1.0s. Her only claim to fame was being a direct descendant of their founding leader. It was a thankless job with little future, but none of that seemed to phase her.

Avery sighed and took a seat at a meeting table in the corner of the room. She had been fretting since the team had left on the mission. So much could go wrong, but it was a chance she had to take. If there was even a shred of truth to her father's words, it was worth the risk.

Finley sat next to her. "Well, he's about twenty-five, male . . . white." He said the last word with a bit of disdain. "Said his name was 25. Oh, and he seems about as useless as parsley on a steak."

"Okay, but I like parsley on my steak." Avery's expression encouraged him to say more.

Finley shook his head before continuing. The corners of his mouth tipped slightly upward. "He speaks English and can run pretty well. Mostly, he was all broken up about losing his partner."

Avery nodded and let his words process. "Thanks, Finley. Go get cleaned up and have him brought to me . . . and good work."

Finley shook his head and left the room.

25 banged his head against the metal rim as he was tossed inside the cage. The door was closed and locked as he rubbed his skull. He watched with contempt as the two soldiers walked away, joking about a girl named Penny. He spun around, taking in the foreign world around him. Soldiers moved and worked, mostly oblivious to his presence. His wire pen was just short enough; he could not fully stand. There were two boards next to each other on one side of the floor to keep him off the dirt when he slept. In the corner was an older galvanized bucket with a rank smell. He moved away from it and sat tentatively on the boards. His nerves and emotions were shot, but his survival instinct still hummed.

The base had a weathered, overused, and unmaintained look to it. Across from him was a small alcove carved into the sandstone wall. Three soldiers knelt mid-prayer on small rugs facing east. A cross and the Star of David could also be seen on altars nearby. None of the soldiers here wore protective bio-suits over their clothes. Containers and supplies were stacked wherever space might allow. A bang to his left spun 25 toward a grizzled man in a bordering cage. His hair and beard were all one big ball of fur, leaving bloodshot, crazy eyes as the only greeting.

"Hey."

25 gave the man a simple nod.

"You here to be executed?" he asked with unmasked excitement.

"Is that what they do to prisoners here?"

The man cocked his head in confusion. "You're new, aren't cha?"

"Yeah, I get that a lot. New guy just dropped in from outer space."

The man suddenly stepped back from the bars.

"Outer space? Are you from planet Naulis?" He started to chant undeci-pherable words until a large man in fatigues walked by and slammed on his cage. "Shut it old man, or I'll cut your tongue out and give you a reason to speak gibberish."

The next-door-crazy curled into a ball, suddenly silent.

25 shook his head and turned away from the man. He sat back and looked around. The military base, or whatever they called it, was mostly hidden in a red sandstone overhang that doubled as a sunshade. Several buildings were con-structed into the side of the cliff, with only the front wall and windows showing. It was a symbiotic relationship between technology and the earth. To the right, it opened up, revealing a blue sky and the city he had seen on the way in. Buildings within view were in various stages of completion or disrepair. An assortment of drones flew through the air, each with a single-minded mission. To the right were a large landing pad and a collection of vehicles and drones all built for war. Many were foreign to the research and training 25 had been following.

He tried to process his situation. It had taken almost half a day, from the time they had taken off and landed, all the while heading almost due west. He soon realized this information did him no good. All he had done was change prisons.

He had no clue where he was or who had captured him, but at least he wasn't in a restraining bag, just a metal cage.

President Caleb watched through the glass as the body bag was laid on a table in the secure lab. A wizened doctor in a stage-four bio-suit stepped up and removed the body. The doctor was short and a bit thick around the middle, with smokers' lines for a face and penetrating eyes that never missed a detail.

The room was white with a sealed double-door entry and two examination tables inside. There were medical tools and machines against the walls and several red buttons mounted around the space that could flood the space with aerosolized sodium hypochlorite at a second's notice. It would kill every living organism not protected by a suit. Powerful lights from above illuminated a lone female, 24, as Doctor Hastings, on loan from Pharma One, cut away her clothes. The saddened look on her face, just above the slit throat, was still on display for all who would notice.

Caleb turned to his assistant Cin, who stood next to him in the viewing room.

"What do you think?" he asked.

"You don't pay me to think, just to get things done," Cin replied.

"Humor me."

Cin's upgraded yellow irises set against her dark skin and short white hair made her stand out, and she used them to regard her boss for a moment. "I think you should burn the remains and be done with it. At the very best, nothing will come of this, but at the very worst, powers will fight to control whatever they find," Cin said, rather boldly. "And you will lose that fight."

Caleb took a clearing breath and considered her words.

A voice from in the lab squawked over the speaker next to them.

"Orders?"

"I want a full spectrum analysis and complete DNA breakdown," Caleb said. "and keep this hush, hush. No one—and I mean no one—gets wind of what you find, understand?"

"Of course, Mr. President. I should have everything by EOD," Dr. Hastings replied.

President Caleb turned from the viewing glass and headed down the hall to his next concern.

Cin watched him go, trying to decide if she should follow or not.

"Cin," he bellowed. She ran to catch up.

Caleb missed the days when the war was just that: a war. Now, it had become a convoluted business venture with so many hands reaching out, he couldn't keep track of them all. Unfortunately, some of those hands were very powerful. *Hands*. It made him think of his late wife. She had the most beautiful hands—long and delicate, with smooth, perfect skin. He had lost her to a variant of Marburg-G that had ravaged the city so fast, even Pharma One was surprised. She had died in his arms, separated by the plastic shield of a Gen2 bio-suit, as her organs liquified.

The memory still haunted his dreams and under the right circumstances, his days as well.

A soft constant beeping filled the background as doctors huddled around their patient, working the problem. Commander L. Weng was still on the operating table and, mostly, out of danger. Two specialists in bio-mechanical upgrades and bionic technology waited patiently as the medical doctors carefully removed a section of Weng's arm, taking it back to the undamaged section. They prepared it to receive a replacement arm just above the elbow. Once it was ready, the specialists would attach the bionics to working muscles, bones, and tendons. It was a delicate operation but not new territory for them. The difference was the man watching from the other side of the room.

President Caleb had requested the most up-to-date artificial limb and had stopped by to see how it was going.

"This is the TX2204, sir. There is nothing quite like it."

President Caleb nodded his approval.

The TX2204 was held up to the commander's arm and the specialists began the timely fusing of tissue and bionics. President Caleb watched, and his mind flashed back to the last time he had been in a hospital room with the commander. The accident that had taken Weng's wife and nearly his child.

The machinations it had taken to save and rebuild the little girl were cutting-edge. It seemed such a happenstance that the commander was having a similar experience.

If only he could have anticipated the response that night would have on his friend. Perhaps there could have been another path. Now, they were connected by something they both had in common: grief. It was as good a tool as any, Caleb surmised. Now, if he could just end this war, maybe the planet could start healing.

"Carry on," he said as he turned and left.

Two serious-looking soldiers escorted 25 into the Council leader's office. They had forced him to sit and held him tightly. Doctor Patel, a middle-aged doctor with brown skin, hair, and eyes, approached. She tried to give 25 a smile, but she was not well practiced at that. He squirmed, trying to free himself from the two men who held him.

"Stop fighting. I'm not here to hurt you. I'm just going to take a few samples." She took hair, blood, and skin before scuttling off back to her lab. Once she left, they released 25 and stepped back, ready for a fight. 25 rubbed his arm where they had taken his blood and looked around at his surroundings.

Avery's office was made of reinforced concrete and angled out over the base, with a large armored viewing window. An organized desk sat next to the window, and a striking woman with curly brown hair and dark eyes watched his every move from its corner. There was other furniture in the room—polished wood and leather and a small round work table off to the right.

Avery watched the proceedings with curiosity, trying to read the new man's intent. He did a good job of giving her nothing but resentment.

"Leave us," she ordered.

The two guards reluctantly turned, leaving the room in awkward silence.

Avery stepped over to the windows that overlooked the operations below, intentionally turning her back on the man.

25 stood, fists tightening with anger, but curiosity holding him at bay.

"I'm sorry about your partner," Avery voiced.

Silence.

"We didn't know when to expect you, and the 2.0s control most of the territory you landed in. It was costly and complicated."

"Is that an excuse?" He finally spoke.

She turned back to face him. "Perhaps. But we have been monitoring the skies for a long time. So your unexpected arrival caught us a bit unprepared."

"When you say 2.0s . . . Is the Vaxxer War still going on?" he asked.

"Oh, very much so. Although, of late, it is more of a business for them and a case of survival for us." She let her eyes roam across his body. He looked tired and haggard, as if this world was just too much for him. His white jumpsuit was ripped and dirty with 24's dried blood painted across the front. Cuts were prevalent on both his hands and face. He had kind eyes, something that she had almost forgotten could exist. For this world was not made for the kind at heart. Terror and anguish, certainly. That was a daily thing.

After so much war, humans, both the 1.0s and the 2.0s, had become just numbers . . . cannon fodder, a commodity used, abused, and cast aside once they were no longer of value. Here was a man that had never seen or felt war—until today.

Well, welcome to the party.

"Quick history lesson for those that have been isolated up in space." She sat down across from 25 and gestured for him to join her.

25 had quickly learned to distrust Earth-born humans and sat with a dose of caution, his fists still clenched, his body ready to bolt.

"The 2.0 leaders have systematically targeted our governing Council of Twelve. You are looking at the last. That means eleven cities filled with 1.0s have been destroyed."

She paused before changing the subject. "I'm curious about what you know, your training. Perhaps you could tell me a little about yourself and what Dr. Honeywell taught you?"

"You know Dr. Honeywell?" 24 asked as curiosity replaced some of his anger.

Avery looked down. She saw no reason to lie. "He was my father."

The memory of losing 24 flashed across 25 thoughts. "*Was* . . . I'm sorry."

"Thank you. He was a great man." She stood and started to walk as she talked.

"We have concentrated here in Zion to make our last stand."

"Zion?"

"It's the name of this city. It means 'promised land,' which reminds me, 25 . . . that's not a real name. That's a number. Have you given any thought to a proper name?"

He watched as she looked him over.

"Okay." She gave him a focused stare. "Hmm. Let's see . . . born next to the moon. Jer . . . Jericho! That's your new name. You look like a Jericho."

"What does a Jericho look like?" he asked.

"Like someone willing to brave incredible feats to get himself all the way to Earth from the other side of the moon."

"Jericho . . ." He tried the name out for himself.

"It means 'city of the moon.' Yes. It suits you." She turned away, still not comfortable being too close to her father's creation. "We'll have more time to chat later. Let's get you cleaned up. Are you hungry?"

A slight twitch of his eyes answered her question.

"Of course you are. We have a room for you so you can get some rest and shower, and I'll expect you for dinner. I'll have someone bring a plate to tie you over until then."

She watched as his light brown eyes met hers. There was something there. He was more than just a manufactured man. There was a spark behind those eyes.

"We have a lot to go over, and I'm guessing you have questions, as do I."

Avery turned back to the window. Her memory of her father seemed to be fading. A man who had done so much for her and the 1.0s' cause. It was his efforts and ideas that started the Tenant Project. It had given her people hope and a purpose—a way to end the war and bring humanity back together. A solution for both the 1.0s and the 2.0s to put sickness and disease behind them. They had built and launched the SS Hollanbach as a backup, a safeguard. They were in the middle of building the SS Brookstone when the 2.0s destroyed the lab, the launch site, the city, everything. Dr. Honeywell's closely guarded secret was lost. It was all lost, leaving a black husk in its place and a rip in her people's souls. It meant the SS Hollanbach was their last and only chance.

Within a few months, the 2.0s had overrun and destroyed several more of their cities. New Kansas had grown into a mega-city, filled with 2.0s, and now that the war was turning in their favor, 2.0s were being sent out to other locations, repatriating the world with their fear and prejudices. If she was going to make a push and turn the tide, it had to be dramatic, and it had to be soon. Holding back and waiting was a death sentence. Her desperate act to capture and bring Jericho here might shift things in her favor. She reflected on the last message her father sent her. "Hollanbach holds the key." *The key to what? Was Jericho that key? Was it still on the ship?* It was all so cryptic. She never got to see her father again to understand the message. It was like unplugging a newscast mid-sentence. She turned and let her frustration go. It would not help.

8

New Kansas was lighting up as the sun went down. The silicon solar grids across the city had stopped making electricity, and now, banks of charged fuel cells would carry the city through the night. It was a never-ending dance of charging and discharging. One the public took for granted.

Advertising billboards strobed for attention with messages designed to satisfy even the pickiest of consumers. Even the government had a hand in it with health and safety messaging designed to create concern and provide solutions, all in the same ad. As the last mega-city, New Kansas had its share of problems. Overcrowding, crime, and extreme class separation were just a few. The once great bastion of modernity and progress was starting to show her wrinkles.

Sci Officer Katrina and three friends walked the overcrowded pathway that led past a neon alley and all its vices. They chatted and laughed, unconcerned with their surroundings. Each wore the off-duty uniform of military personnel: a black form-fitting jumpsuit with cuffed sleeves and leggings. Their assigned unit's logo was on the front right pocket. It would keep the lowlifes from bothering them and the street callers from getting too aggressive.

Derry and Faith were both part of Katrina's Sci unit and had made this outing many times. Scotty was a new warrior recruit out on the town for his first earned leave. The four of them meandered through the pedestrian-only section as they talked about coworkers, pay, and politics.

They had met randomly in the commissary and had become good friends spending time together when possible.

"What's the over-under on tonight's action?" Scotty asked.

"You can't bet on the Ion-Dome; no one ever wins."

"You can bet on anything, Derry."

"Okay, five to one odds the Ion-Dome takes 'em all."

Scotty looked at her sideways but said nothing.

"Like I said," Derry muttered.

"You've never gone before, have you, Scotty?" Faith asked.

"I told you. I grew up on the outskirts. My parents never let me come downtown."

"They were smart," Katrina said. "I had a heck of a time growing up here."

"That's why we're all here tonight. For a *heck* of a time," Derry exclaimed.

"Heck of a time!" they all shouted in unison.

The city was alive tonight with a parade of citizens trying to one-up the other with their obvious upgrades and fashion choices. There were high-collared coats and glimmering jeweled tops. VR glasses, heads-up displays, even a polka-dot jumpsuit with lit polka dots. Eyes in every color and faces and figures that hid the originals. Upgrades were the norm and the talk of the city—a city that held no love for its occupants, just ingress, egress, and a place to stay, as long as the money flowed.

Large light strips lit the streets and local businesses tried to outdo each other for attention by decorating in the most outlandish ways. Like a carnival sideshow, they rarely used taste. Above was a pathway that required special access to use. It was the place the wealthy occasionally strolled and shopped. Above that were the drone lanes, giving the city depth and layers. Buildings reached for the sky. Lower for commercial, mid for lower rent housing, and upper for those with connections and money. One of the tallest had an upward curve to one side that accessed a series of ascending outdoor spaces, which held pools, gardens, and patios for the occupants of that level. Each was more exotic as you increased in height.

Just above Katrina's head was an Octadisplay, a giant floating 3D head that spoke. It was projected from both sides of the street via eight electric beams. Katrina reached up her hand and passed her fingers through it, distorting the image as it spewed something about a forty percent off sale. No matter where you were in the street, it looked like he was talking directly to you.

The general flow of patrons headed in one direction, toward the Ion-Dome. Katrina's group had managed to score four tickets, and tonight promised dazzling entertainment filled with real-life drama, good food, and music.

Having grown up so close to the Ion-Dome, Katrina had never been interested in going, but tonight, she was bound by the group's whims.

"Hey, a LIFE-ARCH. I'm due for an upgrade," Katrina called out.

Off to the left was one of the many LIFE-ARCHes throughout the city. People could be seen entering and exiting it from left to right.

"Me too. Come on," Derry said, as she started across the street. "You guys wait here."

This section of the city was open for street traffic. Katrina and Derry jogged between the many vehicles that plied the lower street. Each slowed to a crawl with the influx of pedestrians. Some vehicles were occupied, some automated. There were pizza delivery cars, taxi drones, overcrowded beaters, and a few nicer rides showing off in the lower world, all interspersed with two-wheel conveyances darting in between.

The LIFE-ARCH was white and about eight feet high. It was shaped just like its name, an arched tunnel running six feet in length. Lights flashed on the outside, grabbing the attention of anyone looking.

Katrina went first. She stepped into the middle and lifted her arms, doing a slow turn like the icon in front of her showed. After a second, a bio-chip implant under the skin of her wrist flashed green. The arch beeped, and an automated voice confirmed, "Science Officer Katrina, your vaccines are up-to-date. Have a nice evening." A money symbol replaced the rotating human icon to show $50 dollars had been automatically withdrawn from her account. Katrina smiled, and exited the LIFE-ARCH, waiting for Derry to go next.

Everyone in the city had a bio-chip implant. It allowed you to make purchases, prove your identity, upgrade your health, and interface with your home security. Bodies could be identified with the implant and, often, the cause of death determined. The bio-chips were even used to help select compatible sexual partners, although many still refused to follow that protocol. The heart wanted what the heart wanted.

The crowded streets got worse as they moved closer to Edison Avenue.

"Hey, follow me," Katrina called out. She turned down a narrow alley. It was surprisingly empty.

"What's with the back alley tour, Katrina?" Scotty asked.

Katrina didn't respond. Instead, she bounded down a few steps to an old weathered door.

"Sack up, Scotty. It's just a deserted alley with Jaggers waiting to pounce," Derry taunted.

Katrina jerked the handle, and it popped open.

"Okay, now you have my attention. Is this where you keep the serial killers?" Faith asked as they cautiously followed Karina into the dark room. Katrina slipped behind a boarded-up wall and disappeared.

Her three friends stopped in their tracks.

She popped her head back out. "Come on."

They followed her around the wall and into a large, abandoned tunnel, heading off in the direction of the Ion-Dome.

"Whoa. This is very cool," Derry said.

The old maintenance tunnel had grating above that allowed the glow of the city in, just enough to see by. Curved concrete walls and a dank smell beckoned, with the occasional rat squeal for a soundtrack.

"This way. It's a shortcut." They all followed Katrina down the tunnel, not sure this was a good decision.

The Ion-Dome was alive. Its glass-like ceiling sparkled with energy like a disco ball and a plasma beam had a giant baby. The tall, oblong dome was surrounded by stadium seating that held forty thousand people. From above, it looked like an evil eye, twitching and pulsing with electricity.

Katrina followed the signs directing them to their seats, and soon, the show started.

A man dressed in a silver jumpsuit was lifted up to the top of the dome, making the bolts of energy on the glass above him go crazy. He seemed to float in the air, without any visible wires or support. The crowd cheered. He raised his hands and spoke through the public address system. "Welcome one and all to the Dome . . . The Ion-Dome!" He waited while the fans' cheering died down. "Tonight, we are processing over twenty 1.0s," he shouted. Again, he waited for the crowd to settle. He knew how to control them with just his voice. "First up is a mother-child combo. Carla and Bridgette were captured while trying to steal vegetables just outside this very city."

Boos filled the air as two forlorn-looking humans were led into the center court by a mountain of a man in all black holding a six-foot-long electrical prod that zapped and sparked just behind them. The mother grabbed her daughter and held her away from the sting of the prod. They were herded into the center of the Dome, across the polished black floor that reflected the light show from above. Both mother and daughter were poorly dressed and dirty, with disheveled hair and fear in their eyes.

The man backed away, and the door he had come through closed behind him, leaving the two cowering females in the center of the arena.

Music blasted from above, and a visible electrical grid closed in from two directions, like hands coming together; one red, the other blue. They enveloped the two 1.0s and lifted them up into the air some thirty feet, into the perfect viewing position for the excited crowd. The mother and her daughter—who looked to be about eight—seemed unharmed, but the terror on their faces was very real. The two bisecting grids then rotated to a horizontal position, bleeding together and becoming purple. Now, the mother and child looked like they were floating on a carpet of purple energy. Slowly, the mother stood on shaky feet, realizing the energy field was solid enough to do so. The crowd cheered her efforts as the music played for the action.

She pulled her daughter up and ran. The energy field moved to counter her efforts, and all she did was run in place. She tried a different direction and got the same result. The crowd roared with laughter.

"It's Processing Time!" the man in the silver jumpsuit, still floating well above the action, yelled with zeal. This got the audience on their feet as screams and whistles filled the air.

A green undulating light the width of a street lane appeared below the two 1.0s and began its ascent. The mother was unaware of its presence, but the crowd could see it, and they went wild. It passed through the purple energy floor and touched the mom's feet. A screech filled the air as her body began to burn away. She snatched her daughter away from the danger and held her tightly. The green beam continued until the screeches died out, and nothing was left of them. Jumpsuit guy yelled his pleasure, and the crowd echoed theirs.

The Ion-Dome's beam super-heated matter and transmuted it into a gaseous state. What was once solid became gas in an instant. It made for a visual show without any gore, and the city's population thrived on it. In addition to the disintegration and purification of 1.0s and their myriad diseases, there was something else at work in the Dome. As the beam burned away human matter, it collected and transmitted each kill's genetic code into the computer database at Pharma One. This information was used to make vaccines and thwart future sickness—all done without the dangers of taking samples by hand. Pharma One made big money by collecting samples and safely destroying the infected. Though not all were infected, or even 1.0s, the populous would never be the wiser, and Pharma One had a way to feed any public dissenters into the pipeline—no questions asked.

The music ended with a crescendo and then a wild laser-light show hit the Dome.

"That, ladies and gentlemen, is the power of the Ion-Dome. Remember, all 1.0s' genetics here tonight will be used for science to help make our world a safer place to live. Okay. On with the show! Our next 1.0 is a real piece of work. He killed three guards before he was captured. Give it up for Landry!" A broad-shouldered man was escorted by the beast in black into the ring, under a chorus of boos. He seemed relegated to his situation as he walked with slumped shoulders. As soon as the guard got too close, however, he flipped the tables and pried the electric prod away from the surprised big man in black and a scuffle ensued. The exit door quickly closed, and Landry ended up zapping the handler into oblivion. The fans ate up the violence as Landry posed in victory, holding the prod high in the air, but his fate was already determined. The red and blue grids closed on him. Katrina had seen enough and excused herself.

Giles Favreau leaned back in his chair in the chairman's suite and watched from the raised platform in the back of the room, his interest scarcely registering on the action below. When he first envisioned the Dome and had it built, he paid particular attention to the construction of this room. It was a large half-circle of glass that stuck out above the main seating section, giving him the feeling of floating above it all. The front part of the floor was glass for a perfect view of the action.

The red and cream lavish appointments and plush seating included couches and two rows of reclining chairs. Displays around the room gave off 2D and projected 3D images of the Dome's action. There was a set up for food and drinks, including an L-shaped, fully stocked bar. Overlooking it all from the left corner of the room was a five-foot platform. This was a work area—Giles's work area, a throne of sorts—where he could survey his guests from above.

Giles had not invited anyone to share in the festivities tonight, as his morose mood had been with him for the last two days. This often happened when things in his life got too predictable. The sameness of day-to-day was not for him. He was a man of change. A man who worked and looked to the future because change didn't happen when things stood still.

The exception to his empty guest list was Dr. Millie Hastings. He looked at the older woman, who had an intense stare and intelligent eyes. She was the genetics brain behind Giles's operation. Her mind was focused on the data readout happening on the screen in front of her, totally consumed by her work.

Giles's eyes shifted from her salt-and-pepper shoulder-length hair to the show going on outside: the music, lights, and entertainment. The Ion-Dome had been one of his greatest inspirations. It had grown in popularity after a few initial protests and, well, frankly, some botched disintegrations.

As the only sponsor for the Ion-Dome, Pharma One was not here just to sell tickets and a few beers. With each death, or ionization as the marketing department had named it, genetic samples of the deceased were harvested and digitized. The screen in front of Dr. Hastings gave a complete readout of the DNA and genome makeup. It had provided Pharma One with so much raw data and gene collection; it had more than paid for itself. Add the ticket prices and concessions and he had a literal cash cow. Well, a digital cash cow. Nobody used cash anymore.

"Sir, this is interesting," Dr. Hastings said, interrupting his thoughts.

"What have you got?" Giles asked as he leaned over to take a look.

"Look at this deformity on Landry's adenine structure."

Giles noticed the familiar composition that looked like two connected stop signs. Only the image on the screen had two extra posts sticking out.

"What could have caused that?" he asked, almost to himself.

"Most likely a mutation from some type of viral infection."

"I'm surprised he was still alive," Giles said without emotion.

"He must have been asymptomatic. Very interesting," Dr. Hastings surmised.

"Can we use it in some way?"

"Give me a minute."

Dr. Hastings opened a keypad and punched in a code. The structure moved from the screen to the air in front of them, almost like a tangible 3D model. She used her hands to zoom in and rotate the model to show the deformity. She tapped twice on the spot.

"Analyze."

A readout on the screen followed. She had full access to the main lab from here, and once the genetic code was captured and input, she could run almost any test remotely. A string of information appeared on the screen. Dr. Hastings swiped the model away, and it vanished. She leaned closer as she read.

"It appears to be a variant on the adenovirus 11 that swept through here six years ago."

"That was a nasty one," Giles said.

"Yes, and if I'm not mistaken, this mutation is even worse."

"See if you can isolate and grow it. This could be the next big thing for us." Giles's sour mood lifted in an instant. He stood, lifting his bulk suddenly, ready to get out and have some fun. "It's time for a celebration, Doctor. This is excellent news."

Dr. Hastings marveled at her boss's ability to go from one emotion to another in an instant.

Giles left the suite, his mind on his newest acquisition waiting for him at home. A young street urchin he had grabbed, cleaned up, and vaccinated. It was time for some fun.

"Commander Weng, you'll want to wear this for the next two weeks. It blocks the nerve pain receptors to your brain. After that, you should be healed enough to take it off," the doctor said as he placed a strap with a small electronic bulge on one side around Weng's left upper bicep. They were in a small hospital room with one bed and a host of equipment around it. Some were made to beep and others to display text, graphs, or numbers.

Commander Weng sat at the end of the hospital bed, finally disconnected from everything. He was wearing black loose-fitting drawstring pants and no shirt. His torso was covered with scrapes and bruises and a couple of old battle scars. His left arm ended with a visible connection where skin met lab-grown tissue. The trauma to it was still very obvious.

"You're a lucky man." The doctor pressed a button to engage the EMS strap.

The pain in Weng's arm faded away. "Luck favors the prepared, Doctor."

"And sometimes, luck is just luck," the doctor said as he finished up his exam, before stepping from the room.

He was replaced by a technician with an electronic tablet and bug eyes. "Commander Weng, I'm Tech Officer Cruz. If you give me a few moments, I can have your new arm fully functioning so you can get out of here."

Weng scratched at a phantom itch on his missing hand. He watched as the tech wirelessly connected to his arm. A graph on the screen highlighted various motor and reaction functions. "What you now have is a titanium skeleton with lab-grown bionics over it." He used a pin to poke the tips of Weng's fingers, dialing the reaction signal that was sent to the brain. "The skin we grow here is touch, heat, and cold sensitive. On the order of five times more efficient than your previous . . ." He let the words fade, trying not to be insensitive. "I realize the color match is a bit off, but you should see the pigment stabilize in about a week or so. In time, only those close to you will be able to tell, Okay, make a fist."

Weng did as asked. Two fingers refused to properly curl.

Again, the tech modified muscle control until all of Weng's fingers were curled into a tight fist. After a few more tests and calibrations, the tech sat back and disconnected from the arm. "Okay, one last thing. I like to call it the lightbulb test." He handed Weng a sturdy yet small stainless-steel box.

"Why do you call it that?"

"Squeeze."

Weng's hand crushed the heavy-duty chunk of steel.

"Because now you know what your arm is capable of."

Weng nodded with satisfaction. "What are the chances someone could hack my arm and control it?"

"Virtually nonexistent, sir. This tablet comes with the arm. It has your unique code programmed into it, so if you have a problem down the road, you'll need to come to me for a tune-up."

"I see." Weng snatched the tablet from the tech's hand with lightning speed and smashed it to bits. "And now?" he asked.

"Imp—impossible, sir." The tech turned and ran from the room.

"Good."

Sci Officer Katrina stirred her food around on her plate, trying to let the morning's events and especially the night before fade. She had been through three after-action meetings with finger-pointing and twenty-twenty hindsight on display. That she was not in charge of the operation to recover and destroy the ship and its passengers had worked to her advantage, and the higher-ups eventually returned her to active duty. *What a waste of a morning.*

The base cafeteria was a spartan place with rows of stainless-steel tables with surrounding hard-backed chairs. The soft music piped in was flat and the lighting harsh.

Katrina couldn't help but think about the two strangers from outer space who had landed on Earth. What was their mission and where did they come from? The girl had been killed and the man—who knows? They both spoke English. That was weird. *The 1.0s probably killed him themselves. It was anyone's guess, but why sacrifice so many for one?* Something was off, and she intended to find out more. She still had the samples she had collected stored in the freezer at the lab. Maybe they would shed some light, but she would have to be careful how she proceeded.

Commander Weng entered the chow hall. He was back in uniform and most of his visible wounds were covered. The young officer jumped to attention, her eyes quickly going from Weng's battered face to his new arm.

Weng picked up on this and moved his arm freely as a demo. "Good as new. Actually, better than new," he added. "At ease, warrior."

"I—I'm not a warrior. I'm a science officer, sir," Katrina stuttered.

"You're a warrior to me. Please, sit."

Katrina sank back into her seat as Weng took the chair across from her. He looked at the gray, mushy pile on her plate. "What is that? Oatmeal?"

"I think it is supposed to be fish, sir."

"Okay, do me a favor and call me Larry."

"Ah, I think it's better if I call you, *sir*."

"I heard what you did for me, and I just wanna thank you for your bravery." He looked back down at her plate, and his nose couldn't help but turn up a bit. "Are you sure that's fish?"

"That's what it said."

Weng slid her tray out of view and looked up at her face. Something was there that consumed his attention. It took a bit to realize it, but her chestnut eyes drew him in. Not bedroom eyes, but something more captivating . . . intellectual. He made a decision right there. "Okay, that does it. Sci Officer Katrina, I'm asking you to go to lunch with me. I know a nice little place that serves real fish."

"I think that would be a bad idea, sir," Katrina said, with a defensive frown.

"You don't like me, do you?"

"It's not that, sir. Let's just keep things professional," Katrina said.

"I can do professional. Sci Officer Katrina, I'm ordering you to go to lunch with me."

She let out a sigh and stood. "Yessir, but I think I've had my fill of fish today, sir."

"Well, they serve other things there, too," Weng said. He gave her a disarming smirk.

"That would be fine." Her frown nearly turned upside down.

For the first time since his accident, Weng smiled.

Avery was a mover, not a sitter and spending. Her life on the move had served her well, but now, as the leader of what was left of original humanity, she was all bunkered up in the city, trying to stay alive like the rest of the 1.0s. It was a dismal and desperate move, one with a limited future. They needed to do something bolder, more aggressive, and they needed to do it soon.

She downed the food on her plate, using it to power her body—not for taste—something the times had dictated. Soldiers sat around the metal table making small talk. The officers' mess hall was always a place to gather and people watch, but today, it was empty, save one table. The room had wood paneling and wall sconces, giving it a private club feel. In the corner was a small bar and collection of liquors, all unfamiliar to Jericho.

As Jericho was shown in, she studied him. He was wearing a mottled camo outfit that still had creases on the shoulders and pants. It stood out against the well-worn and earned clothes of the others at the table. It didn't go unnoticed either, as he slunk into the last available seat between Avery and Finley.

Many of the soldiers sitting around the table had lost friends while getting Jericho there, and they still couldn't understand the benefit. If Avery was honest, neither could she.

"Well, I have to admit, you clean up nice," Avery said, breaking the silence. She made introductions around the table until all ten names were shared. Jericho recognized a few faces from his hasty extraction from the 2.0s.

A plate was filled and passed to him, and Jericho ate like he might not see food again. His last few days had been a bit lean on caloric intake.

Avery cleared her throat and began. "So, since you left Earth . . . or since your biological essence left in a spaceship," Avery continued, "a lot has happened. My father had a parochial view of life. Very black and white. He, along with a few others, grasped the writing on the wall."

Avery pushed herself back from the table and stood. "After the first virus, humankind was encouraged to get vaccinated. Some were all about it, but others, not so much. As other viruses swept through the masses, a division grew, and civil unrest between the two factions divided humankind like a gorge. Fighting amongst a polarized humanity intensified until a global war broke out. The powers in charge quickly realized the opportunity this war provided—a chance to consolidate their power."

Jericho looked around the table; most were busy eating and not paying attention to Avery's speech. Not the first time was she giving this chat, he deduced.

"You see, this war, the Vaxxer War, was never about a virus or vaccine and who had it and who didn't. It was always about power and control. Big Pharma. Well, that's what they used to call it. They used the first virus to plant fear in the public. Then slowly, over the next few years, a string of suspicious outbreaks continued to hit."

"What kind of outbreaks?" Jericho interrupted.

The girl from the trek with the scar, Major Christine Helen, spoke up. "Let's see, first there was COVID-22; then there was Hanta8, followed by Marburg-G, and so on. About six different outbreaks, one after the other. Always somewhere between six and twelve months apart."

Finley put his fork down. "And each time humanity gave more and more of their freedom away until Big Pharma got control of it. Initially, it was a race between competing companies. First to the market with a patented vaccine, etcetera. Then the companies started fighting amongst themselves until one came out on top. I know; I was part of it for a while . . ." His mind drifted for a second. "Pharma One eventually ended the competition and soon, other corporate giants from different disciplines followed, giving rise to a corporate war within the war that decimated the planet."

"Now, five major companies control just about everything that's left." Avery finished as Finley stuffed a chunk of meat in his mouth.

Jericho deduced, "Except Zion?"

Finley nodded while chewing.

"You mentioned five corporations? Like what? Power, finance, health, food, and . . ."

"Consumer products. Exactly," Avery continued, "Big Pharma learned long ago, a cure to a disease or sickness is not nearly as profitable as a maintenance program. Take measles or polio, for example. You pay one time and get a shot; presto, you're cured." She let the words hang in the air for a beat. "But imagine having to pay every year to keep it away . . . or every month? The new vaccines changed our DNA structure, making some humans more dependent and less tolerant to new disease."

"Hence the term, Human 2.0?" Jericho asked.

Off her nod, Avery continued, "Plus, they owned the whole downstream. The vaccines, the hospitals, the doctors—all of it. And if you believed that you would die screaming in pain or sucking your last liquid breath in your bed, then you had to get the vaccine, and that's when they had you. Once injected, Pharma One owned you."

Finley added, "No vaccine, no admittance to a hospital, or any other public place, for that matter. It was fear-mongering at its finest."

"A very hostile takeover," Major Helen added.

"So you're all banned from even going to New Kansas?" Jericho asked.

"Shot-on-site banned," Avery said, leaning toward Jericho. "Unless you are willing to submit. You see, the vaccines were more than just an immunity boost against a virus. It was a subscription to health. It changed key markers in your immune system. As long as you kept up with your monthly payments, you were fine."

The shaved-head guy, Sergeant Kay, who had threatened Jericho with a knife, interrupted. "That's a kind of control where *you* pay someone else to have it. Pharma One has control over your health *and money,* your life. And if you miss a payment . . . well, the system's rigged."

"That's what we are fighting for. To take back our lives. Not just for us." Avery moved across from Jericho. "The 2.0s aren't bad; the problem is they are so indoctrinated, they believe exposure to just one of us 1.0s would kill 'em. It's bred a fanaticism that's impossible to hurdle." She moved left and placed her hands on Finley's shoulders.

"Not everyone was willing to blindly accept their solution. Some of us . . ." Finley waved around the room as an example, "Preferred to let our immune systems fight and strengthen the way nature works and God intended.

"God?" Jericho said.

"Yes. He is alive and well, right here in Zion. We have Buddhists, Christians, Muslims, Hindus, and Jews all working and living together."

"That seems impossible from what I've learned," Jericho voiced.

"It was. Organized religion had been a source of death around the globe throughout history, but it's funny what happens when your belief system is about to become history. All the great religions fell during the war, but individual faith grew stronger, and here in Zion, all are welcome to intermingle and worship as they please, even our atheist friends. When you're busy trying to just stay alive, criticism of other religions fades away."

"You won't find that in New Kansas," Kay added.

The others around the table agreed.

Avery walked over and activated a Hollowvision image of the continents. "None of this matters if we don't survive the war. Look." She pointed. "Here is a map of the earth as it currently stands. 2.0s control New Kansas, the world's only mega-city, and a few growing pockets, known as sister cities to the East. Europe and Asia are in shambles, as the worst of the war's weapons hit there. The few that remain grovel for existence. The Middle East ran out of oil and without money, returned to an unlivable desert. Africa is still viable, and many have fled there, but most are engaged in a series of civil and territorial disputes."

Finley added, "Some things never change."

"England, Australia, and South America—that's a lecture for another time. Suffice it to say, those who don't pay attention to their history are doomed to repeat it." She turned off the projection and sat back down. "We represent the last large pocket of 1.0s on the planet."

Commander L. Weng let his PCD R-2 drone do the flying while he voice-programmed their destination. "Just for the record, you are free to say no. I am not really ordering you to have lunch with me . . . just hoping."

Katrina decided to let her experiences with male officers slide; the commander seemed genuine. "Thank you for saying that."

The PCD lifted off and banked right, then rose into the highest lane.

"I've never flown in lane four before," Katrina said as she looked out over the city from the highest skyway.

It was afternoon, and the sun was kicking off everything reflective, giving the tarnished city a new luster. The symphony-like moves of the city were on full display out of the drone's windscreen. It was beautiful. Everything she cared about was within sight. Since she was a child, Katrina had played and connected with the people around her. The street level was her home and comfort zone, like an extended family—the family she chose—and this perspective made it all look so small and insignificant.

"It's funny," Katrina said. "You would never know we were at war the way citizens go about their daily lives. Laundry, shopping, cooking, and shagging . . . the circle of life keeps going. All while we're out there getting killed, just so they can do it all over again tomorrow."

"Believe it or not, the simple freedom to have that routine is what we are fighting for," Weng said.

"Oh, I believe it. Those are the things I love most."

Weng cocked an eye, wondering if the shagging part was on her list. He dismissed the thought as fast as it materialized. Katrina was a beautiful woman, with a rare natural beauty—something that seemed on the extinction list these days.

They flew past a collection of bronzed high rises, built for the super-rich. Next to the shiny towers was a collection of crumbling brick buildings that looked to be occupied by squatters. There were clothes hanging to dry on rusted balconies, and boarded-up windows and the stench of poverty sat just outside the cockpit.

"War is good business," Weng said, interrupting the moment of silence.

"And once the 1.0s are gone, it will be great business for all," Katrina added.

Weng looked over at her. "Sounds like someone stayed awake during one of the Citizen Alert propaganda broadcasts."

"You don't believe that?" Katrina asked.

"I believe politics and money dictate what comes next. There is no doubt the 1.0s are dangerous, but once they're gone, someone else will have to take their place," Weng said, "if we are to maintain the status quo."

"Like who? The poor?"

"Maybe. There's a lot that goes on above my paygrade, but it seems like a new viral strain or variant cycles across the globe every six months or so and as long as that happens, we need to fight it with every technology possible."

"For all we know, Pharma One is growing and distributing variants related to these viral outbreaks, just to keep *us* dependent and their pockets full."

"That's dangerous talk," Weng said.

Katrina lowered her head and gave a brief nod. She knew better, and to be honest, it was the one thing that scared her the most, catching some disease from a 1.0 that would leave her drowning in her own sauce.

"I'm curious. Why the military?" Weng asked.

"What, you don't think I can handle it?" Katrina said a bit too defensively.

"Just the opposite," Weng replied, with a half-smile.

"I grew up in a house with three brothers; there was always a competition between us. They all went on to do mundane things, but not me. After my mom died, my aunt got me the introduction and interview. I did the rest."

"Your aunt?"

"Dr. Millie Hastings," Katrina replied. "She was head of the weaponized bio division for a while."

"WBD, wow . . . was?"

"Now she's working for Pharma One. Same crap, different master. She still can't talk about any of it."

"So your aunt gets you in the military, and you . . . what? Follow in her foot-steps? Science division?"

"After an initial detour. I tried out for the warrior class. Not for me, and yes, I love it," Katrina said.

"It shows," Weng said.

"What does?"

"Your passion for the work. So you mentioned your mom, aunt, and your brothers. Any other family, a father?"

Katrina looked away for a moment, her emotions building.

"Sorry, didn't mean to . . ."

"It's okay. Not my favorite subject," Katrina confessed.

"Change in subjects then. So, besides seafood, what else do you like?" Weng asked.

Katrina cocked a glance his way and took a clearing breath. "I like to watch the moon from my rooftop with a glass of white wine. The city is quieter at night, and the air seems more . . . crisp. It's my unplug time. Away from all the crazy. Sometimes, I play a little jazz."

Weng let the words breathe as the drone dropped from the sky and landed on Delaney's hover pad. *Unplugging sounded nice.*

The restaurant was fabulous, and Katrina enjoyed the company even more. She surprised herself and ordered the fish. Small talk about work and family peeled back an easiness that grew more personal.

The drone ride back to the base was quiet but comfortable. The kind of comfort where two compatible souls are happy just being together.

"That's where I live, over there," Katrina pointed out.

Weng hovered over the row of red-brick military housing just off base, before landing. Katrina unbuckled and looked over at Weng. "Lunch was really great."

Weng nodded with a semi-smile. "I have something for you."

Katrina shot him a sideways glance in response.

He handed her a small brown box.

"What is it?"

"Open it and find out."

Katrina lifted an eight-inch knife in a thin scabbard from the box. "A knife? You sure know the way to a woman's heart, Larry."

"Not just any knife. A boot knife. It might be the difference between living and dying. Mine's saved me a few times."

"And you want me to stay alive?" She asked, with a bit of coyness.

Weng couldn't find the right response, so he blurted out something lame. "Of course. You saved my life. This may, one day, let me return the favor."

There was a beat of silence before Katrina reached for the door. "Thanks," she said. "I had a good time." She paused and looked back at him with a genuine smile.

Weng wanted to respond in kind, but he failed to find his voice.

Katrina exited the drone.

Weng shook his head. *Do I like this girl? What is that burning feeling that just shot through me?*

He voiced his next destination, "Home," as he tried to shake off the emotion. Below, Katrina made her way from the landing pad as his PCD R-2 lifted off and banked left. Weng watched until he could no longer see her, then turned his thoughts to Ruth.

Katrina tossed her things onto the kitchen table and went to her input panel. With a few swipes and taps, she was in her lab's database. She opened the file relating to her last mission. Her plan was to do a little research of her own on the samples she had collected in the field. The problem was the file had been deleted. Everything relating to her samples was gone. She double-checked everything, but a sinking feeling was all she had. Someone far above her was covering their tracks or hiding the truth. She stepped back, letting her mind ferret out an answer, but nothing obvious came to her. Maybe her aunt would have answers. She made a mental note to ask her the next time they got together.

As the drone powered down, Weng stepped out and hurried past the small hedge that surrounded the home landing pad.

"Thanks for helping out," he said, as he walked through the door into the kitchen."

A female trainee had been assigned to watch his daughter, Ruth, until he was released from the hospital. She saluted her superior officer and left through the front door, carrying a small overnight bag. Weng placed his gear on the island and let out a breath as his shoulders lowered. It was good to be home.

"Dadda, Dadda!" Ruth called as she ran across the open floor plan and threw her arms around his neck, relieved at his presence. She had been so worried when he hadn't come home; the fear of losing her only remaining parent had nearly been too much.

Giant tears flowed as Weng held her tightly, then carried her over to the modern leather couch. The home was decorated all white with a few dark pieces contrasting the clean look. Carlyle watched from his charging port over in the corner.

They sat together, and he allowed her emotions to cycle. After a time, her sobbing calmed.

"I have something to show you," he said in a whisper.

Eventually, the tears were wiped away, and she pulled back to see what he had brought. Weng pulled a plush stuffed platypus from behind his back. It was the one animal Ruth had been consumed with ever since learning about the unique egg-laying mammal. She had a collection in her room: statues, pictures, and toys. The duck-billed platypus had gone extinct, along with several other species, during the early years of the Vaxxer War, but that had just made it more interesting to Ruth.

"A platypus! I love it," she said as she hugged it.

"You'll need to think of a name for her."

"It's a she?" Ruth asked.

"Yep."

"How can you tell?"

"No venomous spurs . . . and she told me," Weng said with a wink.

"Okay." Ruth looked up to the ceiling, letting her mind think, the tip of her tongue sticking out as she did. "Patty."

"Patty the Platypus."

Ruth giggled, and the two made the moment last. It was just what they both needed.

"I have something else to show you." Weng rolled up his sleeve and showed Ruth his new arm.

"Is that?"

"Yep, now we're twins."

"Did it hurt?" She asked.

"It's just an arm, honey."

9

President Caleb stepped into the secure VIP conference room, leaving his personal device outside in a specialized slot in the wall. His ever-present assistant, Cin, followed behind him. He sipped at a coffee that was still too hot to drink. The space was the size of a large living room with angled soundproof lead-lined walls and several closed-circuit heads-up displays. In the back was a spread of food and drinks on several polished white cabinets. There was a central elongated steel and glass table surrounded with chairs and a few more comfortable stuffed chairs along the walls. Just above the table was a realistic projection of Zion.

Caleb looked over at the three serious-looking generals waiting for him, each with their own agenda. These were men he kept close but never fully entrusted with too much power. To the left was his right-hand man, Commander Weng, a man who had proven himself time and time again. This was someone he could trust—rare in his world.

"Generals," Caleb said.

"Mr. President," they replied, standing as he entered.

"How are you feeling, Commander?" the president asked.

Weng held up his new arm and moved it about. "I'm good, sir."

"Glad to hear it."

"So let's get to it. Have a seat, please."

They did.

"What do you have for me?"

"Mr. President, as you know, we have a mole inside the upper echelon of Zion." General Tran, on his left, started.

"As I understand it, your 'mole,' as you call it, reached out to us," the president corrected.

General Tran paused, a bit flustered, then continued, "We now have in our possession a means to disrupt the laser containment grid protecting the city."

This grabbed Caleb's full attention. "How?"

"Blow it up, sir. Well, actually, the power source for it. As you know, they have an old-school dam and generator plant that powers the entire city." He pointed them out on the projection in front of him as he spoke .

"Go on."

General Rice, to the right, jumped in, trying to get noticed. "If we take a small team and link up with our mole . . . here." He pointed near the dam, south of the city. "That team will have a good chance of getting to those generators."

General Phelps, across the table, added, "Timing's critical. The city will be vulnerable for about twenty seconds before the back-up system kicks in."

"A lot can happen in twenty seconds," Caleb said.

"Exactly, and we'll launch a full warrior regiment on the ground from the west, where they won't expect it, and a fast-attack airborne division from the east." His fingers showed the two points of entry on the miniature city in front of them.

"Put Zion in the middle and squeeze," General Tran added, using a hand to demonstrate.

The president stood and placed his hands behind his back as he moved through the room, letting the information simmer. "This is good news. What's the expected damage?"

"We won't destroy the generators, sir. Just take 'em out of commission. The military base will have to be hit pretty hard," General Tran said.

"Of course."

"But I see no reason we can't mop up the civilian population without destroying the infrastructure," General Phelps added.

"I want as much of the population corralled and captured as possible—not killed," the president said.

"But, sir?"

"An empty city to fill eventually is good, but a working, breathing city we can control is the goal here. Put measures into place to pen up the citizens and vaccinate them all. Any who refuse you can kill or bring here for the Dome, understand?"

"This just got a whole lot more difficult and unsafe for our warriors," General Phelps said.

"That's why I keep you lot around; figure it out," the president said, with finality.

"Yes, sir," General Tran replied.

"Excellent." The president moved to the table, grabbed a grape, and popped it in his mouth. "When can we launch?"

"Anytime, Mr. President. Just give the order."

Caleb turned to his friend. "Commander, I need you to personally run the sabotage operation on the generators. We can't have any margin for error. This can end the 1.0s, once and for all. We can finally rebuild this world in our own image."

Knowing what this meant, Weng could only give a brief nod. His mind spun with thoughts of Ruth—her future and her place in the new world that was to come. She deserved a future, and he could now guarantee that.

The conversation continued around him as he stayed lost to his thoughts. Weng barely heard his name being called by one of the generals.

"Commander?"

"Sorry, yes; it's a solid plan. I'll lead the advance squad that takes out the generators."

"Excellent. Concerns?" Caleb asked Weng.

"The 1.0s are a filthy lot. All we can do is make sure our warriors have their vaccines up-to-date. Unfortunately, the advance squad won't be able to wear a bio-suit into the city. It would be a sure tip off we were 2.0s. That would put an end to everything before we even started. So there is a solid chance that some (or all) of us will be infected."

General Rice added, "We don't know what the latest strains are or if they are even active in the city."

"Thank you, generals. The risk is high, but we are talking about ending the war here once and for all, with a final 'shock and awe' to their last standing city."

President Caleb leaned over, placing both hands on the table. "Okay . . . make it happen, but remember, there are spies everywhere. This information stays right here in this group until the last possible second."

His words were met with a round of nods and grunts.

Giles had listened to the meeting with interest from his office. He processed what actions he would take should the war between the 1.0s end. After all his previous attempts and scheming, it looked like a lone person on the inside would tip the scales and open the door to Zion. An entire city, ready to be occupied and controlled. Hundreds of thousands of 1.0s would be vaccinated and soon put in line, making monthly health payments to him. It was a potential boost to his bottom line. The loose jowls on his face tightened with the rare hint of a smile. He let his MindLink connect with his computer and quickly made a to-do-list, then distributed it to the relevant parties.

After a moment, he paused to think about how far he had come and how much he had lost. Before the Vaxxer War, the world had been accelerating technologically at light speed. Quantum computing had just passed testing and been implemented in one of his facilities. Global warming had been reversed, the population had stabilized, and humankind was planning a mission to start terraforming Mars.

One of the first things destroyed when the war started was the brains and infrastructure of his quantum computing lab. That single incident had set the world back by many decades, and as the war dragged on, nearly every advancement took a hit. It had taken a Herculean effort to maintain the technology they currently had. Scientists, engineers, and specialized facilities had been targeted and eliminated by both sides. And now, weapons systems were repaired instead of improved, and his facility with nanoscale fabrication tools was just starting to be rebuilt. Humanity and his company were many years away from matching things as they were before it all started.

Giles's thoughts shifted to the idea of getting control of Zion and what steps he would need to implement to make sure that happened.

A quick MindLink message was sent to his chef and staff to set up for a celebration. Goose foie gras, caviar, and a bottle of Opus One from his private cellar. He needed a quiet place to think, so it would be a private affair—with only the king attending—but first a bit of business.

Giles connected to President Caleb on a secured connection. The president picked up with a slightly annoyed tone.

"Giles?"

"I've been giving this little war of yours some thought."

"Okay, glad to hear. What now?" The president asked, skeptically.

"A city of nearly 400,000 can be used to our benefit," Giles said.

The president quickly countered the conversation to see what Giles was really getting at and just how much he knew. "The way I see it, we need to eradicate all the 1.0s and the best and safest way to do that is once the containment grid goes down, we bomb the city out of existence."

"Perhaps, but I'm thinking we save the city infrastructure. If we were to give the 1.0s an option to be vaccinated, we could double our power base in just a few weeks."

Caleb's face flashed red. One of the generals must have passed on the details of his secret meeting with Giles. The man had his tentacles in everyone's business and was now playing him.

"Imagine being the leader and president that brought these warring factions together. The two largest and most profitable cities in the world, united. It would be a historic event for the ages."

The president calmed as he recognized the words for what they were, an opening to negotiations. He stalled for more. "That would mean street-by-street fighting. You're talking about a lot of 2.0s dying for a race of people we have only tried to eradicate. I fear it might not be worth the risk for our warriors."

"Warriors will do what they are ordered. Nothing more." Giles tossed almost the same words Caleb had used as he leaned closer to the screen. "Take Zion, but leave it intact. Convert as many 1.0s as possible. I suggest you drop pamphlets or use loudspeakers to blast their options as we move through their city like smoke in the wind. Do this and I will make sure you spend the rest of your life as president of not just one city or two, but a whole new world."

Caleb let the words weigh heavy on his face by showing reluctance, but inside, he was savoring the outcome. Sharing the city was not all bad, and he would never have been able to control it all by himself. The rest of the CEOs could fight over the scraps. He gave Giles a curt nod in agreement.

Giles disconnected the link. He would reconnect with Cin to make sure Caleb carried out his wishes. She was as clever as she was smart, and that kind of person could be counted on to do what was best for them—a predictable and therefore controllable person. He had promised her Caleb's job. It's been a tactic that had bought her loyalty but for only so long. If things went well and Caleb delivered, he could always manufacture a new position for her that would nullify her ambitions for a time.

Jericho woke feeling like he was hungover. It took a moment before his memory kicked in as to where he was and how he got here. He sat up and rubbed his eyes. The bedroom reminded him of his personal berth on board the SS Hollanbach. He wondered how many other subjects before him had the same hopes and dreams, squashed by a deadly gas in the night. His thoughts turned to the reoccurring nightmare of 24's throat being sliced, each time waking him up to a racing heart and drenched in sweat. It had been a long night. He shook the thoughts away and slowly got dressed. Dreaming was no longer an escape for him.

Reaching into his old pants pocket, Jericho pulled out the ring he had taken from 24's finger. The shiny aluminum had a few specs of dried blood, so he washed them off, then held it up to the bathroom light. A never-ending circle symbolizing their life together, with no beginning and no end, yet it had ended, horrifically.

Jericho let the emotions build and a burning in his heart overwhelmed him. Tears flowed without restraint as he sank to the tile floor. His body shook in uncontrolled convulsions as he let grief take over.

After a time, his feelings quelled, and he stood. The reflection in the mirror was haunting. He looked haggard and worn out, not like the promising young man ready to restart the Earth he was a few days ago.

Jericho pulled a Kevlar thread from his torn jumpsuit and threaded it through the ring. He then tied it off and placed the necklace around his neck, tucking it under his shirt. He would carry her memory with him always.

As he stepped from his room and turned right toward the mess hall, a voice stopped him.

"Morning. I have a full day planned for you."

Jericho turned to see Avery walking down the hallway.

"Hi. First, we need you in the lab for a few more tests and then perhaps a little training?" Avery said as she approached Jericho.

"Training?"

"Yeah, it'd be good to get some type of evaluation of your skills and how we can best use them," she added.

"Sure. I just hope you're not disappointed. My training on the ship was cut short."

"I'm sure it will be just fine. My father put everything he had into you, and I intend to follow through with his wishes."

"And I don't have a say?" Jericho asked.

Avery just glared at him.

"I don't have a father, so this might sound a bit jaded, but what if yours was wrong?"

"The lab is at the end of the hall on the left. Dr. Patel is waiting for you."

Jericho dropped a sigh and headed down the hallway to the left.

Avery watched him go. She had a lot riding on this science experiment from outer space, and time was not something she could waste.

The double doors into the lab pushed open, and Jericho looked around. It was a collection of unfamiliar equipment, samples, and smells. This was not an area he had been trained in. He watched as a lab tech used a machine to look at the molecular structure of a sample. It all seemed so complicated and foreign.

"Please, have a seat. I'm Doctor Patel," a woman said.

Jericho glanced up to see an older, white-haired woman with olive skin and a curious expression. She was standing near a bench looking at an e-chart.

Jericho sat and tried to make himself comfortable, but this place made him feel vulnerable. He didn't like it.

Dr. Patel pulled up a chair and sat across from him. "Let's start with life back on the SS Hollanbach."

"Okay, so no pleasantries." Jericho took her through everything as he remembered it, from right after his birth to 24 and the subsequent destruction and escape from the dying ship.

The doctor didn't seem interested in his life after the Hollanbach, and she turned the conversation back several times.

"So, you said that Doctor Honeywell and this AI, Azraelle, never told you your purpose other than repopulating Earth with humans?"

"Everything we did was to get us ready for that. The fighting skills, the survival training, and our education."

"I see . . . And no mention of a weapon system, virus, or bacteria?"

"As far as we knew, Earth's population had been destroyed. There were supposed to be no 2.0s, or very few," Jericho replied.

"Well, that didn't happen."

Jericho stared at the doctor.

Dr. Patel cleared her throat and looked away for a beat. "The 2.0 . . . they live in fear. Fear of getting sick, but frankly, getting sick is part of life. They vaccinate for everything. Overcoming sickness actually helps build our immunity for the future. It is the way the human body is meant to work."

"What about the cost of life for you to get your immunity up as a whole?" Jericho asked.

"Well, that's the debate, isn't it?"

"Just sounds like the other side of the same extreme coin to me," Jericho surmised.

Dr. Patel ignored his comment and leaned toward Jericho, taking her glasses off as she did. She began a careful examination, starting with his hands.

"Once you start down the path of vaccines for every little sickness, your body's immune system starts to rely on those vaccines and their updates. The 2.0s love their updates. That's when Big Pharma has you, trapped between fear and a sickness that is now very real."

She looked in his ears, nose, and mouth. "Say *ahh*."

Jericho did.

"You have no choice but to continue or roll the dice, and the longer you wait, the riskier that becomes. If I was a 2.0, always getting the latest viral update, and then suddenly cut it off, I doubt I'd make it through another year. That's the core of the problem. They can't stop. 'Course, you wouldn't know anything about that, would you?"

"Well, Doc, I do now," Jericho replied.

"Sorry, I sometimes get on my soapbox. If it's all right with you, I'd like to check your vitals."

"Okay, but make it quick. I'm beginning to feel like a lab rat here."

Dr. Patel did a cursory check of Jericho's vitals and reviewed the lab's notes from the blood, skin, and hair samples collected previously. Nothing popped out as unusual.

"In my opinion, Jericho, you are extremely healthy. So get out of my office so I can focus on someone who needs me." She finished the words with a coy smile, and Jericho relaxed for the first time since he had arrived.

A soldier standing in the hall intercepted Jericho as he exited the clinic. "I've been asked to escort you to the training grounds."

Jericho lifted an eyebrow. "Any chance I can grab breakfast first?"

The soldier just stared at Jericho.

Jericho let out a heavy sigh and gestured to the soldier. "All right, lead the way." He followed the young man in fatigues down a hallway decorated with fading paint and a worn floor to an exit door. The soldier then led them along a narrow path surrounded on both sides by a high fence. Men and women were training on both sides. To the right, there were weapons being fired at humanoid targets. Hand-to-hand combat and a few calisthenics were on the left. They entered a gate at the end and stepped into an open dirt space.

"Oh, good. You're here." Avery paused what she was doing and stepped over to Jericho and gave him a smile. "We'd love to get an idea of the kind of training you did on that ship. I'm afraid we have become a bit more *low-tech* over the years."

The dirt area was roughly ten-by-ten meters, with a fence around it and several fighting weapons on a rack to the left. A group of two dozen soldiers stood along the fence, watching Avery interact with the new man, each carrying a different expression—some curious, some resentful. Word of his capture from the 2.0s and the cost of lives had sped through the base.

Jericho recognized several of the soldiers from his rescue team and a few from last night's dinner. He gave a little wave but was met with only a scowl from Sergeant Kay. Jericho looked at Avery. "I'd be happy to show you what I can. Did some E-Chung . . ." A few of the soldiers snickered at the mention of the decades-old training system. ". . . and some virtual weapons and combat gaming."

"Well, we are in real life here. No games or pre-programmed strikes," Avery said, trying not to sound patronizing.

Jericho nodded, suddenly doubting his abilities.

"Pike. Front and center," Avery called out.

An average-sized soldier stepped from the group with a sneer on his face and a scar from his eye to his throat. "I'm gonna wipe that smile right off your face, maggot."

Jericho frowned, then realized it was all part of the soldier's act, so he let his smile grow even larger and took a fighting stance. "Let's see you try."

Pike took three quick steps to close the distance before letting a round-house kick fly.

Jericho dropped and fired his boot into the man's groin, sending him spiraling into a pained clump on the ground behind him.

Jericho stood and dusted himself off, his smile even bigger.

"Bravo, Jericho. Pike has always been too full of himself," Avery said. "Paris, your next."

A much larger man stepped from the group. He cracked his knuckles as he approached. The rippling muscles on his arms pulsed with anticipation as he bounced effortlessly on his toes. He was focused and ready.

Jericho resumed a fighting stance, moving and countering as the big man closed. This time his expression matched his opponent's: all business.

A few of the watchers cheered their fellow soldier on.

This soldier was careful, unlike his predecessor, and used jabs and crosses to look for weaknesses in his opponent.

Jericho blocked and ducked most of them, getting a few glancing blows as the fight progressed.

Shouts and cheering from the crowd intensified for their own as Jericho countered a cross from Paris with an elbow to the bicep.

Paris, named after his hometown, shook his arm at the pain and reengaged. Jabbing and crossing with increased intent, always moving and bouncing on his toes.

Jericho was patient, and the moment he detected the pattern, he used it against his foe. The man seemed to do three jabs and then a cross, followed by a couple more jabs. Jericho slipped the cross and came in under the man's swinging arm, then up around it to lay a devastating forearm into Paris's throat as he simultaneously swept the man's unbalanced feet out from under him.

Paris went down hard, and Jericho followed with an elbow to his chest, knocking the wind out of the man and ending the fight.

Once again, Jericho stood. This time, with a quarter smile. Before he could react, ten soldiers rushed in, pummeling and kicking him to the ground. They were angry. Angry at the loss of their fellow soldiers, his attitude, his good looks—you name it. No test-tube freak from outer space was welcome here.

Avery cried out for them to stop, but it took several minutes before emotions calmed.

She kneeled down next to a dirty, bloody, and beat-up Jericho. She could see the hatred in his eyes. This had not gone as planned.

President Caleb looked over the report from the body they had recovered in the forest. It was interesting but a disappointment. Dropped into one of his over-stuffed chairs in his office, he swiped through the data. The mDNA and RNA markers were normal, and the evidence of viral antibodies from myriad diseases that had swept and panicked the planet was nonexistent. This was effectively a virgin 1.0. That certainly corresponded with the arrival of the escape pod, but why go to all the expense and trouble of the SS Hollanbach's operation, just to make two virgin 1.0s? They should have put all that money and effort into advancing their weapons tech. The fallout between Giles and Doctor Honeywell that ended it all was devastating. He would never want to get on Giles's bad side. It was a place from which you never came back.

The one thing the 1.0s had done right was to develop the laser containment grid over the city. That was something totally new, and as of yet, he and his generals had not been able to defeat it. He wondered how much of that was Doctor Honeywell's genius. The thought that it might all now be coming to an end raised the corners of his mouth. A second city far from the prying eyes of the chairs might give him working room and help cut a few strings from the CEOs and their position of power. Hopefully, this was more than just wishful thinking.

It was all still to do, and if Weng and his warriors failed, it would amount to nothing but a fire drill. Even so, his faith in the commander's abilities was encouraging. So he would plan accordingly.

"Mr. President?" Cin walked into the room. Her eyes, the yellowest he'd ever seen, always garnered his attention. Caleb loved her efficiency and appreciated her body, which she shared with him on her terms. He pulled his eyes from her chest and looked her in the face.

She quickly went through his schedule for the day, pretending not to have noticed his impropriety. She tweaked and adjusted the schedule based on his responses. "And Chairman Favreau is requesting a link."

Caleb looked at his watch, a bygone piece that was rarely used by most, except for decoration. "Patch him through; I'll take it here."

"Very good, Mr. President," she said as she cast the call into the room.

"Caleb." The image of Giles Favreau was unusually chipper as it materialized.

"Chairman Giles Favreau. This is an unexpected pleasure," Caleb said with no small amount of sarcasm.

Giles held back a frown. He hated it when Caleb used his whole name with a dose of mimicry. "I know you're busy winning the war and running the country, so I'll make this short."

Too late, Caleb thought.

"I wanted to give you a heads-up. There is a new strain of adenovirus 12 making its way to our city, and it is a nasty one."

"Our citizens are getting tired of running to a LIFE-ARCH every week for an update, Giles. Maybe it's time to dial that back," Caleb offered.

"Its genome makeup is different enough that a simple LIFE-ARCH update will not do the trick," Chairman Favreau continued as though he never heard

Caleb's concern. "It will take more than software. Pharma One has developed a next-generation, two-step vaccine that will boost your immunity and stop the sickness dead in its tracks. The science behind it is all a bit tricky, but those who don't get this vaccine will probably perish."

"You don't think it's a bit soon for another outbreak? Our citizens might suspect you are creating them for your bottom line."

"Don't be so dramatic, Caleb. We are launching a strong campaign with some pretty horrific images of victims' bodies turning to jelly, that sort of thing. It'll be happening at our outpost in New Memphis."

"I haven't heard anything about that," Caleb said with concern.

"Well, you're hearing about it now. . . . We'll dial up the fear-mongering and counter that with a safety message about the vaccine's efficacy. I would be surprised if the demand for the inoculation isn't off the charts within a week. I also propose we post a video of all the upper echelons getting the shot. That will boost confidence among the masses. Of course, we'll need to have a few die here to help complete the story."

"Of course," Caleb monotoned.

"I was wondering about your thoughts on using this latest wave to cast off a few of our undesirables," Chairman Favreau asked.

"You're talking about street level?"

"Give it some thought. We can bring it up at the next chair meeting, but I will expect you to back me."

Caleb cocked his head slightly but did not give a verbal answer.

Giles looked at the president, trying to get a read on his non-reply. After a beat, he changed the subject.

"I understand you've acquired a pure 1.0."

The words did not surprise Caleb as much as they disappointed him. He had been very secretive about the recovered female body from the escape pod. The level of spying at the highest levels was sickening. He had no choice but to come clean.

"You are well informed, as usual."

Chairman Favreau grinned with a hint of victory. "I want unfettered access to the body and any samples you have collected."

"Of course. But this is a military matter; may I ask why?" Caleb queried.

"No, you may not. I'm sending a team over to collect her. Make sure they are afforded every courtesy and good luck on your upcoming battle." He hung up before Caleb could answer.

Giles turned from the screen. He had witnessed President Caleb's rise to power and the backdoor deals that had gotten him there. Now, the president was pushing back. A little lesson in humility might be required. It was a natural progression, after all. He had seen it before. As one doles out power to another party, that party tends to forget it was given, not earned, and something given can always be taken back. Giles was never afraid of a man who craved power or wealth. It made them predictable and controllable. It was the man who wanted none of those things that he feared. For that man had no strings to pull.

He let his mind turn to the corpse that had crash-landed here, all the way from the other side of the moon. What secrets might it hide? Was there a way to monetize it? His thoughts would have to wait until his people had some time with the body. He activated a secure COMMs with his MindLink and waited for a reply.

"Hello, sir," Cin replied.

"I have a small package I'm sending you for your boss. See that he gets it," Giles said.

"Certainly."

"Cin?"

"Yes?"

"I know what you've done for me, and I won't forget it. Your days of playing second fiddle to nothing more than a face will soon be over. As the first woman to hold the president's office in our growing world, you could be a real force for change." Giles knew the phrasing of his words would be irresistible to Cin.

A soft smile twitched across her lips, but she said nothing.

"Look here." Dr. Patel pointed to the screen that held a medical DNA display in 3D. "Jericho's DNA seems normal. No signs of RNA or mDNA."

"Plain speak, please, Doc," Avery requested as she grabbed a lab chair and rolled over to the doctor. She had always hated the smell of this room, with its biological samples mixing with harsh chemicals. It looked white and clean, but the odor belied a different story.

"He isn't modified. He's a pure 1.0, just like us. There's no sign of viral or bacterial trauma, and he seems perfectly healthy," Dr. Patel added.

"A 1.0 that has never been sick?"

"Seems so."

"I don't understand. My father was very specific," Avery said, trying to find an angle.

Dr. Patel lowered her glasses and looked over at Avery, waiting for something more.

"Right before my father died, he told me the SS Hollanbach held the genetic key to our survival. He spent his whole life trying to improve the human condition. Make us better, faster, stronger. He was determined . . . gung ho." Avery looked down for a moment. "When my mother died, all that changed. He could see the writing on the wall. The end result of what we were doing to ourselves."

"That's when he left New Kansas and started working with the 1.0s in Topeka?"

"I was young, but I remember the change. The way he used to look at me like I really mattered. He never did that in New Kansas. My father was never the same man again. Still driven but for one and only one purpose. To preserve humankind in its original form."

"Isn't evolution a natural thing?"

"Of course, when it's natural, but the 2.0s are not evolution, they are orthogenesis. Lambs guarded by wolves jacked up and modified far beyond evolution. There's no end to what awaits us on the other side."

It had been a long day, and nothing throughout had paid off. Avery's frustration was at its peak, and she took a calming breath before continuing. "There has to be something I'm not seeing. . . . Maybe it was destroyed on the ship."

"I don't know about any key to our survival, but as far as I can see, Jericho is just a normal guy with very limited real-world skills. And no antibodies for anything, including the common cold."

Avery put her head in her hands. She'd taken a chance, and it had failed.

"Okay, thanks, Doc. Run everything again. Deep dive, just to be safe."

"Okay, but I don't expect to find anything different."

Jericho washed the blood from his face, examining the cuts and bruises left behind. It was just another layer to the things that had happened since landing on Earth. He left his dorm and headed for the mess hall. Dinner helped revive him as he sat in the corner by himself. Questions about his place in this world bounced around in his mind once more. Without an obvious answer, he dismissed them after a time.

Once back in his dorm, a soft knock on his door was followed by Avery stepping into his quarters without waiting for a reply.

"Jericho, I'm sorry about what happened today."

He stood near his bed with his arms crossed. "This is the *army* you command?"

"Yes, but commanding and controlling are two different things. "

"I didn't ask to be brought here."

"I know. Those men lost close friends to get you here, and they don't see the scales balancing, and unfortunately, neither do I."

Jericho stared at Avery. They were harsh words. "What do you want from me? You bring me here against my will, and you have yet to say what it is I'm here for. So I ask again: what do you want from me?" He was learning to control his anger, but some reactions seemed beyond him.

Avery took the chair by the small desk against the wall and moved it to the center of the room.

"I honestly don't know. My father said you would be the key to everything, just before he died. But I can't figure out what he meant."

Jericho sat on the corner of his bed. The room had no windows and was lit by a single warm glow from the ceiling, creating a harsh shadow on Avery's face.

"Honestly, you don't fit in here. I'd ask you to help us with our fight . . ."

"It's not my fight," Jericho interrupted.

Avery took a slow breath, nodding. "And I can't guarantee that today's events won't be repeated. I can't always be there to protect you."

"I don't need protection. I don't need any of you," Jericho countered.

"Perhaps not, but you know nothing of this world or its ways."

"I can do you one better. I *care nothing* for this world and its ways."

Avery stared at Jericho, vacillating at her final decision. The disappointment of her father's words weighed heavy. She stood and placed a stack of credits on the dresser next to her. "This will get you through the next couple of months—till you find your place." She stepped for the door without turning back. "You can stay the night, but after that, I can't be responsible . . ." The last part she whispered before leaving the room.

10

As the city awoke to another day, Jericho left the base and walked amid the Earth-born 1.0s in the city. He watched as they scurried about their daily lives and routines. Their concerns were not his. Zion was a city built on a city, in a city. Like an onion, it had layers. The original metropolis dated back to the 1950s, with classic box-style architecture, some still standing here and there. A few had been restored, giving them a desirable vintage feel. The next layer had roots in the turn of the century, where 2000-style glass and steel overshadowed the smaller buildings. The last and far more practical layer was mostly concrete structures with boxy windows. This layer was built in the last five years and had a rushed, non-planned look to it.

After the destruction of the other 1.0 cities, refugees had flowed into Zion in hordes, leaving a severe housing shortage that required some emergency thinking by what was left of the Council at that time. The new builds lacked style, height, and luxury but put a roof over so many desperate people who were living in the streets.

Jericho walked along the river that flowed through the city, which made its way to the small lake on the southern end. Small crafts darted back and forth, carrying goods and passengers. He made his way across one of the three bridges connecting the east side of the city to the west. Rusting steel girders supported the ground-based traffic. The streets were filled with moving bodies, all in a hurry. Jericho was the exception. He had never been among so many humans. It was overwhelming and exciting all at once. Old, young, and a mix of everything between, living and working together.

His mind moved to the map he had been shown. It looked like a city divided by neighborhoods and streets, but citizens here shared equal freedoms and respect for their neighbors. It was a homogeneous collection of misfits.

Street-level life was a congested affair. Each burrow came with its own smells: curry, paprika, even excrement, and attitude. Cars and autonomous vehicles weaved in and out of myriad bodies, all plying the many shops and sidewalk vendors scattered throughout the city. It was a symphony for Jericho, and he couldn't get enough.

The tech running Zion was dated but well-maintained. Streets and alleys were worn but not filthy. Powerlines haphazardly crossed the sky above like rogue spiderwebs. Repeater boxes were on every corner and most commerce took place right along the crowded sidewalks. Jericho marveled at the selection. Things he had never heard of before and things he had always wanted. He could get virtually anything, from freshly grilled meat to a resoled pair of shoes, 30 percent off with a trade-in.

Jericho looked up, shielding his eyes against the rising sun. Above the fray was a flow of drones coming and going. Some small, others carrying multiple passengers. Overarching everything was the laser containment grid, an almost invisible shield capable of stopping even the most hardened explosive from passing through. It shimmered like a heatwave in the sun, as power coursed through it. It was something the 1.0 scientists had developed and perfected just over a year ago, and it was the last level of protection between Zion and the outside world.

Zionists were aware of the war, but most were not concerned with it, as they had other priorities, like life. Jericho paused to get a snack from a vendor grilling on an open fire. It was called a "taco," and its flavor consumed him, so he bought another. Everything around him had a well-used quality to it, from the clothes on people's backs to the hand-built stalls selling goods stacked along the streets. The people who plied these streets were his people—fellow 1.0s—but he felt no connection to them. Their concerns and desires were not his. Jericho was a man without a family or a home. A one-off bastardization with no hope of ever connecting—no parents, no childhood memories, no belonging.

The sun was out, and the heat seemed oppressive, filling the air, ripening it with the sickening smells of rotting food and body odor. Jericho's self-guided tour of the city had left him sweaty and a bit lost.

Every block or so, a street caller cried out his message of hope or destruction. Everything had a price, from love to salvation. Jericho stopped to listen to a few, wondering if their words held any truth. "God has a plan for everyone. He cares about you personally."

"Life without liberty is a prison sentence."

"Love is real and for the next ten minutes, it's only twenty credits. Right here."

"Who dares to meet a Reeker and survive? Cannibals of the highest order." That guy was just plain crazy. He had no reason to believe anything or anyone after his first few days here on Earth, and he wouldn't be fooled now.

Avery had told him he knew nothing of this world, but what he did know was discouraging. So many people. It was crushing, and he started pushing his way through the bodies faster and faster as he felt panic rising, taking control. He ran through the throng, leaving angry cries and shouts in his wake. He didn't look back, only forward.

After several minutes, he turned a corner to a less crowded area. This was an older part of the city, with warehouses and squatters. Jericho found an empty alleyway and paused, leaning against a red brick wall to catch his breath. The sun was now directly overhead, cooking the ground around him. The air was particularly foul here, and most of the street's population had vanished. Rusted beams and boarded-up windows decorated a dead end.

It was at that moment the weight of the world hit him: 24's death, the failed mission, being a prisoner, having been cast away like a piece of trash, and his very existence to serve as a savior to humankind.

It started as sorrow and turned to uncontrollable sobs as he slid to the ground, letting it all out. Eventually, he course-corrected his emotions and focused on something more useful: anger. Wiping the tears from his face, Jericho stood. He let one of Azraelle's lessons run through his mind.

Feeling sorry for yourself gets you nowhere. It is only through forward motion that you will progress. Hurdles will be part of every experience. It is what you do with them that will make you successful. If you fall down, get up; try again. Your mind can help you overcome anything. It can also be your biggest hurdle.

Jericho needed to get back up and start anew. He let his fingers caress the credits in his pocket. He would take this money and find his place in this world.

"What do we have here?"

Jericho spun to the voice.

"Looks like a lost puppy."

Three men in worn clothes appeared out of nowhere and surrounded Jericho.

"Oh, and he's been crying."

"Did your rich daddy throw you out?"

"Or maybe you just got lost?" Each had a homemade shiv as a weapon, handling it threateningly.

"Nice new clothes."

"Yeah. Take 'em off, or we'll gut you and take 'em, anyway."

They were skinny, malnourished, and had a jitteriness to everything they did.

Jericho let his training with the E-Chung kick in. He pushed his back to the wall and raised his hands while lowering his stance. Then his world was filled with pain, and he fell sideways. Everything went dark.

The three street rats cackled. Their fourth teammate had dropped a large brick from the roof of the building. It had glanced off their target's head, ending him.

They quickly went about kicking the corpse before stripping his clothes and boots. One of the gang members stepped up to stab their victim in the heart when the credits in the pants pocket were discovered. A fight broke out over the money, and it quickly turned deadly. Before anyone could fully claim their share of the spoils, two were bleeding out in the alley. The leader grabbed what he could and ran. The rooftop assassin chased after him for his share, leaving two members of their gang behind without a second thought.

Cin opened the small package that had just been delivered. It contained a vial with a clear liquid. A handwritten note next to it read, *Handle with care.* She picked up the vial and held it to the light. It could be water for all she knew. Cin slipped it into her pocket and headed for the president's office.

"Good morning, Mr. President. Working on your speech for tonight?"

"Cin. Yes, it is just about finished."

She let her yellow eyes roam around the room until they found what she was looking for. A small ever-present fruit plate on the corner of his desk. She stepped closer, fingering the vial in her pocket.

"So, what else is on my plate today? Remember to keep it light."

"Oh, I have." Cin began her patented description of the day's meetings and planned appearances. As she spoke, she moved the vial out of her pocket, keeping it hidden in her hand.

Caleb stood as he listened and grabbed his handheld screen with the speech on it.

"Good, Cin. How's this for an ending?" he asked her as he transitioned into his speech. "Citizens of New Kansas have a right to their health and freedom . . ."

As he droned on, Cin, in a choreographed motion, removed the cap and poured a few drops onto the fruit. The president remained occupied with practicing his bi-annual speech.

". . . to live their lives to the fullest and contribute to the greater good."

Cin turned to face him, holding the vial behind her back.

"It's good. Direct and hopeful," she said with manufactured conviction. In reality, she was not thinking about Caleb's speech at all. She was afraid some of the liquid might have touched her hand, so she finished up with Caleb and quickly ran to the bathroom to wash them several times. She made a mental note not to go anywhere near the president for the rest of the day.

After a quick message to Giles, she allowed herself to relax.

The last two years had been a journey through darkness for Cin. Giles became aware of her when her partner, Jenni, had been killed in a lab accident at one of his facilities.

Cin and Jenni had made a home and a life for themselves. Both were career-minded and focused on their lives together. Cin had always been the ambitious one, while Jenni was more nurturing by nature. It had been a perfect pairing. When Jenni was killed and no answers were forthcoming about how it happened, Cin had gone to an angry place where only action could calm. She needed an outlet, something that could make a difference.

Cin took an idea and, like a weed needing to find a way to take root, let it grow. It was a way to fight back against the rigid status quo without weapons. Cin began a public awareness campaign against the monopolies of her world, naming it FreedomCall. It had grown legs and the underground movement had expanded, taking on a life of its own.

Normally a faction like this would be shut down with a swift and deadly control action, but Giles had plans for the enthusiastic and determined female with a background in business management.

He had negotiated a meeting and taken the time to express his sorrow for her loss. It was not real sorrow—just a sociopath's version, but only a real expert could tell the difference. Giles then played a doctored video that showed Jenni sacrificing her life to save two coworkers when an accidental exposure to a deadly pathogen hit the lab.

Tears crept down Cin's cheeks as she watched the footage.

"She died a hero. I wanted you to know that," Giles said.

Cin gave a noncommittal nod.

"Unfortunately, this pathogen is highly classified and cannot be discussed outside this room. If the 1.0s were to get wind of this, it could be our undoing. Jenni was a true believer in the work."

"I know that. She loved her job," Cin added.

"I have a proposition I would love to discuss with you." Giles laid out his plan, using words like *movement* and *save the planet* and *humanity*. They appealed to Cin's sensibilities, and she took to the idea like a mop to a spill.

Within the month, control had raided FreedomCall and killed everyone behind it. Cin was President Caleb's new executive secretary and a conduit back to Giles. She had been forced to switch-hit for a time as she wormed her way into the president's inner sanctum. A most distasteful requirement but the future of humanity was at stake, and she would help Giles save the planet. It was a path she could get behind because the promise of real power and control was now within reach.

Commander Weng buzzed just over the treetops on the hoverboard drone. His squadron consisted of six other warriors, four of them also air-surfing the highly mobile tactical drones. Each hoverboard consisted of a strap-on standing platform the size of a small surfboard. At each corner was an articulating propeller that could vector the board in any direction. Top speed was just under 68 kpm, but their low profile and small size made them almost invisible to any tracking technology until they were right on top of you. The moon was just a sliver, casting a dim glow on the dark branches below. The heads-up displays they wore made navigating through the dark easy, casting the moving world around them in a light and dark blue contrast.

His second in command was a six-foot-tall female named Singh. She had short green hair and matching chocolate skin and eyes. During the battle of Denver, Singh had proven herself by leading a squad through one of the densest sections of the city, killing all in sight. A surveillance drone had caught her decimating a superior force with nothing but a half-charged EM1 and sheer will and determination. It had put her on the radar of her major, and soon, her career was on the rise.

Commander Weng had chosen her first among the serious fighters who now flew alongside him. He knew her allegiances and methods aligned with his.

The two remaining warriors rode sky cycles, carrying extra supplies and gear. The sky cycle was a motorcycle with two horizontal discs that were propellers instead of wheels. Each rotated in a different direction to give the bike stable flight, much like the old helicopters with a tail rotor from the 2000s.

Weng had left Fort Camden with a margin of apprehension. Katrina had vanished. He had set up a real date with food, drinks, and everything, and she had no-showed. The military was notorious for changing its mind and sending people running for no apparent reason, but they were also overzealous about paper trails for everything. When Weng had learned she was assigned last-minute to the task force heading for the West Gate of Zion, he understood two things. A) It wasn't her that stood him up, and B) someone with some real horsepower had diverted her to that mission. For now, his own mission would need to come first, but the image of Katrina's sweet face still lingered in his brain. There was something about her he just couldn't forget, and he would get to the bottom of her reassignment once he returned.

The squad skirted around Zion and continued arcing west until battery warnings on the hoverboards forced them to land. They knew it was a one-way trip but getting there undetected was mandatory. Between the battle soon to come and the contamination each one would face in the city, none believed they would come out the other side unscathed. This was likely a one-way mission for more than just their transports.

Once safely on the ground, Weng ordered the hoverboards to be buried and the sky cycles unloaded before covering them in branches.

"Fan out. Look around," Weng ordered.

They searched for a place to set up an E-Marker for the ground forces to assemble—somewhere they could gather and not be easily seen. According to his readout, they were just over twelve kilometers from the west gate of Zion.

"I think I got something," called a warrior on his left.

About 200 meters north was a shallow bowl surrounded by trees. Weng looked it over. "Nice find. This will work." They set about installing the E-Marker in the middle of the meadow and camouflaging it in case a passerby came through. The E-Marker would pulse a scrambled signal out about every sixty seconds. The two platoons making their way here would be able to track it like a moth to a light. Once it was operating, the squad moved off through the forest, heading back toward the west side of Zion.

Weng had them post up for the night just beyond the sight of the wall. That meant a quick five-kilometer hike to the west gate was on the menu in the morning. Their contact had made it clear where and when they would meet, as the carefully guarded West Gate was only operational during certain hours.

The group bedded down for the night, each with their own thoughts of home or family, knowing they were stepping into a city filled with an invisible pathway to death the following day.

Weng let his mind go to the day he had taken off and spent with his daughter, Ruth, before this mission. It was always a bonding experience when the two were together. They had gone on an adventure around the neighborhood, collecting bugs for a jar she carried. Unfortunately, it had ended in tears when Weng confided in her he was leaving again. He held her close and rocked her sobbing body as she let her emotions go. He leaned into her ear and whispered, "I need you to be brave for you and for me, one last time, understand? Daddy can't make the world a safer place if he's worried about you, and I promise . . . this is it. No more missions; no more leaving."

After gathering herself, Ruth had looked up into his eyes and given the slightest, bravest nod. Weng knew right then that she would be okay. No matter what happened to him.

It was an extreme sacrifice but always done on her behalf. *Just help make the world a better place for her.* He had repeated the thought in his mind several times since leaving New Kansas.

Jericho cracked his eyes to a blurry world. The sun was just peeking into the city. His head pounded, and his fingertips soon found matted blood at the source of his pain. Someone or something had hit him on the head. He felt his body suddenly roll to his back, and his blurry vision was filled with a curious face.

"You okay?"

Jericho blinked the vision into reality. An older man with a trimmed gray beard and no hair on his head stared at him. He had muted blue-gray eyes filled with concern and a host of well-earned wrinkles across his face.

Jericho slowly sat up, using the wall to support the effort. Two very dead bodies lay next to him in the alley, their dried blood covering the pavement.

"I thought I heard a commotion last night. Figured I'd take a stroll early this morning and check it out. You sure you're okay?"

Jericho looked himself over, realizing he was naked but somehow still alive. "My clothes . . . my credits?"

"I'm afraid that ship has sailed, sonny. Guess God had other plans for you because somehow you're still alive. Oh, I'm Santos, by the way."

A further look around revealed Jericho's pants lying a few feet away in the hands of one of the dead muggers, but that was all that was left of his belongings.

"Here, let me help you up," Santos offered.

Jericho stood with his help and grabbed his pants. The pockets were empty. He went about gathering what he needed from the dead—shoes, a shirt, an old coat. They wouldn't miss them. He no longer looked like a fresh recruit ready to start his life but a jaded street rat with a bad headache and a worse attitude. His plans for the future had been snuffed out in a single moment.

The two men left the corpses and the alley behind.

"I've got a small shop just over here. You're welcome to rest there for a spell."

Jericho followed the old man whose shoulders had just begun to hunch over with age. He noticed he wore an unusual belt around his tattered jeans and flannel shirt. It was extra thick and had a collection of gadgets, the likes of which Jericho had never seen.

"What's with the belt?" Jericho asked.

"Oh, this is my multi-belt. It has everything I need to stay safe." He whipped out a hidden pistol and flourished it for a second before slipping it back out of sight. "And can fix just about anything too." This time, he pulled a self-ratcheting driver from a slot and hit the button. It spun up.

Jericho looked up to see a lit sign above a battered gated entry. *NCW.*

Santos hit a button on his belt, and the gate opened. "This isn't the safest part of town, but the rent's cheap and since I cater to the poor . . . gots to keep my prices down." He stepped into the warehouse and raised his hands. "Welcome to NCW."

Jericho looked around, a bit baffled. Two dirty skylights cast a brown glow on two rows of what looked like four-wheeled garden carts, the sizes of small cars. The wagons were built out of an aluminum-framed skeleton and were currently see-through, except for the installed floors. They had four large spoked wheels with aggressive tires and a small tailgate. Materials were stacked and organized on shelves around the space, and the back of the shop looked like someone was living there.

"New Covered Wagons. I design 'em and build 'em." He grabbed and tossed a container to Jericho. "Here, have some water. Never did catch your name."

"Jericho, sorry. Not quite myself yet. What are they for?" he said, pointing to the carts before taking several gulps of water.

"Not everyone likes living in Zion. There's been an increase in families heading West to restart their lives, away from all this." He used a sweeping hand gesture. "There's quite a bit of open land out there that's becoming quite livable again. Nature has a way, you know. An industrious person, not afraid of a few risks, can start over. I provide those with few means a way to do that."

"That is admirable. So how many actually make it?" Jericho asked.

"That's not my responsibility. Everyone is warned of the dangers. The whippers will kill you for a sandwich and the Reekers . . . pray you never meet one. I make sure families get to the trailhead at Cedar Breaks, and then it's up to God and luck."

Jericho let his defenses down. He took another drink of water and paused. "I don't know a 'God'."

"The All-Mighty Caretaker, son. He keeps just enough of an eye on us to lend a hand from time to time."

"Sounds far-fetched," Jericho said, as he handed back the water container.

"Oh, he's real, all right, but you gotta believe, and that takes faith."

"I don't have time for faith. Besides, God's done nothing for me."

Santos nodded his head in understanding. "I get that, but doing everything all by yourself gets awfully lonely."

"What's that smell?" Jericho asked, changing the subject.

"Oh, that's the livestock barns. They're just a block away from here. You'll get used to it. . . . Say, you wouldn't be looking for a job, would you? I've been a bit too busy lately."

"Job?" Jericho was confused.

"Yeah . . . say, you musta been hit pretty hard on the head. Either that or you're from outer space."

Jericho hid a look of concern.

"You know, work, get paid, and drink it all away each night—a job."

"No. I don't think I want a job, but thanks." Jericho looked over the progression of wagons. Some didn't have wheels yet, and others were only partially constructed. "I gotta go. Thanks for the water, Santos."

"Sure. Just take it easy. You probably have a concussion," he said as he raised the gate for Jericho to leave. "If you change your mind, I'm taking a train out through the West Gate in the morning."

Jericho nodded and left.

Santos closed the gate and watched as the man from the alley walked off.

President Caleb looked at himself in the mirror. He was twenty minutes away from his bi-annual speech that would, he hoped, galvanize the public and ensure his continuation as their beloved president. He would love to predict an end to the war, but the whole operation was still unfolding. Getting it wrong or having word leak to the 1.0s would do him no favors. Maybe a few well-placed investments, however, would pay off. He did a few word exercises to get his mouth working and then looked more closely at his reflection. His eyes seemed sunken, and his ears were red. Worst of all, he felt bad. He would just have to suck it up. He could call his doctor after the speech. Right now, he had a duty to his people. He popped two pills as a "pick me up" and finished adding oil to his dry hair. The gleam made it look healthy and young again. His impossibly white teeth smiled back against pitch-black eyes. He adjusted his posture and then, without warning, threw up. The vomit ricocheted off the mirror and splashed across his new suit. The sudden pain was so violent that he collapsed onto his own juices.

Five minutes before he was scheduled to broadcast, he was found quivering on the floor. His doctor was called, and he was rushed to an isolation chamber, along with the man who found him.

Cin had monitored all the action from a safe distance, wondering what Giles had given her. Would Caleb die or just be incapacitated? She would need to step up in the president's absence. First and foremost, she had his office cleaned and disinfected.

Without missing a beat, Chairman Giles Favreau stepped up to the microphones and gave the president's impassioned speech as if it was his own. His opening words were geared toward the unfortunate sickness that had overtaken his friend and colleague. His heart and mind were on a speedy recovery. He added his concern about the newest virus heading for the city and his plans to thwart it.

After the speech, Giles met with Cin to give her his instructions for the next few days. She would be effectively running things in the interim, and there was no time like the present for a few course corrections in policy. It would be good practice for her.

His COMMs buzzed with several attempts by the other chairs, wondering what was going on. Seeing Giles unexpectedly give the bi-annual speech had their political Spidey senses jangling. Giles ignored them for now. Once things were in place, he would pacify them.

The day passed without incident, including Jericho's complete failure to obtain food. It seemed this world only ran on credits, and Jericho was flat broke. He tried asking, begging, and stealing, to no avail. One ended with a foot chase.

As the day wore on, he became more desperate. Maybe Avery would take pity on him and give him some more credits. There had to be something she could do to help.

Jericho walked up to the entrance to the military base at the south end of the city. The same gate he had left less than twenty-four hours ago. The guard gate was closed. A single-guard shack sat to the left. Tall walls closed on either side, making it the only option for entry. His tattered clothes and worn-out shoes made Jericho look desperate and out of place in the harsh afternoon sun. To top it all off, his stomach grumbled loudly with hunger.

"Halt. State your business," a large guard ordered as he stepped from the shack. It was Sergeant Kay, the man who had tried to slit Jericho's throat.

"Kay, I need to see Avery," Jericho called out.

"Councilwoman Avery is too busy for the likes of you," he replied.

"It's me, Jericho. Tell her I changed my mind; I'm here to sign up."

"You had your chance. Besides what do you think this is? If you want to send a message to Avery, go to a center. This is a military base, and no one gets in without *my* say-so."

"Kay, quit screwing around. She'll want to see me." As he said the words, he stepped forward.

Four rifles from on top of the wall suddenly cocked and pointed in his direction. Jericho stopped and raised his arms.

"Like I said, I ain't no messenger. I'm on guard duty because of you. So please, take one more step in this direction. Those boys up there will send a message by shooting you dead. The choice is yours." A nasty smile crossed Kay's face, daring Jericho to take that step.

Jericho's shoulders slumped, and he turned and walked away.

"Good riddance, space freak!" Kay called after him.

The sun set on a hot day leaving behind no breeze to cool the air. Different people came out at night, and Jericho wandered among them, numb to their presence.

He eventually settled on a small hidden space between a closed street market and the wall of a building, squeezing inside. He chewed the last of an apple core he had picked up off the curb and lay down, hoping to get some rest. The concrete was still warm but hard on his aching bones. He had tried and failed to fit into this world. Now he would dedicate himself to another course of action. Exhaustion soon won out, and he drifted off into a restless sleep, dreaming only one dream—leaving this city and its people behind. He was trained to survive, so he would.

The sun peeked up for the day, with a promise of something better. Jericho woke to a broom hitting him in the chest and the shop owner demanding he go away. The man was large, with beefy hands and a bull-like attitude. After the third strike, Jericho grabbed the broom and turned it on the shopkeeper. He hit him in the chest with two quick bursts, sending the man sprawling on his back.

"How do *you* like it?" Jericho asked, looming over him.

"I'm sorry. I thought you were a street—"

"Someone you could push around?" Jericho interrupted. "Well, I've had enough of that. From now on, I'm the one that does the pushing!"

The man wasn't sure what Jericho was talking about, and the fear in his eyes was obvious.

"Is there a problem here?" A policeman with his hand on his weapon called out from the end of the block.

"No. I was just leaving," Jericho called back as he threw the broom next to the shopkeeper and walked off.

Near the West Gate was a jamboree of twenty-two New Covered Wagon carts ready to begin their journey. Their frames were covered with a rugged, rain-proof canvas, and the rooftops beveled in the center with a collection of silicon-based, flexible solar panels. The front of the NCWs had a yolk that maneuvered the carts via a few simple controls. Rotate the grip for forward and reverse and flip a switch for a right or left turn. The carts carried belongings at walking speed, and the panels were powerful enough to do it on a cloudy day. Most of the NCWs were decorated uniquely by each family, some with ribbons and others with various identifying signs. There were children playing and adults looking anxious to get started. The NCWs at the front and back were colored red and were used as bookends to keep everyone together during the trek.

These families had packed up everything important to them and were leaving civilization behind to start anew. Santos stood next to the front cart and called out as the West Gate opened for the day. "All carts, prepare to depart!"

The train of handcarts slowly rolled out of the city—adults guiding or walking alongside their wagons as children rode inside.

Jericho stepped up to the display of vehicles as they rolled past. Many people had come to see them off and watch the spectacle. Leaving the safety of the city was risky, but there was strength in numbers, so hope seemed to fill the air.

Exiting was easy; it was coming into the city where the guards scrutinized everything, and that was harder.

Jericho pushed past the onlookers and, in a single moment, made a decision. He dropped to the ground and rolled under a wagon, grabbed hold of the framed undercarriage, and rode past the gate and out of the city. Once outside, he pulled his way into the cart and hid.

The warrior squad watched as the wagons left the city and passed them by. Weng guided them to a line forming to enter Zion. The group carried a couple of cases between them and were dressed like outlanders with old clothing, unkempt hair, and dirty faces. Weng's purple eyes were hidden behind brown contacts, and any trace of the 2.0s they were was covered up, including a few tattoos.

Jericho ducked further into the wagon, just missing the face he would never forget. The man leading the squad . . . the man who had killed 24.

"Chairman Favreau, right this way, sir."

Giles followed the lab assistant down a long, white corridor populated with doors and frosted windows. Each door had a letter-number variant but no other markings. At E-23, they stopped and entered.

Inside was a small space filled with screens and two workstations.

"Please, have a seat. Dr. Hastings will be with you momentarily," the assistant said before leaving the room in a hurry.

Giles refused to sit and instead looked over the readouts on the screen. He huffed with frustration; he never liked having to wait for others.

"Sorry to keep you waiting, Chairman," Dr. Hastings said as she entered the room a moment later in a practiced hurry.

Giles looked over the fiftyish black-haired woman with smokers' lines across her face. "What was so important that I had to come here personally?" Giles asked.

"This." She sat in a chair and pulled a pair of reading glasses from her head to her nose. A press of a button brought up an image of 24.

"The girl from the spaceship?" Giles asked.

"Yes. As requested, we ran several tests and took biopsies and samples of everything."

Giles took a chair and sat next to the screen. The chair strained with the extra weight. Images populated with a top-sheet results page.

"You can see she is a pure 1.0, with none of the markers of infections or contagions."

"Interesting, but I still don't see why I had to—"

"This is why," Dr. Hastings interrupted. She changed the screen to another readout.

Giles leaned in, his eyes narrowing as he read the information. "Is this real?"

"One hundred percent. Checked it twice myself," she replied.

The screen showed a broken DNA chain. At the end of the polynucleotide chain was a small tail. She zoomed in more. On the tail, between the phosphor-diester linkage, was a cluster of compounds sticking up.

"Somebody used a CRISPR-Cas9 editing technique to cut and modify the DNA chain. Then a modified RNA to re-engineer the structure."

"To what purpose?" Giles asked.

"This purpose. An RSAD2 protein modifier. Her body has unusually high levels of viperin."

"So, she was what, immune to sickness?"

"Looks that way. Now, check this out." Dr. Hastings zoomed in even further.

"What is that?"

"I'm not sure. Never seen anything like it. My best guess is a biological code of some kind. Like a computer code, only saved in living tissue."

"Can you read it?"

"Not with anything I know of," Dr. Hastings replied.

"Fascinating and baffling."

"Exactly."

Giles leaned back and crossed his arms. He processed the possible meaning the modification might present. "Burn the body."

"What?" Dr. Hastings exclaimed. "Sir, she very possibly holds the key to a cure for all viruses. Known and imagined. If we can replicate this tail, we can eradicate human sickness. No more vaccines and no more quarantines. 1.0s and 2.0s could live together without fear. You could be the author of a whole new world."

"Dr. Hastings, unless you want to be the body that's burned, I suggest you follow my instructions to the letter. No one is to know about this. If word got out that we could end these vaccinations, I'd be ruined. Understand."

Dr. Hastings looked up, her eyes filled with fear. *Of course, he didn't want this. It would mean the end of everything he has built. Power, money, control.* The implication of everything dawned on her. "I will see to it personally, sir."

"And destroy all the files. I want no evidence of this discovery left." Giles stood. "When you're done, I want you refocused on the adenovirus 12 that we got from that Landry character. I want an effective delivery system and a vaccine to go with it. That is the future of this company."

"Absolutely," she said with mock excitement.

Giles exited the room. His mind filled with concern. There was another person like this out there, and he was in the possession of the 1.0s. It was time to light a fire under the president—if he ever woke up.

11

Major Christine Helen was not herself. The fever had given her shivers and body aches over the last two days. This was not the first time she'd been sick since moving here to Zion, and it was always a nuisance. As a survivor, she was willing to go the extra mile to make sure her needs and future were met, and today's mission was bigger than any cold or flu.

When Denver had been destroyed, Helen had managed to escape, leaving behind thousands of dead and dying. She knew there was no future for her living out in the wilderness like an animal, and her only hope was to make it to another city. Zion was the closest, and the two weeks it took her to get here nearly killed her. The 2.0 warriors had strafed the refugees multiple times, forcing her to watch in horror as people right next to her had fallen, like some kind of evil lottery. Water was in short supply and food almost nonexistent. It caused infighting, and no one was truly safe, especially at night. She would never forget the screams of the weak being taken advantage of by the strong in so many ways.

One night, they came for her. Three hungry, desperate men looking for whatever they could get. Helen was not a fighter, but when it came to logistics and planning, it was different. She had scattered dried sticks around the hard ground where she slept, and the first snap from an assailant's shoe woke her from her restless sleep in an instant. The fuel cell on her pistol was long dead, and her only weapon was a short piece of steel pipe she had collected along the trail. Without waiting for the attack, she swung the pipe down as hard as she could on the closest predator's foot. A satisfying crunch of small bones was followed by a screeching sound the whole camp could hear. But hearing and reacting to the violence were two things. Helen knew no one would come to her aid. Every night, there were screams in the dark, and every night, the tried and numb refugees turned a blind eye, grateful it wasn't them. After all the killing and the destruction of their city, the survivors were wary, run-down, hungry, and completely apathetic to the violence in their lives. It was astonishing what humans could do to other humans.

Helen kicked out with her foot and tried to stand. A knee to her temple spun her around, but she still managed to hang on to her pipe. A wide arc connected with a knee, leaving another attacker swearing in pain. The third man used the heel of his boot to stomp Helen into a daze. He kicked the pipe from her hand and followed with a second kick to the head. Helen had lost the fight and her senses as the world around her spun and went dark.

The coppery smell of blood was strong, and Helen woke with a start. Her clothes and shoes were gone. They had taken the small knapsack that held mostly keepsakes and memories, along with a small stash of nuts she was surviving on. On closer inspection, she had been marked by the mugger with a slice to her face. It would leave a scar. Luckily, for a reason she would never know, they had not raped her. A small blanket was handed out by a stranger, the incident quickly forgotten by all but Helen. The next five days nearly killed her, but somehow she stumbled through the West Gate into Zion.

As a major in the 1.0s military, Helen was added to the strained resources at the base and placed in charge of logistics. The problem was she was a leader who had lost her commitment to the cause. Major Helen knew they were fighting a losing battle, and after watching Denver get destroyed, she needed a conduit to get her through her current situation into a proper life beyond. Her alliance was now to herself only.

It hadn't been difficult to make contact with the 2.0s. The trick had been communicating with someone who had real horsepower. Over the last year, she had carefully worked her way right to the top, while still doing just enough to be useful to the military at Zion. A general in New Kansas guaranteed her safety and a life on the other side of the 1.0s once she had been vaccinated. She just needed to do this one small favor. It was the first time in a long time she had felt hope.

As Helen approached the West Gate, one of the guards noticed her and stood to attention.

"As you were, soldier."

He relaxed and looked at her curiously, wondering why she was there.

Helen ignored him.

The three other guards at the gate did careful inspections of everyone who entered. A fourth guard held down a "dead man's switch" inside an armored room that could drop the heavy gate in an instant, should the need arise.

"Prepare to be inspected. No weapons allowed in Zion. Make sure you check them here and get a chit for their return when you leave," one of the guards called out in a repetitive monotone. There were merchants, farmers, and families, all hoping to find or sell something in the city. Off in the distance, a cloud of dust followed the wagon train as it slowly disappeared around a bend in the road. The squad of warriors carried a collection of well-used guns that fit with their legend as outlanders. They passed the weapons to the collection guard, who gave them a ticket for their return when they left the city. The guards then started a secondary inspection for each person.

"Glasses off. Show me your eyes," said a guard.

Weng removed his dark glasses to reveal brown eyes. He and the other warriors had taken the precaution of wearing specialized naturally colored contacts, just in case they were checked. The guard looked closely and even waved a sensor across his eyes.

"Larry," Helen shouted to her pretend brother as the group approached.

Larry called back, "Helen." He recognized the woman with the scar on her face from an E-Pic he had committed to memory and gave her a friendly wave.

The guards, realizing this was a friend or the Major's, did little more than finish up a cursory inspection. "All good here," one of them said.

The guard next to him had more concern. He didn't like the hardened look of this group. "What's inside the cases?"

"Fuel cells. I can make you a great deal. Two for one."

The guard checked the cases until satisfied. "Move along," he ordered, before turning his attention to the next group trying to enter. "Prepare to be inspected. No weapons allowed in Zion. Make sure you check them here and get a chit for their return when you leave."

Helen gave Weng an overzealous hug. "I'm so glad you could make it," she said, making a show of her actions for any onlookers.

Commander Weng tried not to freak out while being hugged by a 1.0 without his bio-suit on. He forced a smile across his face and held his breath.

Major Helen led them back through the city to her apartment. Weng marveled at the differences between cities. The team tried its best not to jump out of the way in fear of every 1.0 who passed by or coughed.

Helen placed her palm on the reader, and the door unlocked as the lights came on. The squad quickly entered and closed the door behind them. They gathered around the kitchen table as she laid out her plan on a chart with a drawing of the dam and generators. Two of the warriors opened the fuel cell cases and revealed false bottoms hiding modern weapons. They quickly distributed them.

"Commander," one of the warriors called as he threw Weng his customized tanto sword from the bottom of a case.

Weng grabbed it and slid it into a holster on his back.

"The explosives are under the couch," Helen added.

Singh collected the high-impact explosives and surveyed them.

"This is the main entrance to the dam here." Helen pointed to a spot on the map. Her fever was somewhat controlled by her medication, but her eyes were still watering. She removed a cloth from her pocket and blew her nose.

The group flashed concern as fear spread across their faces.

"She's infected," Singh said.

The team backed away from Helen. One pulled his EM1 and pointed it at her.

"And you hugged her," another warrior said, backing away from Commander Weng.

"Relax. It's just a cold." Helen was met with several confused and fearful looks. "Just because you all have never been sick in your lives doesn't mean getting sick is a death sentence. Your Pharma One Corporation spreads lies thicker than chunky peanut butter on toast. A cold is nothing more than a mild illness for a few days. So stow the weapons, and let's get back at it."

There was a moment of silence before Weng finally nodded.

"Just walking through the city was probably a death sentence for all of us. We knew that." He stepped back up to the table. "Okay, show us."

Major Christine Helen shook her head at the extreme belief on display. "The first guard station is here. This is the main building that houses the generators. Three guards cover the doors. Inside are two engineers that maintain the facility rotating on twelve-hour shifts. We will need to get inside here before sunrise and hold out until the attack. This is a problem because any daytime operation will be quickly discovered and shut down. But going in at night makes things much easier. We will have to . . ."—she checked the time—"hold the position for eleven hours."

"A long time to hold a position with only eight bodies," Weng commented.

"Yes, it is. We'll need some stealth and a lot of luck. I recommend we get some sleep. It's gonna be a long night."

Giles stepped through the doorway to the isolation room with the president. Caleb was writhing in agony on the other side of the protective glass. This action alone brought great satisfaction to Giles. Cin had played her part perfectly and put Caleb at a crossroads.

The president looked at his visitor. He was dripping with sweat, and his body was wracked with pain, but he could still make out the joy in Giles's eyes as he stared back.

"You did this," he croaked.

Giles stepped closer to the protective glass.

"I see you've met one of my new creations. Not quite as deadly as the one I'm working on now but still very robust, especially the way you were infected."

Caleb burned what little hatred he could muster in Giles's direction.

"I have to thank you. Your death will be my launching platform for the new vaccine. Video of your suffering will be the catalyst I need to take total control." He pointed to the small recording device in the corner of the room.

Caleb looked up and was disgusted to be a lab rat for Giles's ambitions, but in truth, right now death sounded like a merciful release.

"No more rigged elections to deal with. Allowing the public their illusion of an opinion. Just policy and enforcement, all coming from one man, one mind, one source. . . . Hmm, sounds like a campaign slogan."

Caleb had tuned out the rumblings of Giles as another level of pain took hold.

Giles reached into his pocket and held up a small vial with a yellow liquid. "Looky here. I brought a gift."

Caleb swallowed hard and tried to focus on the change in the narrative.

"It comes with a few strings, however, including full backing on my next roll-out of a little something called adenovirus 12 and policy enforcement to go with it. Interested?" Giles asked as he held the vial like a doggie treat.

The chance to reverse his plight was more than he expected. "You want to force everyone to buy your vaccine?"

"I see the brain is still functioning, but you sound surprised. It's not the first time," Giles said.

The president gave a single nod and whispered, "Anything."

"Good. By the way, your little operation in Zion is just about ready to kick off. You should be just well enough to watch it all happen once we get this in you."

Sci Officer Katrina dozed softly as the transport shook and bounced. They had been on the road for two days, making their way in a giant semi-circle around and behind Zion. As they moved in one direction, the other half of the regiment mirrored their actions to the South, hoping to meet back up on the other side. 2.0s attacking Zion at the West Gate would be totally unexpected.

Katrina let her mind wander to a moment just before leaving Fort Camden. Commander Weng had unexpectedly come by her apartment and requested the pleasure of a dinner with her. She had felt a rush of excitement as she tried to answer with poise and grace, but all that came out was, "Sure."

The commander didn't seem to mind and stammered a bit as he relayed the time and place for the restaurant that night. That was before she had been recalled and reassigned to this mission. They had left just before dusk under radio silence. The smile on her face faded. She wondered if he would forgive her for the no-show.

Katrina looked around the Stryker. She had been assigned to the Green squadron, consisting of eleven other warriors—all males, all the time.

Keeping her eyes closed was helping her not engage with the testosterone-filled dialogue, but her ears picked up on every little nuance aimed in her direction. Some things never changed.

Their route mostly consisted of old roads that were still navigable. Every so often, they would have to stop while a tree or landslide was cleared from the path. This was when the regiment was most alert. Clearing the obstacles was Green squadron's job, while the other teams looked for an ambush or trap of some sort. The presence of fifteen Stryker IIs, all armed to the teeth, kept the curious away, but this was a "no man's zone," and anything was possible.

In a coordinated effort, recharge stations had to be air-dropped every 380 kilometers, synchronized with their campsite locations for the night.

A sudden stop had everyone in the cab awake and on edge. The male banter came to a stop.

"Contact dead ahead." the gunner in the front passenger seat called out from the first Stryker. The message was broadcast to everyone at the same time.

Several commands shot through the communication system until the man in charge called out, "Stand down." Colonel Smyth was a no-nonsense officer with concern for his men. The two rarely went together. This was his first field operation, and after so many years behind a desk, he hoped to make the other officers who had called him Colonel Desky behind his back see him in a new light. He sat just behind the gunner in the first Stryker. What was called the widow-maker position, as it was often the first vehicle—and seat—targeted.

"Blue and Red squads, form a perimeter," ordered Smyth.

Warriors from the third and fourth Stryker exited and formed a protective ring facing outward.

An old pickup truck had been slammed into a tree, blocking the road up ahead. The forest here was a mix of conifers and deciduous carpeting, rolling hills, and a few valleys.

"Green, we have an obstruction. See to it."

The squad from the fifth Stryker ran to the front of the column to deal with the problem. Katrina was handed an EM1 to keep a lookout as the other warriors rocked the old truck back and forth, trying to roll it onto flat tires. Divots caused by where it had been sitting for some time made physics work against them. Katrina listened to her squad strain with effort as she kept her eyes on the trees around them. A chant started up in the distance. Quiet at first, then louder and louder.

"Quiet," Katrina called out.

The men paused.

Silence returned, then slowly again, the chanting rose in volume.

"Reekers," the lieutenant spoke, just loud enough for Green squad to hear. He connected to the colonel. "This is Lieutenant Rice. We have what appear to be Reekers closing in around us, sir."

Reekers were more myth to some than reality. Myth because the stories told about them couldn't possibly be true. The scavengers had turned cannibalistic some years ago and thrived on others' misfortune. They loved to torture their captives before consuming them, thinking the meat tasted better that way. The mere thought sent shivers down Katrina's back.

The stories told about them were only fit for night terrors. Most wore piercings and jewelry made from their victims. They had distended stomachs and missing teeth. It was a branch of humanity that had long since fallen from the family tree.

Reekers lived in tribes that had taken over abandoned towns and a few mines in the area. Only the strongest of their victims were given a chance to join, instead of becoming dinner. Most had skin sores and hair loss because of their filthy living conditions and poor diet. With their lack of hygiene, some say you could smell them coming from a mile away. It was your best defense at staying safe—a good sense of smell. If you were to categorize them with just one word, it would be *violent*. Their ferocity was unmatched.

"Freakin' Reekers," Smyth said to himself, before pressing the mic button. "Send a volley in their direction to warn them off. And get that truck out of the way—now!" the colonel ordered.

Twenty warriors holding the perimeter fired their EM1s, sending the super high-speed flechettes out in a covering sphere. Katrina slipped her EM1 over her shoulder and helped push the truck. They desperately rocked it back and forth, using the steering wheel to finally push it from the road. They watched as it rolled down the hill and crashed into a tree at the bottom.

A sudden rambling from up ahead grabbed Lieutenant Rice's attention. An old Abrams tank from a bygone era appeared on the road ahead. It was smoking as the old diesel motor tried to carry on. Where they had found the fuel for it was anyone's guess.

"Sir, you're gonna want to see this," Lieutenant Rice said as he and his squad started running back to the Strykers.

Smyth looked out the front of the armored windshield with curiosity. "An Abrams. Straight out of a museum . . . shame," he said to no one in particular. The turret turned and line up with the lead Stryker. "Target and destroy, Sergeant."

The gunner in the front passenger's seat dialed up and fired the mini rail gun from the roof, and in less than a second, the tank turned to scrap metal.

Katrina could have sworn her hair puffed as the projectile passed overhead.

The chanting quieted down and backed off.

"Back on board, now! Get us out of here," Smyth ordered.

The Red and Blue squads piled back inside, and Green ran for their ride.

The sudden movement had the chanting quickly back up to full volume.

The Strykers moved out in rapid succession.

That's when hundreds of scarcely clad shapes closed from the rear and sides, firing their older guns and screaming like banshees. Two warriors from Green went down while trying to get back. Return fire from the plasma cannons on all the Strykers filled the air, and body parts flew in every direction. Katrina dove up the ramp and rolled into the safety of the armored metal shell. She heaved lungfuls of air as what was left of Green made it to safety.

Once onboard, the vehicles tore off down the road, leaving an angry mob behind, with the sounds of bullets harmlessly pinging off the Strykers and a roar of success because though they had scared the soldiers off.

A broad-shouldered figure in a loincloth stepped to the front of the group and screamed. The rest of the Reekers quieted. He had a short mohawk with black eyes and a massive necklace made of teeth.

He spoke in a guttural version of English they called Tuk-Tuk. It was clear he was the leader, and they were not done with the warriors who'd run off with their tails between their legs. Any chance to get their hands on just a few of the more advanced weapons would be worth any cost. They would pay for coming into their world—in blood.

A call from the front stopped the train. "Hold."

They'd traveled all day, and the NCWs were slowing as the sun started to dip below the trees.

"Gather the wagons. We'll camp here for the night," Santos called from the lead position. They had come to a clearing along a small river that bubbled past. The wagons formed a rough circle, and the dust of the day finally settled. A burned-out shelter stood nearby, its black remnants telling a sad story for the former occupants.

Jericho slipped out from the wagon he had hidden in and mingled with the group as if he belonged. The camp was filled with mostly desperate families trying to improve their place in the world. A few were running away, and one expressed his plan to build a utopia far from all the madness to anyone who would listen. Despite their circumstances, the people seemed energetic, fueled by the promise of something better ahead.

A young girl in pigtails and a frown rubbed her backside from the long day's ride. She had been against leaving her meager home in Zion. At eight and a half, Geena was an outspoken heartbreaker with a pug nose and a dimple on her left side. When the family had taken a vote, hers was the only one against the trip. She didn't like change and taking a wagon train across the country was nothing but change. She huffed over to the river and threw a rock she had picked up into the clear water, watching it disappear. Her left arm held a small stuffed doll with braided locks, named Holly, in a death grip. It was the one extra item she was allowed to bring. Geena looked back at the camp that was forming. She watched as Santos moved to his wagon and started to unload it. Her curiosity won out, so she headed his way.

"How much farther?" Geena asked Santos as he set up a small table.

"Dear, we are just on day one. We'll reach Cedar Breaks trailhead tomorrow, and then you're on your own. If you're planning on going to the coast, I'm guessing eighty more days like today."

"Whoa."

"Yeah, whoa."

The girl turned away and ran off to tell her brother. Santos smiled at the simplicity of youth and how precious it was.

"You wouldn't still be lookin' to hire, would you?"

Santos plopped his bedding down and turned to the voice.

It took him a second to put the pieces that were so out of context together. "Jericho?"

"Good memory."

"How'd you get here?" Santos asked.

"Hitched a ride."

"Well, I'm not set up to take a person on the trail right now. But if you're willing to learn the ropes, I would sure be grateful to have another trail boss down the road that I can send on these trips."

"Okay, I can do that," Jericho said with a growing smile.

Santos debated for a second and then made up his mind. "Best you can do right now is watch and learn."

Jericho nodded.

Santos pulled an E-match from his belt. "Here, get some dry wood and build us a fire. I'll figure out something for you to sleep on."

Jericho stacked the wood he collected and quickly started a small fire. After learning how to build a fire in his survival training back on the ship, this was the first time he had done it in real life. "I made fire," Jericho called out with pride.

Santos looked him over, trying to decide what made him tick.

Dr. Hastings hurried from the lab, looking over her shoulder. She let her index finger graze across the SIM hidden in her purse. She had recorded their meeting on a concealed capture module, then done exactly as Chairman Favreau had requested, with one exception. She had made a copy of the data before destroying everything. Now, she needed to get out of the office with the information before being added to Giles's growing pile of bodies that made up the pathway for his ascension to godhood.

Before the propellers from her commuter drone stopped, she was off the roof's landing pad and into her apartment. She could hear the drone take off for another fare as she ripped a suitcase out of her closet. A quick packing job later, she was out the front door and into the crowded street below, trying to blend in. The city was alive and busy as citizens moved in every direction, buying, selling, and just looking. She kept her suitcase close, not wanting it to fall prey to a desperate character.

Dr. Hastings went on foot, enduring the overhead sun, hoping to hide her trail. Street-level surveillance was fraught with broken cameras and faulty bio-scanners. Her heart seemed to beat out of her chest as the severity of her actions tried to overwhelm her. A reflex had a lit cigarette in her mouth, sucking the nicotine into her system, encouraging it to do its magic. Each step required a reminder of why she was doing this. The word *traitor* spun through her head, and she tried to replace it with *whistleblower*, but her fear would not allow the transfer.

Her first stop was her niece's place—a precaution. She punched in the code on the door pad and quickly entered Katrina's tiny apartment next to Fort Camden. She used her back to close the door and let her perceived safety calm her nerves, allowing her breathing to slow. One more drag on the stub of her cigarette, pinched between nicotine-stained nails, helped her focus her thoughts.

Dr. Hastings has been here many times, and the plan, her plan—once just a seed in her mind—was now full-grown. She pulled a small computer from her case and fired it up, then spent the next hour running tests on the data, making sure she was not connected to any network. As with any scientist, one hour turned into six, and by the time she was satisfied with her results, it was late in the day. She output everything to the data SIM card and cloned it for good measure. Now she was sure of her hypothesis. There was a way to stop disease for all humankind.

She scribbled a note to Katrina and slipped the first of two the data cards behind one of the many pictures on a small end table next to a gray couch. She paused to look at the picture of the two of them—Katrina, only six years old at the time. Their smiles sat frozen as they posed near a large bed of flowers.

Dr. Hastings stepped back, satisfied with her actions, and packed everything back up before leaving. The transportation terminal was just a few blocks away, and she planned to purchase a ticket for one of the off-city transports to a smaller sister city in the East. Maybe from there, she could find a way to disappear.

As she approached the terminal, she spied several control officers with their eyes on every passenger. *They're looking for me.*

Dr. Hastings continued past the terminal, her mind racing with the sudden change in her plans and a sudden need for another smoke.

"There she is!"

A call out from behind sent a chill down her spine, but she was no runner. Just an older doctor with a lifetime of sitting and a mountain of cigarettes to her credit. She stopped and lowered her head. What would be, would be.

"Hands in the air, Dr. Hastings. Don't make me shoot you!"

Tears streamed as she raised her shaking arms.

After two hours of slogging along a battered road, the regiment came to their planned stop for the night. Fifteen rechargers had been air-dropped into a small clearing; without them, this would be the end of their trip. The rear ramp lowered on the lead Stryker, and Colonel Smyth stepped outside. His dark green eyes matched his uniform. With a simple look to his number a bevy of orders filled the COMMs as the regiment set up camp for the night and arraigned for the recharging of the vehicles.

They were now only one day from reaching the rendezvous point.

"I want extra security tonight. No surprises, understand?" Colonel Smyth ordered as other warriors hustled to obey. The recent run-in with the Reekers nestled fresh in his mind.

"Yes, sir," his second replied before passing on the orders.

The camp comprised a few tents and a mess area, all erected inside a barrier of Strykers. A simple latrine was dug on the edge, and a laser alert perimeter was established 200 feet out. The boys in demolition left a few surprises for anyone stupid enough to approach. Finally, things were calming after their earlier encounter.

The usual guard number was doubled to eight, each positioned within sight of the other and operating on a rotating schedule. They wore their headsets with active night vision and kept their heads on a swivel.

As darkness enveloped the area, groups formed around the camp, based on mutual interests. There was a poker game, a wrestling match, and a singing group. Eight of the fifteen women in the group gathered to read from a book one of them had brought with her, one filled with a mix of romance and intrigue. The colonel held court by a small campfire, and many warriors shared their war stories there. The colonel listened, knowing in just two days, he would be able to add his own.

Katrina listened to the stories of bravery and slaughter as the flames painted ghoulish shadows across their faces. Being one of only two survivors from the recent mission, she was asked to share her version. She was hesitant at first, but enough encouragement had her recanting her meeting with the two humans from outer space and saving Commander Weng.

Seventy-eight men and women double-timed it through the forest. They were wraith-like quiet, with only one thing on their mind: payback. The Reekers used a plant they grew called Betel nut that boosted their energy and added to their crazy look by making their mouths and teeth red. It was all-natural but addictive. The energy it gave them pushed them forward with little fatigue, even after three hours at pace.

As they approached the lights of the camp, the Reekers picked up the pace, as if an unspoken command had been issued to the group. They spread out, forming a curved arc that would engulf the camp. This time there was no chant, just soft footsteps that closed the distance quickly.

The outer perimeter alarm was the first to go off, alerting the camp it been tripped. Then, several explosions followed by screams confirmed it. The camp was under attack.

"Form up. Weapons hot!" The guards pulled back and joined their other warriors who were scrambling for weapons, helmets, and bio-suits. The gunners hustled to the Stryker, trying to get the weapon systems online, while others took cover behind the armor plating.

Katrina bolted from the campfire as the first few old-school bullets pinged the camp. She grabbed her bio-suit, trying to stay calm. The air seemed to change as a musky, moldy smell hit her nostrils, carrying with it fear. It was the fear of being tortured and then consumed. She slipped her legs into the suit and pulled it over her shoulders, shoving her arms inside. A quick zip, a helmet don, and she was back out of the Stryker, ready to fight.

A battle screech sounded, sending chills down her spine. The camp was in chaos. Homemade smoke grenades exploded, filling the air and obscuring the battlefield. Warriors returned fire, and soon the sky was lit up with plasma pulses. A giant man blindsided Katrina, knocking her off her feet and slamming her head against an ammo case. Her helmet exploded off her head, and her world spun for a moment. A sudden shot of pain jerked her head to the right. She was sliding across the ground at a fast pace, being pulled by her hair.

As her eyes focused, she saw it was the massive man who had knocked her down. He had a dangerous gleam in his eyes as he pulled his prize away from the camp. The smell made Katrina want to puke, but she fought the feeling off by fighting back, like an ant against a rhino. Anything she tried had no effect on her situation. The guy had a vice grip on her hair and pulled her along the ground as if she was on wheels.

She remembered the boot knife Commander Weng had given her for her bravery and tried to focus her will on reaching it. Her fingertips brushed the hilt several times before she grasped it in her right hand. With a single motion, she swung the blade forward and embedded it into the forearm that held her hair in the vice grip. A grunt was followed by a sudden stop as he released her and reached for the knife to pull it out.

Katrina scrambled back across the ground, trying to put distance between herself and the monster. He pulled the knife from his arm and closed on her, his towering body a mountain of muscles. He stomped her to the ground with one foot, which left her breathless. His original idea of taking a live captive for pleasure and food quickly died with the wound she had inflicted. He could still have pleasure with a dead woman. He leaned over to slit her throat and be done with it. Katrina was helpless, still trying to find her breath as the man reached down to flick his wrist across her throat.

A random plasma burst from the fight caught the giant mid-shoulder, removing his entire arm in a millisecond. It fell to the ground still clutching the knife. The wrist still twitched in a slicing motion. Katrina spun to her hands and knees and forced air back into her lungs. She scrambled away, toward the camp, as fast as she could. Had she looked over her shoulder, she would have seen her demon carrying his arm away—still clutching the knife. It was a fair trade, the knife for her life.

The battle was intense but only lasted a few more minutes before the sound of gunfire died out.

"Cease fire!"

By the time the smoke cleared, there was no Reeker to be found, not even a dead one.

"Colonel, we're missing eight warriors."

"What do you mean missing?" he asked.

"There is no sign of them. I saw Walters take a hit right over there. You can see the blood, but his body is gone, sir."

"Reekers," Smyth said it like a swear word. "Everybody load back up. We're not staying here."

"Sir, the batteries are only half-charged."

"Okay, everybody back inside; we'll hold up until we get fully charged."

Katrina wobbled up the ramp to her Stryker. She was spent and still dumping adrenaline.

Someone handed her the helmet she'd lost, and she placed it on her head and sat. Warriors piled into the Strykers—some bloodied, and others still hopped up and ready to kill. They all wore their bio-suits, still sweating with exertion. They closed the doors and gunners stayed on guard for a possible return visit. It didn't take long before the air inside turned sour. It was going to be a long night.

The tribe had taken several casualties in the attack, but they had grabbed six of the killed or injured armed soldiers, including their modern weapons.

Anyone injured in the tribe dared not reveal it, as once you were unable to keep up with the group, you were expendable . . . and expendable got you eaten. Including their own dead, they carried eighteen bodies. Each would be put to good use.

Jericho rubbed his hands against the flames. Several campfires were scattered around the site, along with a few bio heaters. Groups formed and friendships grew as like-minded souls got to know each other. This was the beginning of a grand adventure and a new way of life, far from the politics and war that seemed to be a constant in the city.

"This is my favorite time," Santos said, without looking up.

"What. Nighttime?" Jericho asked.

"No. The time all these strangers with common goals start to bond. No matter where they come from or what their past is, they find a way to mesh and work together. It gives me hope for humanity."

"I was once hoping for humanity," Jericho mumbled.

Santos lifted his head curiously.

"I wasn't born here."

"None of us were, son."

"No, on Earth."

This got Santos's eyes to widen.

Jericho shared his story with the only man who had not tried to kill or use him. After he was done, there was a silence that only the crackling logs broke.

"Well, you're either one heck of a storyteller or bat-crap crazy," Santos laughed.

"Do I look crazy to you?"

Santos's laugh died out, and he looked away, uncomfortable with Jericho's stare. "I'm gonna get some shut-eye . . . and no . . . you don't."

Jericho stood and strolled through the camp, watching the interactions between the families. There was a young girl in pigtails refusing to eat her dinner, and her mom seemed beside herself.

Families were a mystery to him. He took the time to observe and digest what he saw.

This was not a totally harmonious group of people. There was some arguing, and one person sat off by himself. How were all these different people and mind-sets supposed to form a compatible group? Children seemed like the biggest wild card. They didn't listen and often misinterpreted their parents' requests. It seemed like a mishmash of personalities and agendas, surely a doomed prospect for their future. Whoever thought creating a family unit was a good idea had obviously never tried to maintain one.

"How'd it go?"

"Piece of cake," Finley replied as he closed the door and entered Avery's room. Unlike most of the concrete living quarters, Avery had taken the time and expense to paint her walls a lavender color and hang some art. She had comfortable furnishings and an extra bedroom. A couple of throw rugs and soft lighting gave the room an inviting feel.

Finley pulled his shirt off and tossed it over the back of a padded chair. His dark ripped back and chest had myriad scars, every one of them telling a story.

Avery stepped up to him and ran her fingertip along the trail of imperfections. They had both sacrificed so much to get here, and now was not the time to be shy about it. Finley had wanted Avery for some time, and it wasn't until she had seen him in a different light that she let him into her life.

He had been on a mission to rescue a group of 1.0s that had fallen prey to a band of Whippers. The fight had cost both sides, but Finley's forces prevailed, rescuing most of the hostages and eliminating the Whipper threat in that area.

Avery had watched as Finley carried two young boys, now parentless, in his arms through the East Gate as the team returned. He had tear stains on his face and spent the next two days making sure he placed the young boys in a good home.

For all his rigid exterior, Avery had seen into his heart that day, and it had changed the way she now saw him.

Lately, Avery's days were filled with the complications of being a leader, but her nights were her own, and she could do with them as she chose.

"You oversaw the latest graduating recruit class in thirty minutes?"

"Sometimes, it's good to be the boss. I got people," Finley replied.

"I see, and they did your job for you?"

"Wow, harsh! They did their job as instructed by me," Finley countered with a smile.

Avery playfully nodded at him. "Fair enough. Now, what about your job for me?"

"Job? I wasn't aware of another job?" Finley said, with a perplexed expression.

"This job." Avery pulled his face down to her level and kissed him. Their lips and tongues commingled as a warm, comfortable feeling spread between them.

"Hmm. Not sure you could handle the kind of job I can do," he tossed back, trying to regain the upper hand.

"Is that right?" She reached her hand down and *handled* his goods, grabbing on tight.

"Oh, I might have been premature in my estimation," Finley recanted.

"Ya think," Avery said as she pulled him close with her new handle. They kissed for a while longer, letting the emotions of the day fade and their passion take over. This was the only time Avery completely lost herself. No more thoughts of work, saving humankind, or leading her fellow citizens. Right here, right now, she was lost in the moment. She pulled her shirt and pants off in a frenzy. Her figure was in stark contrast to Finley's—soft, white, perfect skin against firm muscles in an hourglass shape. She guided Finley to her bed.

"I could get to like this job," Finley muttered.

"Too bad the boss is a ball-buster," Avery whispered in his ear, before clamping down on a sensitive area.

"Ow!"

"That's more like it."

12

Commander Weng led the way as the squad moved along the edge of the road that led toward the south end of the city. All was quiet in the pre-dawn darkness. The lake held behind the dam was small but deep, giving plenty of pressure for the generators below. A sliver of the moon's reflection danced on the dark water. Helen used her pass card to open several gates as they moved along. Up ahead was a lit entry post with a single guard blocking the way. It led to the access road down the side of the dam and to the entrance doors of the generating plant.

The plan had been mentally rehearsed several times and everyone knew their part. The squad ducked down and took positions in the dark as Helen casually walked up to the guard.

He snapped to attention when he recognized the major.

"Relax, Corporal, I'm just out for a stroll, checking security. Couldn't sleep."

"Yes, ma'am . . . but procedure dictates I call this in."

"Good. You follow your orders, and I'll follow mine."

"It also dictates I detain you until authorization is given to me to do otherwise." He pointed his rifle in her direction.

Helen lifted her hands slightly in supplication. "Corporal, I am Major Christine Helen. Lower your weapon, or I'll have you manning latrine duty before the night is over."

The man's hands shook as he tried to make a decision. "Just let me call it . . ."

A shot rang out, and the corporal dropped his weapon and fell to his knees. A strange look crossed his face before he slumped to the ground. Seven warriors dressed in all-black approached.

"That was not part of the plan," Helen angrily hissed. "I had it handled."

"It's handled now," Commander Weng replied. "Lose the body. Come on," he ordered his squad.

"If someone comes by and there is no one on duty . . ." She let silence finish her thought.

The body was stripped and tossed over the fence into the dark water. One of the men put the guard's clothes on and replaced him at the gate.

"There, happy?" Weng asked.

"No," Helen said as she unlocked the gate.

They jogged down the empty lane to the building at the bottom of the dam.

As they approached the well-lit entrance, two guards could be seen chatting and sharing a smoke, and a third leaned against the doors. The 2.0 squad didn't hesitate and made quick work of them.

Helen opened the doors, and they shoved the bodies inside.

After rounding up the engineers and locking them in a storage closet, Weng and his team set about placing the timed explosives in the most vulnerable spots on the generating system—vulnerable spots that would stop all operations but only require a reasonable amount of time to repair. Once mounted and set, they would detonate, no matter the situation. If someone tried to remove them or disarm them . . . *kaboom*. The team took up positions to defend their hard-earned territory.

Now came the waiting game.

It took about twenty minutes of sunlight before the wagons were charged enough for the day. Santos showed Jericho how to control the lead wagon, capable of hauling nearly three tons across uneven terrain, at up to seven miles an hour. Jericho twisted the grip forward on the T-bar and began walking with the wagon. It was like pulling a cart, without the pulling or steering. The controls handled all the work. All he had to do was maintain the speed and direction he wanted it to go. The wagon train continued west along the river before the trail moved away from the water and up an incline. Most of the travelers remained excited, and the mood across the camp was good. Even the children seemed to be looking forward with little complaint.

A fork in the road led to an overgrown paved road that made the going easy for a spell before it became so full of potholes, they steered back into the dirt. Trees dotted the surroundings, opening up occasionally to grass-filled meadows.

Santos walked to the front. "You picked that up easy," he said, pointing to the controls on the wagon.

"It's not complicated."

Santos had to agree with him since the design was his.

"So, how did you end up here?" Jericho asked.

"Used to be a schoolteacher back in the day. Then lost my family to Marburg-G . . . nasty way to go. Jenni was just four, and my wife, Karen," he said with a far-off look. "I had consigned myself to the same fate when I became their designated caretaker. For some reason, it didn't like me. Never had one symptom. It was not easy being left without even a scratch. I miss 'em and think about them every day." He walked in silence for a bit.

"Then every time a sickness passed through, more friends and family left town or died. I got tired of saying goodbye, so I did it myself. Never did like giving control of my life to someone else, so New Kansas wasn't an option."

"You ended up in Zion?"

Santos reminisced silently before he began. "After a bit. Fought in the war for a while, trying to defend our freedoms. That was a bust." He looked up for a second remembering. "I remember the day clearly. The 2.0s had us cornered in an old part of New Orleans."

Jericho gave him a quizzical look.

"Big 1.0 city in the South. Had mosquitoes the size of hummingbirds. I'm not kidding. They were huge. Anyway, we were cornered and gave as much as we got. Then out of nowhere, the skies filled with these automated drones about the size of lawnmowers." He used his arms to demonstrate. "Hundreds, and they just started firing on every 1.0 in sight. I tripped and fell down an open drainage pipe, or I wouldn't be here. It's just a matter of time if you ask me, so I just try to help people and pray every day for a miracle."

"Does that really work?" Jericho asked.

"What, prayer? Heck yeah, it does." He walked for a few seconds, letting his words hang. "At the very least, it makes me more accountable for my actions."

"What do you mean?"

"Well, let's say I pray for the safety of this wagon train. It would be pretty stupid for me to, then disregard keeping an eye out for trouble. You see, prayer is like a reminder that I still gotta do my part. God does his part, and I do mine—like a partnership. God helps those who help themselves."

"But bad stuff still happens," Jericho said.

"All the time. All we can really muster here on earth is to make things better than we found them."

They shared a smile as the two friends walked along.

"So what about you?" Santos asked. "What are you doing here?"

If he was honest with himself, Jericho didn't have an answer.

Santos didn't wait for a reply. "I can tell you one thing: hanging on to all that anger like you do, it'll eatcha up. The first step in forgiving others is to forgive yourself. You can't move forward until you do."

Colonel Smyth watched as the wagon train moved up the incline in his direction. There were twenty-two of them in a line. A dust cloud bloomed behind in the morning sun. He zoomed in and saw a host of families, some riding and some walking alongside their precious possessions. The sight of so many 1.0s made him sick. He lowered his view scope, turning back to his men.

He had positioned his Stryker force in an arc along the tree line, awaiting the other half of the regiment to arrive. That group had taken a southern route, and he expected them by mid-day, at the latest. Then it would be a full-court press to the city wall to coordinate their timed ground attack with the destruction of the laser containment grid and the aerial bombardment.

Katrina leaned on a tree, letting the sun's rays warm her face. The previous night had been a real nightmare as they waited in their Strykers, wondering if another attack from the Reekers was coming. The fear of being someone's lunch sat heavy in the air. An hour after the initial attack, they disconnected from the fuel cell rechargers and continued the mission. It was a rough night with no sleep, each warrior ready to deploy at a moment's notice against a possible Reeker assault. By sunup, they had arrived at the rendezvous spot, thanks to the E-Marker, and established a holding defensive pattern. So far, all was calm.

Commander Weng came to her mind. He was a handsome and strong man who could take care of himself and those around him. She wondered what he was up to right now and let her thoughts drift to the possibilities of a second date between the two of them. She would like to spend more time with him. From there, who knows? He was not what she was looking for in her life, but there was something about him that made her feel safe when he was around. She looked at her commanding officer standing on the lead Stryker with a view scope pinned to his eyes. His face focused on something in the distance.

Smyth battled with a decision. Should he hide the regiment and let the wagon train pass, or should he do his duty and kill as many 1.0s as he could? They were distant enough from the city that the odds of the battle being discovered were low, but there was still a chance. A random explosion could give away their position. In the end, he sent ten of his best fighters through the trees on an intercept path. They had bio-suited up and jogged toward their objective with confidence. These impoverished pioneers would put up little resistance, and a ground assault would keep him off Zion's radar. Besides, he might as well start things off with a victory. It would do the troops' morale good after their recent Reeker encounter.

Jericho felt them before he saw them—shadows moving quickly through the forest and coming their way.

"Santos. We got visitors with bad intent."

Santos was quick to react. He called out for the families to circle the wagons and take cover. Adults grabbed for weapons as drivers pulled the wagons into a defensive circle.

Before all the wagons stopped in formation, Santos had the rear tailgate down and was throwing out his bedding. He kept some more modern firepower packed with his supplies. With a yank of a lever, a tripod-mounted plasma gun cleared its container. At the same time, the canvas sides rolled up to allow an unrestricted shooting profile. He climbed up and activated the weapon. Jericho moved behind the wagon, looking for someplace to post up when the shooting started.

"Here," Santos called as he threw his pistol to Jericho. The weapon felt comfortable in his hand after so many hours of virtual combat gaming.

"Come and get some, you greasy crud suckers!" Santos cried out as he blasted the forest and the warriors in front of him. Bullets flew against flechettes in an unequal tug-of-war. The poorly armed pilgrims were no match for trained warriors. The devastation was almost instant, but the 1.0s were fighting for their lives, and no one in the group would just let go. Children picked up guns as fathers and mothers dropped. Santos took a round to the shoulder, his arm nearly amputated. He continued to fight, using his other arm until another round sent him to the dirt, gasping.

The warriors, for all their training and superior firepower, still took casualties as bodies dropped left, right, and center.

Jericho knelt next to Santos and lifted his head. The old man struggled with something, and Jericho realized he was trying to take off his multi-belt.

"This . . . for you. Now get up on that gun, son, and give it back to 'em."

Jericho let the belt drop to the ground. "This ain't my fight."

"Look, space boy, if these aren't your people, then you got no people." He coughed up some blood. "Make a choice, but do it soon, or you'll die alone . . . and that's no way to go." He coughed again through a blood-red mouth and murmured a prayer that died on unmoving lips.

"Santos? Santos."

He was gone.

Jericho laid the head of his only friend back down in reverence, letting his words hit home.

Someone from the group yelled, "They're 2.0s! Murdering scum. Kill 'em all!"

Jericho looked up to see a male adult firing off his gun repeatedly as he ran toward the enemy. He was cut in half.

Jericho climbed up onto the wagon and took the plasma gun in his hands. He was filled with anger as he fired with an intense focus, taking out warrior targets from right to left. The intense fighting died out, and the dust settled. Jericho lowered the weapon and climbed numbly from the wagon. He knelt down and took the time to close Santos's eyes before picking up the multi-belt and putting it on. He placed the pistol back in its spot and stood.

The devastation was complete, with bodies strewn around the wagons and across the battlefield. He counted ten heavily armed men dressed in black, all dead. Many by his hand. These were the types of soldiers who had killed 24. He felt nothing for them. He turned his attention back to the wagon train. No movement.

He collected a backpack and filled it with a few supplies before turning and walking away, never planning on looking back.

A muffled sound caught his attention, and he paused, struggling with indecision. These were not his people, but he had fought with them. Fought against a common enemy.

Jericho turned and followed the source of the sound until he came to a small child trapped under her mother, a mother who had died trying to protect her.

Jericho lifted the corpse off the little girl and helped her up.

Her hair was matted with dirt, and there was blood on her face, but it looked superficial. She had a shattered expression along with a cute little pug nose.

"What's your name?" he asked, trying to get her attention back to the present.

The girl blinked a few times before a hoarse voice squeaked out, "Geena."

"Geena, I'm Jericho." They looked at each other for a beat before the little girl spoke up. "I want my Holly." She started pulling at her dead mom's arm. "I want my Holly."

"I'm sorry Geena, but Holly didn't make it."

"She can't die. Dadda told me." As giant tears flowed, she pulled on her mom's dead arm.

Jericho had no experience with children. He tried to pat her on the back and even convince her that Holly was dead and that was that. It only made her more hysterical. Jericho considered leaving her there, but then he decided on a dose of reality. "Fine, I'll show you."

He rolled the dead mother over. There was a hunk of her face missing as dead eyes gaped at the sky. Jericho held back the urge to vomit, but Geena seemed numb as she reached and pulled her stuffed doll with braided locks from the dirt. She held it close, and her emotions calmed; only tears flowed.

Jericho turned her from the ghastly vision as he put two and two together. "Oh, your doll Holly, of course. Yes, she can't die, but we can, so we need to get moving. Understand?"

A simple nod came in reply, and the two orphans moved into the trees, leaving the massacre behind.

Colonel Smyth waited for a reply from his men that never came. He zoomed in on the wagon train. There were bodies clearly visible, along with a few fires. No movement. He sent another ten warriors to follow up. A few minutes later, he got his answer.

"They had a plasma cannon in the lead wagon. Made puzzle pieces out of our men."

"Any survivors?"

"None, sir."

That did not go as planned. "Return to camp," he ordered.

Katrina heard them before she saw them. Fifteen additional Strykers pulled into the meadow and stopped; the other half of the regiment had arrived. The sun was high in the sky, and the heat index soared. She watched as Colonel Smyth reconnected with his counterpart and reviewed the plan.

The southern route had not been without its complications. Whippers had taken on the squadron, and both sides suffered damage. The Whippers were an organized group of lawless outliers who used violence and outdated weapons to control their small part of the world. It would be the 2.0 leaders' next problem to eradicate after they finished off the 1.0s.

Katrina could see burn marks on a few of the Strykers, and it looked like one of the roof-mounted rail guns was missing.

Lieutenant Rice stepped next to Katrina, startling her.

"Sorry, I've been asked to keep an eye on you when we hit the city."

"Oh, really?" she replied.

"I guess someone up there likes you."

"Someone?" Katrina raised an eyebrow at the lieutenant.

"It was Commander Weng," Lieutenant Rice confessed. "How do you two know each other?"

Katrina let a small smile cross her lips. "I saved his life once."

Lieutenant Rice looked at Katrina with new eyes. "Seriously?"

Katrina nodded, and if she was honest, after her last battle, appreciated the concern.

"Once we take the city and everything is secured, you'll be part of a squad that will neutralize any and all 1.0 corpses. Anything biological remaining, disintegrate. When that is complete, the whole city will have to be sterilized before we can begin sending our people or the vaccinated 1.0s to re-habitat it."

"What are our plans for the 1.0s we vaccinate?" she asked.

"I'm guessing some'll be taken to the Ion-Dome for processing. Everyone likes a good show. The rest will be processed and put to work. Someone's got to clean up and rebuild this world."

"Form up!" The command was shouted across to all warriors. It was time to do what they had come here for. Katrina and Lieutenant Rice jogged to their Stryker.

Now that the regiment was recombined, they lined up and moved out toward the city. With the clock ticking, the warriors no longer needed to worry about a stealthy approach. Timing had become the critical element. When the laser containment grid went down, the 1.0s would be fighting a losing battle. The plan called for a focused strike on Zion's military base first. Once the base was neutralized, they could spare warriors to clean up the remaining civilians across the city. It would be a block-by-block effort.

Thirty Strykers moved two-by-two, closing on Zion at a pace that would put them within 300 meters of the West Gate just before the shield went down. That would allow for a fast attack on the entrance, destroying it and the neighboring walls so that even if the laser containment grid was reestablished, they could still get into the city.

The protective grid over Zion was a two-sided sword. Only weapons on the outside could fire when it was up. The 1.0s had placed a few towers outside for additional protection around the city, but they were not designed for the level of attack that was about to take place.

Colonel Smyth could feel the energy in his men as they grew closer. This was a battle he would savor. He inspected his bio-suit for holes; after his two previous skirmishes with Reekers, he didn't want to risk contamination. It made him wonder how Commander Weng's advance team was handling the myriad diseases among the 1.0s without suit protection. He had respected the commander's skills and determination, but he would never see the man again. That was war in a nutshell. Do your duty and move to the next one, with or without your mates.

The morning had passed uneventfully—so far, so good. Weng's squad was down to five more hours of holding their position before the main strike force would arrive. The goal was to have the ground force come out of the setting sun since they would be identified first. That would have the city's defenses scrambling to address them. When the containment grid failed, the ground forces would battle their way to the gate as the aerial threat crashed down from above and behind. It would be a decisive advantage and practically guarantee a favorable outcome. Weng looked up as the radio squawked.

"Two soldiers coming my way. Looks like a guard exchange. What's the call?" a voice over the earpiece said. It was the replacement guard they had left behind at the gate by the lake.

"Eliminate and dispose of," Weng replied.

"It won't be long till we get company here," Helen said.

"One thing at a time," Weng responded.

They listened to the sounds of flechettes firing off, and then a few minutes later came the "all clear." The warriors visibly relaxed and settled back into the waiting game. The temperature had climbed to well above 40°C, and everyone was dripping with sweat inside the generating room.

"Major, what's your deal? Weng asked, trying to pass the time as he wiped sweat from his brow.

"What do you mean?" she countered.

"Why are you helping us, betraying your own kind?"

Helen paused before answering. "I'm just backing the winning side; nothing more. There's no future here in this city. Just a bunch of misguided people who believed freedom and rights are worth dying for. If you ask me, nothing is worth dying for."

Weng looked around at his squad. "We all came here on this mission knowing it was a death sentence because we believe ending this war will bring peace and a future humankind deserves."

"That's your decision, and honestly, none of you are going to die from any sickness, maybe a flechette. You might get a flu, cold, or a sniffle, but that whole vaccine and upgrade thing you all do is bologna. It lines pockets and keeps your citizens under control. There hasn't been a true outbreak from nature in years."

"There's been an outbreak almost every six months," Singh countered.

"Not here," Helen said.

The concept was not sitting right with the squad. How would a disease just impact their city? It was preposterous, but the idea they might not die from some horrible 1.0 disease—that was something worth considering.

The front door slammed open and closed. Weng and Helen spun their weapons in that direction.

"Don't shoot!" the guard called out with one hand in the air. "We're busted. A squad of five is following up to see why the guards didn't return. Once they see the blood on the ground, things are going to get even hotter."

"I'm guessing we have maybe twenty minutes or less before we have company here," Helen said.

Weng had taken a radio from one of the dead guards to listen in on their communications. It squawked, followed by a request. "Station 12, please respond."

"That's us," Helen said.

"Station 12, responding," Weng spoke into the radio.

"Access code please," came the reply.

Weng looked at Helen. She whispered the code to him, and he repeated it back into the radio.

"Good, copy," came next, followed by silence.

"That should buy us a bit more time," Helen added.

They hoped she was right, but a fight was coming, and they needed to be ready.

Avery stepped into the operations room and took the call personally. A guard had left their post or there was something very wrong. She called Finley as she waited for the report to come in.

"No sign of the guard anywhere, and we have what appears to be blood here."

"Secure the area. I'm sending a full squad to check it out."

"Copy."

Finley walked in just as Avery was giving orders. "What's up?"

"Something's going on down by the dam. It could mean the power station. It could also be nothing, but I need you to check it out thoroughly."

Finley made a quick salute and left to gather his force.

Ten of his personal commandos escorted Finley to the gate in question. There were five soldiers standing there on duty, awaiting them.

"Any sign of the missing guard?" Finley asked.

"No, sir. Nor his replacement."

"Where is the blood you reported?"

"Right here and here."

Finley moved over and inspected the splatter. He carefully followed a minuscule drip trail that led to the fence surrounding the lake. He focused on the top of the fence and the other side. "The bodies were thrown into the water," he said.

The group looked at each other, suddenly aware that something was very wrong.

"What's the Freq-ID for the guards at the generating plant?" Finley asked.

"26.78."

He dialed his COMMs system to the specific frequency.

"Station 12, this is Finley."

He waited for a beat before a reply came.

"This is Station 12."

Finley went through the process of confirming the day's passcode. Once complete, he still had that uncomfortable feeling in his gut.

"Heading over for a hard confirmation," he added.

"Copy that."

He let his mind consider his next steps.

"Finley."

"This is Finley."

"Yeah, this is Major Christine Helen. I'm on-site and have your hard confirmation."

"Helen? What are you doing there?"

"Heard about the trouble and didn't want to take a chance. Took five men and headed straight to the generators. We have everything secured here. No problems to report."

"The guards were on station?" Finley asked.

"Yes, all present and accounted for. The trouble must be on your end."

"Okay, copy that. Stay there until I get a better idea of what's happened. I'll send two additional warriors over in support."

"Copy that."

Finley pointed at two of his men. "Let me know what's going on down there."

They nodded and ran off through the gate, down the angled path to the bottom of the dam.

Helen placed the radio they had taken from one of the guards back in her belt. "Two coming in hot."

"Let's make them welcome," Weng said as he positioned his warriors.

"How much more time?" Helen asked.

"Just under an hour," Singh replied.

"It's gonna be close."

"That's how I like it," Weng said.

Helen, along with the warrior in the dead guard's uniform, stepped outside and took up positions. They watched as two highly trained operators moved along the path, carefully approaching. They took nothing at face value as they closed on Helen and the faux guard.

"All good here?" one man named Dixon asked.

"All good. Just like I said," Helen replied.

"Where are the other two guards?"

"They're inside helping my men search the premises for . . . well, for anything not right. You're welcome to join them or stay here and help keep an eye out."

"I'll need to check in first," said the one on the right.

"Finley. This is Dixon."

"Go ahead, Dixon."

"Just like she said. Helen is here, and they are blanketing the facility. I'm gonna have a look inside and report back."

"Copy."

Helen stepped up and pulled the soldier's attention from his conversation. "Dixon, is it?"

"Yes, ma'am," Dixon replied.

"Right this way, men."

The two soldiers followed her into the huge generating plant.

As they passed the entrance, several muffled shots rang out, ending the 1.0s' lives before their eyes could compensate for the difference in light.

Weng's men moved the bodies out of the way and waited for what would come next.

According to Einstein, time is relevant. Right now, time was relevantly slow, but what seemed like an eternity was less than five minutes before the radio squawked.

"Dixon, this is Finley. Do you copy?"

Nothing. Finley tried a few more times before Helen's voice returned. "Don't think he can hear you. He's in the back part of the facility."

Finley considered the major's words. "Have him call me in the next five with the new code word I gave him."

"Will do." Helen slammed the radio down. "They're on to us."

"Well, we knew this was a possibility." Weng called out to the other warriors, "Get to your spots. Things are about to boil over."

The men hustled to their positions, each ready to die to make this mission a success. They didn't need to survive. Just hold out long enough that the 1.0s couldn't thwart their plan. The bombs needed to go off at an exact time. Nothing else mattered.

Finley waited to hear from his man, Dixon. After more than five minutes passed, he knew something was wrong. There was no new code word, and he expected Dixon to call him back with that information. He tried connecting with Helen one more time, knowing in his heart it was futile. The generating plant was in jeopardy.

13

The last two miles were done in creep mode, and it seemed to take forever. Thirty Strykers blasting toward the city would be heard and seen for miles away; the dust cloud alone would give them away before it was time. But creep mode allowed the vehicles to fan out into their attack positions and move through the trees in a careful and silent approach.

The wall around Zion was nearly eighteen feet tall. It was made of stone and steel with a slight angle from the bottom up. There was a protected pathway on top with several access points along the inside, including a troop monorail for quick repositioning. The trees had been cleared back to 300 meters, leaving an empty field surrounding the city's fortifications. With living space in the area at a premium, small shanties and huts had popped up within the open space, along with agriculture. Beyond that lay the forest with myriad risks and problems. About every 500 meters, a large tower made of wood stood high above the wall. It held spotters and defensive weapons that could be fired while the grid over the city was still in place.

As the sun dipped low on the horizon, it lit up the forest in a golden glow, making it difficult for the spotters to see anything. This was the time Colonel Smyth had been waiting for. They had held up about a half click from the city, back in the trees enough to avoid detection. Once the sun was low enough, they continued forward until they were just a few trees back from the clearing. It was now just a matter of minutes before the attack would begin. At that point, it would be a mad dash for the gate.

Katrina leaned on her left butt cheek. Her right one had gone numb. The time spent riding in a metal can was wearing on her, and that they were finally going to assault the 1.0s was more of a relief than a case of nerves. Metal creaked as the afternoon sun heated up the Stryker and one warrior muffled a cough. Every detail of the moment played out as her mind raced with anticipation.

The HollowVision projector was rolled into the room. Now that President Caleb was no longer contagious, he had been moved to his bed in the presidential apartment. Cin had been by his side, covering for him and carrying out his orders. The near-death experience had quelled much of his passion, and Caleb was just covering the basics, but the battle ahead had his full attention.

"It's time, Mr. President," Cin announced as two workers finished setting up the projector and tested it. Multiple images started streaming from the field.

Caleb leaned forward. He could just make out the walls of Zion through a copse of trees. Next to it was an aerial view as fighters moved west, the sun casting a bright glare.

"Twenty minutes out, Mr. President."

"Everything is in place?" Caleb asked.

"As far as we know. The real test will be from Commander Weng's team. We have no way of knowing how they are faring, and, as you know, without them, this will be nothing but a ding, dong, ditch."

The president sat up in his bed. He teetered for a second before gaining his balance. His fever was gone, and he was waiting for his energy to return. "Have my transport readied. I'm going to get a closer look as soon as it's safe to do so."

"Are you sure you're up to this?" Cin asked.

"Yes, I'll be okay. Besides, there is no way I'm gonna let Giles run the battle." He stood and moved closer to the pre-battle images. "And I'll need you to come with me to help make sure everything is running smoothly."

Cin nodded and left to make the preparations.

Caleb let his mind go to all the careful planning that had been a part of this operation. Cin was right. It all hinged on Weng's success. This was one thing

Caleb had no concern over. Commander Weng had always come through. His dedication to the cause and unwavering focus on a task's end was unparalleled. The thought brought a smile to Caleb's face—something that hadn't happened in a while. He considered the orchestration Weng must be going through to make that happen.

Caleb remembered the woman who had turned Weng against his duty two years ago. Not her name, per se, but the fact that she was Weng's wife. The woman had wanted a normal family life, far from politics and war, and her corrupt thoughts had affected Weng's performance. It was only a matter of time before Weng quit the service. . . . Not acceptable.

Caleb had been forced to take drastic action. A drone accident was all it took. Unfortunately, the little girl had survived. She was badly damaged but alive. It had forced Caleb to pull out all the stops to save her, making the little girl a miracle of modern medical technology.

He had never considered how that might affect Weng. The man was now more loyal than ever, with a passion to make a safer, better world for his little girl. It had all worked out perfectly in the end. Caleb swelled with pride at his genius, just as a small coughing fit consumed his thoughts.

No, Commander Weng would come through for him today. Caleb headed for the closet to dress.

Avery paced in the operations room, waiting to hear from Finley.

"Avery, this is Finley. We have a potential breach at the dam. Send one more squad, and you better get things ready topside, just in case. There might be more to this than we can see."

"Copy that and you better get back here. . . . I need you."

Finley processed her request. Where would he be the most useful? "Negative. I'll clean up here first and then return."

A shot of adrenaline spiked through Avery with his words. This was the one thing she feared most. She was in the starting blocks, and the gun had sounded. It was go time, and, ready or not, she needed to be a strong leader or her city and people would be lost. She called for one more squad to help and activated a recon drone to give her an aerial view of the proceedings.

The squad double-timed it down to Finley. He tried to reach Dixon and Helen, but there was still no reply.

"Okay, we are heading into hostile territory, and we need to consider that Major Christine Helen is compromised in some way. So heads on a swivel, and if it comes to it, make your shots count." He set an assault plan in motion, and the soldiers moved off to comply. Twelve men would repel down the dam onto the roof of the generating plant. From there, it would be a short drop from above onto any resistance they encountered at the front door. The rest of the force would approach the front and deal with problems as they manifested.

He waited ten minutes to give the forward operating team a chance to get into place on the roof of the plant. The support squad then started down the ramp toward the steel double doors.

Jericho adjusted the multi-belt around his waist for the third time that day. Santos had been much wider, and Jericho had yet to find the right fit. Geena had done a solid job of keeping up as they put distance between themselves and the 2.0 warriors who had murdered the wagon train. Jericho had vacillated on which direction to go. Back to the city so he could unload his charge or away from the city and try to find a family he could sell or pawn her off to? The further they walked, the more he was convinced a cute little girl like this was worth some credits, food, or favors.

In the end, they headed north, away from the wagons and the city. Zion had brought nothing good to his life.

Maybe distance from humanity was the answer. Jericho absently fingered the ring hung around his neck.

"What's with the ring?" Geena asked.

Jericho self-consciously put the ring back under his shirt. He walked a few more steps before answering. "I gave it to someone once."

"Your wife?"

Jericho thought about how to explain his and 24's relationship. She wasn't a wife or a girlfriend. She was his partner. "Someone I cared about."

Geena glanced up at Jericho, waiting for more.

24 was a strong, smart woman with the best smile and the kindest eyes. She had connected with Jericho on some sort of deep level, and his heart ached for her. That's why moving in any direction was so important to him. It kept the painful memory just behind him. In this case, the path was a mix of game trails and overgrown roads, long since abandoned, but it did the trick—until the little brat brought it up.

"Aren't you a little old to be playing with dolls?"

Geena looked at Holly for a second, considering his words. "My mom made her for me."

Jericho understood, and they walked in silence for a while. He let Geena lead, as it was far easier to keep an eye on her that way. He had no intention of letting this possible meal ticket get away.

"How old are you, by the way?" he asked, hoping to get some information from her that might enhance her sale.

"Eight and a half," Geena replied, looking back over her shoulder. "How old are you?"

"I'll be one in a month," Jericho replied.

Geena stopped walking, and her eyes narrowed as she processed his answer. "That doesn't sound right."

"I get that a lot. Come on." They continued walking, only this time side by side.

"What kinds of things do you like to do?"

"I like stories that aren't scary . . . my doll Holly and fried chicken. Why? Are you making a list?"

"No," he said a bit too defensively. "Just curious."

"How is it you're not even one year old yet?" she asked.

"It's a long story."

Geena used her hands to convey *we got nothing but time.*

"I'd rather hear about you," Jericho added.

"Fine. My name is Geena Callister. My mom, Diana, is dead. My Dadda, Paul, is also dead, and my little brother, Stevie, dead. Happy? I have blonde hair and blue eyes, but you already know all that." She continued rattling on for most of the next hour.

Jericho was sorry he'd asked.

The first sounds of flechettes flew in their direction as Finley and his squad rounded the curve to the sightline of the generating plant's entrance.

Each of Finley's soldiers carried the venerable FN-USPLs, Fabrique Nationale Ultra-Short Pulse Laser rifles. They fired an energy beam, invisible to the human eye, that could blast through even the most advanced body armor. Much like firing a bullet, the laser pulse could only be seen by the result of its impact. It traveled at the speed of light, making it a much faster weapon than a plasma or even a flechette gun but less destructive on impact. The modern weapons had the advantage of being quieter than a traditional discharge bullet gun, but each had its unique sound and drawbacks. With the FN-USPL, you needed a fair amount of power. That required extra fuel cells to be carried, like in a clip. Plasma weapons were similar in their power needs and had limited range and speed. The advantage was their devastation to almost any material, from armored steel to human flesh. KRISS Vector EM1s used power to generate the EM pulse that fired the flechettes, so it needed ammunition and power as well. Of the three, it was the lightest and most durable under battle conditions.

"EM1s. We're dealing with some serious folks here," Finley said as he took cover from the withering destruction of the weapons fired.

"2.0s?" the soldier next to him asked.

"If they are, then there is more to this than possible sabotage." Finley connected to the base. "Avery, we have heavy resistance at the generator plant. Possible 2.0 infiltration."

"Copy that. Stay on them and don't let them damage the generators." She knew it was a request based on hope and not logic, but things were spinning out of control. It was time to take some back. She watched the overhead drone feed as soldiers took cover from aggressive fire coming out of the power plant. Several fighters on the roof prepared to repel over the side into the fray. She called for the base to be put on DL1, for Defense Level One. That would put all troops at the ready and recall any that were not currently on base.

"We need to get inside the generator room now and secure it at all costs," she said over the COMMs system.

Two shooters were firing from behind the partially open double doors to the facility. Beyond the doors was a concrete cavern where three generators, powered by the force of water coming from the bottom of the dam, provided enough electricity for the entire city and its defenses. Each generator was roughly the size of a small apartment building, humming to its own tune and loud enough to hide the sounds of the battle outside. The turbines that spun up the generators had large pipes, which allowed the pressurized water in and out. Pipe conduit and control boxes littered the rest of the concrete space, illuminated by harsh HID lighting.

Once Finley's forward team repelled enough down the wall of the plant from the roof, they were able to dispatch the two fighters covering the front doors from above. Within seconds of that, the doors closed with a defining slam and lock. Finley and his soldiers charged forward, keeping an eye out for anything unexpected.

It took a moment to attach explosives to large doors and clear back to safety along with the soldiers who had repelled down. Finley gave the command, and the entrance doors blew off their hinges, opening a maw to the space inside and sending a cloud into the air. The heavy doors cartwheeled away and Finley followed that up with an SB3, a remote Stun Bomb. It zipped into the facility on four wheels and detonated. That was their cue to get inside and quickly, before any fighters on the other side recovered.

"On me," Finley cried as he charged into the building and dove right. Half his squad followed while the other half went left.

When the two shooters at the door fell, Weng ordered the doors closed and locked. He had his force pull back to predetermined defensive positions and prepare to be breached.

Once the doors were blown, he ordered all his men to fall back in anticipation of some type of non-lethal explosion. Sure enough, as if he had planned the assault himself, a small remote bomb on wheels whizzed into the room and exploded. The intensity was off the charts, leaving several men who had closer positions incapacitated. As their brains tried to reboot from the concussion and bright flash, Weng and his men reset to their forward positions. They let loose with a barrage of fire as bodies poured into the room. Two went down almost immediately before the rest found cover.

It was now a matter of tactics and luck as each side fired at the other from protected positions.

"Time," Weng yelled.

"Five minutes," came the reply from Singh.

"Okay, controlled retreat. I want everyone to work their way back to Charlie position. Covering fire as we go."

Charlie position was a large metal transformer near the roof access ladder. As weapons fired back and forth between the two groups, occasional screams told of the slow but steady attrition of bodies on both sides. This was not a war Weng could win with only six warriors and a major who had flexible alliances. That versus the twenty or so fighters bearing down on them.

Singh let out a humph as she fell to the floor with an arm wound and rolled out from her place of cover. She was dispatched where she lay with a laser blast from the left. Weng had no choice but to retreat, as the rate of fire in his direction was withering. He fired over his shoulder on the run, leaving Singh behind in a growing pool of her own blood.

"Make your shots count. I don't want to be responsible for taking out the power grid." Finley ordered, as his team slowly advanced on the smaller enemy.

Avery listened to the COMMs's chatter as she tried to figure out what was happening with Finley and his squad. The view from the overhead drone showed nothing but a dam and a power plant. Did she need to send more soldiers? That was unclear, but what was clear was the need to act and act now. She raised the threat level to DL2.

That would put pilots in their fight suits and gunners hauling ammunition and fuel cells to their weapons. They could react at a moment's notice, should something happen. Soldiers reported to their commanders for orders and disbursement. Armored vehicles started their engines and ran full checks on their weapons systems.

Dr. Patel stepped into the room and approached with concern on her face. "I may have made a rash judgment. I need to talk to you right now."

"Not a good time, Doc," Avery said as she looked over to the soldier manning the drone on station.

"Lieutenant Merrill, see that Dr. Patel is escorted back to her lab and stays there."

"No. I need to talk to you right now about Jericho."

"He's no longer my concern."

"He needs to be, Avery."

"That's an order, Doc." Avery turned her back on Dr. Patel and refocused on the action taking place down by the dam.

Helen couldn't wait any longer. She dashed to the back of the facility where there was an access ladder to the roof. It was the only other way out.

Movement caught Finley's eye, and he tracked a form behind a row of conduits and squeezed the trigger just as a target moved between pipes, heading for the rear of the facility. A cry was heard as the body dropped to the ground, but it rolled out of sight before Finley could finish them off.

Helen's leg felt like it had been blown off, but when she looked down to inspect the damage, only a hole the size of a golf ball was evident. It wept blood, but most of the wound was cauterized by the laser blast. She was very familiar with this type of injury, and a close inspection revealed the blast had missed her femur. A small blessing. She looked around for her weapon. It had skittered off somewhere when she had been hit by her own side . . . well, her *old* side. She tried to stand, but her leg failed her, so she crawled away, toward the ladder. Each movement of her injured leg shot pain through her body.

The return fire seemed to die out, and Finley used the lull to advance their position, calling his troops forward.

The inside of the room was a labyrinth of steel and concrete, all built around the three giant steel generators. A person could easily hide here, and it would be difficult to find them.

Using a classic pincer move, Finley and his squad moved from two different directions, closing in on any saboteurs. One of his soldiers had discovered the engineers locked in a utility closet, and Finley put them to work, verifying the generators were okay.

Weng waited at the bottom of the ladder, making sure his team made it up and out. He was down to two warriors left out of the six he had brought.

He noticed Helen crawling over.

"Help me," Helen called out.

"Help yourself, Major," Weng said.

"I am the reason you are even here. You owe me."

"Owe you what? You turned on your people. What makes me believe you wouldn't do the same to us?"

"I wanna live, and you can believe me. I would never do that," Helen replied, the sweat on her face growing.

Her words seemed a bit desperate to Weng. "Okay, prove it. Get yourself up this ladder and I'll make sure you're taken to safety."

"I lost my weapon," she said.

Weng turned and scampered up the metal rungs without looking back. He felt no guilt for leaving the major behind.

Helen hissed at him, "Don't leave me!" She watched helplessly as Weng flew up the ladder. It made her double her efforts. She grasped the bottom of the ladder and pulled herself over. Then, one by one, she climbed the rungs. She used her hands and one leg to move up, while the other leg dangled painfully, dripping blood.

Weng cleared to the roof and slid over to his warriors staged behind an electrical box the size of a small car. On the other side were three soldiers looking over the roofline, focused on the fight below and covering their flank. He took aim. It would be like shooting fish in a barrel.

Three soldiers fell from the roof landing in front of the blown-out entrance. They were shot full of holes and hitting the hard ground from that height did the corpses no favors.

Helen made it three-quarters of the way up the ladder before her body was spent. She hooked an arm around the rung and hung there, catching her breath. Below her, soldiers that had once been under her command were now trying to kill her. She held still, hoping they would not look up and identify her.

A young soldier, clearing his section carefully and methodically, came around a control panel. His eyes saw a few drops of blood, and he followed the trail. It led to a ladder on the wall. His eyes tilted up, and he noticed a silhouette hanging about twenty feet up.

Helen closed her eyes, hoping the soldier would just go away.

Finley and his troops took their time, confirming the room was safe. There was no sign of the saboteurs.

"They didn't just walk out of here. Find them."

"Sir, I have someone on a ladder on the back wall."

Finley's eye shot to the back and scanned the wall. Sure enough, there was a person hanging on the ladder.

"Help me! I am Major Christine Helen. I was kidnapped and forced here against my will. Then shot and left to die. They went up the ladder, and this whole place is wired to blow."

Finley stepped over to the ladder. He considered Helen's plea for a few seconds and then pulled his weapon and shot her. The body dropped a bit and twitched, hanging there caught by an arm hooked on the ladder's rung.

"Sir, she was one of ours," the young soldier said.

"Would one of ours give up the access code to save her own skin? Would one of ours conspire with 2.0s to deceive us or would one of ours shoot back at us?"

"Never, sir," the young soldier replied.

"They're on the roof," Finley said without emotion. "Go." Three soldiers started to climb.

Avery had heard enough over the COMMs in the operations room. She hit the button for DL3 and took the base to the highest alert level, Defense Level Three. She had watched the surveillance drone's image as Finley's soldiers repelled down the face of the dam and onto the roof of the generator plant. Then additional troops moved toward the main entrance as some of the soldiers on the roof lowered themselves over the side of the plant. She could make out fighting from both sides and ordered the drone closer to get a better view of the action.

If the generators did go down, it would take about twenty to thirty seconds before the backup system would reset. Twenty seconds in a war could be a lifetime. Avery ordered several armored vehicles into the city to prepare to repel any unwanted guests. An alert to the outside guard towers had everyone in the bubble. All gates around the city were ordered closed and locked. Troops were sent to man the wall at key positions, and fighter drones were warming up in anticipation of an attack.

Finley could hear the klaxon in the distance. The entire base and city had just locked down for battle.

Once the fighting went inside, her surveillance drone moved up on station and hovered over the generating plant. There were three soldiers on the roof leaning over the wall to cover the exit in case a few squirters got out.

Everyone in operations was intensely listening to the words on the COMMs. Finley announced they had retaken the generators and everything was still working. A cheer went up, and Avery let herself breathe. Perhaps she had been overreactive to the situation but better safe than sorry. She reached for the switch to take the base back to DL1 and recall the soldiers back to base. Her hand paused above the switch, refusing to move. Something just didn't feel right.

As soon as the fighting stopped in the plant, Finley and his soldiers secured the generators and searched the premises for survivors. "Careful when you exit," he called up to the three soldiers nearing the top of the roof access ladder.

"Sir, you might need to see this," one of the engineers said, his body shaking.

Finley spun and followed the engineer with the scared look on his face. There was an electronic device attached to the panel, and it was ticking down. *12, 11, 10 . . .*

"Everybody out! We gotta bomb!" He didn't wait to see if his orders were being followed, and he didn't have time to transmit a warning over the COMMs. He just sprinted for the exit as fast as his legs would carry him. *3, 2, 1—*

The explosion was a hard, concussive blast with no flames. It was so violent that it disintegrated the panel it was mounted to. Several other blasts occupied the same second in time, leaving devastation and a complete failure of the electrical generating room. Finley was blasted out the door and through the air. The power of the detonation concussed him to blackness. His limp body rag-dolled across the pavement of the roadway, coming to a stop against the chain-link fence.

Weng and his men moved to the corner of the roof's building, hoping if it collapsed, they would be spared. They had placed the explosives specifically to do damage, not destroy the generators themselves, but when it came to explosives, there was always the unknown. Despite the power of the blast, the roof held, and Commander Weng and what was left of his team officially completed their mission.

Avery saw the explosion on the drone's camera just before alarms blasted through the control room. It was total chaos, followed by silence as the power shut down to the entire facility. A flash of fear cut through Avery as Finley's mortality became a reality. She pushed the emotion aside and called for the backup fuel cells. The confusion in the operations room quieted as everyone waited as the twenty-second reset ticked down. Time slowed, making each second seem like an eternity. Until the power rebooted, they were blind and helpless, but most of all, the protective grid over the city was down. Avery screamed orders, most of which could not be followed until the power was back on. The screen she had been watching was black, and she continued to stare as if that might help speed up the transition of power.

Colonel Smyth began firing at the defensive towers the moment his Stryker cleared the trees. A force of thirty Strykers was no match for the four towers set up near the West Gate, and within ten seconds return fire ceased. One burst into flames and another toppled over. Several of the Strykers tried their hand at firing on the West Gate, but their weapons were ineffective against the laser containment grid.

"Concentrate on the gate," Smyth ordered, as everyone raced for the entrance.

The first few seconds of focused fire on the gate resulted in complete failure as the grid absorbed the heavy fire. Then, as if a curtain had been lifted, damage started to show on the gate. The laser containment grid was down; however, soldiers on the wall could still shoot. The sky lit up with crossfire as the sun set. Several Strykers were hit and disabled, but the intense fire on the West Gate collapsed it, along with a section of the wall.

"All units get to the other side of that wall, stat!" Smyth called out over the COMMs. He knew they had a limited time to get inside before the grid was back up. They bounced across the plowed fields and through a few shanties before crossing the roadway into the city. His mental countdown dropped below eight. The people living just outside the city ran for their lives but were picked off before they could get to safety.

Katrina held on tight as the Stryker bounced and swayed. She could do nothing more until it was time to exit the vehicle. For now, it was hang on and pray.

Captain Yellin was young for his rank but had made his way up the ranks of the 2.0s Fighting Air Force with a natural leadership quality quickly recognized by his commanders. He watched as his two squadrons of manned drones flew low into the late afternoon sun. Their formation was that of an upside-down *V*, keeping low just above the terrain. The ships were loaded with weapons as part of the pincer movement on Zion City. An umbrella of unmanned drones was up front, leading the way. Further back, Vortex TT transport ships carried more warriors for the hard fighting that would be inevitable on the streets of the city. It would be close, but most of the fighters and drones would clear the grid when it went down for twenty seconds. Timing was hard, and today, it would offer no leeway.

The transports who didn't make it in before the grid re-powered up would have to hover and hold until ground fighters could take the military base and turn it back off permanently.

Their orders were quite clear: minimal damage to structures unless absolutely necessary. Someone up the ladder wanted to reuse this city when the fighting was over.

Three drones hit the grid and blew up. Captain Yellen was about to order a holding pattern when the next one flew harmlessly inside and began its pre-programmed routine, destroying as many enemy drones at the base as possible.

"The grid's down. All fighters, begin your attack procedures!" Captain Yellin ordered before banking right and heading for the defensive towers firing in their direction. The first transport of troops entered the city's airspace. The second was cut in half as it approached and the grid powered back up. The other troop carriers pulled up. They would have to wait on station until the grid was down again.

Plasma blasts and rail guns from the Strykers cleared a path through the city and over to the military base. Several Strykers encountered resistance from armored vehicles lying in wait. They exchanged fire, ending one or both, depending on the circumstances.

Smyth listened on the radio as hot-shot pilots and two squadrons of attack drones dove into the city and lit things up. Now that the laser containment grid was reactivated, they would have a limited altitude with which to fly in, and anyone going too high would be disintegrated. They used the first few seconds to blast from above before dropping down and getting more personal. It was like fighting in an upside-down cauldron.

"Emergency power restored," came a voice over the COMMs in the operations room.

It was followed by a bevy of voices, all overlapping as multiple attack warnings filled Avery's ears. "Get our fighters up! We are under attack! How long till the grid reboots?"

"Sixty seconds," called a voice behind her.

Avery noticed the screen in front of her had switched back on. It showed the surveillance drone's image, on station just above the power plant. She could see Finley's unmoving body and three men on the roof.

"Get me a closer view of those men," she ordered as she pointed to the screen.

The drone swept in closer. The tallest of the group moved into view. She could see his dark purple eyes and rugged American-Asian features just before he lifted his weapon and shot the drone out of the sky. The screen flashed black, and Avery flinched. She spun to see several 1.0 fighter drones leaving the base, just as a formation of 2.0 attack drones buzzed the tarmac and destroyed anything not yet in the air. It was followed by a second wave, concentrating on the facility's defenses and vehicles. "Get everything we have in the air now!" she cried.

The sky all around the base was filled with fire as fixed guns countered against fast-flying fighters—everything now trapped inside the containment grid. All of Avery's plans and training for this moment seemed suddenly irrelevant. She ran to the armored window overlooking the base below. Some soldiers ran for their lives; others ran to help out. Explosions and blood seemed to fill her vision. Movement ahead caught her attention as a large drone fired two missiles in her direction. Avery only had time to yell and dive right. "Incoming!"

The explosion that took out the operations room left Avery cut and bleeding. Several of the soldiers around her were dead. A smaller drone followed the devastation and flew into the room, dispatching anything left alive. Avery gathered herself and did the only thing that came to mind: run.

Within minutes, the base's defenses were no longer firing back at the attackers. Automated drones swept in, cleaning up any remaining resistance. The rest of the 2.0 forces shifted their focus toward the city. There would be only one outcome: the complete surrender of the city.

Commander Larry Weng and his two remaining warriors sat on the edge of the dam and dangled their feet off the side. They had a solid view of the battle going on across the lake at the military base and some of the city beyond. Weng popped the brown contacts out of his eyes, glad to be rid of them. He was no longer a man in hiding; he was a warrior, proud and true. Reaching into his breast pocket, he pulled out a small case and opened it. There were several cigars inside, which he passed out to his fellow warriors. They fired them up and watched as the city burned.

"To our fallen brothers and sisters and the peace their sacrifice will give us." He spoke the words with conviction. The other warriors joined him in sentiment.

"It's been a pleasure serving with you." The two warriors gestured with their cigars.

Aerial battles from manned and unmanned drones and fighters took a toll on both sides, leaving a little over half of the 2.0's drones still in the air. Most of the 1.0s were down, but they fought on with win-or-die programming. Avery pulled a rifle from a fallen soldier and grabbed his COMMs gear. "This is Avery; condition green, I say again, condition green. If you can hear this, get to Echo."

The coded message was a last desperate plea to save any remaining souls within the base. Dying for your cause was always worse than living for your cause. They would regroup and live to fight another day.

Avery turned and ran for escape tunnel Echo.

Smyth watched as his ground force of Strykers cleared out the more hardened defensive positions. Plasma weapons were the most effective against the Strykers' hardened armor, so the 2.0s concentrated their attack on any such weapons.

Once they cleared the West Gate, the division of Strykers had moved in a coordinated ballet, each following their orders set out in the battle plan. Half the Strykers headed for the military base to eliminate any resistance and take command of it. The rest split up, going street by street until there was no more serious return of fire. At that point, the warriors exited the Strykers and went door to door for the final pass. Any return fire was met with severe aggression. The street fighting would take many hours. As the return fire grew silent, groups and families surrendered en masse. There were fewer 1.0 survivors than expected. Those who complied with the loudspeakers demanding their surrender and promising life were gathered into large groups. The plan was to place them behind ten-foot-high ion-fenced pens that would kill any airborne germs coming from the filthy humans and keep them contained. Some of the more troublesome were assigned transport numbers and awaited a trip back to New Kansas for Ion-Dome processing.

The lab was white and stainless steel, with a collection of modern equipment. But the equipment was only as good as the people using it, and the loss of the traitor, Dr. Hastings, had Giles behind schedule and out of sorts. He huffed as he stormed out the door, his girth making his breathing ragged. The remaining scientist, now properly motivated, shook with fear of failure. Giles knew they would find a way to meet his needs or die trying, as that was their only option. A quick look at his precious pocket watch did nothing to squelch his guile or his patience.

The latest outbreak, adenovirus 12, was not quite ready. They had successfully extracted it from its host and were able to grow it in the lab. Initial human testing was remarkable. It was very contagious and had a relatively high mortality rate, but releasing it without a proven vaccine would be catastrophic. The lab techs had assured him a finished working vaccine last week, but the computer sim runs showed a few flaws still present. They were close but not yet ready.

After his tirade, Giles was assured they would have something by the end of the week. Right now, good scientists were hard to find. He already lost his best. *If only Dr. Hastings hadn't . . .* He flicked on the wearable screen on his wrist and clicked through several angles and perspectives of the war in Zion. It all looked very positive. At least that was going well.

Giles decided he needed a distraction. Using his MindLink he called for his personal drone to take him home. A little debauchery for the next few hours would calm his angst. He let his mind drift over the latest girl he had picked off the streets. She had been sanitized and was now ready for a little fun. Though a bit younger than the rest, he was sure he could train her up or enjoy the pleasure of watching her expire right before his eyes if she displeased him. Both were a win for him and his libido. He could check back on the battle after he was appeased. His need to act wouldn't come until the fighting was over.

14

Katrina jogged down the Stryker's rear ramp and formed up into her squad. She was part of a team of twelve Sci Officers, tasked with moving through the city and eliminating any leftover biowaste that might be contaminated. That meant all humans and animals in their path, the wounded and the dead alike. The commander formed the team into three groups and assigned them each a section of the city. Any 1.0 that was down would get hit with an XL21 plasma-based discharge weapon and be ionized into atoms. She looked up. A multi-drone dogfight was going on in the air above her. They were dodging and diving in an attempt to best each other. And firing on civilians and other flying objects. The sky was alive, like a laser victory celebration with consequences.

The squad moved from street to street, staying behind the warriors who were clearing out the city. Katrina did her best to eliminate any possible contaminations. Families had been cut down running for their lives or standing their ground and fighting. It didn't matter. The smell of plasma-burned flesh filled the air, but once Katrina hit the bodies with her XL21, there was nothing.

Any 2.0 killed in the attack was tagged and readied for transport back to New Kansas.

A couple of times, stragglers opened fire on the various sci teams, but the warriors made quick work of the resistance, and the squad continued their mission, one block at a time.

After all the heavy fighting and lack of sleep over the last few days, Katrina was near her breaking point. She headed back to the rear support for fresh fuel cells. Her weapon had grown hot from so much use. She guzzled some water, then pulled her bio-suit helmet off to get some fresh air. There was none to be found as the harsh smell of battle stung her senses.

The body count was staggering, and even though the people they were killing looked just like them, she knew they were dangerous to her existence. She would take every precaution.

Soon, the 2.0 warriors controlled the military base and shut down the laser containment grid. Now, it would be easy coming and going for the rest of the troops. Attack drones finished their runs and landed on the tarmac of the base. Resupply drones were on the way, and it would be a matter of minutes before the fighters could be reloaded, recharged, and put back in the air. The transport ships dropped off additional warriors to help across the city.

Avery fired at three 2.0s who were closing in from behind. Her head pounded and there was blood streaming through one eye, but she didn't let that stop her. As she neared the emergency escape tunnel, Echo, military and civilian 1.0s could be seen entering. Some limped; others held tightly to wounds leaking their lifeblood onto the ground. It was bad and only going to get worse. A nervous guard at the entrance seemed antsy to leave.

"Make sure we get everyone out before you seal the entrance, understand?"

The soldier nodded at the councilwoman's orders, feeling his spine straighten. He would do his duty. As the last few bodies approached, he heard shots following them. Without hesitation, he hit the self-destruct button and ran for the other end of the tunnel. A muffled explosion collapsed the entrance to the tunnel behind him, sending a cloud of dust hurtling for the only exit.

Finley forced himself to sit up. He had somehow survived the explosion of the power plant and was now witnessing a brutal attack in the skies above Zion. The sun had gone down and only emergency lighting was in effect. He tried the COMMs but got no response. Grabbing a weapon next to a fallen mate, he stood and checked the other soldiers around him who had also escaped the blast. Only one was still alive: Carmine. He rousted him up, and the two stood for a moment, watching the battle in the sky. They climbed the fence and headed for the stone and steel wall that surrounded the southern tip of the city. The troop and weapons monorail that circled the wall would not operate on emergency power, so they would have to get back to the base on foot. The wall was still the fastest way, and being up above the fray would give them a tactical advantage. Every hundred yards, there was a staircase giving access to the city's protective wall from the inside. Finley led the way and paused just before the top to make sure it was clear. No 1.0s or 2.0s in sight. All the fighting was now concentrated on the other side of the lake. Once on top of the wall, the two soldiers did a clockwise jog, unsure of what they would find ahead.

Colonel Smyth stepped from the ramp of his Stryker. His men fanned out and made sure the area was safe. He had led his regiment to victory, and only a few shops and homes were left to clean up in his sector. He wanted to take part in the action before there was no one left to kill. A lifetime of leading without boots on the ground had earned him the moniker "Colonel Desky." It was never said to his face, but when he was not around, it was a different story.

Smyth was determined to prove himself as a true fighter, and today was that day. He pulled his EM1 out and followed as his men cleared a small apartment building that was putting up some resistance.

The warriors opened a path through the front doors and went door to door as they eliminated any threats. Emergency lighting gave the rooms a dim red glow. Those who'd surrendered were already being processed. The remaining occupants felt they had nothing to lose and battled for their lives and families. It was a give-and-take of bodies on both sides of the fighting as the warriors moved through the building.

On the third floor, the last of the shots rang out. They had lost two men, and another was wounded, but the building was cleared. The problem was Smyth never had the chance to fire his weapon. Every time he saw a target and pointed his gun, someone else beat him to the shot. A cry from an apartment on the left caught his attention, and he entered it, ordering his men to wait for him. He would clear this one himself.

There were an adult male and female dead in the kitchen and a small baby crying from a baby-walker in the adjacent room. Smyth was afraid to touch anything in the 1.0's apartment but his bio-suit made him feel safe enough to be inside with a crying baby. Who knows what it was carrying? He pulled his weapon up and aimed it at the infant. This would be a good way to finish his part of the city's assault. His orders were clear: the complete eradication of any 1.0s fighting back, and this baby was putting up a heck of a wail. He looked at the filthy creature, helpless and angry. It would be an easy kill.

Smyth flexed his finger, but before he could watch the results of his action, something tugged at his back. He looked down to see a hole in his bio-suit. A feeling of shock coursed through his body as thoughts of contamination flared. He backed away from the crying baby. As he spun around, he saw a small child of about five holding his parents' weapon. That's when he realized he had been shot. Before he could re-aim his weapon, the child fired again, and Colonel Smyth fell to the ground. He watched as his warriors streamed into the room and eliminated the child. The last thing Smyth heard before his world went black was the small baby stop crying and start laughing.

Weng tossed his spent cigar into the water below. The sky was a darkening shade of purple as the last of the sun's light disappeared under the horizon. Emergency lighting popped on around the city, giving his new world a reddish-orange glow. He stood up and looked down at the two men who had risked everything to help make this day happen, good men with fighting spirits and brave hearts.

He knew all three of them would have to be quarantined before being allowed back into society. Worst case, they were contaminated and wouldn't live another week. Best case, they would be bored to death in a confined space for the next week or so.

Right now, they could join their brethren in the fight for Zion. They would have to procure bio-suits of their own first, but Weng was done fighting. He had sacrificed enough, and it was time to focus on more important things. He had promised Ruth an end to the war, and that was all but assured now. Peace would soon follow, and a warrior commander during a time of peace was a paper pusher—something with very low appeal for Weng.

"Should we try to link back up and see if we can lend a hand?" one of the warriors asked.

Weng let the words hang in the air for a bit before answering. "Let's find command and see what's needed."

The three warriors headed across the top of the dam toward the wall on the far side. Smoke from the downed generator plant climbed into the air behind them.

Giles ducked as an explosion took out the front of a building. The image was so realistic, he had forgotten he was still back at his office watching the fighting.

"Phew, that was fantastic!"

He was feeling good again after his self-induced respite from the day's regimen. The young girl he had enjoyed lay in the corner, bruised and weeping softly; she would recover.

An alert on Giles's MindLink connected him to a virtual image of Cin.

"Looks like he's done it, sir," Cin said. She was standing in some type of concrete bunker, obviously away from prying eyes and ears. "The fight is going our way."

Just then, a Stryker blew up on an image to the right as a squad of warriors ran into a large high-rise, weapons raised and ready. To the left, on another projection screen, was a scene of families huddled together and being escorted into one of the many holding pens set up around the city. It was a cornucopia for the eyes with so many images, and Giles had a hard time focusing on any one for very long—let alone Cin's face.

"Yes, I think you're right, Cin. Get back over to Caleb's side. I want to be informed of everything he does from here on out. Use the secure text."

"Of course. What do you want done with the prisoners?"

"I'll be sending clinicians and injectors to administer the latest vaccines as soon as the fighting has died down. We'll also be erecting LIFE-ARCHes throughout the city, and I expect the president to pave the way for that."

"I'll make sure he does."

"See that you do. Oh, and Cin? I know you've been patient and loyal. The timing for a change is close; you are not being led on."

"Understood, sir."

He watched as her firm figure vanished. He'd once had a taste of her, some time back. Now she was too valuable to waste on physical pleasure. He planned to make her president of Zion. It would weaken Caleb's position and strengthen his. Two puppets for the price of one.

A large collection of go-bags and survival gear were stored in a side shaft at the end of the escape tunnel. Avery put on a backpack and flowed out with the others doing the same into the darkness beyond the wall. It was a good 300 meters to the forest, where they could disperse into the night. The open field between the woods and the city would give them no cover. To her right, one of the guard towers burned like a Roman candle. The first shots from the top of the wall dropped fleeing 1.0s as they ran over the uneven ground. It was target practice for the warriors now occupying the higher ground. Some bodies dropped as others, unharmed, ran for the safety of the tree line. It was anybody's guess who would die and who would make it.

Finley heard the EM1s being used up ahead on the wall. He and Carmine sprinted to intervene. Eight warriors on top of the wall were so focused on the running human heat signatures on their heads-up displays down below, they never saw

Finley and the soldier approach. They wasted little time eliminating the 2.0s where they stood. Soon, eight bodies were piled like a teenager's dirty laundry.

Finley pulled one of the heads-up displays off of a dead warrior and looked over the wall. On the field below, he could see the remnants of a once proud human force dedicated to the survival of original man. It was heartbreaking. He spied Avery moving among the lost souls, and his heart skipped a beat seeing her still alive. She had nowhere to go and nothing to fight back with; it was over, and so were they. All they could do now was run, hide, and survive.

"Carmine. See if you can find a rope or something to get us down this wall."

Carmine searched as Finley watched Avery make it to the tree line. At least he could go out fighting by her side.

A series of shots from behind lit up Carmine, and he collapsed in front of the heap of bodies. Finley dove behind the corpses, out of sight. Three men were heading in his direction, firing as they went. He checked his weapon. Its battery was at five percent, and he had no more fuel cells. Carmine's gun was on the other side of the corpses, but he would never get to it unscathed.

The EM1s the warriors had been using would have to do. He grabbed one of the fallen weapons and took aim to return fire. Nothing. It was personalized to each warrior through thumbprint and biometrics. He pulled the hand from the fallen warrior toward him and placed it on the gun—still nothing. No pulse, no weapon.

During all this drama, the three warriors had closed the gap significantly. Finley grabbed his old gun and returned fire, hoping it would last.

The three warriors had little coverage on the top of the tower, and it didn't take long for Finley to pick two of them off. That's when his gun showed E, with one more warrior hunting him. He pulled the trigger several more times, hoping it might give him a last random shot, but nothing. The warrior on the other side stood and approached. He recognized the desperate actions of his prey. Keeping his gun leveled, he stalked toward the man hiding behind the pile of bodies.

"This is the end of the road for you," Weng called out.

Finley stood up; there was no place left to hide, and frankly, hiding was not how he wanted to go out. It was time to face his enemy head-on. "Who are you, and why do you not have on a bio-suit?"

"I don't fear what I can't see."

Finley was a formidable man made of muscle and experience. He stepped slightly sideways, trying to make himself a smaller target.

Weng stopped about twenty feet away. The emergency lighting was poor, and Finley's silhouette hid his expression. On the other hand, Weng was clearly illuminated.

"Was that you back at the generators?" Finley asked.

Weng gave him a slight nod, never lowering his weapon.

Finley marveled at his foe's distinctive purple eyes. The man's face held nothing but confidence. "Why do you hate us? All we want to do is exist."

"Your existence means our extinction," Weng replied.

"You look too smart to believe that. We are not who you think we are."

"What I believe is irrelevant. I have orders, so what I do is what matters," Weng said. "Today, it's the end of your kind."

"Said the robot to the human."

"You 1.0s are so caught up in your 'original man,' you can't see the future standing right in front of you. We were meant to evolve."

"How's that working out for you? Slaves to the big corporations and those with the power and money? Sounds more like de-evolution," Finley said.

"Every society has its problems," Weng replied.

"True. I just don't think hatred should be one of them."

Both men stood in silence for a second. The sliver of the moon waned in the sky. Growing fires from the battle below added a ghoulish glow.

"I could give you a chance," Weng said as he gestured to his weapon, lowering it slightly.

Finley was no slouch and at six-foot-four and 230 pounds, he stood taller and wider than Weng. His opponent had just made a fatal mistake. "I'm a soldier sworn to protect the people I love, and I'll kill you for what you have done today."

"You can try," Weng replied. "But killing me won't change the outcome of today. Maybe neither one of us has to die for our cause because soon, the only cause will be mine."

Finley took a fighting stance.

Weng looked at the man. His opponent was filled with emotion and ready to act. All Weng felt was apathy. He had killed and murdered in the name of his president and his people. He just wanted it all to end, but as soon as the man across from him moved into the light, Weng could see in the man's eyes what was going to come next.

"Okay, you asked for it. Soldier to soldier, I'll give you that." Weng lowered his gun and leaned it against the wall.

The two titans moved cautiously back and forth, each waiting for the other to attack first. Weng had the advantage of his upgrades with muscle speed, advanced eyesight, and a new arm, capable of removing the roof from a car.

Finley led out with a front kick to the chest. Weng knocked it away and took a step back to reset his distance. Fighting for him was all about range. Distance to target, based on weapons and location. He would keep close enough to strike his opponent but not too close, where he might get trapped by the massive arms of this man. A choke-out would be a death sentence, no matter how good his enhancements were. He snapped Finley's head back with a few lightning-quick jabs and followed them up with a cross from his new arm. Finley went flying, barely able to keep his feet.

Finley shook his head, and blood poured from his mouth. He'd never been hit so hard in his life. "What in the world was that?"

"Just one of my many upgrades," Weng responded.

Finley stood, tasted the blood streaming from his lip with a finger, and moved back into the fight, feeding on the pain.

"Okay, so you got a few upgrades. Let me show you what a real man can do." Finley faked a punch, then followed it up with a dive to Weng's torso. Weng sent a forearm blast into the man's spine, but Finley resisted the jolt and grabbed Weng up in a vice-like grip, lifting him up in the air before slamming him down on the ground.

An audible sound flew from Weng as his back and head smacked stone.

Finley jumped on top of Weng and pummeled his face.

Weng found himself on the wrong end of a beating and needed to put a stop to it, quickly. He used his new arm to catch and crush Finley's left hand. It was enough for him to roll away from his predicament, and he stood quickly to reengage.

Finley cradled his useless hand and realized the true danger he was in. This was not what he thought it would be. He continued to fight with just one hand and two deadly feet. It was enough to make mincemeat out of almost anyone else.

Weng hadn't liked the turn of events that had put him on his back and nearly caused him to black out. He changed tactics and went on the offensive. No more playtime. He used his speed to ring Finley's bell with a barrage of punches. Some so fast, Finley never saw them coming. Within a few moments, Finley was losing focus and starting to stagger. His arms were heavy, and blood covered his right eye. Finley wobbled, took one more hit, and fell to the ground.

Weng stepped over his opponent and pulled his tanto sword. This 1.0 had been all he could handle, but handle him he did. He wiped some blood dripping from his forehead. A flash of regret passed for just a second before he placed the point over the man's heart and pressed down. A sudden alertness from Finley had him fighting and grabbing to hold the blade at bay. "Your kind will never win. Your hearts are in the wrong place," he said with a final effort.

The razor-sharp blade sliced through his hands and pierced skin, bone, and heart.

"But your heart is in the right place," Weng said as he watched the man. Finley closed his eyes for the last time. Weng lingered for a moment. A brief feeling of regret came and went. He dropped to the ground and placed his hand on Finley's chest. "I'm sorry . . ."

Weng was conflicted. Everything he had been taught and believed seemed to be in jeopardy. He should be shaking with a deadly fever right now. These 1.0s weren't monsters, just humans who believed differently and were willing to die for those beliefs. *Beliefs.* What a waste of life that was.

Slowly, Weng stood, his eyes filled with doubt. He reached for his sword but stopped short. This was the last comparable 1.0 he would ever meet. He left the sword where it lay, a sort of memorial to the soldier. From here forward, he was done with killing. Unfortunately, killing was not done with him.

A boom in the distance sounded off, waking Geena.

"Is that thunder?" she asked as she held Holly close.

"Could be. Go back to sleep," Jericho answered, wondering which direction the sound had come from.

A small campground with a withering fire was set amongst trees. A large boulder, shaped like a dying mushroom, reflected its heat back. Jericho was on one side of the fire, and Geena was on the other. The fear on her face was illuminated by the meager flames.

There was silence for a moment as Jericho strained his ears to hear more—nothing but a few crickets and an owl off in the distance. Humankind might have nearly wiped itself out, but nature was quick to recover.

"I need a story," Geena voiced.

"What?"

"I need a story to go to sleep. My mom always told me a story."

"Do I look like your mom?" Jericho replied.

Silence followed, and soon a soft crying started.

"I'm sorry. Too soon, I know. . . . What kind of story?" he asked.

"A kid's story."

"You're the only kid I know."

"Really?" Geena questioned.

"Really."

The fire popped, and Geena sat up further. "Any story then."

Jericho leaned over with a sigh. "Well, there was this intelligence that I used to work for."

"Intelligence?"

"Like a computer."

"You worked for a computer?" Geena asked, suddenly curious.

"Look, I'm telling the story. That means you shut up and listen, okay?"

Properly chastised, Geena came back with a meager, "Okay."

"So I used to work for this computer, and she was a real hard-nosed boss. Up at six every day. Lights out at ten. Always asking me questions and pushing my buttons."

"You have buttons?"

Jericho gave Geena a stern look.

"Sorry," she said meekly.

"Anyway, she was always on me . . . what about this or what about that."

"Sounds like a mother," Geena said.

"Yeah. Well, I tore the arm off an E-Chung and beat her sensors to death with it. That was a good day. No more questions."

Geena just stared at Jericho. Her big, open eyes filled with fear, waiting for something more, something that would comfort her, but she was met with only silence. She rolled away from him, holding Holly tightly, trying to forget his story and go back to sleep.

After a beat, a small voice croaked. "It must have been lonely."

"What?" Jericho asked.

"Having a computer for a mom."

Jericho felt a surge of emotion course through him at all the memories.

"Yeah, it was." He lay back down, his mind returning to the many possibilities the *boom* could have been.

Katrina sat on an ammo box in a spot of shade at the 1.0's old military training grounds. Her team had been recalled to the base about an hour ago, awaiting reassignment. She was totally spent. The night had come and gone, and the sun was beating down from above, cooking anyone who spent too much time in a bio-suit under its heat.

Her squad had ionized so many bodies, she'd lost count. A moving shadow from overhead caught her attention, and she looked up to see the presidential transport escorted by three fighter drones lowering to the ground. Dust and hot wind made her squint as she watched it land on the tarmac just to the left of her. Curiosity won out, and she moved to get a better look.

President Caleb was all smiles as he peacocked down the ramp of his craft. A collection of the high and mighty seemed to gather and fawn over his presence. A woman with a sleek figure and short white hair was orchestrating data collectors documenting the President's arrival.

Katrina figured today was the day for cashing in on publicity and handing out "atta boys" from the boss. It seemed as though everybody wanted one.

After searching the crowd for several moments, her heart sank. There was no sign of Commander Weng. She owed him an apology for her date no-show, and if she was honest, maybe more. The knife he'd given her had saved her life.

Katrina returned to her ammo box, no longer interested in the politicking and speeches that would come next.

The 1.0's operations room was a mess of blood and glass. Sanitation crews were doing their best to make it usable. Caleb walked past them into the adjoining office, once used by Councilwoman Avery. He was back to his old self after his brief bout with death as he listened to the reports streaming in from the clean-up actions around the city. Orders were dispatched as fast as info came in. Sporadic fighting in the city continued, but with each hour's passing, it lessened.

Caleb knew it would be critical to maintain a large force here to prevent any undesirables from moving back in. Once they got the power permanently back up, they could reengage the laser containment grid and protect the city. He had ordered a team of engineers to repair the power plant with all haste. In the meantime, declining anarchy seemed to be the order of the day. He put Cin and a few generals in charge of getting his wishes followed, hoping to add some sanity to the transition of power. Cin left the room, eager to get started, including adding a few demands of her own on the downstream, knowing Zion would soon be hers. Giles's promise meant this city would need to be remade in her image, not Caleb's. With a bit of cleverness and back-door deals, she could get things started.

Calls soon came in from the CEOs, congratulating Caleb in the first sentence and clamoring for their share of the new city in the next. Once they had converted Zion to a safe place for 2.0s to live, they could start collecting on their investment. It was going to be a busy few weeks, and those responsible for the numbers were trying to get an idea of what they were dealing with.

Cin rushed back in with an anxious face.

"What is it?" Caleb asked as he swiveled from his view of the window.

"Mr. President, I think you can officially claim a complete victory. The city is officially ours. There are some minor holdouts, but it is over."

"Great news, Cin. Get me in contact with my generals. I want to congratulate them personally. Today is the beginning of a whole new way of life for our people."

Cin nodded but didn't move.

Caleb gave her a crooked glance.

"Sir, he is requesting your presence," Cin said.

"He is huh?" Caleb replied. "I guess I might as well get this over with." Caleb left the room and followed her down a stairway to a lower floor. They went through several hallways and turns before coming to a door with the label *Security*.

Caleb stepped through the door and paused. On the other side of a plexiglass wall was the hero of the day . . . Commander Larry Weng. He was secured in a small room with a cot and a pot.

At the sight of Caleb, Weng stood and approached the glass.

Caleb kept his distance. "You continue to surprise me, Commander."

Weng watched the president, not sure how to take the comment. Caleb looked unusually tired, but there was no mistaking the manufactured veil he portrayed on his face.

"How are you feeling?" Caleb asked.

"Actually, I feel great," Weng replied. "Doc says I have five days in quarantine before I can go home."

"I might be able to do something about that." Caleb smiled. "Your actions made all this possible, and I won't forget that." Caleb took a tentative step closer to the plexi-wall separating the two men. He was still leery after his recent exposure and sickness, compliments of Giles's latest power play. "We have reports of a fairly large contingent of 1.0s moving west from here. Apparently, they had an escape tunnel, and many got out before we could stop 'em."

"Is it really worth sending more men to die over a small batch of 1.0s that can do us no harm?" Weng asked.

"Harm? Are you kidding me? I nearly died from one of their viruses. No 2.0 will ever be safe as long as there is even a single 1.0 out there, carrying around a death sentence."

Weng kept quiet.

"You, of all people, with your precious daughter and her future, should want the same thing."

"Yes, sir." Weng deadpanned. "I was wondering if you could arrange for me to talk with her?"

"We currently have just over thirty warriors in quarantine from various incidents during the last few days." Caleb continued without responding to Weng's request.

Weng looked at Caleb as he finished his sentence for him. "And you want me to lead them in a cleanup mission?"

"Exactly right. I have made arrangements for you to use a section of the base separated from the rest of us to plan and execute your new mission, Commander."

"Why not just send in some drones and take 'em all out?"

"We could do that, but once the shooting starts, the 1.0s will scatter, and we'll have a devil of a time rounding them up. Computer models estimate a forty percent reduction in their population using drones. I want one hundred percent. You go in there, surround 'em, and make sure no one gets away. You can use the drones as support and initial engagement, understand?"

Weng thought about the ragged 1.0s he'd seen from the wall, running from Zion in the night, and the man he had killed with his sword. Killing refugees seemed below him. *After all, I helped bring an entire city to its knees. Let someone else mop up the stragglers. This wouldn't be war, it would be murder.*

"Let me know what you need, and I'll make it happen," Caleb said, interrupting Weng's thoughts. "We are *this close* to being done. Help me get over the finish line for us and your daughter. What was her name again?"

"Ruth," Weng answered.

"Of course, such a lovely girl."

"She means the world to me. You *are* taking care of her while I'm away?"

"We're not barbarians. She is safe. In fact, I would be happy to set up a COMMs link so you can speak with her."

"Yes, please," Weng said. "I would also like to see a Sci Officer Katrina if you could arrange that."

Caleb paused before answering. "I'll see what I can do," Caleb added. "Out of curiosity, who is this Katrina to you?"

"She saved my life when I lost this." Weng held his enhanced arm up. "And beyond that, it's none of your business."

Caleb looked Weng over, trying to read between the lines of that statement. He nodded slightly and left the room, trying to decide his next move.

Weng watched him go. *Another mission.* When would his sacrifice be enough? He had given everything, and his mental picture of a better world was changing.

15

The sun rose on a hazy, smoke-filled Zion like a blanket being lifted from a bed. The sound of fighting was over, and the city's normally active rhythms were eerily left behind. The battle for the precious city had taken less than twenty-four hours. Clean-up and sanitation crews were going street by street. A few random acts of looting and violence took place overnight, but most were put down quickly with deadly prejudice.

There were still concerns about infection, and no safety measure was overlooked. Stacks of fallen warriors had been labeled and readied for transport back home on ships that cycled to and from New Kansas with regularity. Any dead 1.0s were disintegrated where they lay, and those still left alive were gathered in large groups the size of a city block. Ion fencing was erected around them with the current set to kill. Anyone coming within two feet of the fence beams would not survive it. The 2.0 guards were taking no chances.

Cin stepped from the concrete building, shielding her eyes from the bright morning haze. The air was still foul. She led President Caleb to his waiting transport, and the two climbed on board. A soft humming rose in volume as they strapped in. President Caleb looked out the window as they lifted off, getting his first real look at the post-battle city. Most of the fires had been dealt with, and he was surprised by the number of buildings still standing throughout the city. The warriors had really come through for him. He would make sure they had a robust meal tonight.

If reports were correct, this was the first city not totally destroyed by a battle between the 1.0s and 2.0s. Zion would be up-cycled in the image of New Kansas and help alleviate overcrowding. Caleb also wanted to get a good look at the laser containment grid. He had envied the technology, and now it was his. With two major cities to run, protect, and control, he would be the face of the new world.

Cin looked out the other window as they flew toward the city. This would all be hers soon. She let her mind fill with the many things she would implement once in power. Giles was known for being loyal to those who served him faithfully, and she had strived to do just that, sacrificing her own needs and wants along the way. She let a small smile dance across her lips at the thought of what was to come.

The military base partially built into the rock moved from their view as they passed the small lake and dam on the southern end of the city. Caleb had a team down in the generating plant, trying to get it back up and running after Commander Weng's squad had successfully sabotaged it.

As the transport arced, she saw the city to the north. It was compact and had a balance of modern and old, the river drawing a line through the middle like a fence. Here and there, buildings were destroyed; a couple of the taller ones had taken out other buildings next to them as they collapsed. They both saw points of smoke billowing in the north. Overall, the city looked remarkably intact.

"Reports have seventy percent of the infrastructure still intact. Another ten is repairable, and the rest will have to be demolished and rebuilt," Cin announced.

"Seventy percent, huh? That's good news," Caleb replied, without turning his head from the window. "Get those fires out and more manpower down there. I want this city ready for occupation as soon as possible."

From Caleb's vantage point, it looked like a board game, ready for him to set up the pieces and dictate the players and profits.

Cin nodded more to herself than the president.

Jericho paused and called for Geena to do the same. He was sweaty and hot. They had hiked most of the day and were getting tired. It was time to look for a place to stop for the night. He looked around, sticking his nose in the air and inhaling.

"What is it? Geena asked.

"You smell that?"

Geena sniffed the air and came up empty. She shook her head.

"Smoke. And where there's smoke . . ."

"There's fire?"

"People," Jericho corrected. "The question is, what kind of people? Come on, stay close."

They carefully made their way through the trees and over to the top of a wedge-shaped ridge. Down below was a small town, and it was occupied. People roamed around doing various chores, while others sat and chatted with each other. The buildings looked weathered and beaten, but one could expect that in a place like this.

Geena started to stand and head down. "People . . . we're saved."

Jericho pulled her back down abruptly.

"What's your problem?" she hissed.

"Something's not right. See that fire by the stack of barrels?"

Geena let her eyes roam to the spot. A man was cooking some meat over a fire.

"Yeah, so what?"

"That looks like a human leg on that fire," Jericho said.

"Gross."

"We gotta get outta here. And now. Move," Jericho said, pulling Geena with him.

They backed away and turned, almost running into a group of eight scary-looking men from a hunting party. They were wearing loin-style clothes made from human skin. The one in the middle had a distorted face on his covering. Several sets of human teeth necklaces were around his neck, and his hair was shaved into a short mohawk. But most memorable was his size. He was huge. The man to his left smiled. His teeth were sharpened to points like some kind of animal. Each was armed and pointing a weapon at Jericho and Geena. That's when the wind changed directions and the smell became overwhelming. Geena bent over and puked.

This got a laugh from the group.

Jericho was trussed up like a pig on a pole and carried back to town. Geena had a noose placed around her neck and was escorted to the front of the group. They chatted back and forth in a guttural language that only occasionally resembled bad English. Jericho's arms ached as he swung from side to side as they walked down the trail.

As soon as others from the town saw the hunters return with food, they gathered around to see what was on the menu. Several poked at Jericho to see if he was meaty enough to eat. A few of the women circled Geena, stroking her hair and admiring her youthful beauty. After a few moments, an argument broke out, followed by a fight between two women. Everyone formed a perimeter to watch it. The two women tore and clawed at each other, ripping clothes and skin as they battled.

One had short, curly hair, shaved on the sides, and the other had long straight hair tied in the back. They were filthy, animalistic, and hadn't seen a bath in months. The fight lasted about five minutes, ending up on the ground as most fights do. The one with the short hair got a leg around the other's neck, and after much rolling and flopping in the dirt, snapped it. Cheers exploded as the audience approved. The long-haired woman went limp. Knives quickly came out from the bystanders, anticipating more meat. The short-haired woman walked over and claimed her prize: Geena. She pulled on the rope around Geena's neck, and as was her right, claimed the head of the woman she'd defeated.

Geena struggled to keep up as she was led back to a small shanty. The short-haired woman held her other prize by *its* hair.

Jericho tried to object, but a club to the back of his head finished his objections.

Geena was chained by her neck and locked to a post that supported the center of the rickety house from collapsing. She was given some unidentified meat and a bowl of water. The woman grabbed Holly, still clutched in Geena's arms. She looked it over and gave it a few sniffs, amid cries and protests from Geena, then without concern, threw the doll into the fire. Geena melted to the floor, her emotions raw as Holly burst into flames—the last vestige of her family burned to ash.

The woman turned and began braiding the dead woman's hair.

After a few minutes, half the dead woman's hair was braided into long rows. Geena squinted, her tear-stained face in disgust, as she watched, transfixed by the morbid display still softly crying.

Once the woman was finished braiding, she cut off the braids and wove them into her own hair, along with a few sun-bleached finger bones she had been drying outside. Now she could wear her victory every day. A smile came through rotting teeth as she turned and left Geena behind to strut through town with her new crown.

Jericho woke. One eye cracked open, followed by the other. It was dark. He was lying in some kind of room. He could just make out two other people staring at him from across the hard-packed dirt floor. They had ragged clothes and hollow looks on their faces. Jericho sat up and rubbed the knot on the back of his head. He was assaulted with the overwhelming smell of urine and fear.

"Hello?" he said, cautiously. His voice was dry and almost unrecognizable.

One of the prisoners scooted over next to him and reached out to touch Jericho. He swatted the hand away. That's when he realized it was a woman.

"How long have you been here?" Jericho asked her, the words making his head pound.

"Three days," said a voice from the other prisoner in the room.

Jericho could tell it was a male.

"What do they want with us?" he asked.

"They're gonna eat us. Yesterday, there were four of us. Tomorrow, they'll be one, and then none."

The woman reached out to touch Jericho again, and instead of swatting her hand away, he distanced himself from her. "What's her deal?"

"Estelle ain't right in the head. Ever since they hit her, she's been like this. Can't talk; can't stand up or walk."

"Did you know her before this?" Jericho queried.

"She's my daughter. I'm Tim."

"Sorry, Tim. I'm Jericho. So, how do we get out of here?"

The woman cackled.

"We don't. The walls are solid adobe; there are bars on the windows, and the door is made of metal."

"I see you've given this some thought."

"Yeah, I have, and if there was a way out of this place, I'd be long gone by now, but let me tell you something . . . if, by God's mercy, we did get out of here, there are at least eighty of those creatures out there, ready and willing to do anything to recapture us. Our best action forward is a merciful death, but since they like to torture their food before they eat it, that ain't gonna happen." He whispered the last words in total defeat.

Jericho stood and walked around the room. He noticed they had taken his multi-belt. The door was indeed made of metal, and there was no lock or handle on the inside. He gave it a good kick just to see; nothing happened but a throbbing in his foot. There was definitely a distinct smell of urine coming from somewhere.

He looked back around the room. It was small, maybe three by four meters. There was one small window, and it had steel bars across it. A soft, orange glow from a fire somewhere outside was the room's only illumination. The ceiling was beamed with chain-link fencing mounted to the wood as an extra precaution and just out of Jericho's reach. The floor was rock-hard, compacted dirt from too many years underfoot. He went to the window and leaned out. Several people dressed like the hunters who had captured him were out and about. There was a campfire off to the left, and he could see a group gathered there. One of them, the large man with the mohawk. He was wearing Jericho's multi-belt and seemed to be the center of attention. Jericho turned back from the window. "Do they feed us or give bathroom breaks?

The man in the corner finally stood up. He was tall and stooped from a lifetime of manual labor, but the things that caught Jericho's attention were his eyes—vacant. He was already dead, just didn't know it. "Are you kidding me? No water or food, and if you have to pee or whatever, we do it in the corner over there, like an animal." He paced for a bit and then sat back down. "Hope is not a part of our world anymore."

"Hope is a state of mind," Jericho said to himself.

"God has forsaken us." The man started weeping.

"A wise man told me once that God helps those who help themselves." Jericho moved to the corner where Tim had pointed during his rant. Sure enough, the smell of urine was strong there. The ground was wet from multiple people over the course of time using the corner to do their business. He unclasped his pants and added to it. As he sat there relieving himself, a thought born of desperation grew. He let the urine soak in for a few minutes, then tested the ground with his heel. It was soft, not like the hard pack on the rest of the floor. Jericho used his shoe to remove a few disgusting clumps and then dropped to his knees and started digging.

The bolt on the door slammed open, and the door swung in. Jericho sat, quickly covering the hole he had been digging with his butt. During the night, the firelight had been replaced by a silvery shaft from a nearly full moon. Finally, the warm glow of the morning sun appeared. The two creatures that opened the door never entered. They just beckoned to the father-daughter team, who exited the room as if in a trance. The girl crawled on her hands and knees. They were tired of living and looking forward to the possible peace of what lies beyond. Why they had only taken the two was a mystery to Jericho. *I guess there is some kinda cannibal priority system.*

Jericho had heard the father softly praying in the night and watched as he submitted himself to his end. It seemed like proof to him that prayer was useless—until he remembered Santos's words. *You have to do your part.* That's when he'd started digging.

He gave it a try and silently prayed that he might find a way out. The door slammed shut halfway through his thoughts, and Jericho cracked an eye to see he was alone. Immediately, he flipped around and began digging again. He was about two feet down from the bottom of the wall. His fingers were raw, and the ground had lost its moisture. What he needed was something to dig with. After a search, Jericho found a cracked piece of adobe block in the shape of a wedge. He pried it loose and used it to chip away at the hard-packed dirt. Inch by inch.

Geena rattled her chains. They were locked tight. She was hungry, but the meat in the bowl was putting off a foul odor. Luckily, the water next to it, though cloudy, tasted fine. The night was filled with terrors and haunting dreams. Eventually, Geena drifted off to sleep. She was awakened with a kick to the ribs, sending her from a fitful dream to a crueler reality, as yesterday's events came rushing back. Some muffled screams were heard, and the woman with the funky braids left the house.

Geena's situation, illuminated with the rising sun, had not improved, and no amount of wishing would change her circumstance.

Her new guardian was in and out of the hut all morning, constantly checking up on her *new pet* and even patting Geena on the head a few times. Geena stayed docile and calm, biding her time, trying to imagine a proper plan to escape. The keys to her prison were hanging above the door frame, a good five feet beyond her reach.

Geena stretched herself to the limits of her chains to get a look at what was happening outside. A gaunt man and a pale woman were being pulled to the center of a group of people. The male was being strung up on a post mounted in the ground, while the woman was strapped to a steel shaft and hung like a rotisserie. A small fire was built under the woman, and Geena looked away, hearing the pleading moans of the man.

Geena pulled back, having seen enough. It took some time, but soon the air was filled with shrieks and screams the likes of such Geena had never heard before. She muffled a few sobs and tried to concentrate. The room was dark; the only light coming through the open doorway. She could hear the crowd get excited. *Focus!*

To her left was a table with the shaved head of the dead woman. Her dry eyes still gazed at nothing. To the right were a bed and a frayed blanket. The walls were aged wood, and the few shelves around them were filled with everything from dried plants and chipped pots to metal shears and rusty tools. A small shelf on the right held a collection of human trophies, like earrings and a couple of gold teeth. There were several buckles—one had a silver *A* with a leather belt attached—next to a small engraved flask.

She was a prisoner but not helpless. Geena remembered a game she used to play with her dad called "IF." They would set up a scenario starting with the word *if,* and the other person would have to come up with a solution to that scenario using only their mind. One time, her dad had asked her, "If you were taken by pirates and forced out onto the gangplank, how would you get away?" Her answer had been typical of a young girl. *Grow wings and fly away, of course.* She had then gone on to ask her dad, "If you were trapped in a spooky basement with a locked door and a ghost what would you do?" The thought of her dad rushed raw emotion to her frayed nerves, but she focused on his response. "Ghosts can't hurt you, so I'd forget about the ghost and find something in the room to help me open the door, like a hammer or screwdriver."

Geena let her mind fill with the things in the room. A plan formed as she asked herself, *If you were chained to a post in a small house and the keys were just out of reach, what would you do?* Once it became a game, she was able to think more clearly. Taking off her shoes, she stretched herself to the max, getting a toe on the blanket across the small bed. She curled her toes tightly and pulled back. The blanket moved a foot before she lost purchase.

Geena repeated the process several times before she was finally able to grab the blanket. She pulled at the corner and a thread started to unravel. After a few moments, she had ten feet or so of thread. She tossed the blanket back and proceeded to tie a small human bone she had collected off the floor to the end of the string. It was a simple knot made by small delicate hands.

She used the weighted end to swing and toss the bone toward the keyring hanging on the wall. It was a good three feet short. She pulled back the string and tried again, next hitting the wall. She continued for several more minutes until one of her tosses actually hit the keyring. It gave her renewed hope, and she tried to repeat the throw without success.

After twenty minutes of frustration, she stopped and let her emotions take hold. Hopelessness spouted tears that flowed until there was nothing left. Then, from the very bottom, she found herself and willed one more try. The crying had solved nothing.

After another ten minutes of frustration, there came the *clink.* The small bone caught on the keyring. It was the most glorious feeling.

She pulled carefully on the end of the string, taking out all the slack. A subtle tug wiggled the keys to the edge of their holder, but they refused to release. She

16

Sci Officer Katrina stepped into the room that used to be the 1.0's command center. Most of the battle's destruction had been cleaned up, but you could still see the blast marks on the walls. She was escorted into a side room, and the door closed behind her as she looked around. A silhouette of a tall, older man boldly scanned her body before stepping away from the window and into the light. It was President Caleb. Katrina released a verbal gasp and came to attention, saluting him.

"Mr. President, sir."

A sudden concern coursed through her body. *Why was she here?*

"Science Officer Katrina, nice to finally meet you in person. I hear good things about you," he said as he stepped closer. Caleb looked her over, taking a moment to size her up. She was a natural beauty who cared little for upgrades, or even makeup. The concern in her eyes was obvious, but the way she stood was bold and intriguing. If he was honest, he would give her an eight out of ten on his sexuality scale—points off mostly for the red hair. He wasn't a fan, but the rest was well within his demanding specifications. He tabled the thought for the moment.

"I've been looking over your file. You have done some solid work for the state."

Katrina had no reply. Something wasn't right.

"I understand you helped get Commander Weng to safety on the New Kansas mission two weeks ago?"

Katrina nodded as a slight squeak of "yes, sir" escaped.

"I'm wondering what is it you two have going?"

"*Going,* sir?" Katrina asked, with genuine confusion.

"Yes, between you."

Katrina saw no reason to lie. "Well, he took me out to lunch, and he gave me a knife for protection."

"And?"

"We've only seen each other a couple of times," Katrina recalled them with fondness. "So I can't really say, Mr. President."

"I see. And do you anticipate this going somewhere?"

"I'm not sure that is anyone's business," she replied, with her chin angled to the floor.

Caleb had his answer. He was fine with the commander and an occasional tryst, but this woman had feelings for him. Something Caleb needed to put a stop to before it became a problem for him.

He stepped closer to Katrina and raised his voice, "It's my business because Commander Weng works directly for me . . . and I have to know his mind and limit his distractions. He already has a daughter that takes up too much of his time. I need him focused and available, here." He pointed to himself. "Understand?"

The strong words scared Katrina, and she quickly covered her fear with a brisk whispered reply. "Of—of course."

Caleb turned and paced. *No, no, no. This can't be happening again. I won't let it happen again.* He spun back in her direction.

"Do you have any idea the mess his last female interest caused?"

"You mean his wife?"

"Yeah, that one. She had him ready to quit and head east for a new start. Had to put a stop to that, and I will do the same to you if you get too . . ." He let the threat fade off. It was better not to actually finish the words.

Katrina was breathing heavily now, not sure whether she should run or get ready to fight. She balled her fists and took a subtle fighter's stance.

Caleb turned and looked her in the eyes. "Keep your head down and your toes pointed forward, understand?"

"Yes, Mr. President," Katrina replied, not totally sure of his meaning.

"Now, get out of here. I never want to see your face again, and if I hear that you so much as looked in Commander Weng's direction, I will end your career and everything that goes with it." He watched her go, letting his mind firm around a proper course of action toward the young science officer. In his mind, she would never let things go, and so, neither would he.

Katrina practically ran from the office and out of the building. She tried to calm herself, but her heart was pumping too fast. Tears flowed against her will. She shook her arms and willed herself to put the last few minutes behind her. Had she heard right? Did President Caleb have something to do with the death of Weng's wife? *Drop it, Katrina. It will only cause more problems. The kind you are ill-equipped to handle. Everything you have worked so hard to achieve is at stake here.*

She let the demons in her mind battle out a resolution. In the end, screw the President; she needed to tell Commander Weng. She spun on her heels, just as two warriors arrived, hands on holsters.

"Sci Officer Katrina, please come with us," the older of the two warriors said. He was wearing sergeant's stripes.

Katrina looked like she might run.

"If you refuse to come. We are authorized to use deadly force!" The words were backed up by the guard on the right pulling his weapon and holding it low, at the ready.

Katrina's heart jacked back up. There was nowhere to run, so she put her hands up in supplication. "What's all this about?"

As the sun dropped for the day, Jericho knew he was close. His mini escape tunnel was three feet long and just wide enough to squeeze his torso through. It dropped down and under the adobe wall, then back up close to ground level, freedom on the other side. All that was left was to punch through the last eight inches or so. He would need to wait till the camp was asleep. His mouth was so dry that he could barely swallow. His mind wandered to a random thought: *Doesn't dehydration make the meat tougher?* He shook it away and refocused on his situation. The pile of loose dirt on the floor was now too large to hide, so he spent the next hour spreading it all around the floor and stamping it down with his feet. Hopefully, any guard feeling the need to check up on him wouldn't notice the subtle change in the floor's surface.

He had listened to the screams and terror of the two prisoners taken just after sunup. It was close to high noon before they stopped, and the smell of burning hair filled the air. It had spurred Jericho on, as no living human, or dead, deserved that fate.

As the camp quieted down, Jericho went back to work. It took another twenty minutes before the hole on the other side was big enough. He took a large gulp of air and committed to the tight tube of dirt, worming and clawing his way down and then back up, bending his torso to the limit. Jericho eventually emerged through the ground on the other side of the wall, like a seedling cracking through the soil. He gulped for air through dirt-encrusted lips as he shook off the excess from his hair and face. A cloud of dust obscured him for a second. He stood and quickly hugged the outside wall of his prison, letting his senses take in the surroundings. A small campfire burned off to the left. A few people sat around it, drinking and chatting. Jericho could not make out their words. The camp was otherwise quiet. Footsteps from the left closed, and Jericho tried to become one with the wall as a Reeker passed by. The man seemed preoccupied and just missed stepping into the exposed escape hole by inches.

Jericho finally took a breath and found an old rusted bucket nearby. He placed it on the exit hole, hoping to hide his tunnel for as long as possible. Then, with a mouse-like quietness, he crept away from the small village. He needed to get some water soon, or he was going to be in real trouble. As he neared the small rise south of town, he looked back at the Reeker village below. He would never wish them on his worst enemy. He turned to go and an invisible hand stopped him. Well, not so much a hand as a feeling. *Geena.* He dismissed the feeling and continued on. Take care of number one. Without another thought, he jogged away, trying to remember where he had last seen a stream.

Katrina was taken to a small room. There were two cots in the corner and a glow from a strip of light on the ceiling. "Remove your uniform," one of the men ordered.

Katrina did nothing.

"Remove your uniform, or we will do it for you." The man on the right pointed his gun at her.

"Turn around."

They didn't.

She slowly began removing her boots, pants, and shirt, feeling vulnerable in her underwear, standing in front of the two strangers.

They shared eye contact at the sight of the beautiful woman, exposed and ripe for the taking, but each knew his orders and the penalty for not fulfilling them.

Katrina held her chin up, trying not to show fear or any emotion.

"Put on these clothes. You have been discharged." The guard pointed to a pile of well-worn civilian clothes on the end of one of the cots. "You can keep the boots."

Katrina quickly dressed, thankful the situation had not been worse. She had placed all her eggs in the military basket and was now apparently a civilian. This would take some real planning, thinking, and determination to hit her reset button and start over. With a casual swipe, the president had tossed her career and everything she had worked for aside.

Once dressed, she faced the two warriors who had enjoyed the show. They escorted her off-base and through the city.

"Where are you taking me?"

Her question was met with silence; the two determined guards could not be bothered to answer. They marched her to the West Gate and waited as it rose. "Our orders are to strip you of your military rank and escort you out of the city. If you try to return, you will be shot on sight."

"I will need water, supplies . . . a weapon?"

The two men stared without passion. They weren't bad men—just had a duty to fulfill. "Go. For your own good," said the sergeant.

"This is a death sentence. A weapon, please," Katrina pleaded.

"Staying here is a death sentence. Out there . . ." He left the words hanging.

Katrina took a final breath of city air and turned and walked through the gate. It started closing as soon as she was through.

She looked back at the walled city one last time, a city she had recently triumphed over. Now she was a woman without a home, a people, or a future.

The heat was oppressive and, mixed with the day's dust, made for some very dirty 1.0s. They moved without hope, migrating away from everything they knew. Most walking and a few riding, some stumbling along, all were numb to their surroundings. They stretched out over a hundred yards, leaving a column of dust in their wake. The occasional cough, clang, or clank from a backpack acted as the background rhythm to a morose soundtrack.

Is that all we are now? Avery thought, *Refugees?* They had made good time heading away from Zion. She had done a rough head count coming in at just under a thousand. Some children but mostly adults between the age of nineteen and forty-five, the strong and fast who could get away. There had been no sign of Finley, and she feared the worst.

Avery let her mind drift to the traitor, Helen, someone she had worked with and trusted. She made the 2.0 conquest of Zion possible. If Avery ever saw her again, no death would be good enough for her. A city of nearly 400,000 taken, with many lives lost.

"What are you thinking about?"

Avery looked up to see Dr. Patel walking next to her. Her normally smooth white hair was matted, and her eyes were puffy and tired. Avery could only imagine how she must look. It had been a long day of trekking. Dr. Patel was holding a small stack of printed paper like it was a precious commodity.

"Nothing," Avery lied.

"That sums us up nicely," she said.

"I guess it does." They continued a bit in silence.

"I suppose it doesn't matter, but I found something in Jericho's genomes that I had missed on my first tests." She gestured to the pages.

Avery shot her a glance.

"It's not something you would ever test for, but you said go deep, so I did. He tests as a 1.0, but he's not . . . has none of the rDNA modifications of a 2.0. He's something in between. There is a tick on his polynucleotide chain."

"What do you mean?" Avery asked, glad for the distraction from her destructive thoughts.

"Like a flea on a dog's tail. Jericho's genomic DNA structure has a small tip of compounds on the end of his double helix, between the phosphor-diester linkage. Some type of genome editing technique using RNA to cut and modify the original DNA chain, boosting his RSAD2s—radically."

"Easy, Doc. In laypeople's terms, what does that mean?" Avery asked.

"Humans have a protein known as RSAD2, or viperin. It's a naturally occurring viral inhibitory protein."

"And this RSA . . ."

"RSAD2. It basically kills viruses in the body without killing us, and for the most part, it helps us get over many sicknesses. Jericho has five times more viperin in his system than any human ever."

"So he can what? Fight off sickness?" Avery asked.

"That and a lot more. He is basically immune to any of the deadly contagions that have plagued our planet over the last twenty years."

Avery stopped walking.

"And there is something more," Dr. Patel said. "Some kind of code embedded in his tissue."

"Code?

"Like a computer code, only biological."

"Living code? Huh, any way to read what it says?" asked Avery.

"I might have a way—if I still had my lab."

"That must be what my father meant when he said Jericho was the key."

Dr. Patel nodded her head. "Yes, and we have to get him back. I believe he holds the genetic material to fix this world."

Avery let the words seep in as the two started walking again. Whatever her father had in mind for Jericho, it was now too late to do anything about it. There was no more lab, no more Jericho, and no prospects for this scattered bunch of original humans. It seemed a host of mistakes had been made lately, and kicking

Jericho out was just one more along the way. The kind of mistakes that could never be rectified.

"He's gone."

The words let the last morsel of hope drain from Dr. Patel, and she faded off the pace, watching Avery walk away with the hopeless and the destitute.

Jericho crawled along the base of the old house and peeked an eye around the corner. The night was dark, as the moon had just dipped below the horizon, revealing a carpet of stars across the horizon. He could just make out the shape of the door to the shanty. It was broken and not fully closed. The slight glow of a dying fire was beckoning him. Creeping closer, he could see Geena sleeping in the center of the room on the dirt floor. A chain wormed its way from her neck to a center post holding up the roof. A small fire crackled in a homemade fireplace near the right wall. A second person—no, make that two more—were sleeping arm-in-arm on the small bed. Jericho watched as one rolled over. It was the man with the mohawk. He could see the multi-belt Santos had given him hanging on the bedpost.

The rest of the town had long gone to sleep for the night. Jericho had wrestled with his thoughts until he could take no more. After hiking for half a day with only a small mud puddle to drink, he spun around and headed back to the town, anger growing with every step he took, but his legs were unwilling to stop. Approaching the village, he was more careful this time and found a berry thicket to hide in until the sun went down. He managed some much-needed sleep, but his thirst required some serious attention.

He tiptoed into the house. His first job would be to dispatch the two adults before he could figure out how to get Geena free. He looked around for a weapon. Over by the glowing embers were several pots and a large cast-iron spoon. He reached for the spoon but changed his mind as he drew closer. Next to the pot was a large femur bone with a pointed end. He picked it up and carefully padded to the bed, ready for anything.

He raised the bone over his head and was about to drive the sharpened point into the woman's heart. She was the closest to that side of the bed. Jericho hesitated. He had never killed anyone before, and even though the circumstances warranted it, he couldn't. He rotated the bone in his hands and, using the knobby end, he blasted her in the head. The woman went from sleeping to out cold in an instant. Jericho quickly moved to the other side of the bed to repeat the process. Before he hit the sleeping mohawk-man, he opened his eyes with a curious, pained look. "Ahh." Jericho re-cocked the bone and swung again, this time with all his might.

Mohawk moved like lightning, and Jericho's blow hit an old pillow that burst into feathers. The man brought a foot up and unloaded it into Jericho's midsection before he could club him again. Jericho doubled over and dropped the bone. The man then rolled over his sleeping partner, all the way out of the bed, and faced Jericho from the other side, but not before noticing his woman was not moving. This elicited a deep growl of anger.

Jericho tried to find some way to get his breath back.

Mohawk looked at Jericho and hissed as he leaped at Jericho like a frog. He cleared the entire bed. Jericho ducked out of instinct and the man flew over him, crashing into the trophy case and sending the hominid keepsakes flying around the room. Geena grabbed the belt with the large silver *A*. She held it at both ends as she waited for her chance to help.

Jericho spun and faced his attacker, taking up a fighting stance. His breath returned to him in ragged gulps as he let his training take over. Mohawk was huge and built like a human tank. He swung several high-speed haymakers at Jericho, meant to incapacitate him with a single blow. Jericho ducked and weaved out of the way, trying to keep his distance. He tripped over a pot that clanged loudly. If this kept up, the whole town would soon be awake and investigating. He had to end the fight and fast. He spied the bone he had used earlier lying on the floor near the bed, and he tried to angle his way over to get at it. The man had other ideas and no regard for Jericho's abilities. He ran straight at Jericho, ready to grab him and tear him apart.

Jericho used his front leg to lock out against his opponent's knee. The man's forward momentum came to a sudden stop, and a cracking sound followed as his knee buckled backward against Jericho's locked foot. The big guy went down with a grunt and a howl but quickly crawled back to his feet, grimacing with hatred.

Jericho scrambled to the bone and grabbed it. He stood ready to drive it into his prey.

Mohawk was now limping, his face red and intense. He darted at Jericho, who was trapped between the bed and the back wall.

The bone weapon suddenly seemed too small for the task at hand, but Jericho held his ground. He realized he had not injured his foe as much as he had ticked him off.

Mohawk ran at Jericho with a battle cry. A rattle of chains to the right was followed by a decibel drop in his scream of terror. The big man lost his footing and went from running to falling. Jericho swung his arm forward just as he was knocked from his feet. The two men collided in a cloud of dust and hit the floor, Jericho cushioning the big man's fall with his body. Jericho let out an involuntary *humph* as his breath was knocked clean out of him—again.

Before he could recover, the Reeker placed two meat-hook hands around Jericho's throat and squeezed. Jericho was trapped under him and could only wiggle. His eyes bugged as he scratched and pounded against the steel flesh of Mohawk. The lack of air soon took Jericho's strength and focus, his fist-pounding having had no impact, whatsoever. Dots appeared in Jericho's eyesight, and his limbs felt like lead, eventually falling to his sides. He cursed himself for coming back to get Geena, but then, even that thought took too much energy.

The man on top of Jericho let a crooked grimace grow as his foe gave up the fight. It would only be a few more moments before it was done for good. Then, for no apparent reason, his hands loosened and surprise graced his face.

Jericho's vision faded. He tried to understand the expression on Mohawk's face just before he collapsed on top of him. Jericho got his breath back in small doses. His sight and some of his strength returned. He eventually wormed his way out from under the dead weight of the big man and sat up on the dirt floor next to him. He turned to see Geena, sitting on the floor. Her hands still holding the end of the belt she had lassoed around the cannibal's ankle. It had been her actions that had tripped the big man. He let his eyes continue around, finding blood spreading slowly in his direction across the hardened dirt. The sharpened bone that was once in Jericho's hands was sticking out of Mohawk's torso. He was dead.

"You okay?" Jericho whispered hoarsely.

Geena nodded with glistening eyes.

Jericho slowly stood and tested the chain around the post; it was solid.

"The keys." She pointed to the door frame.

Jericho found them and quickly unlocked the chain around her neck. He grabbed his multi-belt off the bedpost and a few other supplies, stuffing them into an old backpack. He found some water in a bottle and guzzled it. Geena ran to him and threw her arms around him. She hugged him for all she was worth. Jericho stood still. Not sure what to do with the human child. A feeling of warmth spread through his body. He lowered himself and returned the hug. It was nice. No, it was something more than that.

"We need to get out of here," he whispered.

A simple nod returned, and Jericho stood back up. He grabbed her hand, and the two turned. Geena suddenly stopped, let go, and went back into the room. She pulled and twisted until the belt with the silver buckle popped loose from the man's ankle. Rolling it up in one hand, she then ran back to Jericho, and they left the sleeping town of cannibals behind.

After the last debacle during the bi-annual president's speech, Caleb was keen to repair any lingering damage to his image. He had selected a warrior's uniform and the words *commander-in-chief* were placed on his right pocket. He stepped in front of the data collectors and cleared his throat. The image was broadcast to every screen and projector in New Kansas. Caleb let a couple of seconds pass, knowing people never heard the first few words of a speech. He needed everyone's attention.

"Citizens of New Kansas, it is with great honor and excitement that I announce the end of hostilities between us and the 1.0s." He thought he'd lead off with a bang. "We have killed or captured every living 1.0 in Zion and now hold the city."

Citizens throughout New Kansas gathered around viewscreens and Hollowvision projectors. Workers in factories, offices, and homes paused to watch the message. There was an initial shout when he announced the end of the war. Then curiosity took over as people wondered what was next.

The president continued, outlining his plans for the future and basking in the good news—more room for expansion and safer conditions for all. He knew the city would hold a giant celebration tonight, and he wished he could be a part of it. The ego-stroking handshakes and pats on his back he would get, but sometimes a president had to act like a president. He still had work to do in Zion. His speech only lasted for ten minutes, but it galvanized an entire city and put his face at the forefront of their joy. After his last no-show speech, he was once again riding high with the masses, the one sure way to keep himself at the heart of power. He'd like to see Giles try to replace him now.

Cin watched the speech, and with every word, a feeling of dread grew inside. The president just supercharged his Q rating, and it would take some doing to change that now. Even Giles would have to tread lightly for the next few weeks, before disparaging Caleb in the eyes of the public. A new war was beginning, and she was in the crosshairs—from both sides. A war of three. It would take some very careful maneuvering from here on out.

After several hours of trekking, Jericho stopped for the last bit of daylight before darkness. He had not properly slept in two days and had nothing more to give. They found a hollow log, and he and Geena curled up inside. Geena wrapped her arms around Jericho.

"You did good," Jericho said.

Geena looked up.

"The most important thing out here is to survive. Keep moving forward. And you did that. You found a way."

"Thanks, but I'm never going to see my family again, am I?" Geena said softly as she nuzzled into Jericho's chest. Jericho saw no reason to lie. "No. We're family now. You and me, understand?"

There was a slight nod against his chest. "For how long?" she asked.

"For as long as we can . . . as long as we can."

Geena nuzzled a bit before falling asleep.

The words that had popped out of his mouth weighed heavily on Jericho.

A late morning exit had them traveling southwest, hoping for greener grass. The ordeal with the Reekers had left Jericho and Geena weakened and on edge. They moved as fast as their bodies would let them, fearing a reprisal. The forest thinned and then disappeared for a time as they moved through knee-high grass set against red cliffs on the right. A small stream along the cliff face was a welcome treat, and they gulped all they could before moving on.

Jericho paused and eyed the red sandstone towering above him. "I'm gonna climb up there and see what I can. You wait over there in the shade till I get back, understand?" Jericho said while gesturing.

"No! You can't leave me. You said we would stick together," Geena cried out.

"I'm not leaving you. I'm just going up there to get a look around, make sure we're not being followed, and more importantly, heading to a better place."

Geena shook her head in fear. After all the other adults had left her behind, she was still trying to trust the man who had now saved her twice.

Jericho could see the fear on Geena's face, and even though he felt it was unwarranted, he understood it. "Look, hold this; it will keep you safe till I come back." Jericho took off his necklace with 24's ring on it and held it out. "You know how much this means to me, right?"

"Yes," Geena replied.

"So you know I'll come back for it, right?"

She grabbed the necklace and held it tightly. After slowly nodding her approval, she stepped into the shade.

Jericho made his way up the cliff, using his hands and legs to maintain three points of contact with the steep, rough wall as he climbed.

Geena strained her neck to watch, the ring held close to her chest.

At the top, Jericho paused to catch his breath. Looking back, there was no sign of anyone following, which gave him great relief. He turned back around and shielded his eyes from the sun. The earth was deformed. Nine huge craters in the ground, each bigger than a city block, were all that was left of a once-large city in the distance. Only a few scraps of buildings and debris remained. The red earth around it was permanently scarred, dimpled for life. In the distance, he could see two distinct clouds of dust. A large one to the front and a smaller one following from behind. They were on a collision course with the path he and Geena were currently trekking.

Jericho knew they needed to connect with people—if nothing else, for Geena's sake. The question was, what kind of people were up ahead? From this distance, there was no way of knowing. A quick estimate in his mind put them at just over a day's journey before making contact.

He climbed back down with a new reading in mind, but first, he would need his ring back.

17

Commander Weng sat in the Stryker, his purple eyes fixed on the floor and his mind somewhere else. *Ruth.* Just as the president had promised, Weng had been allowed to chat with her over a secure line before leaving for this mission. His emotions had almost gotten the better of him since Weng assumed the mission to Zion was most likely a one-way trip.

Now, with the end of the war at hand, he felt eager to return home. Ruth was excited about her ideas and plans for when he returned, the sparkle in her eyes making him a proud father. She was truly destined for something more. The woman Caleb assigned to watch over Ruth was nothing if not professional, and Weng was confident things were fine at home. It had gone a long way to focus him on the task ahead.

A darker emotion crossed his mind. Katrina. *What happened to her?* He had tried to reach out just before leaving, without luck. Weng had even asked Caleb to look into it. Her complete disappearance baffled him, especially when Caleb had come back with no results. The more he thought about her, the madder he became. What was it that had him so consumed with this woman? His mind continued to spin.

Was it possible she was one of the battle's casualties? That seemed hard to believe as he had talked to her just after the main battle. It is uncommon for a sci officer to go down; they brought up the rear, but it could happen. The strange part was that there was no body or report attached to her, even with the medics. It was as if she had just disappeared.

A bump in the road returned Weng to the present, and he refocused on the attack plan. He would give his best once more and investigate what happened to her upon his return.

"Ten mikes out," the navigator called back, breaking Weng from his thoughts.

"Gear up," Weng ordered over the COMMs, and the warriors prepped for the upcoming fight. Thirty hardened fighters in five vehicles, all plucked from quarantine, to do one more run on the 1.0s. Some put on their bio-suits, but several of the recently exposed didn't bother. It was the first time Weng had seen anything like it, and he stopped mid-donning and took his off, as well. He had been exposed more than most and was doubting the validity of the current sick-1.0 mindset.

The energy in the cab was not quite the same as when they had attacked the city. These warriors had done their job and were sated with killing. The only reason they were here was their bio-suits had failed or been damaged during the fighting. It was like drawing the short straw. They would do their job, but that was it.

"Any heat signatures?" Weng asked his navigator.

"Nothing showing on the screen, except the group we see straight ahead. It's like they are giving up before the fight, sir."

"Or they are in position and ready." Weng eased himself forward in his seat. *Is it really going to be this easy?* "Keep a lookout. One thing they are not is dumb." *Surely, they have some defensive capabilities, or did that go with their precious city,* he wondered.

"Send in the drones," he ordered over the COMMs. He would let them do the heavy lifting before closing to within shooting distance.

Gravity seemed to stop for a second as Weng was lifted into the air, just before slamming back down abruptly. The lead Stryker dropped nose-first into a giant hole with its butt sticking up in the air, coming to an abrupt stop.

Avery and a band of soldiers had been hiding behind a wall of dirt. Two trenches had been dug on either side of their planned ambush point. They stayed out of visual and thermal sight, letting the thick dirt block any scans of their presence.

She ordered her soldiers to open fire. Since their flee from Zion, she'd been weary, placing watchers along their flank. At the first sign of the dust trail following them, she had lain a trap for the 2.0s trying to sneak up on them from behind. Avery knew the chasing 2.0s would assume they held all the cards after taking Zion. She would use their over-confidence against them. The 1.0s might be down, but she would do everything in her power to give them a fighting chance, here and now.

Fighter drones fired from the roofs of the Strykers flew toward the heat signatures in the distance. The remaining 1.0 drones were launched in return. They quickly engaged each other in a spectacular aerial ballet of combat tactics, diving, spinning, and firing without fear.

Avery peeked up and watched as the lead Stryker drove into the pit they had dug and covered over in the road. It came to a crashing halt, blocking the way forward for the rest of the attacking force. The rear Stryker was hit with an EMw weapon the minute it stopped. The weapon was designed to emit powerful electromagnetic microwaves through the air, killing all electronics and acting like a type of microwave oven to its occupants. Within fifteen seconds, the men inside were screaming and flopping in pain and, shortly thereafter, cooked to death.

With the front and rear blocked, the three Strykers in the middle were trapped but not helpless. They fired relentlessly at any target they could find. They took out the EMw before it could be turned on the next Stryker full of warriors.

Handheld plasma weapons counter-fired, making holes like Swiss cheese out of the other Strykers. The cannon on top spun and engaged, as did the rail gun. It was a fierce but short-lived battle that went from zero to a hundred and back down to zero again within two minutes.

Back at camp, the surviving 2.0 drone fighters swooped in, firing a barrage against the poorly armed civilians, decimating their ranks. Vehicle-mounted automated ion cannons returned fire. Each 2.0 drone tried to out-maneuverer the deadly fire and still complete its mission of destroying any remaining 1.0s. After a few minutes, there was only one drone left, one with a damaged prop. It flew erratically, trying to engage the targets in the camp, but on one of its return runs, clipped a tree and spun off out of control, exploding. Cheers around the camp went up. This was the first victory over the 2.0s since Zion.

The casualty list was surprisingly low as the remaining soldiers surrounded the lead Stryker that was nose-down in the pit. Weng and five other warriors emerged with their hands in the air. Sergeant Kay lined them up in a row and placed them on their knees with their hands secured behind their backs. They removed the bio-helmets from two and mocked them for their unfounded fears. Kay then moved down the row of warriors, executing them one at a time.

"Kay. Stop!" Avery screamed as she ran up to the spectacle. The veins in her face popping red. "This is not how we do things."

"These men killed everything. Family, friends, our homes, and I, for one, want justice," Sergeant Kay said.

"This is not justice, just plain and simple murder. Now, stand down, Sergeant."

"If just one of us dies because you don't have the marbles to do what needs to be done. I swear to you, I'll—"

"You're relieved of duty, Sergeant Kay." Avery interrupted. "I need two men to escort Sergeant Kay back to camp and relieve him of his weapon.

Kay held his weapon, pointing it at Avery. She stood her ground, knowing any sign of weakness now would send those left into complete chaos. Several other soldiers hesitated, trying to take a side. They believed in their societal structure as a whole, but Kay made a bloody good point. Slowly, they moved their weapons, targeting the sergeant. He finally lowered his gun and stormed off, not waiting to be escorted. "You just made the biggest mistake of your life."

Avery released the small breath she'd been holding. "Corporal, take these men to camp and see that they are secured and well-guarded."

"Yes, ma'am."

"Collins, see if you can get these Strykers up and running; we could really use 'em."

"On it."

Avery watched as the three remaining warriors stood. One was familiar to her, and it took a second for the poor context to connect the dots.

Weng stared at her with unflinching purple eyes.

Eyes Avery would never forget. This was the man from the roof of their generating plant. The one who conspired with Major Helen to destroy them from the inside and quite possibly, was responsible for whatever happened to Finley.

She should have let Kay kill him.

Weng spun as he and his other two men were escorted away. Avery watched as anger coursed through her body.

The camp was busy collecting their dead and organizing what was still of value after the strafing runs that had blasted through the camp, taking the lives of several and leaving three critically wounded.

The work stopped as three 2.0s were marched into camp. Anger and hatred flared, and several citizens had to be restrained from outright killing the prisoners as they passed. The entire camp sparked and united with one mindset: kill the 2.0s. Kay watched it all with interest. This might present him with an opportunity. He began to share his viewpoint with anyone who would listen. His words grew into a word-of-mouth campaign that spread through the camp. Politics were not working anymore. It was time for a strong and powerful leader, and that leader was him.

"Citizens and fellow 1.0s," Avery called out in an attempt to calm the rising storm. She stood up on a crate so all could see and hear her. "I have been your council leader for eight years now—since the death of the twelve. We have accomplished many great things together. Now, in our most dire of circumstances, we must stay together, trust and love one another." A few grumblings followed her words. "There is a path forward, and we will find it together, but our only hope for this to happen is unity. To stand as one, fight as one, and move forward as one." People pressed closer as she spoke, even those who had grumbled now listened. "I realize now is not the time for speeches. It is time for action. And believe me when I say, we will get to the other side . . . but only if we are one. Murder without justice is not our way forward. Please look to your emergency unit advisors for guidance, and we will update them as needed. Thank you and may God bless us all. Now, please tend to your wounded and bury the dead. We will leave at first light."

Another voice interrupted. It was strong and confident. "Or I say it is time for a new leader." Kay had stepped up onto a log across from her and was using the moment to his advantage. "One that has what it takes to pull the tail out from between our legs and kill those who killed ours. I say—"

A blast rang out across the camp, and Kay slumped and fell off the crate to the ground. His treasonous lips still moved, but no sound came forth.

"The time for discussion is over." Silence filled the camp. Avery stood tall, holding the EM1, and waited. A few murmurs started, then were drowned out as people turned back to their duties.

Her words and actions were just strong enough to quell the tempest for now.

Jericho woke with a start. Images of Reekers eating his leg while he was still alive faded, and he tried to calm his breathing. The sky was just starting to turn orange, and he decided he was done sleeping, or whatever that had been. They had made camp early, and both had fallen asleep where they first sat, too exhausted to even make a fire.

He coaxed a flame to some kindling, nursing it to a fire while contemplating his next move. This world started off full of hope for the life he and 24 had ahead. Now he was jaded and soured by the humanity that occupied it. His future was drab, and his charge, mostly helpless. He needed to find something better and find it soon.

Looking down at Geena's still sleeping form, Jericho was envious of how happy, peaceful, and rested she looked. None of those things would be true when she awoke. His stomach rumbled with hunger. First, they needed to eat, then . . . that part was still a bit murky. He pulled the gun from his multi-belt and headed off in search of food.

Two quail, barely recognizable after being blown apart by his gun, cooked over the fire. Geena's nose was the first to wake as the smell of roasting meat filled the camp. They ate till there were two small piles of bones in front of them.

Jericho didn't relish traipsing through the wilderness at night, but they were getting close to the source of the dust trail he had seen.

A crunch from the left had Geena and Jericho scrambling for cover behind a clump of brush.

A woman with long, curly, strawberry-blonde hair and a dirt-smudged face tripped over a root and landed hard by the fire. Her lips were cracked, and her desire to get back up low. She looked like she had been crying and wandering, which she had.

Geena ran out from cover before Jericho could stop her and knelt by the woman, who smiled weakly at the young girl.

Jericho stepped out, and the woman started to scramble away, her fear evident on her face. He held his hands up and called out, "We won't hurt you."

She stopped scrambling and looked between Geena and Jericho, trying to size up her situation. Her heart pounded with the proximity of two 1.0s, likely carrying a death sentence with every breath they exhaled.

"I'm Geena. I'm eight and a half years old, and I like fried chicken, and this is Jericho. He saved me."

The woman swallowed weakly, trying not to move rudely away from the young 1.0. This was not the place to announce your past or prejudices. Her life was now forfeited and death assured, so she might as well go out on her terms. She would embrace any and all humans until the plague claimed her, and she slipped beyond this realm. After taking a calming breath, a hoarse voice croaked. "Hi, I'm Katrina, and I like fried chicken, too, but would love some water if you have any."

Jericho cautiously stepped forward and dug a bottle out of his pack and handed it to her. She guzzled it until there was nothing left.

"Oh, thank you. I was really struggling," she said as she wiped her dripping chin, wondering if she could feel a contagion moving down her throat and into her body.

"Where are you headed?" Geena asked.

"Away," Katrina replied.

It was a response Jericho could understand.

"Zion's been destroyed, and there is no place left for me," Katrina mumbled.

Jericho was taken aback—an entire city gone, the few decent humans he knew with it.

"We are on our way to link up with some people moving out west. You are welcome to join."

"That is very kind of you." Katrina stood and held her hand out.

Jericho stared at it for a beat before reaching out and taking it in his hand. They shared eye contact and the jolt that comes with touch, but the context blocked any chance at familiarity. In reality, the two had briefly crossed paths in the forest outside of New Kansas—one in a containment bag and the other overwhelmed by her first off-base mission. Neither looked like their former self.

Moving through darkness seemed safer as a trio. They shared stories to pass the time. Most of Katrina's were made up as she feared being outed as a 2.0. The occasional laugh was a welcome sound after so much terror. Jericho used a small direction indicator on his belt to keep them on an intercept path to the human activity he had seen from the hilltop.

After an hour of trekking, they stopped by a small creek to refill their water containers and take a break.

Jericho opened his pack and tossed two containers to Geena. Katrina sat down and tried to catch her breath. She watched Geena carrying back the water and noticed the silver buckle with an *A* on Geena's pants. Her face lost all color.

"Where did you get that?" she suddenly demanded.

Geena paused, looking a bit bewildered. "Get what?" she said, sheepishly.

"The silver buckle," Katrina said, pointing with her finger.

"That's her good luck charm," Jericho replied, not answering her question.

"We got it from a camp full of really bad people," Geena said.

"Cannibals," Jericho whispered to Katrina. "Why?"

"May I see it?" Katrina asked more politely.

Geena took off the buckle and tossed it to Katrina.

She looked it over carefully. Turning in her hands like it might be precious. "This was my mother's."

Both Geena and Jericho waited for more.

"My mother and father left the city heading west for a better place to live, away from all the disease. They left me and my brothers with my aunt and were going to send for me once they found someplace safe. That was the last I ever saw them. I remember my mother wore this buckle to hold up a belt with a pistol and a knife on it. She was a tough woman, much more so than my father." A tear fell from Katrina's cheek, just missing the buckle. "I guess they never found what they were looking for."

"Does anybody?" Jericho added rhetorically.

Katrina held it back out for Geena.

"You can keep it," Geena said, with a smile on her face.

Katrina returned the expression.

Once the camp was reorganized and the bodies buried, the remaining 1.0s took a moment to reflect on those no longer with them. The hurried exit from Zion had left them desperate and forward-thinking. Vulnerability and fear were dangerous viruses among sheep, but this group was filled with strong souls still willing to push themselves. Avery would need to keep a close eye on her people and choose her actions carefully. The worst thing that could happen now would be their infrastructure unraveling.

The chains they used to cuff Commander Weng's arm to the captured Stryker were too strong for his enhanced arm to break, but that didn't keep him from trying—every time a guard's attention was distracted. He had pulled and banged till the veins in his neck nearly popped, finally relenting and letting sleep take him for a while. The other two warriors were tied to the other side of the Stryker, out of sight from Weng.

The camp had been restless, and Weng was sure he would not survive the night, likely dying at the hands of an angry 1.0. Weng reflected on the battle he had lost. The 1.0s set a trap that was unexpected and clever. He had lost consciousness when the lead Stryker suddenly dropped and come to an abrupt stop in the disguised hole dug in the road. The sudden shift had launched him into a support beam. By the time he regained his senses, the fight was over. The choices were to die or surrender.

Now, Weng needed to convince them to trade him for something the 1.0s needed. For him, it was no longer a case of finishing off the 1.0s, but getting back to Ruth at all costs. His taste for this war was soured. He would do what he had to, and if he did get back, he would be done with the military. The president would surely understand he needed to be a father to the one person still innocent in this whole calamity, Ruth.

Survivors started pre-packing their meager belongings just before bed so they could get a jump on an early exit in the morning. They would need to put as much distance from here as possible if they were ever again going to feel safe.

The camp quieted down, and some drifted off to a restless sleep, filled with dread that the 2.0s would never just let them go. Others stayed alert and ready, guarding over family and loved ones. What they had was gone, along with any hopes of what tomorrow would bring.

Crickets carried a tune on a soft breeze that cooled the warm night air. An ion lantern moved through the camp like a floating ghost until it was close enough to reveal its holder, Avery. She set it down just out of reach of Commander Weng, letting the cool glow illuminate his face and his trademark purple eyes. He leaned up on one elbow and stared back at her as she sat across from him.

"I know who you are. You were at the dam," Avery said.

"Congratulations," Weng replied.

"We were betrayed."

"Yes, by one of your own," he added.

"After all that has happened, it still seems impossible to me."

"She was weak and saw her future as bleak. Major Helen brought her worst fears to fruition."

"You're talking about self-fulfilling prophecy . . ." Avery's words faded at the end.

Weng nodded. "And ultimately killed by one of her own."

"Well, that's something."

Weng looked at his captor. "You are deciding what to do with us?"

"Anything less than execution, and I'll lose my position here."

"Queen of the dung heap," he said.

"Better to rule in hell than serve in heaven."

"Is it though?"

"Probably not. I might be better off just walking away." Avery pointed to the rest of the camp. "They might be better off."

Weng sat up, and Avery moved back a couple of inches.

"When I first entered Zion, I was sure my mission would end in some fatal disease that would leave me begging for death. Then after it was all over . . ." He held his one unchained hand up as a gesture. "Nothing. I'm fine. Makes me wonder if this whole thing between the 2.0s and the 1.0s isn't all bollocks. Now, all I care about is getting back to my daughter."

"Neither of those is going to happen, and as for your opinion, it's a little late for that kind of sentiment," Avery said with conviction.

He looked down at the ground as he spoke. "I suppose so."

"There was a man . . . I sent him to stop you at the generating plant."

Weng cocked his head to the side.

"He was strong and brave. The kind of man who puts his heart into his actions."

Weng knew who she meant, the battle-hardened man who had chased him down after the explosion. "He didn't make it."

Avery let her head fall as she tried to handle the surge of emotion that swept over her. She had suspected as much, but now she was sure. A single tear pushed past containment and fell to the ground. She lifted her head. "Did you kill him?" she asked, without realizing she had said the words.

"He died well."

Avery gave the slightest of nods. "Your actions caused the deaths of thousands of people, families, friends, co-workers. The loss of an entire city and way of life. People I loved. . . . The man I loved." She took a breath as she regathered her strength. "I have every right to shoot you where you lie, but I'll let my people witness your death for their good." Avery stood and took the lantern, leaving Weng in the dark.

He let the words burn through him. She was right. He was responsible, and he would need to pay for his actions. There was no going back. He just needed to place a period at the end of his story. Death was probably too good for him. Regrets started to fill his mind, and he embraced them.

Giles watched as the little blue dots engulfed the green, spiky ball. It tried to fight back but was quickly overwhelmed and withered. The lab tech glanced at his boss, trying to get a read on his facial expressions as the antibodies killed the adenovirus 12 cells in the computer simulation.

"And you're sure there's no side effects?" Giles asked.

"There are always side effects, sir. No one vaccine works for all," the lap tech said.

"I'm aware of that," Giles replied, with a bit of disdain.

"Yes, sorry. I, ah . . . there are no side effects outside normal parameters. There is, however, a twist to our usual protocols."

"Oh?"

"Adenovirus 12 is quite tricky to kill. It takes more than just an injection. What you saw here today was the result of an injection, followed by a digital augmentation once inside the host."

"So you're saying they will have to get a shot, then go through a LIFE-ARCH, as well?" Giles queried.

"That's correct. It's critical they do both within twenty-four hours of each other, or the vaccine will be ineffective. In fact, the closer to the twenty-four-hour mark, the better."

"Understand. Good job . . ." Giles looked at the lab tech's coat for a name tag. There was none. *So much for his atta-boy*, he thought. "Mass produce it. I want the vaccine ready to roll out just about a week after adenovirus 12 hits."

"When will that be, sir?" The lab tech asked.

"Tomorrow."

"Is there a time you would like it to hit?"

"Let's go with a lunchtime release. That will give us maximum potential hosts."

"Very good."

Giles left the lab feeling good. His latest virus was nasty, and after the public saw its effects, they would be clamoring to get their shot and the necessary twenty-four-hour-later LIFE-ARCH upgrade. His first step would be a demonstration for the masses. He and his fellow leaders, along with business associates and other key personnel, would join together for a press vaccine event. A way to show the public how safe the injection was. He would also hammer the public with videos of how deadly the disease was to those without the vaccine. It would inspire confidence in Pharma One and have the public anxious to follow his lead.

Then, two days after his vaccine party, when there'd be a few deaths reported in New Kansas, Pharma One would release en masse. Two weeks after that, he would do the same to Zion.

Giles reveled in his genius for a moment before using his MindLink to update Cin on his progress and console her after Caleb's speech. He needed her focused on his needs, not lamenting this temporary round won by the president. This next month would be very profitable. He stepped into his office, lit only by the city skyline through the tall glass walls. It was one of his favorite times—alone in his office at night on top of the world, with the lights out. He couldn't decide whether he wanted to eat or do something more primal. He leaned forward and pressed his forehead to the cool glass that gave way to the city beyond. His city. His creation.

18

Some of Zion had emergency lighting up and running, but most of the city was still without power. The last few 1.0 holdouts were reduced to hiding and small skirmish guerilla warfare, making the darker parts of the city a dangerous place to be. Caleb had been promised full power within the next couple of days. Apparently, Commander Weng had done a first-rate job on the generators. His squad had taken them out without damaging the main components—quite remarkable.

The real task for the next two weeks was food and sanitation within the fences. There were twenty fenced-off areas holding thousands of 1.0s, all waiting to be vaccinated and then redistributed throughout the city. Each one had to be identified and selected for a job that best suited their skills and Zion's needs.

"Cin, what's the word on the inoculations?"

Caleb's assistant pulled up an E-doc and referred to it. "One hundred thousand vials will be here tomorrow, and the rest in the next two days. We have been using fire hoses to wash off the prisoners daily to keep them clean."

The last thing Caleb needed was a breakout of some disease from the crowded conditions. The feeding alone was a massive undertaking, and he needed these bodies back in the workforce, no longer a threat to the city's safety or a drain to its resources.

"Let's use the vaccines on these three pens here." He pointed to his map. "Once they are empty, we can shift some of the other prisoners over and relieve the overcrowding."

"At some point, you are going to have to stop calling them prisoners," Cin said.

"I suppose you're right. What should we call them? They're not 2.0s, and they soon won't be 1.0s."

"How about just *citizens*? It will help to heal the line that's been carved in stone between us and them."

"Okay, makes sense. Have the *citizens* who have been vaccinated distributed to this section. We'll need to get them to work as soon as possible. New Kansas can't keep feeding a city of this size. It needs to be self-sufficient and soon. Plus, I want to clean up Zion and modernize it."

"A New Zion?" Cin asked.

"Exactly. I like the sound of that."

"There is one thing you should be aware of, sir."

Caleb looked at Cin, waiting for her to continue.

"I have a report on the adenovirus 12 that is making its way from out eastern towns."

Caleb almost paled at the thought of another sickness after his recent brush with death. "Let me guess . . . you got this report from Pharma One?"

Cin nodded. "They have a working vaccine, and the prognosis is good for a minimal event."

"Fine," Caleb said, almost under his breath. He had something else in mind for Giles, and one more virus running through the ranks would not alter his plans. He stepped over to a large map of New Zion with a patterned overlay on the projected screen. He had been busy divvying up the city. It showed colored areas for new citizens, old citizens, and a more modern transportation system. It would take time, but soon, New Zion would be the next New Kansas. That would make him president of nearly a million people. Not bad for a kid raised by a single mom who worked two jobs just to keep a roof over their head. He only wished she was still alive to see how far her son had come.

The chip on his shoulder that screamed he had something to prove had quieted down years ago. He was now lining his nest egg and hoping to keep the chairs out of his business and plans for a while, especially Giles. Maybe this latest outbreak would keep the nosey CEO distracted.

In Caleb's mind, the best way to do that was to pit chairperson against chairperson. He could let them fight it out for their piece of New Zion while he sat back and controlled it all. He picked up a COMMs and connected to Simon Bogachev, the chairman of All Goods back in New Kansas.

"Good evening, Mr. President. I hear congratulations are in order."

"Well, thank you, Simon. It was always a matter of when, and sometimes things just go right. How's the celebration?"

"The city is alive tonight. Biggest party in the universe."

"Sorry to miss it but duty and all."

"What can I do for you?" Simon asked, cutting to the chase.

"I am sending you a breakdown for New Zion. It details All Goods' proposed factories and distribution locations. I am having a small issue with Pharma One over some of the buildings. Giles seems quite adamant, but I'm sure you two can iron that out."

"Oh, really?"

"Not a big deal. I assure you."

"Well, I appreciate the heads up."

"My pleasure, Simon. Talk soon." Caleb clicked off and let a smile spread across his face. Now, he just needed to change the overlay slightly in the other direction and do the same thing to the other chairs, each version thinking one side was getting more than the other. Soon, they would be bickering and then fighting amongst themselves. Leaving Caleb to mold the city how liked.

"Cin, can you get Karla Brown of Grocery Giant on the COMMs?"

The glow of the camp ahead called like a moth to the light. Jericho and his two charges watched for a good twenty minutes before they felt safe enough to advance. Fifty meters out, they were met by two armed soldiers, hiding in the shadows.

"That's far enough. Identify yourselves," came a voice from the right.

'My name is Jericho, and this is Geena and Katrina. We're . . . we were from Zion."

"Hands where I can see them." One guard stepped up behind them with his weapon trained while the other looked them over with an ion lantern. Its cool color gave everything a bluish glow.

"We've been getting stragglers all night. You're lucky you found us," he said.

After a careful inspection and a few more questions, the trio was let into camp to join the rest of the retreating 1.0s. Katrina was glad she had never popped for upgraded eyes, or this would have been the end of her journey. If she could get past her fear of being contaminated, a fear that was starting to ebb with each passing day, she could fit right in here, and maybe, just maybe, start over.

A quick look around revealed a large group of people. Some slept; some were hunkered down, and several stared at nothing. Most were in various states of trying to put their current situation into some kind of order, mental or otherwise. There were small groups gathered around lights or fires. Several were engaged in cleaning their weapons, while others surveyed Katrina suspiciously. A feeling of fear and hopelessness filled the air, but under it was a solid vibe of determination. These were the survivors; the ones who had escaped and found their way here had grit.

Jericho glanced to his right and saw a familiar face. "You."

He charged without thinking and slammed his body into Weng's, sending both men sprawling—Weng, only as far as his restraints would allow. They both popped up and reengaged. Other 1.0s heard the commotion and clambered for a view of the action.

Kicking, punching, and gouging went on in an angry fray. Weng's enhanced arm was limited by the chain, but he got in a few devastating blows that sent Jericho hard to the dirt. Jericho used the pain to fuel his anger and reengaged without concern for his well-being. This was the man who killed 24, and he must die here and now.

Katrina recognized Weng, and her heart skipped a beat. Without thinking, she went to his aid, trying to break up the fight and save the commander.

Within a few minutes, several guards arrived and put a stop to the foray. Avery pushed through the gathered crowd and looked on with interest.

Geena clung to Jericho's leg, worried sick. He knelt and placed an arm around her. One of the guards piped up. "I think she's a 2.0."

The look on Katrina's face confirmed his accusation.

"You're one of them?" Jericho said, confused, as he stood back up.

Avery then noticed the third person in the scuffle.

"He killed 24. He needs to die," Jericho yelled.

"He did a lot more than that," Avery replied.

"Why is he still alive?"

"We're not murderers here. He will be tried and sentenced, according to our laws."

"Your laws are over. Can't you see that? Everything about your civilization . . . it's over."

The words hit Avery hard, and it took a second to recompose herself. Others from around the camp waited to hear her response.

"Compromising our beliefs because of what's happened is not who we are. The law, our ways and philosophies, are more than a city, group, or person. It's the essence of who we are and what we stand for."

"Your essence is crap," Jericho spat.

"Be that as it may, it's good to see you again, Jericho," Avery said. "I wish it was under different circumstances."

"What are you talking about? You threw me out."

"I set you free. To find your own way and place in this world."

Jericho stared back at her with fury in his eyes.

At an impasse, Avery looked away, no longer willing to meet Jericho's accusing eyes. She had had her fill of that kind of energy. For the first time, she noticed the little girl hanging on Jericho's pant leg, watching the adults with caution. She knelt slightly. "Hello, who are you?"

"I'm Geena, and I could really go for some fried chicken."

Everyone turned to see a little girl with one dimple and a hopeful expression. Her hair was roughly braided, and her expression of innocence at a time like this was priceless. The tension broke almost immediately.

"Okay, Geena. I'm Avery. Let's see what we can do." Avery spun her attention back to Jericho. "Can you control yourself so we can let you go?"

Jericho gave her a short nod, and she signaled the guards to lower their weapons.

Immediately, Jericho dove at Weng, swinging his fists.

Jericho pulled against the chain that bound him to a tree some ten feet away from Weng. Katrina was bound a few feet away, to the right.

"You okay?" she asked Weng.

"You should have maintained your cover," Weng said.

"I'm sorry. I saw you fighting, and I . . ."

"It's okay. I am right where I belong."

Jericho glared at Weng, thinking captivity was too good for him.

"There's something you need to know," Katrina whispered.

Weng scooched closer to her on his butt. "I know what happened to you on our date."

"Not that. President Caleb is not who he pretends to be."

"What do you mean?' Weng asked.

Katrina went on to tell Weng about her treatment, expulsion, and suspicions about his wife and daughter.

Weng's head spun; his world imploded. He gritted his teeth and pounded his hands, trying to process his new reality. "I'll have his head for this." He had never felt so helpless before, and the feeling consumed him.

Jericho wasn't sure what was happening, but seeing Weng in anguish was satisfying.

Katrina looked at Jericho. "President Caleb is the one who ordered the death of your friend."

"Katrina, I can fight my own battles," Weng said.

Katrina nodded, slightly embarrassed. Her emotions were erratic at seeing the commander. "Caleb threw me out like I didn't matter. Everything I worked for was stripped with a single command."

"Welcome to my world," Jericho spat, as he looked back and forth between them.

"I brought you some chicken."

All three turned to see Geena carrying a plate filled with cooked chicken.

"It's not fried, but it's really good." Geena sat next to Jericho and handed him a leg-thigh combo. She reached into her pocket and slipped him a key to the cuff that bound his left hand to the tree. She did it in such a subtle way, Jericho wondered if she had spent time on the streets. A simple smile followed; then she was off, distributing chicken to Weng and Katrina before sitting back down next to Jericho.

"Avery told me we are going out west. There are some settlements out there that we can join."

Jericho pulled his focus off of Weng and back to Geena, the little girl who had wormed her way into his heart and mind. "That's good news. Maybe you can put all that's happened to you in the past. You can start over." His words were meant for Geena, as he had other plans for himself. They started with the elimination of Weng and this president who had ordered 24's death.

"I'm going wherever you're going."

"That will not be possible, Geena. There is something I have to do alone before I can go west, and I need to make sure you're not in danger while I'm away."

"But you said you'd take care of me."

"And I will; as soon as I finish my business, I'll join back up. This is my way of taking care of you right now."

"Promise?"

Jericho removed the ring from around his neck. He moved it around in his fingers, taking one last look before handing it to Geena. "You know what this means, right?"

"You'll come back for it?"

"Always, but in the meantime, I need you to watch over it for me."

Geena held the ring in her little hand and looked up to meet Jericho's eyes. Tears were on the verge of spilling.

He matched her look with genuine concern. "I'll be wanting that back." He shared a soft smile that helped console her, and she gave a hopeful nod in return.

"Come here."

Geena scooched over, and Jericho put his arm around her. He held her there until she fell asleep, the long day finally catching up.

Weng watched the tender display, eventually clearing his throat. "So they call you Jericho now?"

Jericho looked up at Weng, the anger in his heart still evident.

"It's a strong name. Look, I'm sorry about 24. I was just following orders, and I'm not that guy anymore. It was a terrible act, and I can never take it back."

Jericho tilted his head. "People don't change. Your words are hollow."

"Understandable, but I disagree. The one thing that makes us human is the ability to change. I have a daughter about her age." He gestured toward Geena. "She is the world to me, so I did everything in my power to make her world a safer place to live."

"By killing others?"

"Since I was very young, we have been taught the dangers of the 1.0s. A standing kill order has been in effect for years. It appears we were lied to."

"That's how dictators and kings keep their power," Jericho said.

"Yes, it is. I was blind."

"And what? Let me guess, now you can see?" Jericho mocked.

Once everyone in the camp had gone to sleep, Jericho slipped the cuff off his wrist. He moved over to the dying fire and discovered a cooking knife lying on a stump. With knife in hand, he tiptoed back to the place where Weng was sleeping. And Jericho didn't hesitate. He placed the knife up to Weng's throat and tried to slice it open, the same way he had watched 24 die. He tried again . . . nothing.

"It's not so easy to kill a man up close and personal. Don't worry, I won't stop you. Just press and slice." Weng never opened his eyes. Instead, he tilted his chin up. "You'd probably be doing me a favor." He opened his eyes. "Come on, do it."

Jericho's hands shook. He wanted to, but something about killing a person in cold blood was too much for him—even for the man who had murdered 24.

"I'm not long for this world, Jericho. It's time for me to pay up. No one will fault you for your actions."

"Jericho, don't." Avery appeared, her empty hands outstretched. "I won't stop you, but killing him will change you. I know you. You're a good person, and there are far too few good people in this world. Please."

Katrina and Geena both woke to the drama. Neither dared to say a word.

"If I could take down the man that killed my wife, I would," Weng added. "But that is not in the cards for me. Maybe it will be for you. Before I go, I want to say in all sincerity, I'm sorry for my actions."

"Good to see you're all getting along." Dr. Patel threw out as she stepped over to the drama, unaware that Jericho had a knife on Weng. It broke the tension with unplanned triumph. Jericho slowly pulled the blade from Weng.

"Oh, my," she added.

Avery crossed her arms as she looked over the situation. "I might have a way for you to make amends," Avery said to Weng, "And for you to get back at the man responsible," she tossed to Jericho. "Maybe we can put an end to all this hatred, but it will require you two to work together."

Dr. Patel hurried over to Avery's side, holding several printouts she had carried with her since leaving Zion. The two women shared an uneasy glance.

"Not a chance," Jericho said.

The captured Stryker bounced along the path under a cover of a dark, starry night. Avery had pulled a small team together and left before anyone from camp could stop them. Her number two had watched them leave and was now in charge of getting the rest of the group to safety. Avery had one last card to play and was hoping it was an ace.

Weng let his mind go back to the drone crash that killed his wife. *Was it more than just an accident, like Katrina had said, or was it just Caleb manipulating her like he did everyone else?* He started picking up on details he had overlooked. The way Caleb had ordered him to his office so he wouldn't be with his family at the time of the crash and the overzealous investigation afterward that Caleb had personally led. All of it so he could control the narrative. Weng had been overwhelmed with grief and anger, and the clues had slipped by. The disappointment in Caleb's eyes when Ruth survived her surgery. He had originally interpreted it as sadness, but that was wrong. Caleb had bent and molded Weng into a killing machine, built to serve his purposes . . . his wants and needs, not the people's. Weng's rage grew with every turn of the Stryker's tires.

"I don't trust him," Jericho said as he stared down Weng, who was sitting across from him on the thinly padded bench seat.

"That's a big improvement from wanting to kill him," Avery countered.

"I just want my chance at Caleb," Weng said.

"We all do," Katrina added.

Weng and Katrina sat on the left-side bench, between two armed soldiers wearing warriors' clothing. They kept stealing glances back and forth. Jericho, Dr. Patel, and Avery sat on the other bench, facing them. Up front, there were two more 1.0 soldiers in warrior uniforms driving and navigating their way back to Zion.

The desperate plan was simple, but as with most plans, the final outcome was unknown. It put Jericho right in the middle of everything. That did not appeal to him in the least, and he would have to be careful as they proceeded. What he really cared about was his chance at Commander Weng, but when given the chance, he failed. He was not a cold-blooded killer. Revenge didn't suit him. He was built to be a survivor. Maybe he should just head off on his own and start fresh, but it was probably a little late for that now. He had cast his lot in with refugees, prisoners, and the damned.

Jericho let his mind re-process the flurry of information he had been given before leaving the campsite.

Dr. Patel had been very specific. "There is some kind of code or message hidden in your DNA. I might have an idea of how to read it, but we would need a high-tech lab to do that." She had gone on to tell him about his high viperin levels, making him immune to almost all sicknesses. "If I can recreate your genetic makeup in others, together we can change everything." She had then turned to Avery. "This is what your father meant."

Jericho leaned his head back against the bulkhead. If his body really did contain the genetic code to put an end to disease and the rift that had started a war, maybe it would be worth the risk. It was not like he had unlimited options. Even Weng had been encouraged by her words and verbally committed to the plan, as thin as it was.

One thing was for sure, whatever came next, it would take some luck and a heck of a miracle to pull it off.

He glanced at Commander Weng, trying to feel anything but the hatred. The man was strong and confident, with connections and power. He would be critical to their success, but trusting a man like him would come hard for Jericho. He tried to force out the image of Weng slicing 24's neck—futile. He would have to tread very . . .

"We're coming up on Zion. Now might be a good time to change out," the navigator called back.

Weng and Katrina cuffed the rest of the group and took control of the Stryker. Katrina spun and put her arms around Weng, hugging him for a moment.

"Okay," Avery commented. "Didn't see that coming."

"Sorry," Katrina said to Weng. "I just wanted you to know how I feel about you—in case we don't get out of this."

Weng took her arms in his hands and stared directly into her eyes. "We'll get out of this and . . . thank you for that. It means a lot." He gave her another quick hug and pulled back. "Now, let's focus."

Katrina nodded in reply, too overwhelmed to speak. They were now on the very edge of the razor.

"Commander," the guard said with some surprise as the Stryker rolled to a stop and Weng stepped out of the driver's seat wearing a bio-suit. The West Gate had been sealed ever since Weng and his troops had rolled out of it two days ago.

"I have a collection of HV prisoners for containment. Any trouble with the gate?"

"No. Since we took the city, it's been quiet."

"Good to hear."

The guard called for the temporary gate to be opened, which was a large vehicle parked parallel to the wall.

Weng stepped back into the Stryker and drove past the guards into Zion. The fire and smoke that had dominated the battle for the city were gone. Crews worked around the clock, repairing the damage. Electricity seemed to be flowing again over much of the city, and a few shops were open.

The sky pinkened, introducing a new day. Avery looked out the windshield as they passed thousands of 1.0s locked behind tall fences. She could see a couple had been pulled outside and were being severely beaten by guards in bio-suits.

She closed her eyes at the brutality, knowing this had happened on her watch. Her people, her city, were all now at the whim of a tyrannical society. She had run away and left them to suffer this fate. Maybe it was good she was back. At the very least, if they failed, she could pay penance for her failure as their leader.

A few more turns and the Stryker entered the base at the southern end of the city. It was escorted past the guard tower and over to the holding cells. As it pulled to a stop, several armed guards ran to assist with unloading the prisoners.

Weng and Katrina watched as the "prisoners" were escorted and locked behind a fence with about fifteen others. These were the high-value prisoners (HVs), political or military.

A small group appeared from the main building. Amongst them were President Caleb and his assistant, Cin. The president stepped over and saluted Weng. "Good to see you back. You had me worried for a minute there." He stared at the embattled look on the commander's face.

"Not every path is straight," Weng said.

"No. I suppose not. I sent a squadron of drones out, but there was no sign of the fleeing 1.0s."

"We killed and ionized everyone that we didn't bring back," Katrina lied as she stepped out of the Stryker and stood next to Commander Weng.

"The traitor Katrina," Caleb said in a quieter voice, his eyes on the female he had booted from his world just a few days ago.

"That might have been due to a misunderstanding," Weng said. "You banished her, but we picked her up along the way, and she saved the day."

"I see . . . prisoners?" Caleb asked with curiosity, as this was not part of the commander's orders.

"Yes. Their Council leader and the other half from the spaceship who got away. Along with a few of their remaining infrastructure."

"Well, you are full of surprises, Commander. Perhaps I was rash to judge. Why don't you report back to quarantine with your friend? Get cleaned up, and we can grab some lunch while you tell me all about it."

"Of course, sir." Weng gave a quick salute and headed for the quarantine area with Katrina in tow. He couldn't wait to remove his bio-suit and clean up.

"What do you think?" Katrina asked as they walked away.

"So far, so good, but I've got about thirty minutes to come up with a story of how you saved the day."

"Oh, yeah? Shouldn't be hard. I've done it before," Katrina replied with a half-smile.

"Yes, you have." Weng smiled back.

Avery watched the conversation between President Caleb and Commander Weng. She couldn't hear specific words, but their facial expressions had her suspicions growing. The problem was doing something about it from inside a guarded ion fence.

The pen they were in consisted of double-walled, ion-charged chain-link fencing with roving sentries. There was a small facility in the corner with water and a few outhouses. The prisoners around her looked forlorn, but none of them seemed to have been tortured. That was something, at least. One by one, they came over to Avery and expressed their sorrow or angst at the situation.

"So what do you think?" Dr. Patel asked no one in particular.

Jericho was quick to answer. "I think he will sell his mother's soul for a chance to look good to his bosses."

"He wouldn't do that," Dr. Patel countered naively.

"I hope you're right," Avery said, not sure which way this thing was actually going, only grateful that the rest of her people had escaped.

"If I'm wrong, we're all dead, anyway," Dr. Patel added forlornly.

"Hey, there's not much we can do behind this cage, so just stick with the plan." Avery turned back from the fence and sat on the ground facing away, her mind spinning with scenarios. None of them good.

Once through the quarantine door and past the guard, Weng escorted Katrina to her room before turning back for his. It was an older section of officers' quarters that had been sealed off from the rest of the base. No windows, poor ventilation, and concrete gray everywhere. Still, it was better than the cell Weng had been assigned before. They walked down the hall, filled with something they had never even considered a possibility: treason.

"What are you going to do with the 1.0s we brought back? Their plan is a hope, at best," Katrina whispered. "Sacrifice without a real chance of success is—"

Weng lowered his voice, interrupting. "Not here," he cautioned.

Katrina understood and gave a delicate nod, then changed the subject. "I know you're concerned about Ruth. Go call her."

"You read my mind. Thanks."

"For what?"

"For just being you," Weng said with a growing smile. "It's very appealing, and things will work out. I'm just not sure how yet."

Katrina watched from the door as he headed to his quarters. *Dang, he has a good-looking swagger.*

Once in his room, Weng tore off his bio-suit and connected to his home's data center. Soon, a realistic image of Ruth was projected in the air next to him. She was overjoyed to see her father, and he did everything he could not to show the tears of joy swelling in his eyes. Less than twelve hours ago, he had given up the thought of ever seeing her again.

"Have you gotten taller?" Weng asked, hiding the emotion in his voice.

"I don't know—maybe," Ruth replied.

"You look taller . . . and faster to me."

"I did win the school race yesterday."

"You won? Wow."

"And I'm going to a special school soon," Ruth added with pride in her voice.

"What are you talking about?"

"The lady that is watching me, Ms. Geller, said I was going to go to a special school for gifted kids."

A flash of concern hit Weng in the heart. Had they already been planning to ship Ruth off to a boarding school when he had been late to report back? This was the final nail in the coffin, but Weng hid his anger. "Well, we can talk about all that when I get back."

"Pizza for dinner?"

"Yes, we can have pizza for dinner," Weng answered.

"Yes . . . 'cause Ms. Geller doesn't like pizza."

"Well, I do. Love you, pumpkin."

"Love you too, Dadda."

"Ruth?"

"Yes, Dadda?"

"I need you to do me a favor. Do you remember protocol three?" Weng asked.

"Yes."

"Initiate."

"Okay."

Weng was slow to kill the connection. Just the sight of a healthy, happy Ruth was all he needed right now. The goodbyes lasted another couple of minutes before they finally disconnected.

A soft knock on the door was followed by a familiar face. Katrina strode into the room. Weng had just finished cleaning up and had just managed to put on a pair of pants. He held his ground as Katrina stepped closer to him, letting the door close behind her. Without preamble, she leaned up and kissed Weng gently on the lips. A million emotions flowed through him as thoughts of his wife and more recent stirrings about Katrina jangled about his system, threatening to overload it. It felt right and just when his arms moved to caress her, she pulled back, eyeing him closely.

"I've been meaning to do that for some time now, and with all that's been happening, I didn't want to miss my chance," Katrina said, trying not to make direct eye contact with Weng, in case she had overstepped.

Weng's lips curled up slightly as his heart raced. "For a woman who prides herself on the scientific method, that was not exactly by the book."

Katrina relaxed and owned her actions. "Books are for students. I'm more of a throw-it-out-there-and-see-what-sticks kind of scientist."

Weng bored into her chestnut eyes, taking in every beautiful detail. "Well, it stuck." He pulled her toward him slowly and embraced her in both arms. He held his gaze at her natural beauty for a long time before slowly pulling her lips back to his. They kissed, letting their tongues explore one another. The room around them seemed to heat up and disappear at the same time. A hunger that burned to the very core consumed them as they let desires take control. Right now, it was time to act. No more glances from afar, so act they did.

Passion overtook reason, feeding their gratification like an old itch desperate for a scratch. Soon, there was nothing left of time, mathematics, physics, or logic. Only chemistry and biology.

19

President Caleb carefully studied Weng. He was dressed in clean clothes, and the smudges that had covered his face were gone. He radiated a calm and satisfied expression as he sat across from Caleb.

The two men stared at each other in the same quarantine room President Caleb had previously visited with Weng. Now, there were two small tables and chairs butted up on either side of the plexiglass wall that separated them.

"You were ambushed by a bunch of refugees?" Caleb asked, with a small degree of sarcasm.

"Highly trained and armed refugees. They set a trap, analog-style, and I fell for it."

"Hubris can be a dangerous trait," Caleb added.

"So I've learned. Luckily, we were heavily armed and had someone on the outside."

"You're talking about Sci Officer Katrina?"

"Yes, sir." Weng sat and picked up his wineglass by the stem and swirled it. "She cleared a path for us to retreat and then reengage. Once their plasma cannon was down, they had no counter for our weapons. It was a rout."

Caleb placed his elbows on the table, confident in the security of the partition between them. "Well done."

Weng did a modest air toast with his wine and took a sip. "Talk to me about Zion," Weng asked, changing the subject.

"So, thanks to you and your team, the grid went down and we came in, capturing just over three hundred thousand 1.0s. They are still in quarantine, awaiting their vaccinations and indoctrination before being allowed back into their homes. Of course, the best housing will go to the 2.0s we send here from New Kansas."

"Of course. I saw some of the indoctrination on my way here."

"You know what they say about eggs and omelets." He set his glass down and took a big chunk of steak with his fork. "Our scientists think it will be a couple of weeks before they can move here safely. Until then, we need to bio-suit up before interacting with them. At some point, that will no longer be necessary. Most of the city will naturally disinfect over time, as viruses have a limited shelf life outside a host. The trick here will be to disinfect the hosts, and we already have a plan in place."

"That's good news." The words felt like ash in Weng's mouth.

"Good? It's great. Giles Favreau is practically peeing himself. He can't wait to get another quarter-million-plus customers on his balance sheets, and he's been tracking another pandemic coming in from the East. I think he said it was adenovirus 12 or something like that."

"I remember adenovirus 11. That was some nasty stuff," Weng said.

"Pharma One should have the vaccine ready any day now."

Weng put his fork down and looked at Caleb, his eyes trying to see the lies hidden on the man's face, but politicians specialized in betrayal and falsehoods.

"So I assume you will want to get back to your daughter?" Caleb asked, suddenly feeling uncomfortable with Weng's stare.

"As soon as possible, but first I want to oversee the transfer and delivery of those prisoners."

"What's the sudden interest in a group of 1.0s?" the president asked.

"I want to see their faces when I personally escort them into the Ion-Dome. I lost good men on this mission, and these are the people responsible for the 1.0 uprising and all that has followed since. They deserve nothing but a clapping of hands and a few cheers after their molecules disintegrate right before their own eyes." Weng was surprised by the anger in his voice, surely meant for the man on the other side of the plexiglass.

Caleb cocked his head, and a small grin appeared. "I couldn't agree more." He placed his napkin on his plate and stood.

"I'll arrange everything. You can fly back with me in five days. In the meantime, get some rest; you've earned it."

"I look forward to it, sir." Weng watched as the man he now hated more than any other stood and left.

The first person had just died from adenovirus 12. Their lungs had filled with liquid, and no amount of ventilating or pumping could save them from drowning in their mucus. The body was sampled and then cremated. Giles had read the report of the thirteen additional patients that were still hanging on. The vaccine would be announced today, and as soon as he and his fellow chairs publicly received the vaccine, any back-flutter or citizen concerns would die out.

He announced in a special news broadcast that the top one percent of the city would all be vaccinated as a show of good faith. They would also commit to paying for the vaccines of the bottom five percent. It was a propaganda campaign with real potential. If Giles worked it right, he could sell T-shirts with the Pharma One logo on them.

The day was finally looking up after several grueling territory battles with the other chairs. It seemed there was a glitch of some sort in the divvying up of New Zion Caleb had made, and now Giles defended his position against the others. How they had gotten wind of it all was something he was keen to discover. If Caleb was behind it, he would take pleasure in striking back.

His MindLink alerted him to another call. This time, he cast the image up on one of his many screens. Rachel Tee, the chairwoman of UH Concerns, appeared. She had an obvious frown, which did her fifty-five-year-old face little favors. Her matching red irises and hair seemed to glow with fury. It made him think of the nickname he had given her: Firestorm.

"Giles, what the devil is going on? I hear you raided my cookie jar?"

Here we go again, he thought.

The meeting came to a close around the make-shift oval table in Caleb's temporary office. He was finally feeling comfortable with the way things were being handled in New Zion. The reorganized management team running the city had their orders, and each seemed sufficiently confident.

Cin wrapped things up and excused the team to get back at it. She stood beside the president as he shook hands with the line of exiting managers.

"What are the odds I banish a person from the city one day and they show back up in one of our military vehicles a hero the next?" Caleb said out of the side of his mouth, in confidence to Cin. His eyes and false smile were on display for the group as they slowly left the conference room, but his real attention was on the question posed to his assistant. "Thank you. I look forward to your report," he said as the last one shuffled out.

"Mr. President," Cin whispered back, "no one could have predicted that." They shook hands with the head of housing redistribution, a short woman with thinning gray hair.

"That's my point. It seems impossible, and that story about her turning the battle . . . I find it hard to believe." As the last person left, he dropped the façade and stepped to the window that overlooked the base, folding his arms.

She knew his moods and when and where not to interrupt, so she waited quietly to the side. The amount of time wasted by Caleb's indecisiveness was astounding. She would eliminate those inefficiencies the moment she was in charge.

Caleb suddenly turned. "I want you to go see her and find out what you can. See if their stories match up. I place a lot of trust in Commander Weng, and I don't want to be let down or surprised. Their quarantine will be done tomorrow morning, and we can all take the transport back to New Kansas. Find out if I'm stepping into a hornets' nest or not, and make sure she permanently misses the flight back."

"I understand," Cin said as she spun and left the room.

Katrina entered the room. Her eyes focused on the domed ceiling with a single circular skylight at the top. It was good to finally be out of quarantine. The room was made of poured concrete, giving it an industrial look with equipment shelves and gear stored high and wide throughout. The all-seeing eye skylight seemed to watch her every move, as did the woman who had asked her here.

Cin stepped from her perch on a large case and appraised Katrina with judgmental eyes. "I see quarantine has been good to you."

"Five days of rest and food is like a holiday compared to what I've seen and been through."

"I can only imagine," Cin replied with a false smile.

A brief, uncomfortable silence filled the space.

"I'm sorry about what happened. The president is a bit possessive, maybe even a touch crazy when it comes to the commander."

"Crazy as in killed Weng's wife, or crazy as in, banished me without warrant?"

"Like I said . . ." Cin glanced away for a beat, then returned her eyes to Katrina. "What do you say we put all that behind us and start over? I have read your file and am impressed. Highest in your class and this new world has a great need for people with your skills."

"Are you offering me a job?"

"That and a lot more. For one, I can get Caleb to back off the both of you, but I'm curious . . . what happened when you left Zion?"

Katrina paused to gather her words. "Well, as you know, I was kicked out of the city—no weapon, no water. I wandered helplessly for two days, starving and my mouth dry as sand. I stumbled on some travelers who were linking up with the fleeing 1.0s, so I thought I'd try to blend in and see where it all led."

"You weren't afraid of getting infected?"

"I was terrified. But what choice did I have? Starving to death is not how I want to go out."

"Granted," Cin added.

"When Commander Weng got trapped in cross-fire, I used my training to obtain a weapon and clear a path from the outside," she lied.

"Remarkable."

"Why do you want to know?"

"I like to find out things for myself, not depend on the stories of others. Plus, it's good to have quality people with experience and gumption on our side."

The words seemed hollow to Katrina. "I see. What about you?"

"What do you mean?"

"I know a little about you as well," Katrina said.

Cin looked up suddenly. This was unexpected.

"You worked for Pharma One before transferring over to the president's office. A mysterious death opened up a slot as the president's assistant. That's fast for a girl from the streets. A plaything for Giles Favreau that actually made good. That doesn't happen too often. What was it? Brains or body?"

Cin subdued a sudden flash of anger. "Where you start does not determine where you end."

"True. And where would you like to end . . . Mrs. President? or Ms. President?"

"You know nothing," said Cin, defensively.

"Perhaps not, but I can't imagine Giles has cut the strings completely. How often do you report back to him? The real power isn't in a figurehead president."

Cin lost control. Her days on the street came rushing back, and all her cool, calm persona vanished. She lashed out at Katrina. In a single move, Cin knocked Katrina down and had both hands squeezing around her neck. Katrina used her training to knock an arm free, and with her free elbow, she sent Cin sprawling. The two women sprang to their feet, each now on her toes, bouncing, swinging, and kicking out.

"I'll kill you," Cin growled.

"I never believed your civilized act. You're nothing but street trash, clambering for the crumbs doled out to you."

Cin screamed and raced at Katrina, who dodged out of her way at the last second.

At five-foot-nine, Cin had the size and reach advantage. Her yellow eyes were filled with anger as she circled her prey.

Katrina had been startled at first, but was back in the fight and dishing out as much as she received. Fists, elbows, and a few kicks.

Cin sent a wild punch toward Katrina, just missing her target. She followed the move with a leg sweep that dropped Katrina hard to the ground, sending a shot of pain through Katrina's hip and shoulder.

Cin added a kick to the head that left Katrina stunned. She then pulled a knife from her boot and moved in for the kill.

Katrina caught a glimpse of the knife just before it came crashing down and spun away, wishing she still had the boot knife Weng had given her. The stakes of this conflict now clearly stated.

She grabbed an empty equipment case and used it like a shield to parry the knife jabs away.

Cin grew frustrated with how long it was taking to finish off the little redhead. She faked a jab, then dropped low with the knife. The shield dropped to abate the move, and Cin launched a devastating headbutt that sent Katrina to the floor. The case skittered away, leaving Katrina vulnerable.

Cin smiled as she plunged the knife toward her wounded target.

Weng monitored as the political prisoners were loaded into the transport for New Kansas. Avery had a particularly harsh scowl pointed in his direction, and Jericho refused to look his way. Several of the soldiers who had been on the return trip seemed to be missing and a couple had severe bruising on their faces. Once the door closed, he was escorted to the president's ship for an immediate exit from New Zion.

They would be traveling in a diamond formation of four transports. As Weng entered and sat on the self-molding foam seat, the rotors began spinning up. He glanced at the president and his bodyguards.

"Is Cin not joining us?" he asked.

Caleb checked the hatchway and turned back to Weng, seemingly unconcerned. "She knew the schedule. Probably tying up a few loose ends before she heads back."

Just then Katrina climbed on board, and the door shut behind her. She was out of breath and had a few fresh scrapes and bruises.

"Sorry I'm late."

The president gave her a curious look and double-checked the hatch, but there was no sign of his assistant. He tried to connect with her, but the infrastructure for that was not yet in place in New Zion. He would have to wait until they landed in New Kansas.

Katrina sat next to Commander Weng.

"Almost missed my chance to ride back home with the leader of the free world," she said with a forced smile.

"Wasn't sure you would make it. Welcome aboard Sci Officer Katrina." Caleb took a moment to look over the sultry redhead. She had a dainty but full figure, with full, pink, pouty lips. Her eyes looked tired, but there was something more behind that . . . a fire. Yes, she could be a real vixen. He watched the inner play of body language between Weng and her. There was definitely something there.

He leaned his head back against the bulkhead as the transport arced right and headed east. The next two weeks would be revealing, and he needed to stay sharp and at least one step ahead of his opposition. Once his infrastructure was in place and New Zion was running again, he could relax a little. He tried connecting with Cin again. Nothing.

"You okay?" Weng asked Katrina.

"Just a minor misunderstanding with a colleague. In the end, I was able to make my point." She said the last sentence with her eyes squarely on Caleb.

The intense glare made the president uncomfortable, and he was the first to look away. He was also suddenly grateful for the three bodyguards on board with him.

Weng looked out the starboard window as the four transports began their descent into Fort Camden in New Kansas. A large contingent of warriors moved into position to welcome the victorious president back. The sight made Weng edgy, and he motioned to Katrina for a quick look.

Once on the ground, Caleb spent the next couple of minutes on his COMMs, trying to connect with Cin. The rotors powered down, and the hatchway opened before he could connect. Something was not right. At the very least, she would have sent a message to him by now.

As they exited, a band started to play, and two columns stood at attention as Caleb led the small group from the transport. He was waving and smiling in a practiced fashion.

Katrina and Weng followed at the back, the music and festivities calming their fears.

Hu 2.0

The president saluted several warriors as he made his way to a podium set up for the occasion. His bodyguards followed closely, always on the lookout for trouble. Caleb stepped up, and the band finished their tune. Weng and Katrina stood off to his right shoulder.

"Thank you for the rousing salutation. This has been a long time coming, and now that we have put an end to the war, great things are on the horizon." He allowed the cheers and clapping to die down before he continued. "Every soldier who fought or worked behind the scenes in this war has earned a reward, and I will do my best to see you compensated for your efforts and risks. With new housing deals and better pay."

Again, he waited for the excitement to die down. This was his world, and he reveled in it. "I wanted to take a moment and showcase two of my most trusted associates, who deserve to share in this moment as well. Commander Weng and Sci Officer Katrina." He gestured to them with his right hand. "Without their efforts, this mission would have never been possible, and I will see to it they get the recognition they deserve."

Commander Weng and Sci Officer Katrina stood tall and saluted the crowd. The cheers that followed filled Katrina with pride and satisfaction after all she'd been through. Maybe this mission would work out after all. She wanted to hold Weng's hand, but this was not the place.

Caleb finished his speech and left the crowd as he headed for the main offices, waving and smiling. He called for Weng and Katrina to follow.

The main office building on base was called the General H. Simpson building, named after a commander who had died in one of the bloodiest battles of the war, the Chicago Catastrophe. It had devastated the city and its people so badly; it was still unsafe to even fly over the blackened husk of the once-proud metropolis. People referred to it as Chi-char-go.

Weng and Katrina stepped out of the sun and into an open room with ten armed warriors pointing their weapons in their direction. They stopped mid-step.

"What's this all about?" Weng asked.

"I'm sorry, Commander. I truly believe you deserved the credit I gave you outside, but I can no longer trust you to do my bidding. It appears your girlfriend here killed my assistant."

"What?"

"It's true," Katrina said, with strength. "She attacked me for no reason when I accused her of spying on you for Giles Favreau. It was a miracle I was able to turn her blade, meant for me, back against her."

"You see, Katrina was protecting you, not trying to destroy you," Weng added.

"I have always known about Cin's allegiances to Giles. That was a connection I used against them. While you were off resting in quarantine, I was busy getting some answers from the prisoners you brought me, and I know all about your little plan."

"You know nothing about my plan. How do you think I got out of the 1.0 camp? We were captured, exposed. We did what we were trained to do. Lie and manipulate the situation for our benefit. That plan, as you called it, was nothing but a strategy to get back to base alive," Weng countered.

"You were always quick on your feet, Commander. So you're telling me you have no desire for revenge against me for having your wife killed?"

Weng stiffened. He had believed Katrina's words, but now they had been confirmed. He dove at Caleb with reckless abandon. But a rifle butt to the back of his head ended it.

Caleb stepped over to the inert body of the man who had done his bidding to the highest of standards. "Such a shame." He looked up at Katrina. "You should have kept your legs closed and your mouth shut."

"He deserved the truth."

"The truth? You poor, naive woman. The truth is what I say it is . . . and now you will die for your precious truth. Take 'em away."

The first thing Weng saw as his eyes blinked open was a blurry face. It slowly materialized into his red-haired beauty, Katrina, who was crouched beside him in concern. "Wasn't sure you were ever going to wake up. That's a nasty bump on the back of your head. Welcome back."

Weng rubbed the knot on his head and sat up slowly. The instant pain at touching it seemed to jolt him all the way awake. They were in a small, poorly lit room made of concrete with a porthole window and a steel door.

At a closer look, the porthole window was their only light source. Sitting around the room were a couple of familiar faces. Avery, Dr. Patel, and Jericho. There were three others he didn't recognize—one of them an older woman next to Katrina.

"This is my aunt, Dr. Millie Hastings," Katrina explained.

"You look nothing alike." Weng grimaced. Even talking hurt his head.

"Technically, my God-aunt."

"Pleasure, Dr. Hastings, I'm—"

"I know who you are," Dr. Hastings interrupted. "And you better be all they say you are if we're gonna get out of here and put a stop to this."

Weng blinked his eyes a few times, trying to clear his head. He felt like he had entered a conversation at the midpoint and was not getting the gist of it. "What is this place?"

"Holding cell for the Ion-Dome. We are supposed to be ionized tonight."

"Ionized?" Avery asked.

"Disintegrated down to your molecular structure. It is very painful, but luckily, it only lasts about fifteen seconds before you pass out," Dr. Hastings clarified.

"Good news all around then," Weng deadpanned.

The cell door suddenly clanked and opened, and four armed guards entered. "Katrina, stand up and walk out, or we will shoot you and carry you out."

Weng tried to stand and stop what was happening, but his equilibrium was still in the toilet, and he wobbled and fell back to the floor.

"Don't, I got this," Katrina said with mock bravery.

Katrina climbed from the floor and followed the guards out of the cell but not before taking one last good look at Weng.

Dr. Hastings ran to the closing cell door and pounded on it, yelling in frustration. She sank to the floor and sobbed. "This is all my fault."

Avery sat next to her and tried to comfort her.

Jericho and Weng gave each other a death stare but nothing more.

"What happened to your plan?" Jericho said, with a touch of accusation.

"Caleb happened. He sent his assistant to kill Katrina and manipulated me for the last time."

Jericho shared his frustration. It was the one thing they had in common at the moment. This was not the place to start a fight. Nothing would be gained. It was the place to make peace and say goodbye.

"What did you mean . . . about stopping this?" Weng asked, looking over at the doc.

Dr. Hastings tried to control her emotions as she answered Weng. "They're designing viruses to release on the public so they can sell vaccines and maintain control, and up until four days ago, I was a part of it."

"I never believed that so many different viruses and strains could just keep coming. They had to be man-made," Dr. Patel said to no one in particular.

"They are," replied Dr. Hastings.

"Are you serious?" Weng asked.

"Very. I was the driving force behind it . . . until I couldn't take any more."

"What happened?" Dr. Patel asked.

"Who cares what happened?" Jericho exclaimed. "We're stuck here, and I don't see any way out."

"Jericho." Avery gave him a serious look and then turned her attention back to Dr. Hastings. "I care. Tell us."

"A body of a young girl came into my lab. She was blonde with natural deep-blue eyes, the kind you pay a fortune for here. Her skin was flawless, and there were no scars like you would normally see. Except that her throat had been slit. All very sad."

Jericho suddenly perked up and started to pay attention to her words. "Her name was 24."

Everyone looked over his way.

"She was everything to me."

Avery suddenly got it. "Your partner from the capsule."

Jericho nodded.

"I'm so sorry. She was lovely. When I did the gene and DNA analysis, I discovered something unique in the structure of her DNA."

"A coded biological spike?"

Dr. Hastings turned to Dr. Patel sitting in the corner. "Yes. How did you know?"

Dr. Patel stood and moved over to the cell door with Avery and Dr. Hastings. "We discovered the same thing." She pointed to Jericho. "In him."

"Wait, what do you mean?" Dr. Hastings asked.

"I mean I have seen the code, and I think I might have a way to read it."

"Incredible. I was forced to burn the body and all the evidence. She was a real chance at healing the world, and I had to destroy her . . ."

"She was kind and funny. Very smart and had no patience for my disregard of the rules," Jericho recalled to no one.

"But I couldn't do it," Dr. Hastings said, looking at the ground. Everyone glanced her way.

"I hid the evidence." She turned to Weng. "That's why you have to get us out of here so we can escape with the truth."

"The truth is what they say it is. As long as the corporations control the message, we are powerless to effect any real change, and as far as getting out of here . . ." Weng held up his hands. "That ain't gonna happen."

"The truth is Jericho and 24 have the same unique DNA structure, and that structure can be used to save humankind and shift the balance of power back to the people."

Everyone peered at Jericho.

"Don't look at me. I'm done being used. I just want my shot at Caleb."

"What if your actions could not only hurt him but save thousands of others?" Avery asked.

Jericho didn't respond.

20

Katrina tried to move but could only wiggle. She had been taken to a room up on the top floor of Government House. It was a purpose-built space about fifteen feet square, with padded walls, two cabinets, and a few plush pieces of furniture. There was a bed against a wall, and in the middle of the room was a most curious device, bolted to the floor. This was the kind of room you kept secret from friends and, more importantly, your enemies.

The device was an articulating metal sculpture, with four appendages and a central control box mounted to a pedestal about four feet tall. Each appendage or arm could be locked into an infinite variety of positions or be released to move freely. They could be operated in unison or independently. It was quite ingenious. The only problem was Katrina was strapped to it. Her arms raised up, each connected at the wrist and forearm, and her legs slightly spread, attached at the ankle and calf. The pedestal had ahold of her torso, leaving only her head to move at will. She looked like a model for Leonardo da Vinci's Vitruvian Man.

Currently, all four arms on the device were locked, and Katrina was stuck in that position. A light sweat had worked its way through her clothes from her struggles to free herself. Her limited mobility allowed her to only see about half the room, and what she could see scared her.

As the sun set, a rising shadow of her body moved up the wall in front of her. The devil's sundial, a macabre-looking crucifixion of sorts.

Avery paced back and forth to the point she was making everyone a little nuts. The artificial glow from the porthole window had gone blue and dimmed; the room was mostly dark.

Weng, having fully recovered, tried banging the door off its hinges with his enhanced arm. He was rewarded with only a few small dents.

"Can't you see through the door with those eyes?" asked Dr. Patel as she gestured to his purple irises.

Weng looked at her with a face that said a lot more than no.

"How would you go about reading the code?" Dr. Hastings asked, trying to lower the angst filling the room.

"I would need access to a fairly serious lab and time to test my theory," Dr. Patel replied.

"Time is something we don't have a lot of," Weng said.

The three women ignored him and continued to plan. They talked about technology and used medical terms that neither Jericho, Avery, nor Weng understood, but the more they talked, the more their excitement grew. It was as if they were working out a blueprint of action in their minds.

A jangle at the door stopped everything. Dr. Hastings had removed her belt and was using the buckle to scratch equations into the wall.

The door opened. Two guards with weapons stood in the doorway. "Everyone move to the back wall—now."

The rag-tag group complied. Two more guards entered and set plastic food trays with hot meals and boxed waters on the ground. Nothing sharp or metallic.

"Last meal?" Weng asked.

"Everyone at the Ion-Dome gets a last meal. Tonight's something special for our VIPs." The guard started laughing.

"It's going to be a big night tonight. Completely sold out. I guess everyone wants to see the likes of you all doing the herky-jerky dance." The second guard started laughing as they left, closing the cell door behind them.

"We are never getting out of here," Jericho mumbled.

"I know a lab I can still get us into with a bit of your help, Commander Weng," Dr. Hastings said. "I share privileges at the lab in Fort Camden, as well as Pharma One . . . well I did. Knowing Giles, the word is not out about me yet, as that would not make him look good—to have such a trusted staff member be a traitor."

"How does reading a coded message in my DNA help any of us?" Jericho asked.

"I won't know till I read it," Dr. Patel replied.

"So, we're just hoping here?" he asked.

Avery stopped pacing and turned to Jericho. "Don't you see? My father designed you to restore the world. To heal humankind and put an end to sickness and the monopolies that control us."

"You are the one person who can make that happen, Jericho," Dr. Patel added.

Jericho stood abruptly. "Whatever you have planned, count me out. Humankind has done nothing but ruin my life. You're all a bunch of self-serving crazies, as far as I can see. Everyone trying to push their agenda. Freedom, tyranny, salvation—it never ends. This world is wasted on the likes of you all. History proves you just keep messing it up. I wouldn't lift a finger to save any one of you. I only came along to get my chance at President Caleb."

"Get in line. Redemption for having failed to protect 24? How's that working for you?" Weng voiced.

"Don't you see? You are the way we strike back at Caleb and all he stands for," Avery said.

Jericho sat back down in the corner. "We all deserve what's coming. You especially."

"You are probably right. Besides, the future isn't about us. At best, all we can do is open the door for others," Weng's mind flashed to Ruth and what might be happening to her. His teeth gritted in angst.

Dr. Hastings watched with concern. They were nothing but a group of individuals with self-serving interests. "None of this is helping. We need to come together as one if we are going to succeed."

———

The door to her left opened and closed quickly. President Caleb stepped over to his trussed-up prize, with the eyes of a tiger analyzing his trapped prey.

"To the victor goes the spoils," he said while rubbing his hands together.

Katrina tried to fight her captivity for the thousandth time, but it was hopeless. She had nothing to share but a vivid hatred carved on her face for the man.

"You surprised me, and that's not easy to do, Katrina—not easy at all—and besting Cin . . . I'm still trying to decide whether to thank you or something else. Let's go with something else."

Caleb let his eyes take in the woman who had been a thorn in his side recently. "Let me guess, you did it all in the name of honor, duty, love?" He shook his head at the thought. "Those are just words we use to inspire the actions of the feeble. Get them to do our bidding. Like you are about to do."

Katrina's heart pounded in her chest. She flexed against the bindings, and they answered back by digging into her skin.

"But I didn't come here for conversation. Let's just say, I will enjoy this. What you do is up to you."

Katrina tried to stay calm. Panic would serve as no master, and words would just make her look weak.

Caleb picked up a small remote control and held it up so Katrina could see it. He pushed a button. Katrina's arms moved down to her sides. She tried to stop them, but no amount of effort could resist the machine.

"It's called a Dynatrom. I call her Dyana. Unlike most women, she does what I say without complaint. I can give you mobility." He pressed another button, and Katrina's left arm was suddenly free to move. She quickly reached for the bindings holding her right arm.

"Or I can take it away." Her left arm suddenly shot back out, locked straight again in position.

"You're sick." She couldn't stop the words from coming out.

A sudden and intense current shocked Katrina to her core.

"Like I said, I'm not interested in hearing from you, but I can tell you and Dyana are going to be good friends."

Katrina's head lolled to the side.

He pressed a different button, and the Dynatrom reconfigured, forcing Katrina to another position at table height.

"Women are always spouting off about equality and superior intellect, but when it matters, might holds all the cards. Power is, after all, the ultimate aphrodisiac."

Katrina experienced a jolt of fear and panic. She closed her eyes and willed herself to be anywhere else.

Geena rode on the roof of a captured Stryker with two other children—the only children to make it out of Zion and survive the battle at the campsite. There was a dust trail billowing behind them, obscuring her view. After so many minutes spent looking back for the man who had saved her, Geena gave up and turned forward. She was a survivor, and giving up was no longer part of her DNA. She was changed somehow by her connection to him. She had survived the wilderness and the Reekers. Now she would find a way to thrive, no matter the situation.

The trail was bumpy and the heat of the sun unforgiving. They had left early in the morning. Just another day, heading away from everything she knew. The couple who had agreed to watch after her seemed nice, but they were missing the kind eyes Jericho had shown her. Having lost a little girl of their own, they often looked at Geena with accusing eyes, but that was child's play for her now.

Geena pulled the ring out from under her shirt and let her fingers move across the smooth metal. It was nothing special, and she never learned about its significance, but it was important to Jericho and, therefore, important to her. She would keep it safe until his return, the only family she had left.

She moved her thoughts back to the present. Crying had been commonplace over the last week, but now she had no more tears to offer. Geena would stand on her own and do what needed to be done. She had proven herself capable to both herself and Jericho. That was all that mattered. From here on out, Geena would be a force, and that force would do marvelous things.

Caleb hit a button on the remote that put Katrina back in her original position. He placed the remote in his back pocket and stepped over to a burled cabinet. Inside the double doors was a collection of tools. The sight of the collection ended the last speck of hope Katrina had been harboring.

Caleb selected a small knife with a hooked blade and returned to his prize. He used it to carefully remove most of Katrina's clothes. One second she was wearing them, and the next she was in her underwear. It was a very sharp knife.

The whole thing seemed unreal to her—like she was witnessing it but not participating. Her only thought was that it must be her brain's way of separating herself from the horror of what was happening. He hesitated before replacing the knife in the cabinet, moving like he had nothing but time. Then he pulled out the remote and pressed a button. Dyana reconfigured Katrina.

She grit her teeth. Her mind searched, but she came up with no options. There was nothing she could do but try to survive this.

Caleb removed his coat and tie, placing them purposefully on a chair.

Katrina could smell the musty odor of an excited man, and it sickened her. She threw out a desperate idea. "Put your arms around me. Let me hold you."

Caleb paused, not sure he had heard correctly. Was this young trophy enjoying his advances? He looked into her eyes, searching for deception, but she had her head back and her eyes closed, a subtle sigh escaping her lips.

He pressed the remote, and Katrina's arms wrapped around him slightly. She moved her hands along his back, as much as the bindings would allow.

Caleb hit the reset on the remote, returning Katrina to the original position. He stepped back, his heart beating fast. Could this be real?

"Come back to me," she whispered.

Caleb ripped his shirt off and reset Katrina to the reclined position.

"Say we were to get out of here somehow . . . what then?" Jericho asked.

"Well, we would decipher the code you carry and find a way to get the word out to the people about what Pharma One has been doing. They need to know," Dr. Hastings replied.

"That's not much of a plan," Avery said.

"Maybe not, but we can't let them get away with this," Dr. Hastings added.

"They've gotten away with it, and tonight, the last of the evidence will be ionized out of existence," Weng said.

"I have the evidence saved on a drive, hidden in a picture frame," Dr. Hastings said.

"Where, in your pocket? Because unless it's hidden very well, they have already found it," Weng said. "Do you see any goons torturing you for that information?"

"No, but I don't think they know I have it."

"So, what, you just left Pharma One because you were tired of working there?" Avery asked skeptically.

"Even I don't believe that," Jericho added.

"I—I didn't really think it all through. I just knew I couldn't destroy this world's chance at redemption. So I just grabbed the data and ran."

"These people are smart. They have been controlling the masses for so long now," Weng said.

"That's the problem," Avery interjected. "They have been doing it for so long, they have gotten lazy, even reckless. Now that the war is over, they will have their guard down. This might be the only chance we'll ever get."

"What chance? We are locked up and scheduled for execution in a few hours. How are we going to do anything?" Dr. Patel asked.

"As long as I'm breathing, there is a chance. So let's cut the problems and focus on a solution." Weng's thoughts of Ruth emboldened him. He had been in worse situations.

"I like the sound of that," Dr. Hastings said.

"It's better than lying here, waiting to be killed," Jericho added as he stood. The small but determined group took a moment to share eye contact. They were in this together, win or fail.

"Finally." Dr. Hastings turned back to her belt-buckle wall scratchings.

Dr. Patel approached her, watching intently. "This could be a real chance at getting back at President Caleb."

Her words had Jericho's and Weng's full attention.

"Can you free one of my arms?" Katrina asked, seemingly mired in passion.

"I can do better than that." Caleb hit a preset button on the remote that forced Katrina's arms and hands to move all over his back. He then shoved the remote into his back pocket so he could have some fun exploring a few of her more sensitive areas with both of his hands.

Katrina was helpless to fight the movement of her arms as they roamed across Caleb's bare back, but the pattern was not random. It repeated itself, like an elongated figure eight. She used her hips to push Caleb up as her hand lowered to his buttocks. A stealthy grab and her fingers glanced off the remote just sticking out of Caleb's rear pocket. She waited patiently again, enduring his groping. As her hands lowered again, she thrust her lower body up once more, even harder, and grabbed the remote.

"Ah, I see you like that," Caleb commented on her hip movement.

Katrina blocked him from her mind and focused on her task. She figured she would get one chance at this. As her hand came up, she scanned the buttons on the remote and pressed one. Her arms started opening, and she quickly reversed the button. In an instant, she had Caleb wrapped in a bear hug. She used the power of the mechanical arms to help her squeeze.

With both his arms down, Caleb was pinned and helpless. "You're hurting me. Loosen up a bit."

Katrina slid the button even further and locked Caleb in a vice-like hold.

Caleb tried to find his remote in his back pocket but came up empty. A sudden panic coursed through his spine. "I can't breathe; let me go," Caleb forced out.

Katrina whispered in his ear. "Never mess with a woman with nothing to lose."

Caleb instantly knew this was not foreplay; he was in real danger. He thrashed wildly, but the deadly embrace he was in held fast, tightening with every breath, like a boa constrictor with a mouse. The pleasure receptors in his brain turned off as his libido crashed and his fear rose. A beet-red face transitioned to white as he grew weaker and more desperate. The narcissist in him refused to believe this girl was getting the better of him. He squirmed and fought against two women much stronger than him, Katrina and Dyana. Thoughts of negotiation were the first to hit his racing mind. "I'll give you anything, just say it. I'll make it happen."

When that didn't work, threats came out, followed by a string of cursing that ended with his last exhale. Caleb's mind burned for oxygen as his eyes moved in every direction, looking for salvation, but there was nothing. No way out and no way forward. His last thought was dismissed as folly: *Could I have underestimated this woman?*

Then nothing but pain. His eyes finally lost focus, and his muscles stilled.

Katrina was taking no chances and continued to squeeze. The feeling inside her had gone from hopelessness to anger, and she was feeling the rush with the turning of the tide.

"They say the last sense you lose when you die is hearing," she hissed. "So listen closely. I'll take female wit over male might anytime, you misogynist pig."

With that, she slid the button on the remote over and relaxed her quivering arms. Caleb tipped to the floor, a lifeless blob. It took a few moments for Katrina to figure out the remote, but once her hands came together, she could free herself from Dyana. She dropped to her knees, heaving and shaking. Once the adrenaline dump calmed, she dismissed Caleb's soiled pants and moved to the closet, where she found a French maid's outfit. Her eyes scanned to the far end, where a few backup suits for Caleb hung. She put on a pair of his pants and used a belt to keep them up. The French maid's top was a near-perfect fit.

She stepped to his body and removed his COMMs unit and placed it in front of his face. The screen activated. A quick search revealed his last few communications. She scrolled through them, stopping on one that caught her eye. *Bring the redhead to my office.*

The cell wall had detailed scratches on it, including a DNA chain showing the bump on the tail that was part of Jericho and 24. Both doctors were busy discussing the details and making a plan to decipher Jericho's bio-code. He had long ago tuned them out; the idea of playing Guinea pig again was seemingly in the cards, and he tried not to think about it. His mind flashed to Geena, hoping she was not causing problems with the nice couple that had agreed to watch over her. He let the events of his experiences on Earth replay as he tuned out his surroundings. There were many highs and some very low lows. Life was hard at its core, and anyone who tried to tell you differently was selling something.

He let the emotions of his recent past fade and flow in a sort of mindless stew. It was as if for a moment he was no longer in a jail cell, awaiting execution. Santos came to mind. His God-fearing friend, who taught him the power of something greater than themselves.

"I've heard of a place we go to after we die," Jericho blurted out, interrupting the science experiment on the wall.

The room fell into silence for a moment.

Dr. Patel turned and answered. "It has many names: Heaven, Paradise, Valhalla, Good Kingdom. It's supposed to be amazing."

"Would 24 go there?" Jericho asked.

"I'm sure she is waiting for you there," Dr. Patel said.

"And so are Finley and the thousands of others who have been a part of this war," Avery added.

"A better place for all than here, I hope," Weng said, thinking about his wife.

"But we can do nothing for them there. We're all just passengers on this spinning blue ball," Jericho said, with his head down.

"We can do our best here," Dr. Patel said.

Jericho nodded at the sentiment. Maybe he could do more than just get revenge for 24's death. Maybe he could help make a difference.

Weng stood and started pacing. "I know a way to get it to the masses. There's a streaming center on the base that I should still have access to."

"Don't you think the president would have made everyone aware of your treason by now?" Avery asked.

"Like you, Dr. Hastings, and Giles, Caleb would want to keep my situation very quiet until he can blast it to the world tonight. It could be the kinda thing that might blow up in his face if not handled just right. I have a lot of loyal warriors on my side. Plus, he won't take a chance that one of the CEOs gets wind I'm in here and swoops in to use me like a bargaining chip."

"New Zion is still in flux right now, and any way to tilt the table in their favor is fair game for those at the top," Dr. Hastings agreed.

"The president sounds like he's playing all the angles," Avery surmised.

"That man is the devil, and the devil is the architect of all the angles," Weng said.

The conversation died off.

"We still have to find a way to get outta here," Jericho added.

"Sometimes, when things are at their darkest, the smallest light will show the way. If it's okay with you, I'd like to say a prayer for all of us," Avery asked.

"It can't hurt, darling," Dr. Hastings said.

"What do you know of God?" Jericho asked Weng.

"He requires more faith than I have right now," Weng replied.

Avery ignored Weng's comment. "God is there for all of us, Jericho. We can find solace and peace in knowing Him. If we don't believe in something greater than ourselves, we are destined to remain forever small."

"I don't know him," Jericho said.

"It's never too late to know him. He is waiting, and all you have to do is ask." Avery reached out her hands. "Okay, everyone hold hands," she encouraged.

It took a second, but the small desperate group came together as one. Standing in a circle in the middle of the small room, they held hands and bowed their heads.

Avery cleared her throat and began. "Dear God, we come before you, humbled and assembled as one, to thank you for your grace and love."

Jericho cocked an eye skyward, wondering if anyone was up there listening.

"We find ourselves in a difficult situation and ask for your help and guidance. If it be your will, please take this burden from us . . . so we might complete our undertaking. Amen."

"Amen," a couple of others chorused.

Weng looked around, touched by the words and their sincerity. It was mystical and spiritual all at once.

The group awkwardly broke apart. There was a vibe in the room that seemed to grow, and one by one, smiles grew on their faces.

Weng placed his hand on Jericho's shoulder, and they shared a feeling of mutual respect. "If that doesn't do it, nothing will."

The sudden jiggle of the lock followed by the cell door opening grabbed everyone's attention, and the smiles quickly vanished.

"You two come with us. It's time to say goodbye," one of the armed guards called.

Jericho and Weng shared a surprised look, then followed the guards' orders.

"No, please," Dr. Hastings cried. Only Avery kept her faith.

"I think they are going to have a little fun with us before our execution," Weng whispered out of the side of his mouth.

Jericho looked over and added, "Soften us up a bit."

"They can try."

"No talking." The guards marched them out of the cells and took their time, making sure they were manacled, and taking great care with Weng's artificial arm. Jericho and Weng were led over to an elevator and forced to face the walls.

It took nearly fifteen minutes and a shuttle to get them to their destination— the top floor of Government House, where Caleb worked and lived.

Weng and Jericho had been like loaded springs, waiting for a chance to make a move, but the guards were well-trained and used distance and stacking techniques to keep the two prisoners under control. The group stepped through the empty assistant's office and into the president's receiving area. This was the place where he did most of his public business. It, too, was empty.

"Mr. President?" one of the guards called out, somewhat confused.

Jericho and Weng shared a look, ready for a desperate attack on the guards. It was reckless and dangerous, but after the beating they were about to take, there would be nothing left in their tanks to fight with. It was now or never. Weng pushed right and Jericho, left. Shots rang out, and all four guards dropped to the floor, motionless. Jericho ducked, covering his head in protection, and Weng stood, waiting for the shot that would end him. It didn't come.

Instead, Katrina stepped from behind the desk, gun still raised, ready to dispatch any movement from the guards. None came.

"I thought you were dead!" Weng said, more surprised than he expected to be. Katrina ran to his arms and grabbed on like she might never let go. Tears gushed. Weng had to admit, it felt good.

"Are you okay?"

Katrina nodded against his shoulder.

"He didn't hurt you?"

She shook her head.

Jericho stood back up, and Katrina suddenly pulled away from Weng and pointed the gun at him.

"It's okay. We're good. Help us get these chains unlocked. Nice outfit, by the way."

Katrina did a small curtsey in her French-made top and men's slacks.

"Where's the president?" Jericho asked Katrina as he looked around.

"I helped him embrace the other side."

Jericho's shoulders slumped at her words. His entire reason for being here was now gone.

21

The city was bustling at street level as overlapping work shifts finished and started. Bodies jockeyed for food, drinks, or a destination. A small group of citizens pushed their way through the crowd with a purpose. If you were to casually notice them, nothing out of the ordinary would stand out, but on closer inspection, there were a few things off. Eyes roamed, constantly looking for potential complications. Clothes were dirty or ill-fitting, and they weren't engaged in casual conversation like those around them. Several had subtle bulges under their shirts from the confiscated guards' weapons.

The walkway was scattered with vendors and the smell of roasting meat. Promos and public notifications about the impending adenovirus 12 were running on repeat across the many displays throughout the city. Several deaths had already been reported, and word of a vaccine due out soon was followed with well-rehearsed fear-mongering.

Weng had forced them to travel on foot because every transport was equipped with bio-readers. As fugitives, one step inside a transport drone, and they'd be as good as caught. They would literally lock the doors and fly them to the nearest control station.

Katrina led the group around a congested section on the way to her apartment. A warning tone with three red lines across all the city's displays interrupted a commercial for tonight's Ion-Dome annihilation. It caused most citizens to stop what they were doing and look at nearby screens.

The tone was followed by a graphic. *Stand by for an important message from Government House.* The graphic melted away, revealing Giles Favreau wearing a shiny, fitted suit that hid much of his bulk. He carried a practiced, sad expression and used his hands for emphasis as he spoke.

"I am sorry to inform you that our beloved president has passed away from a bout with adenovirus 12. His brave actions in ending the Vaxxer War against the 1.0s, unfortunately, exposed him to this deadly virus and made him a victim to its ravages." He paused for effect. "My good friend will be remembered for his valiant efforts." Giles's expression changed to one more authoritarian. "As of now, I will assume his role until we can put this current outbreak behind us. Fear not, a vaccine is coming soon. And I will be the first to test it."

The view pulled back to show Giles getting a shot from a technician. "Today, hundreds of key personnel and officials are involved in the running of this city; they will demonstrate its efficacy and safety. After a twenty-four-hour incubation period, an upgrade must be done at any local LIFE-ARCH to lock in the vaccine's full potency. Without this upgrade, the vaccine will not be effective. In forty-eight hours, it will be made available to all who want it. Again I am sorry to—"

Katrina turned to the group. "That's not how he died."

Weng added, "Giles used Caleb's death to make a power play that no other CEO will challenge. As CEO of Pharma One and president of the COE, he has almost unlimited power now."

The death of Caleb had put Jericho's motive for revenge out of reach. Life was funny that way. It never followed a script, only a seemingly random collection of events aligning themselves in some predetermined or even random order. His involvement was often *hang on for the ride*. He was left with only their current plan and his role in it, and going back now wasn't an option. Santos's words bounced around in his head. *Make things better than you found them.* He would do what he could.

"The death of the president doesn't change things. It was always about Pharma One. We need to expose Giles for who he is," Dr. Hastings said.

"It might be too late," Weng countered, his mind flashing through several possibilities. What he really needed to do was collect Ruth and get out of the city.

"I say we get the evidence and go from there," Avery urged. "Come on, we need to hurry."

They moved off, each a bit torn up about their current plan. The citizens around them seemed stunned at the announcement, especially so soon after his success with New Zion. Hushed conversations bounced all around as Avery pushed forward, encouraging the others to catch up.

"Hey, hang a right up ahead." Katrina led them through a narrow alley that cut some time off their journey and avoided one of the working bio-scanners in the area.

Two blocks from Katrina's apartment a second alert filled the street displays. It was a collection of all their pictures, save Commander Weng's, with verbiage: "Be on the lookout for these dangerous fugitives."

"That's not a very good picture of me," Dr. Patel said. "I look like my mother."

"We gotta get off the street and get on base, where they don't have this broadcast system. We can buy some time there," Weng said.

"Then what?" Katrina asked.

"Then we'll need to get out of the city for good," Weng said. He put his head down and hurried towards their destination.

"Can I help you?" A young girl with brown hair and matching eyes cracked the front door open. Weng forced it wide, and he and Katrina entered the apartment. They had left the others in the lobby to make less of a footprint in the hallway. Being recognized now would be the end of everything they had planned.

"Hey," the girl cried out as she flew back from the door.

"What are you doing here?" Katrina asked a bit flummoxed.

"This is my new apartment. What are *you* doing here?"

Katrina looked around. There were boxes and a few crates with personal belongings. Some were opened, a few of their contents exposed. None of it was Katrina's. She looked at Weng, then back to the stranger. "I live here. Where are all my things?"

"Well, not anymore, and the last of your stuff left in a carryall about fifteen minutes ago."

"The basement, come on," Katrina pulled Weng as she turned and left, calling back over her shoulder. "Sorry for the interruption."

Weng asked, "What's in the basement?"

"An ion micronizer for trash and unwanted items."

Weng picked up his pace as they raced down the steps two at a time.

The basement was relatively clean, with storage cabinets for residents on one side and a progressive mural on the other. Pools of cool LED light added to the variety of colors on the wall. At the end was a metal bin with a tilt-up access door. A blue light was emitting from the seams as a man in coveralls and a dirty face stood next to it, watching the timer countdown. Next to him was a half-empty carryall with familiar items stacked inside.

"Stop," Katrina called out in desperation, her hand raised.

"Sorry, once I activate her, there is no stopping this baby. What's wrong?" the man said.

"Those are my belongings."

"That's odd; the work order said you'd been KIA."

"Close but not quite." Katrina started rummaging through the leftovers in the carryall. She collected a simple blouse and jeans to replace the French-made-and-slacks outfit and continued to dig.

The man watched her with detached curiosity. "I'm real sorry 'bout that. Had no idea. Just following the work order."

"It's not here. Shoot! It's not here." Katrina's shoulders slumped.

Weng took her in his arms and gave her a squeeze. "It's okay. It was a long shot, anyway."

They had failed.

"What are you looking for?" the man asked.

Katrina pulled her head from Weng's shoulder. "A small picture of my aunt and me. It was in a faded red frame."

The man looked at Weng, then back at Katrina. Then he looked down at his shoes like he might have forgotten to tie them. "You two looked so happy, I—I couldn't destroy it. Was savin' it for my collection." He pulled the small frame out of his back pocket and handed it over to Katrina. "Didn't mean nothin' by it."

Katrina spun the frame and pulled out the data chip. She finally released a breath she had been holding before handing the chip to Weng. Flipping the frame back over, she took a second to look at the photo. A young Katrina and her aunt stared back with silly smiles. "Yes, we were very happy then." She handed it back to the man and followed Weng to the exit.

"What do you want me to do with the rest of your things?" he called out.

"Fry 'em. I guess I did die after all," Katrina called back.

Fort Camden was just as Weng had expected, busy. Warriors and support personnel moved in every direction as transports did the loop to New Zion. He received salutes from everyone he passed. It was a good sign. His arrest had been kept close to the vest by Caleb. It would give the team a few hours of breathing room. He led them to the on-site lab and ordered the techs working there to take a break for the rest of the day.

"Docs, have at it. You got about three hours, at best, so make the most of it. I need to run some interference to keep the heat off us."

With a short nod, they went to work. "Jericho, I need some of your blood and hair," Dr. Hastings called out.

"You really know the way to a guy's heart, don'tcha, Doc." He sat on a chair and let her collect her samples.

"So how did you become Katrina's God-aunt? Is that even a thing?" Jericho asked.

"Katrina was my best friend's daughter, and when her parents died, I was the closest thing to a family she had. Raised her best I could and pushed her out into the world."

Jericho watched as Dr. Hastings drew his blood. Her words were more factual than they were emotional.

Meanwhile, Katrina made a copy of the data chip. She organized and prioritized the information needed to make a public broadcast condemning Giles and his whole operation. She dumbed down some of the language and sensationalized a few points. Once that was done, she added bold graphics and an AI voiceover to tie it all together. Now, all they had to do was get it out to the system for all to see and hear.

The two doctors seemed buried in their world, trying to read the biological code hidden in Jericho's DNA. Dr. Patel used a specialized dye to reveal the code and then a gene splicer to separate and upload it.

Weng knew something was wrong the minute he opened his front door. The lingering smell of smoke filled his nostrils. He pulled his weapon and swept the house, fearing the worst. Ruth's packed suitcase was sitting next to the entry. Carlyle, their home social robot, lay on its side in the living room with several burn marks across its torso. *The source of the smoke,* Weng deduced. He knelt down and did a quick inspection of the dead robot. Its weapon was out, and it looked like it had been fired.

A smear of red by the hallway caught his attention, and Weng quickly closed to investigate. *Blood.* He followed a trail to an adult body lying motionless at the end of the hallway. He turned it over. The lifeless eyes of Ms. Geller stared back.

"Ruth," he called out, no longer caring about being stealthy. "Ruth, honey." He opened the door to her room and called out with less volume. "Ruth?"

A round head with curly brown hair poked up from behind the bed, followed by Patty the platypus. "Dadda!" She ran to him and wrapped small hands around his neck. He hugged her back, letting all his pent-up worry for her finally dissolve.

"I did what you said. I did it, Dadda."

Weng looked at his daughter, not sure what she was talking about.

"Protocol three. She was trying to take me away."

Weng's memory came rushing back. Protocol three was a secret they had agreed on in case things got bad. It consisted of a code given to Carlyle, allowing it to use deadly force on anyone endangering a family member. From the looks of things, it had gotten very real, and Carlyle had sacrificed itself to save Ruth.

"It's okay, baby. I'm here now. You did good. Understand?"

Her little head nodded up and down against his shoulder. "Ms. Geller was going to take me away."

"From here on out, we stick together. Agreed?" He held his hand out like a used car salesman making a deal.

Ruth took it and shook it with a firm grip. "Agreed."

Weng made a quick call to the military engineer he had worked with when planning the attack on the generators at Zion. He needed to know how and where to go about tapping into the public announcement system, and the man owed him a favor.

"So do you think you can use my genetic material to put a stop to disease as we know it?" Jericho looked over Dr. Hasting's shoulder as she worked on a computer model that showed high viperin levels in a cell.

"It's an almost certainty now that I have everything we need to do it, but it will take some time. Thanks for your donations by the way."

Jericho held up a bandaged arm. "It'll all grow back, Doc."

They shared a smile for a beat.

"I don't believe it," Dr. Patel said as she pulled her reading glasses from her head.

Jericho and Dr. Hastings turned to see what was wrong.

"What?" Avery asked, suddenly alert.

They had been in the lab for just over three hours, and the fear of getting caught was growing by the second. There had been no word from Weng, and everyone was getting jumpy.

Unfortunately for Avery, there was little she could do. This was not her area of expertise. Katrina used her as a spokesperson for a few minutes on the broadcast she was preparing, but otherwise, Avery was on guard duty.

"I think this code is a computer virus, but honestly, it's like nothing I've seen before."

"The code in Jericho's DNA?" Avery asked.

"It looks like a crash code. Your father was a real genius," Dr. Patel said.

Avery flushed at the mention of her father.

"Looks like it either overrides or turns something off."

"So what . . . we just need to input this virus into his computer system and then?" Avery asked.

"I think it shuts it down." Dr. Patel said. "Potentially the whole system."

"You think?"

"Yes, that's the problem. I'm not sure."

"Well, I don't have a problem; let's just upload it and see what it does," Avery said. "We're running out of time."

"The thing is . . ." Dr. Patel started, "I can see the code. I can read part of it, but I can't get all of it out. There are embedded layers, and I can't get at them."

"Even if she had the whole code, it would be nearly impossible to upload it where it would do the most good," Dr. Hastings interrupted.

"What do you mean?" Jericho asked.

"Giles is a very careful man. His whole computer system, the one that runs Pharma One—well, at least the important stuff—is all sealed off. Hacking was a weapon used against his competitors in the early days of the war. Something he learned and used to his great advantage. Now, he's so paranoid that the only way to get anything into his system is through a heavily secured room in the middle of his virology facility. Armed guards and a self-sealing room surround it twenty-four-seven. Only one access point in and out. An extremely sophisticated system that includes the LIFE-ARCHes around the city, as well. You wouldn't believe the protocols I had to go through just to upload new samples or data."

"We'll never get into a place like that," Katrina said.

"Is there a way to cut into the information lines somewhere?" Avery asked.

"Everything's shielded with auto-locking protocols. One breach and the system shuts down to protect itself." Dr. Hastings added.

Katrina continued, "The problem with a sealed system is getting into that system. Once you're into a sealed system, however, you can usually have the run of the place."

"So, how do we get into it?" Jericho asked.

"We don't," Dr. Hastings said as she moved back and forth, her mind somewhere else.

Everyone looked at her, feeling like they just had the rug pulled out from under them. Avery, in an attempt to keep hope alive, added quickly. "We can still put the broadcast out."

Dr. Hastings suddenly snapped her fingers. "The Ion-Dome."

"What about it?"

"The Dome is more than just an ion burst of energy that breaks a human down into molecules. It is also an input device, of sorts. It takes those molecules and categorizes and logs all the important data associated with that person, then sucks it right into Giles's upload system. Pharma One has constructed half their viruses based on data Giles has collected from this process. That's why Pharma One built the dang thing to begin with."

"Okay, so how do we do that?" Jericho asked.

"You would need a biologic element to upload," Dr. Hastings said.

"Like a computer virus saved in bio form?" Avery suggested.

"Exactly," said Dr. Patel.

"So what, Jericho gives himself up and gets vaporized in order to infect the system?" Katrina asked in confusion.

"Well . . ."

"Of course not," Avery interrupted. "We need to find a way to get his biology into that sealed system."

"Any thoughts?" Jericho asked.

Both doctors shook their heads with a bit of futility.

"What's going on in here? Dr. Hastings? What are you doing?"

They all looked up to see a colonel and four armed guards enter the lab.

Avery stepped next to the EM1 she'd placed on the counter. From the corner of her eye, she saw Katrina step in the opposite direction, putting space between her and the warriors.

"Colonel Capshaw, we are here working under the command of Commander Weng," Dr. Hastings said, trying to act boldly.

"I thought Commander Weng was still in New Zion," the colonel replied.

"No. We were flown back here to—"

Three shots rang out, dropping the colonel and two of his guards. The other two guards quickly pulled their weapons, but Katrina dropped them before they were able to fire.

"Jeez! I had it handled," Dr. Hastings said, trying not to freak out.

"We're out of time," Avery countered. "Get everything we need."

The two doctors started backing up all their findings, and Katrina output her compressed broadcast.

Weng suddenly burst through the door, slightly out of breath. "We need to get to the Ion-Dome," Weng called out. He looked around, seeing the bodies on the floor. There was no time for explanations. Everyone shared a knowing look, not sure how Weng knew about the need for the Dome already.

From behind Weng popped a small face with brown curls.

"Ruth, honey, these are a few of my friends." Weng introduced everyone, saving Katrina for last.

Katrina held the broadcast data chip in her hand as she hurried across the busy street. Weng carried Ruth in his arms, afraid to let her go. The others were in tow.

"You know how to get this loaded and onto the broadcast channel?" Avery asked Weng.

"Yes, there's a control room on the first sub-floor. The live feed from there is broadcast across the city and to the projectors inside the Dome."

"So the crowd and the city see the same images?" Katrina asked.

"Yes, they have certain in-house feeds that are exclusive for fans, but the main show is combined and sent to both."

"Okay, so say this broadcast goes out to everyone—then what?" Jericho asked as they passed a group of citizens forming a line for freshly cooked street donuts.

"Well, the corporations will do everything in their power to spin-doctor the message. But if the people believe, really believe, it will start a groundswell that can't be stopped," Katrina said with conviction.

"So what, fifty-fifty?" Jericho asked.

"Those are bad odds," Ruth piped in.

"You heard her," Weng said.

"And if it doesn't work?" Dr. Patel queried.

"We're leaving the city as fast as we can," Weng answered, taking Katrina's hand.

"Me too," Dr. Hastings added.

"Okay, we give it our best and plan for the worst," Avery said.

The group seemed to understand, and all agreed.

"If only there was some way of getting Jericho's DNA into the computer. That would double our chances of success. With their computers down or whatever his code does, they might not be able to worm their way out of this," Katrina said, holding up the data chip.

"Any thoughts on that, Docs, besides me being ionized in the Dome?" Jericho asked.

"Still working on that, so no," Dr. Patel huffed as she tried to keep up with the brisk pace being set.

Jericho felt the weight of the team on his shoulders. He was the last piece of the puzzle. The team needed a win—and soon. His mind searched for a solution, some detail that might make a difference.

22

A plasma blast shot just over their heads as the team turned the corner. Sirens could be heard, closing in from a distance.

"We're out of time," Avery called out.

Weng used his size to blaze a trail through a throng of civilians. Some glowered, perturbed; others pointed as they recognized the fugitives, whose likenesses had been repeating across the city on various displays.

"This is a control action. Please stand clear," the authoritative announcement came over the nearby speakers.

"They're closing in," Avery called from the rear. Another plasma blast just missed Katrina in the middle of the group.

"Go, go, go!"

Weng cut left down an alley, trying to gain some distance, but the two out-of-shape doctors were struggling.

"We need to get off the street!" he yelled.

The pursuing control officers could be seen two blocks away. A control drone popped up overhead and tracked the fugitives, issuing orders to give themselves up. "This is Control. Stop where you are, or you will be fired upon."

"We can't outrun a drone!" Avery yelled.

Jericho could feel his heart racing as he pondered a decision. They were out of time and options.

A taxi drone swooped in and landed nearby. Jericho slowed his pace and came to a stop. He watched as the rag-tag team he had been a part of continued on, running for their lives. The passenger exited and stood, gawking at the excitement going on around him.

Jericho had been purpose-built to save humankind. He had tried and failed at his task, an impossible task. Had he ever really belonged here? Not truly. A singular thought seized his imagination, and a small smile spread across his face. Without giving it any more thought, he reacted.

Avery looked over her shoulder just as Jericho stepped into the taxi drone. "No!" she screamed, running back as the doors closed. "What are you doing? We can make this work."

Jericho placed his hand on the plexiglass. "I have to do this. Don't let me down. Get the broadcast working and make sure Geena is safe. It's the only way my life will have any meaning. Besides, there is someone waiting for me."

"We don't even know if this will work. Don't do this Jericho! Please. Your life has meaning right now."

The bio-reader scanned its passenger.

"It is done. Have a little faith, Avery. You taught me that."

Avery placed her hand on the opposite side of the glass from his hand. "I'll pray for you."

"Thanks," Jericho mouthed as a single tear fell.

A tone could be heard inside the cab as the doors locked, lights flashed, and a warning voice warbled. The drone lifted off just as the others arrived, each calling out for Jericho to stop and come back, but he was no longer in control of the situation.

He saluted Weng with purpose, and Weng returned it, warrior to warrior.

The group watched hopelessly as Jericho was taken away on a direct path to the nearest control station. Tears and angst filled their hearts. After all they had been through and the cost, no price could ever match it.

"Halt where you are," came a voice from an approaching control officer a half-block away.

"Follow me!" Katrina screamed.

Jericho sat down in the taxi drone's seat. He fidgeted with his hands, trying not to second-guess his decision. From up above, the city looked peaceful, far from the madness he had just left. He struggled with his thoughts and the way things had turned out. He failed at protecting 24, killing Weng, or taking revenge on Caleb for it. His path to this point was so twisted, he could hardly remember his start—all the way back to butting heads with Azraelle.

It took a mishmash of desperate people on the run to show him what was truly important. That there was something bigger than self. Something he could do that might actually make a difference.

Jericho was not overly brave or fearful, just a man trying to leave things better than he found them, in a world that didn't seem to care. The world was one thing, but individuals were wildly different. They could hate you, surprise you, change completely, even love you. His friends were risking everything to make an epic change they weren't even sure was possible, so he would do his part by playing the final card. To do the one thing he was made for, to save humanity or die trying. That's what he was now doing, *trying*.

"Take a right up there," Katrina called out to Weng, who was in the lead, as several more shots blasted past. Weng returned fire with his EM1 as he turned down a space between two tall brick buildings that was only wide enough for foot traffic. The drone overhead shifted upward to safely get a better view between the buildings. It relayed the fugitives' position to control, and officers closed in from the other side of the alley.

"This way." Katrina guided them down a set of rusted stairs and up to a weathered door. A quick jerk on the handle later, it opened. Everyone slid inside.

"Now where?" Weng asked, setting Ruth down to shake out his tired arm.

"Over here." Katrina slid behind a boarded-up wall and into a tunnel. "It's an old maintenance tunnel. It runs under the city."

Every one hundred feet or so was a grating that let rain and light in from above. Outdated pipes hung from the curved walls and rats scampered at the intrusion. Deep breaths and gulps of air covered the sounds of the city above as the group members tried to catch their breaths.

"How did you know about this?" Avery asked.

"I grew up around here. This tunnel ends at Edison Avenue."

"That's close to the Ion-Dome," Weng said.

Just then Dr. Hastings slumped to the damp floor. A muffled scream from Ruth alerted the group.

"Auntie," Katrina cried as she ran to her side.

A quick inspection revealed a gut wound from a plasma weapon. It was barely seeping blood, but the overall damage was severe.

"No," Katrina said as she held Dr. Hastings in her arms.

"It's okay, dear. My fate was sealed when I crossed Giles." She looked into Katrina's eyes and gave a weak smile. "You have a real chance here to finish what I started." She coughed a bit and then recoiled at the extreme pain.

The others looked on with genuine concern.

"I'm sorry," Dr. Hastings whispered. "I was never much of a mother, but I loved you in my own way."

Katrina smiled weakly. "You will always have a special place in my heart, Auntie."

"Katrina . . . I was the one who deleted your field samples. Didn't want to get you involved. That was stupid. You never could stay out of trouble. Even when you were little. I guess that was something I always loved about you."

Katrina smiled at the sentiment. "I guess that makes two of us."

Dr. Patel did an inspection of the wound and then shook her head at the prognosis. Dr. Hastings took a couple more ragged breaths and her body grew heavy in Katrina's arms.

"Please, Auntie," Katrina said.

"I'm so proud of you Katri . . ." Dr. Hastings closed her eyes for good.

Katrina held her close for a few beats and then gently kissed her forehead before placing her on the floor.

Dr. Patel, a bit shell-shocked at the loss of her new colleague, said, "What are we going to do now?"

Weng stepped closer. His voice was strong and sure. "I'm going to upload the data and try to save Jericho."

A muted commotion could be heard into the alleyway above. Katrina wiped a tear as she stood. "Come on. I'll show you the way out." They all jogged down the tunnel in total silence.

Outside in the walking alley, control officers, aided by the overhead drone began a door-to-door search. The fugitives had gone in the alley but had never exited. One of the officers brought over a SNIF and started to track their scent. It led to an old, weathered door. He tried the door, but it wouldn't open. One of the other officers reached over and yanked the handle hard. Then it opened. They called in the situation to HQ and followed the trail.

Giles watched the feed from the overhead drone on a small handheld device. He was in the chairman's suite at the Ion-Dome with some of his closest friends and a few rivals to celebrate with him tonight. Screens replayed the newsfeed of the high and mighty getting their adenovirus 12 vaccines throughout the day. The whole spectacle had been a tremendous success, and the room was abuzz. There was nothing like seeing yourself on the feed.

The ascendancy to the president of COE made Giles feel invincible, and tonight was going to be epic. He had noticed the stamp each of his guests wore on their wrists—a token given as they received his latest adenovirus 12 vaccine. The temporary die faded from red to blue at the twenty-four-hour mark, reminding everyone to visit their nearest LIFE-ARCH to lock in the vaccine.

The day had been busy with multiple vaccination stations on the upper levels administering shots for the who's who of the city. The event was covered by a press campaign and multiple interviews with leading citizens and doctors. In a couple of days, the remainder of his domain would follow suit. Then the whole thing would move to New Zion.

Around the room, upgrades were on display, as well as fashion statements and wearable technology—for business or pleasure—only a thought away. His

MindLink sent multiple messages out to underlings as he shook hands and made small talk. The more he used his MindLink, the better his brain worked with the interface. He could now multitask like no other human on the planet, at a breathtaking speed.

Giles stepped to his elevated perch in the corner of the room and looked down. These were the power mongers of this world, and soon, every one of them would bow down to his will. He returned his attention to the screen filled with the action going on out on the streets and pressed a button that sent an invisible sonic wall around his workspace, canceling out the noise of the party in the rest of the suite. He switched his view from the drone to one of the control officers as they entered the old battered building.

Giles could see officers scouting around the dark space with their bright ion torches. Old crates and some broken-down machinery popped into view, but there was no sign of the fugitives.

One of the officers Giles was watching went behind a boarded-up wall. An underground maintenance tunnel running off into the distance soon appeared. The rest of the control officers gave pursuit but stooped to inspect a figure lying on the floor of the tunnel. As the camera's view drew closer, a face became clear who it was: Dr. Millie Hastings.

Giles slammed the wrist screen closed in frustration. He had hoped a few nights in the cell at the Dome, awaiting disintegration would bring her back to her senses. He had never planned on killing such a valuable asset. This whole fiasco needed to stop.

He connected to the officer in charge and berated him. "I need you to find and kill or capture the fugitives. If you don't, you'll be cleaning solar panels by hand for the rest of your miserable life."

"Yes, sir."

Giles clicked off and recomposed himself. He turned off the sonic wall and stepped back into his party, a forced smile of perfect white teeth leading the way.

Weng used his credentials to enter the Ion-Dome at the security gate. His weapon was held at the gate until his return. Avery, Katrina, Ruth, and Dr. Patel hid across the street, watching a giant projection streaming live from the Dome.

They saw a man dressed in a silver jumpsuit lowered onto the top of the Dome, making the bolts of energy on the glass below him go crazy. The crowd cheered. Katrina could hear the roar from across the street, and she nervously pulled Ruth closer to her.

"Welcome one and all to the Dome. The Ion-Dome!" There was a pause before a cheer rose up so loudly, the whole city could hear it. "Tonight we are processing some VIP 1.0s," the silver jumpsuit guy shouted, elongating each syllable. The crowd cheered again. "First up is a general, fresh off the losing side at New Zion."

Boos filled the stadium as images of one of Avery's beloved and loyal generals appeared. Avery's hands moved to her mouth to stifle a scream as the announcer told lies about the man who was about to be martyred.

The control officer watched as two men scurried up a steel ladder at the end of the tunnel. The hatch to the street had been secured; there was no getting through. A sudden growing concern washed over him as he returned to the alley to restart the search topside. The image of him bent over a dirty solar panel flashed in his mind. "Move it!" he yelled.

Once the control officer made it back to the street, all signs of their prey were gone. Even the SNIF was unable to find its way with all the conflicting scents from the busy street. Sweat beaded on the officer's head. "Spread out and look for anything suspicious." His words sounded as desperate as he felt.

Music blasted, and the man in silver seemed to levitate in the air. The fans cheered again.

"It's processing time," the announcer yelled with zeal. The audience rose to their feet and screams and whistles filled the stadium.

The general was pushed to the center of the arena, still in full uniform. He made several obscene gestures to the audience before he rose. Boos and jeers turned into applauses.

The general screamed as the red and blue grid lifted him into the air. The grids rotated horizontally, becoming a singular, purple, floating floor some thirty feet in the air. The general tried to run, but he went nowhere. A green beam moved up and began to disintegrate his feet, then his legs. The horror and screams continued amid roars and shouts of glee from the audience. Soon, the general was no more.

"That, ladies and gentlemen, is the power of the Ion-Dome! Remember, all 1.0s' genetics harvested here tonight will be used for science to help make our world a safer place to live. Okay! On with the show!"

Once inside, Weng dropped down to the first floor and followed the E-guide on the wall to the broadcast booth. Muted thumping and cheering mixed with discorded elevator music. He stepped inside the room, where an AI operated the cameras remotely. It also edited between them to give the viewers every angle of action, including slow-motion replays. Two technicians were on station to monitor and override, should something go wrong. It took only a moment for Weng to disable them. He then uploaded Katrina's data chip into the system. Some trial and error took place before he enlisted the help of one of the recovering and very fearful technicians. Once the AI was over-ridded, he programmed the interruption and stood back to watch the countdown before his new content was broadcast.

Jericho suddenly doubted everything about his decision. Getting into the taxi drone was rash. The rough handling at the control office, with a speedy return to the holding cell at the Ion-Dome wasn't surprising. Even the control officer who took charge of his return seemed unusually happy about the situation. What he didn't expect was the rush of hopelessness that filled him to the core once he was back in the holding cell. He was making a sacrifice for humankind and should be feeling good, but he wasn't. Doubts and fears seemed to take hold, just as the cell door swung open.

"It's time," one of the guards said.

Jericho walked out, trying to fight the overwhelming despair that consumed him. His body felt numb and unresponsive, as if he was just a guest in a meat suit. One step followed the other in a trance-like march. A door slid open, and he was pushed forward, stumbling into the arena. The crowd noise seemed distant to him as he kept his attention on his thoughts of 24 and Geena. He steeled himself as he looked up, and the reality of his situation came rushing in. This wasn't a sacrifice for others; it was just cold-blooded entertainment for people who had lost their humanity. The loud audience booing him seemed angry and hate-filled, just with his existence. He harbored no such feelings for them. In fact, he was doing this for them. If only they knew.

Weng looked up at the screen and froze. Jericho was standing in the middle of the stadium, looking overwhelmed. He had his arms at his sides and a child-like, unknowing expression. His eyes focused forward, seeing everything and nothing at once.

"No, no, no," Weng cried out. He grabbed the technician and shook him. "How do I stop that?"

"You can't from here. We just broadcast what happens. The control booth for the beams is three doors that way." He used his battered head to point the way.

Weng tossed the technician like a rag doll, bouncing him off the wall. He was out the door before the technician collapsed into a heap.

Across the street, Avery lifted her hand to her mouth as she watched Jericho being lifted in the air on the screen. Katrina turned Ruth's eyes away and shut her own as well. The crowd thundered. Dr. Patel felt a pang of guilt while watching the horror on the screen. It sickened her.

Red and blue beams pushed Jericho upward, then rotated to a horizontal position, becoming purple. The weightless feeling filled him with memories of his time with 24 in their escape capsule. A single tear slid down his face, distracting him from his reality. He tried to move his feet, but they had no purchase against the beam. Calming his mind, he realized that the decision was already made. Time to fully commit; he was just a passenger now. Raising his hands out to his sides, he whispered a short prayer in a quivering voice. "God, receive me." His stress fell away, and his face became placid. An inner strength filled his soul.

A green undulating light about twenty feet across ascended beneath him. The crowd noise rose with the beam, but Jericho was no longer frightened. As it approached his feet, he could feel the energy in the air, like just before a lightning bolt strikes. He lowered his head in supplication.

Weng used his enhanced arm to bust open the door and crashed inside the Dome's main control room. It took one second to get the lay of the room. A single person with a large touchscreen built into the desk in front of him was moving his finger slowly up the screen. A fader icon followed the motion. Multiple screens lined the far wall, and recessed illumination gave the room a soft glow.

The man looked back, confused by the commotion, but his fingers continued to slide across the touchscreen.

"Turn that beam off or die where you sit," Weng commanded.

"It's automated. Once it starts, I can't stop it.

It took two strides for Weng to cross the room and fling the technician out of the way. He then smashed the screen with his enhanced hand. Sparks and glass shards flew as smoke started to fill the room. Weng looked up toward the screens on the wall, expectantly.

Avery couldn't turn her eyes from the screen as the green beam began, without emotion or concern, to disintegrate Jericho's feet and then work its way up his legs, just doing its pre-programmed duty. Tears flowed for the man she had put all her faith in once and then lost it, only to have it tragically back. She had banished him and turned her back on him, and now, here he was giving himself for her cause, one without a guaranteed outcome. *Faith.* He had asked her to have it, and faith that she would embrace right now. A heartfelt prayer crossed her quivering lips. The sobs that followed were not just for Jericho but a host of others who had paid the ultimate price for this moment, as her repressed grief finally manifested. Grief is funny that way; it chooses the time and place to rip your heart out, and for Avery, it was in total control. She wept uncontrollably.

Weng had done all he could but failed to save Jericho or find redemption. The pain he felt was too extreme to remain upright, and he slumped into a chair, distraught. The path he had blazed, the body count left behind, all done for the sake of the status quo. It was sickening just to ponder.

The image switched to a closeup of Jericho's face. Weng leaned forward, a quizzical look. There was no pained expression or screaming. Jericho's head was down, and his expression was calm. This made Weng feel even worse about his failure. As the beam worked its way up, Jericho raised his head to the heavens.

The microphones aimed to capture the screams of the dying only picked up a simple statement. "I forgive you." Jericho's feet had disintegrated, and his legs were following. The usual green light associated with the disintegration beam had turned bright white. Rays, like trained lightning bolts, shot up and out in all directions, making the domed glass roof dance and shimmer like never before. The unexpected show sent a hush through the Dome as spectators went from cheering to amazement, then to horror at the actions taking place. It was the first time the Ion-Dome had showed its humanity.

Someone yelled, "Turn it off!"

That was followed by other pleas, all lost on the automated programming of the beams.

Weng tried to hold back his emotion. He wanted to look away but owed Jericho his full and final attention.

The screens suddenly blurred, and an image of Giles Favreau appeared. He could be heard in a conversation with Dr. Hastings.

"Burn the body."

"What?" Dr. Hastings exclaimed. "Sir, she holds the key to a cure for all viruses. Known and imagined. If we can replicate this DNA tail, we can eradicate human sickness. No more vaccines and no more quarantines. 1.0s and 2.0s could live together, without fear. You could be the author of a whole new world."

It was time for Weng to leave. He ran from the room with only one thing on his mind: save Ruth . . . and Katrina. *Hmm, that's two things,* he realized.

Avery watched the projected image across the street from their hiding spot. Giles was angry and showing it.

"Dr. Hastings, unless you want to be the body that's burned, I suggest you follow my instructions. No one is to know about this. If word got out that we could end these vaccinations, I'd be ruined. We make sickness and cure it. Understand? That is our business model."

"My name is Councilwoman Avery, from the city of Zion. What you just saw is true. You have been lied to and controlled at the deepest levels. Pharma One and the other . . ."

Once back outside, Weng ran to the waiting group. Katrina wrapped her arms around him, sobbing uncontrollably. "Did you see him?"

Weng nodded as he held her tight. "I couldn't save him."

Ruth watched the display with curiosity and then stepped over to get her hug, as well.

"Jericho was strong to the end," Weng said.

"He sacrificed everything." Katrina asked what was on everyone's mind: "What do we do now?"

"We'll know soon enough if it worked. We have to be strong. He would have wanted that."

Katrina nodded and pulled her head back to look into Weng's eyes. "We never got a chance to talk about the other night."

"No, we didn't, but I wouldn't change that moment for anything." He pulled up and kissed her gently on the lips. They stayed like that for a while as emotion and energy flowed between them. This was not like before, when two bodies hungered for a connection in the night, not knowing what tomorrow may bring. It was a kiss filled with a lifetime of searching and longing finally coming to an end. A kiss that spoke volumes of the future and their place together in it, the kind of kiss that left you weak in the knees and strong in the heart.

As they finally separated, Ruth took Katrina's hand and completed the connection between all three of them. Weng dropped to her level and smiled at his daughter's strength of character. "I love you, pumpkin."

"I love you too, Dadda."

Avery smiled and looked at the doctor, who was grinning like a Cheshire cat. Dr. Patel clapped her hands and exclaimed. "Now, that's how you do it."

The two girls laughed a bit, mostly because of all the nervous energy they had stored up.

The audience in the Ion-Dome was angry and overflowing into the street. Fights broke out in front of them.

"Let's get out of here," Weng suggested, and they slipped away into the crowd.

The night did not go as planned. Giles had left before the video finished playing. It had been a serious blow to his company and would require some significant damage control. He spent the short trip over to his office at Pharma One watching and re-watching the video, picking out key details and facts, storing them away as ammunition. This was no time to panic. It was time to press forward aggressively. He MindLinked his entire marketing team with a red-alert message.

"Boss, you wanted to be notified when it had been twenty-four hours," his bodyguard said.

"I told you not to call me that anymore. I'm Mr. President now and what twenty-four hours?"

"Yes. Sorry, bo—Mr. President. Twenty-four hours since you were vaccinated. You said you wanted to get as close as you could to the time."

"Yes, quite right. Come on."

He stormed out of the room and down the hall. In the lobby of his building was a working LIFE-ARCH for all the employees.

Always a cautious man, he sent his two bodyguards through the arch for the adenovirus 12 update first. He watched as they stepped through and then back out.

"So?"

The two guards were not sure what he was asking, sporting a confused look on their faces.

Giles barked at them, "How do you feel?"

"Fine. I feel fine."

"Me, too, Mr. President. All good," the second one replied.

"I'll give it a couple more minutes." Giles waited one minute and then went through the arch.

"All right, time to get to work. Send my marketing staff up to my office. It's time to fight back, and I know just where to start."

The two guards waited for more instructions, but none came.

"Go. Make it happen!" Giles screamed.

They ran off to make it happen.

New Kansas didn't take long to explode. Angry citizens ran like mobs, destroying property and swamping intervening control officers. LIFE-ARCHes were torn down, and Pharma One was surrounded. Guards and military were dispatched, but neither had the numbers or desire to kill their own. Fires raged, and mobs ruled against an authority that had kept its foot on the neck of its citizens for quite some time. It was fluid and dynamic.

Lower-level citizens stormed the upper levels to get a better look at how the other half lived. The rich were prepared and forced many back down to their station.

It took a lot longer than expected to make their way to Weng's house on the other side of the city. They'd done all they could, and now it was time to slip away amongst the chaos. Katrina's hand found Weng's, and they stayed like that for some time as they walked across the city. Weng carried a sleeping Ruth in his enhanced arm. They initially tried to stay hidden, but no one cared anymore about the fugitives. Even the control officer who had returned Jericho to the Ion-Dome had his hands full, trying to keep his department from being overrun with angry citizens. *How fast the world can change.*

Shouts of anger and joy were heard all around the city as many people gathered together and sang songs, while others burned and looted their neighbors.

Eventually, an apocalyptic sun scorched the sky orange through all the smoke as it made its daily journey.

The group burst into Weng's house, exhausted but filled with hope. The worst was over.

"There's a bathroom down the hall if you want to clean up. My late wife, Janelle, was a big planner for the worst, and she put a bunch of bug-out stuff together. Ruth, show Katrina the storage locker."

The two headed to the back of the house. Ruth called out, "And then I'm making pizza."

"To go," Weng called back.

"I'm in for a shower," Avery said before Dr. Patel could respond.

"Another bathroom through that door." Weng pointed for Dr. Patel.

"Bless you."

"That's far enough." The voice came from the kitchen entry. Weng looked over to see Giles Favreau and his two bodyguards enter the room. Katrina was held at gunpoint by one of the guards. The other guard was pointing his weapon in their direction, and Giles aimed his gun against a squirming Ruth, held tightly against his wide torso.

"Drop your weapons or these two beauties won't be making pizza or anything else," Giles demanded.

Weng slowly placed his weapon on the floor, and Avery followed suit.

"I have no weapon," Dr. Patel spit out.

"You and your little group of lowlifes have done a great deal of damage. I would have never suspected that from the great Commander Weng, defender of the cause, leader of our troops, always gung-ho and ready to fight for his master. I take it you found out Caleb's little secret?"

"How he murdered my wife and maimed my child just to keep me on his string?"

"Yeah, that one. It wasn't really a secret. He was following my orders."

Weng took a step toward Giles, but Giles started to squeeze the trigger on Ruth. "Don't be foolish."

Weng stopped.

"I told Caleb mums-the-word, but you know . . . politicians, all that power he thought he had, went to his head. I'm curious; who was it that squeezed the life out of him?"

"That'd be me," Katrina finally answered.

"Interesting. Well, you did me a favor," Giles said.

"Wasn't my intention."

"No, I suppose not. Now, I would like the three of you to get on your knees, nice and slow."

Giles watched as they complied.

"Scooch over next to each other, hip to hip."

They did. The guard pushed Katrina to the floor and forced her to join them.

"That's better; now I can keep an eye on all of you at once."

Giles handed Ruth over to the nearest guard and moved closer to the three on the floor.

"Let's see if I have this right." Giles pointed his weapon toward each person in the room as he spoke. "Killer of our beloved president. Traitor to his own kind. Leader of the 1.0s. Doctor of illegal gene manipulation."

Weng kept his eyes on Ruth the whole time, ready to pounce and sacrifice himself to save her.

"I have just captured the one collection of bodies that can turn New Kansas back to her former glory. I just need a quick statement from each of you before you go, and to be perfectly clear, if you do that . . . the little one lives." He pointed his gun at Ruth. "If you don't, she dies first and very slowly."

"Dadda?" Ruth sobbed.

"Good girl," Giles responded to her fear.

Weng gritted his teeth, but there was nothing he could do with a weapon pressed against Ruth's head.

"Avery, good to see you again," Giles said with a large dose of sarcasm.

"Drop dead."

"You first."

Weng and Katrina watched the display, transfixed, their heads moving back and forth like a tennis match spectator.

Weng was the next to speak. "You know him?"

"He killed my father," Avery replied.

"Your father killed himself. We built a better world together, and he got all high and mighty and broke away.

"He saw the kind of world you were making, a world just for you."

"Your father was a 2.0?" Katrina asked. The others tried to follow along.

"Was," Giles added. "He lost that right when he betrayed me."

"She wasn't yours to control and own. That's why they left," Avery said in a soft voice.

"Your mother was mine."

"No, she was nobody's, and my father knew that," Avery said with a quiet calmness.

"Your father . . ." Giles's face reddened, and he took a calming breath. He pulled out a small visual recorder. "You first." He aimed it at Avery.

She had no choice. She could watch the child die or let everything they had done, including Jericho's sacrifice be for nothing. "Kill me. I won't say a word."

"Please, Avery, that's my daughter," Weng pleaded.

"Fine, but the people deserve to see . . ."

Giles fired his weapon, and Avery was blasted backward.

"That felt good. She has been a thorn in my side for too long now. How 'bout you?" Giles pointed it at Dr. Patel.

She began with a trembling voice. "I am Dr. Patel from Zion. I was responsible for the virus that shut down the main computer system at Pharma One and—"

"What are you talking about?" Giles interrupted. "The computer system is fine."

"It is?" Dr. Patel looked like she might be sick. *Had she misread the data? Had she made the suggestion that sent Jericho uselessly to his death?*

"Yes, everything is fine except for your meddling video." He fired the stun gun at her with the same results. "Luckily, I don't have to have all of you alive for my plan to work."

He then pointed his weapon at Katrina. "Don't worry, this is a stun gun. I need them for the Dome." He gestured to the two inert bodies on the floor. "It's important the public gets its pound of flesh."

He gestured to his guard, who started to press the trigger on his EM1, and pointed at Ruth.

"But I don't need her. So what's it gonna be?"

Weng started his speech. "My name is Commander Larry Weng."

Giles raised his hand for a second while he fiddled with his recorder. "Whoa, hang on. Okay, recording."

"My name is Commander Larry Weng. I was integral in winning the battle of Zion, but I was also part of a conspiracy to topple your rightful leaders." He stared at Giles with hatred.

"I will keep my word; she will live." Giles looked at the frightened child, then turned back to shoot Weng.

A choking sound from the guard holding Ruth paused his actions. The guard was sweating all over and seemed as pale as new drywall. The pain on his face looked extreme as he was raked with another bout of coughing and spasms. He released his grip on Ruth and fell to the floor, twitching, his gun loose in his hand.

Giles kept his weapon trained on Weng, but he peeked back at what was happening.

The second guard started coughing as well, showing the same symptoms as the first. He had a confused look on his face just before he, too, fell to the floor, convulsing.

The distraction was too much for Giles, and Weng used it. "Ruth, run!" Weng yelled as he launched himself and swept Giles's legs out from under him, sending the big man flying back and hitting his head hard on the floor. Ruth ran for her bedroom. Weng dove for the guard's dropped weapon and grabbed it just as Giles regained his situational awareness.

Giles blasted a line of fire in Weng's direction as he scurried away. Katrina took a glancing round and spun to the floor, dazed and confused. Weng took a hit in his enhanced arm, and it temporarily shorted out, involuntarily causing it to crush the pistol in his hand. Weng's arm shuddered a few more times before it started to reboot. A second shot hit Weng in the foot as he rolled behind the kitchen island.

Giles stood, keeping his weapon pointed at the island Weng was hiding behind. He was a formidable person at over 290 pounds, but a life of leisure had done him no favors. Fortunately, his MindLink, along with multiple enhancements, gave him a response time so fast, it was like he could predict Weng's moves before they happened. If he hadn't been distracted by his dying guards, this altercation would already be over, but he could still rectify that. He shook his head slightly to clear his mind from the impact of the floor and started for his prey.

Katrina tried to sit up, but her short-circuited nervous system was still recovering from the hit she took.

Weng tested his upgraded arm. It seemed to be working again. It released the gun, now smashed beyond use. The shot to his leg hadn't stunned him, but it had left it too weak to stand on. He opened a cabinet and grabbed several cooking pots.

Giles continued to the right, keeping his distance from the island and his gun ready for action.

A metal pot suddenly flew at him at an incredible speed, but Giles reacted so quickly, it was like ducking from a slow-motion object. Child's play. "You'll have to do better than that, Commander. My mind and reflexes work much faster than yours."

Two more pots followed his comment from over the top of the island, and Giles ducked and dodged them with ease. An unexpected third pot flew from the side of the island, catching Giles in his shoulder. A shot of pain coursed through his body, and an audible ouch followed, his gun arm rendered temporarily useless. Giles switched gun hands, firing several shots into the cabinetry.

"When faced with a faster opponent, use subterfuge or distraction."

"What is that some Sun-Tzu crap?" Giles said as he shook his right arm, trying to get it to work again.

Weng didn't wait. He threw another pot to Giles's left as he sprang forward to the right. Giles overcompensated with the pot, which put him right in line with Weng's enhanced arm. Weng used it like a battering ram to blast Giles in the solar plexus, knocking the wind out of him. Giles flew back hard, knocking the back of his head on the floor for the second time. His weapon rolled across the floor, and his MindLink shorted out, leaving a small trail of smoke rising from his scalp.

"No, that was some Commander Weng *crap*."

Giles quickly stood, hunched over on slightly shaky legs. He hadn't felt pain like this before, and it was nearly debilitating, but he knew the stakes and forced the pain behind him as he gasped for air.

Weng moved in to finish off the fight.

A small handheld weapon appeared in Giles's hand. It was an old-school derringer. Capable of firing two 9mm projectiles with the pull of the trigger.

Weng stopped his forward motion. He was caught out in the open. Nothing but a target for Giles.

"Always have a backup to your backup. That's some Giles Favreau crap." The momentum suddenly shifted back his way. It allowed Giles to stand tall and pull in some much-needed oxygen. His derringer remained pointed and ready, and his target, helpless and out in the open. A small grin grew on Giles's face as he started to squeeze the trigger. A cough suddenly racked him, and the first shot went wide. Before he could pull the trigger for the second bullet, he was consumed with a spasm and a full-blown coughing spree. He looked up confused.

Katrina had watched helplessly as the two titans squared off. After several attempts, she was able to stand again, one leg shaking with the effort. The peripheral movement caused Giles to fire his second shot mid-hack in her direction, just missing her ear.

Weng relaxed, knowing that shot was the gun's last bullet. He was torn between tearing off the chairman's head or keeping his distance as the coughing fit started to consume the man, just like it had his bodyguards.

Giles's mind was now more focused on his current symptoms than his quarry. His arms grew weak, and the gun slipped from his fingers as pain filled his torso. Fear gripped him as he searched for an answer to the turn of events.

"*Jericho*. It worked!" Katrina said as she approached. "His code was loaded into your closed system at the Ion-Dome."

Giles stared in bewilderment.

"His biological code infected Pharma Ones impregnable computer system, causing it to reset your precious LIFE-ARCHes to downgrade your most recent upgrade.

"That's not possible," Giles rasped in denial.

"Looks possible to me," Weng said as he watched Giles slump to the floor, wide-eyed, wheezing, and shuddering.

Katrina stepped closer to get a good look at Giles. "You've killed yourself. Greed, power, and ambition—in the end, they count for nothing."

Two minutes later, Giles was dead.

Weng slumped to the floor and lay his head back. He was spent. Katrina dropped and put her hand in his. They shared a worn smile. Ruth appeared in his periphery, and he managed a half-smile as she wrapped her arms around him. Weng's mind flashed to the man who had given them this moment and hope for the future. A future for all, regardless of version, sex, race, or place in this world. Jericho had been an enemy, a friend, and a fellow warrior. *Jericho, may you find peace and 24 on your journey.*

Weng could not take back his actions or wash the blood from his hands, but he would spend every day from here on out doing good . . . and he would do just that.

Epilogue

Two legs moved back and forth in a jittery, unnatural way. A technician with a tablet was adjusting the bionics and fine-tuning the interface. Slowly, they started moving more smoothly until the legs relaxed and came to a rest.

"That should do it," the technician said.

"I'll take that." Weng followed up by snatching the tablet out of his hands and smashing it to the floor.

"Hey," the technician called out. He took one look at Weng and scurried from the room, suddenly afraid.

"What was that all about?"

"You'll thank me later. How's it feel?" Weng asked.

Jericho stood and took tentative steps on his new legs. "A bit wonky, but if you figured it out with your arm, so can I." He looked up and gave Weng a well-earned smile. Weng returned it.

Jericho had woken up in a hospital room with his memory a bit dazed. Flashes of the last bit of consciousness bounced around in his head. The Ion-Dome, the beam, the crowd, and the pain, then nothing but falling and blackness. He had searched himself for meaning and purpose and had come up with a thin but tangible thought. *He still had more to do here.*

Just then Avery burst into the hospital room slightly out of breath. "You're up . . . you're moving. That's fantastic."

"Care for a dance?" Jericho asked, showing off his new legs.

A scowl grew on Avery's face as she scrutinized Jericho's level of sarcasm. She was sure she had lost him to the Ion-Dome, but Weng's actions had shorted out the beam before it could complete its programming, dropping Jericho three stories to a hard ground, with two cauterized stubs for legs. He was loopy but still alive.

Avery ran to Jericho and wrapped her arms around him tightly. She whispered in his ear, "I don't know how to dance."

"That's all right. Neither do I," Jericho whispered back.

"Okay, maybe I should leave," Weng said as he watched the two hug.

Avery pulled back, a bit embarrassed at her rashness.

"There's a song I loved when I was aboard the Hollanbach. Made me wanna move to the beat every time I listened to it. It was sung by some guy . . . Elvis Presley." Jericho started singing some lyrics and trying to move his new legs to the rhythm.

Weng, then finally Avery, joined in. They let themselves go—something that had not happened in a long time. Laughter, smiles, and horrible dancing filled the room. Jericho got a bit carried away, and Weng had to catch him from falling.

"Maybe a little less dancing for now," he said.

"Good idea."

"So what's next for you?" Weng asked, with a hopeful demeanor.

"I have a promise to keep," Jericho replied.

The power structure, as it had been known, with CEOs and a figurehead president came to a crashing halt. Everyone that had taken part in the adenovirus 12 vaccine and its upgrade died rather suddenly within twenty-four hours of going through a LIFE-ARCH. There had been some kind of corruption in the upgrade code, and any person who went through a LIFE-ARCH was actually downgraded—all the way.

It kicked off a reaction in the body that ultimately turned its white blood cells into angry killing machines. It wasn't quick or slow but more like a teapot being pulled from the flame, its whistle slowly growing quiet. By the end of the day, no one was left in charge.

The pens keeping the 1.0s locked down in Zion were destroyed, and families and friends were reunited. Warriors had initially fought back, but it all ended when new orders from the top, one Commander Weng, were issued.

The cities of both New Kansas and New Zion had been at war for so long, no one knew how to change that mindset, but together with Councilwoman Avery, *General* Weng of the newly formed CAF—the Consolidated Armed Forces—would try their best to put an end to that.

Weng and Avery had used the same system they had hacked to broadcast a message to both cities. One of unity, peace, and hope, with the promise of no more fear of common diseases as part of daily life. With a restructuring that would provide the people with a say in their government and leaders who were responsible for their words and deeds. With the monopolies broken apart and the death of the previous corrupt leaders, hope was on the lips of every citizen. The celebration lasted nearly a week before the reality of getting a paycheck for an honest day's work kicked back in.

Dr. Patel was working furiously on a final cure for disease as they knew it and was almost finished. The genes Jericho had provided would help every human boost their viperin levels and stave off even the nastiest of viruses.

From the most humble beginnings, Jericho, the first human not born of man but made by man, had risen up to do more for humankind in a single selfless act than anyone. He paved the way for the return of freedom, health, and choice. His newfound faith in a God capable of loving all things, regardless of their beginnings, set an example for all to follow. His actions made the world take stock of the mysteries of the soul and revisit ethics as an innate right for all. Religion still had a pulse, but the commonality of beliefs won out. The betterment of man by being better and doing better was now at the forefront of all. The beginning of a new age.

Weng entered the kitchen and set his bag on the island. The home had been cleaned and repaired after the shootout. Ruth ran to his arms. And Katrina sauntered around the corner with a smile that reached her eyes as she kissed

Weng with renewed passion. "How's the new gig as general of the Consolidated Armed Forces?"

"Not sure I'll survive a desk job. I mean, it's great giving orders instead of taking them, but as soon as I get things straightened out, the CAF can do without me."

"So no more?" Katrina asked.

"No more. This, right here, is what's important. . . . Oh, almost forgot." Weng released Katrina and picked up Ruth in his arms. "I have a surprise for you."

"For me?" Ruth said. "Yay, I love surprises!" She squirmed free from him and danced around.

It was amazing how resilient she had been after all that had happened. It gave Weng real hope for the future.

The front door chimed, and Katrina went to answer it.

Weng knelt down to her level. "How would you like a cousin?"

Ruth stopped dancing. She took on a serious look. "A real cousin?"

"Real as they come."

Her frown suddenly reversed itself.

Katrina, Avery, and Jericho entered with Geena in tow.

Jericho looked to Ruth and cupped his hands to his mouth, making a trumpet heralding sound. "I present Princess Geena."

Geena walked into the room with a touch of trepidation and a silver ring displayed prominently around her neck.

Weng stood and continued the formal presentation. "Princess Geena, this is Princess Ruth."

The two girls shared a smile and then a hug.

"Welcome, your highness," Ruth said in her kindest voice.

"I know you two will one day rule the kingdom," Weng added with flare.

"To the future," Jericho added.

"Who wants pizza?" Katrina called out.

"And fried chicken!" Geena yelled with excitement.

"And of course, fried chicken," Katrina added as she ran her hand through Geena's hair.

Ruth started their pizza celebration dance and everyone joined in, even Avery.

IF YOU LIKED THIS BOOK

I would appreciate it if you would leave a review.
An honest review helps me write better stories. Positive reviews help others
find the book, fueling my ability to add more books to the series.
It only takes a moment, but it means everything.
Thanks in advance,
Brent

Author's Note

This is a work of fiction. Any resemblance to persons living or dead, or actual events, is either coincidental or is used for fictive and storytelling purposes. Some elements of this story are inspired by true events; all aspects of the story are imaginative events inspired by conjecture. *HU 2.0* was a true labor of love. Like life, the writing process is a journey, one meant to be savored, and to me, it's more about the pilgrimage itself than the destination. I learned a ton while writing this book, and I hope it's reflected in the story and prose. Only you, the reader, can be the judge of the results. Drop me a line if you have feedback or just want to say hi.

Brent Ladd Loefke, 2023, Irvine CA

Acknowledgments

With deep appreciation to all those who encouraged me to write, and especially those who did not. I wanted to thank the following contributors for their efforts in doling out their opinions and helping to keep my punctuation honest: Jeff Klem, Geena Dougherty, Cortney Donelson, Carol Avellino, David Ihrig, Steven White, and Larry Weng. A host of family and friends who suffered through early drafts and were kind enough to share their thoughts: my lovely wife Leesa, who is my first reader and best critic. And my editor, Cortney Donelson.

A special thanks to my publisher, Morgan James Publishing, who helped make this all possible, as writing is only half the total equation. Finally, to Christopher Kirk for the cover design.

As many concepts as possible are based on actual or historical details. Special thanks to the original action hero—my dad, Dr. Paul Loefke.

Lastly, writers live and die by their reviews, so if you liked my book, *please* review it!

About the Author

Writer and Director Brent Ladd has been a part of the Hollywood scene for almost three decades. His work has garnered awards and accolades all over the globe. Brent has been involved in the creation and completion of hundreds of commercials for clients large and small. He is an avid beach volleyball player and an adventurer at heart. He currently resides in Irvine, CA, with his wife and children.

Brent found his way into novel writing when his son Brady showed little interest in reading. He wrote his first book making Brady the main character— *The Adventures of Brady Ladd.* Enjoying that experience, Brent went on to concept and complete his first novel, *Terminal Pulse, A Codi Sanders Thriller*—the first in a series, and followed it up with *Blind Target, Cold Quarry and now Time 2 Die* takes our characters down another rabbit hole. One more in the series followed. *HU 2.0* is a near-future Sci-Fi thriller that is often too close to the truth.

Brent is a fan of a plot-driven story with strong intelligent characters. So if you're looking for a fast-paced escape, check out the Codi Sanders series or Jericho's journey in *HU 2.0*. You can also find out more about his next book, and when it will be available. Please visit his website, BrentLaddBooks.com.

A free ebook edition is available with the purchase of this book.

To claim your free ebook edition:

1. Visit MorganJamesBOGO.com
2. Sign your name CLEARLY in the space
3. Complete the form and submit a photo of the entire copyright page
4. You or your friend can download the ebook to your preferred device

Morgan James BOGO™

A **FREE** ebook edition is available for you or a friend with the purchase of this print book.

CLEARLY SIGN YOUR NAME ABOVE

Instructions to claim your free ebook edition:
1. Visit MorganJamesBOGO.com
2. Sign your name CLEARLY in the space above
3. Complete the form and submit a photo of this entire page
4. You or your friend can download the ebook to your preferred device

Print & Digital Together Forever.

Snap a photo   Free ebook   Read anywhere

Printed in the USA
CPSIA information can be obtained
at www.ICGtesting.com
JSHW022244061023
49809JS00002B/4